LIBERATING

PARIS

LIBERATING

PARIS

LINDA
BLOODWORTH
THOMASON

Doubleday Large Print Home Library Edition

ωm

WILLIAM MORROW

An Imprint of HarperCollins*Publishers*

This Large Print Edition, prepared especially for Doubleday Large Print Home Library, contains the complete, unabridged text of the original Publisher's Edition.

LIBERATING PARIS. Copyright © 2004 by Linda Bloodworth Thomason. All rights reserved. Printed in the United States of America. No part of this book may be used or reproduced in any manner whatsoever without written permission except in the case of brief quotations embodied in critical articles and reviews. For information address HarperCollins Publishers Inc., 10 East 53rd Street, New York, NY 10022.

ISBN 0-7394-4645-2

**This Large Print Book carries the
Seal of Approval of N.A.V.H.**

For my father,
who swam the river with me on his shoulders,
my mother, a rose-maker,
and Pauline and Trav's boy,
Harry

ACKNOWLEDGMENTS

I wish to thank my editor, Claire Wachtel, for her immediate and unflinching belief in this novel and the ideas that inform it. Her expertise and bold commitment have been a source of confidence and encouragement for me. I also want to acknowledge my agents at ICM, in particular Jennifer Joel, who have represented my debut novel with devotion and care. In addition, I am indebted to Pam Spengler-Jaffee for her steadfast guidance in presenting this book to the public.

Many thanks to my literary lawyer and invaluable friend, Tom Baer, for his wise counsel and meticulous attention to the life of this book. I wish to thank my first writing agents, Bernie Weintraub and the late Stu Robinson, for giving me a hand up. Also my agent of twenty years, Dan Richland, for his friendship and steadfast belief in my writing. And many, many thanks to writer and actress Mary Kay Place for her love, support, and encouragement. Most especially, I thank my mentor and dear friend, Jeff Sagansky, who has nurtured this novel from its inception and who, more than anyone else, is responsible for my career as a writer.

I am indebted to my fellow writers, Pam Norris and Paul Clay, for sharing their southern roots and highly original observations that continue to color my own writing. To Calder Clay and Dan Brundidge—many thanks for your memorable stories, which helped to season the male friendships presented herein.

I also wish to express my gratitude to my beloved cousin Dr. Carl Judson Launius, who passed away in December 2003. I stand in awe of his courageous life as a quadriplegic and a poet. And I thank him for inspiring the character of Carl Jeter, as well as for the use of his poem "Woman, Burning in the Air."

I thank my family and childhood friends for the life that we have shared together and the experiences and stories that so abundantly infuse this novel. In particular, I am indebted to my Aunt Lou and Uncle Ed, the keepers of

Christmas, and to my hometown of Poplar Bluff, Missouri, and its cobblestone Main Street and all of its former inhabitants, including storeowners and courthouse employees, for allowing me to grow up a little like Scout in *To Kill a Mockingbird*.

I am grateful to my husband, Harry Thomason, and his brother, Dr. Dan Thomason, for sharing recollections and perceptions of their own upbringing in Hampton, Arkansas. I also thank my brother, R. R. Bloodworth Jr., for his expansive courtroom personality and incomparable ability as a raconteur of small-town southern life.

My heartfelt thanks to Adrienne Crow, my "adopted" little sister, whose razor sharp research and tireless commitment to this book have been a bedrock of its existence. Also, thanks to Douglas Jackson, whose loyalty and caring and uncanny ability to keep everything running smoothly never wavered during the writing of this novel. And my profound gratitude to my assistant, Allen Crowe, who so generously gave up a year and a half of his life to help with this project, whose good and steady disposition kept me going and who has immeasurably enhanced these pages with his brilliant ideas and personal anecdotes.

And finally, thank you to the law firm of Bloodworth and Bloodworth and all of my male relatives who have labored there—first, my grandfather, lawyer and civil rights activist Charles Thomas Bloodworth. I thank him for instilling in me his great love of English literature and for taking a bullet to the chest from the Ku Klux Klan with good humor and grace. I also thank his four lawyer sons—from my own father, a reluctant Japanese war crimes prosecutor, to my Uncle Charles, a zealous judge advocate at Nuremberg, for their fine and fierce ideals about mercy and justice, southern populism, racial equality, and religious tolerance. Although, like Main Street, their voices are quiet now, they continue to be an inspirational mainstay of my writing, with my father's voice, as always, tempered by good whiskey.

CHAPTER 1

Imagine a town that hardly anyone has ever heard of. Yet everyone has seen one like it. It is just before daylight and the Main Street is coming into view. There are cracks in the sidewalk with stubborn little patches of grass sticking through them. Most of the stores are boarded up, but one that isn't has a lot of naked mannequins lying around in the window. A fall breeze comes up and blows some leaves lightly against the cracked glass pane, blows the stoplight where no one is waiting, until it swings drunkenly from its cable.

Just past all this, if you look hard, you will see the fire station and the football stadium and then the interstate where something large and pitifully ugly has been put up. Something to take the place of the town.

There is a fifty-yard banner stretched across the front of it that says: "Home of the new Fed-Mart Superstore."

A few miles beyond that is a much smaller sign, really about the size of a world atlas. It's nailed to a wooden gate, and you can tell by its shabby condition that it's been there a long time. The sign reads FAST DEER FARM, but there aren't any deer around. Just a middle-aged man on a horse. He is wearing some red-checkered pajama bottoms and drinking whiskey from an upturned bottle and riding as fast as he can toward the sun. If you lived around here, you would know that his name is Woodrow Phineas McIlmore the Third. But most people call him Wood, except his mother, who calls him Woodrow. Even though Wood and Sook—that's his horse's name—take this same ride every morning, they are in no hurry to arrive any-where. They already know the bright light on the horizon moves farther into the distance the nearer you get. Well, really, Wood and Dapplegreys Ultraviolet, the granddaddy of Sook, figured this out when Wood was still a boy—*it was the ride itself that was worthy*—the swift exhilaration of speed and spirit, the complete aloneness of two equestrian astronauts hurling themselves through the green space of a thousand velvet acres—cool customers in their youth, now just two old friends trying to prove one more time that they can still ride the ride.

The boy and his horse had once set out for the sun and quickly learned what others had tried to put into words—that becoming is probably better than being, that there is only one thing in between and that is the ride. *The ride is everything—not* the arrival at some distant or imagined spot of light from which you would probably just see another spot of light and then another until you didn't know where you were or maybe you would even fall from the sky like Icarus for flying too near the sun or end up floating facedown in your swimming pool like Gatsby, who had worshipped too closely to the green light at the end of Daisy's dock. No, there was no question about it: *Forget about the light. Just keep your head down and stay on the ride.*

Wood felt lucky to know such a thing. And if his morning workout with Sook didn't make it clear, the walls of his study were lined with the favored novels of three generations of McIlmores. Books that were full of myopic, vainglorious fools who had not only failed to appreciate the ride, they had gotten off, like some fevered hoboes looking for Big Rock Candy Mountain, and wandered stupidly into irony, mayhem, and even the jaws of a killer whale.

That wasn't Wood. He knew what a fine meal had been laid upon his table. He retrieved the whiskey bottle from the hip pocket of his pajama bottoms and unscrewed the cap—"Whoa, slow her down now, girl, that's the way," he coaxed Sook as she adjusted her pace to his need. He brought the flask to his lips, turning it up full tilt and draining the remainder of the whiskey inside. It went down smooth, warming him, like the maple syrup Mae Ethel used to make for his pancakes. Try as he might, he had never been able to reproduce for his own children the thick, sweet texture that flowed like a small mudslide across and then down the lightest, fluffiest pancakes ever poured on a griddle (nor could the cooks at the local Waffle House, despite his meticulous embellishments). Fluffy was not a word Wood used often but that's what they were, damnit; they were fluffy and he missed them! He missed Mae Ethel, too. For some reason he thought of her whenever he drank whiskey. Maybe that was her secret ingredient for the syrup or maybe it was just that the liquor and the woman warmed him, especially on fall mornings like this when he rode without a shirt. Ah, Mae Ethel, his jolly, all-knowing angel who was colored when he first knew her but later became black. The person who used to scoop him up like warm laundry and press him against her huge, pillowy bosom, laughing her high-pitched approval at his simplest declaration.

His parents were equally doting, but it was Mae Ethel who physically loved him up each day, squeezing his flesh, swinging him, holding him. Mae Ethel, filling every inch of the doorway with her hands-on-hips massive presence, a symphony of happy, human noise moving joyfully through the McIlmore house. Mae Ethel, who had no expectations and therefore no judgments of him other than "do right" and "be happy," and who had been born before self-esteem was discovered but had somehow managed to electrify her charge with the simple admonition, "Study hard now, Peaches." It wasn't a warning, really. It was more like a good tip. But by the time she said it, she had already filled him up with so much highly combustible good stuff, all she had to do was light the match and the boy was on fire. He would have slain any dragon, conquered any portal of academia to please her. For Mae Ethel, he would become the greatest this or that who ever lived, the swellest human, the champion, king, and valedictorian of everything.

Once, he had ridden his bike to her house without permission and seen that she had *children of her own*—seen her actually hugging, holding, and swinging *them* in their yard. He was inconsolable for days. He was Mae Ethel's boy, who knew she was a widow and had never even considered that there could be anyone else. That was the power of their connection. That was why he had attempted to immortalize her in his English comp short story at Duke—the one where his professor had unbelievably given him a "D" for "building a story around a cartoonlike character" and "fostering unimaginative racial stereotypes." Well, you know what?—Fuck him. And the horse he rode in on. Who did that asshole think he was, anyway? It was Mae Ethel he was writing about, not

Aunt Jemima! It was the only "D" Wood had ever received and it happened because he was at a southern school where intellectual southerners, the ever vigilant keepers of the new South, were not about to let some rich, smart-ass white kid wax eloquent about colored servants. Wood's dad said he should have gone to Yale or even Columbia, where he had also been accepted. New Yorkers love southerners who write about their mammies. Hell, they would even throw a party for you.

He brought the flask up to his lips again, then, when it surrendered nothing, went back to cursing. It was just as well the flask was empty. He was beginning to feel the whiskey and he had a hysterectomy later in the day, though thankfully, not a full one. Wood hated removing ovaries because doing so made him feel mean, as though he himself had personally snuffed out a woman's femaleness, though he knew it wasn't so. Of course, if medically dictated, he would do it, but he never failed to be surprised by how many of his patients wanted him to make the call—how easily they surrendered their most private places and thoughts to him. Lately, when he was in the middle of a gynecological exam or even surgery, he'd been struck with the overwhelming sensa- tion that he was an impostor. What right did he have choosing chemo over fertility, decid- ing what goes and what stays, and who should or should not have children—all this because you tested well in math and sci- ence?

He was burnt out. That was the reason he was getting home later and later and chan- nel surfing and reading till all hours of the morning, well, not all hours, just till Milan went to sleep. Then he wouldn't have to worry about her pressing her breasts and pelvis into his backside, running her tongue along the nape of his neck, behind his ears, *inside* his ears, and dragging her finger, just one, *slowly* down his spine, then down the back of each thigh, ending at his feet and kissing his insteps for a long, long, *long* time. I mean, who had a wife, who, after twenty years, still relished these things? It was un- believable. Milan, who was so into perfec- tion, got up every morning and put on makeup before she would let him see her, so into her club meetings and small-town triumphs—Miss I-May-Have-Come-from-the- Wrong-Side-of-the-Tracks-but-I-Can-Sure-as-

Hell-Run-This-Committee-*and*-Be-Better-Looking-Than-Anybody-on-It. No one in Paris would have guessed the desire and abandon that poured out of her in bed—desire that he had made it his business to meet in full for their entire married life. The girl who hadn't gotten enough of anything had attached herself to the boy who was overflowing and it was good. So good, in fact, that he had never strayed. Not once. They didn't want the same things—they hadn't even gotten married for the right reason. But who can say what the right reason is? One of his elderly patients got married because he needed someone to drive him to the Rexall and the Dandy Dog.

Anyway, no matter what doubts he and Milan harbored about each other, the raw unrestrained joy of their physical union eclipsed everything. *"Raw unrestrained joy of their physical union"?* Now he knew he was drunk. That sounded like a damn romance novel. But there it was—and this is the truth—it didn't matter if they were even speaking. As long as they could get their clothes off and wrap their arms and legs around each other with him turning her like some flesh-colored kaleidoscope so that they never ran out of sexual configurations, and as long as Milan could feast on him for hours, sometimes, he thought, trying to eat her way into his soul (not that it would do her any good to get there—they were not "soul mates," they were fornicators extraordinaire and Charlie and Elizabeth's parents and that was about it), but as long as the sex stayed so deliciously damn good, well then, they would still have that. But the problem was, he was losing his appetite for it, for her, and she could sense the absence of his enthusiasm, as though he had already been unfaithful.

Wood turned Sook around a wide half circle and started back toward the old meandering farmhouse built by his Grandfather McIlmore. He loved every board and brick of it as much as the house he'd grown up in with his parents. Especially the old back porch with the kerosene lamp (Milan had since converted it) with a tall ship etched on the globe. And the foldout Hide-A-Bed with the feather pillows and dank old quilts where he and his grandfather slept after Belle died. This was where his Pa had read to him *Great Expectations, Treasure Island, Peter-*

son's: *A Field Guide to Birds,* Mary Shelley's *Frankenstein,* and *Tarzan.* Milan had recovered the Hide-A-Bed with some sissy designer animal print because she thought it would please him. He never made love to her on it again. She could nibble on him for the rest of his life and still never understand who he was, is. . . . Maybe he didn't even know anymore himself. But he sure as hell wasn't going to wander around like some self-indulgent asshole in some hackneyed midlife crisis movie. He sure as hell wasn't going to buy himself a new red sports car, or trek up some frozen mountain in Nepal and have to be rescued after his nose falls off, or grow a beard, or file for divorce, or have an affair with the babysitter, or worst of all get in some crybaby men's support group and start sobbing because his Jim Johnson doesn't come out to play as much as it used to.

No, none of these things were going to happen to Woodrow Phineas McIlmore. He had been alive for four decades now. And some pretty fine people had put themselves out a considerable amount for him. Mae Ethel had made him feel like the most important living person while his Pa had shown

him, against a dreamy starlit sky, how in-
significant he was. His Grandmother Belle,
the mad scientist who could put fruit in a jar
and make it last a couple of years, also
showed him, with her skirts gathered around
her knees, whether a snake was worth
killing or saving. From his father, he learned
that a man who puts people together for a
living can still become too soft to shoot a
deer. From his mother, he got the audacity to
be the first white boy to swim at the
municipal pool on "Colored Day." And when
the hate mail began to roll in, his old man
had shown him that nothing looks more
powerful than a simple "Kiss My Ass" on
monogrammed stationery.

No one could deny that Wood had already
had a pretty good run. Maybe not everything
had fallen perfectly into place, but his days
were more than good enough. And he had
no reason to believe that luck wasn't going
to hold. No way he could know that in a few
short moments, the phone would ring and,
within the breadth of three or four spoken
words, start a chain of dramatic events that
would change his world forever.

Wood and Sook lumbered past the house
toward the barn, bathed in their commingled

sweat. "That's my girl. My girl, you know you are, now." He patted her like a fond, old lover. Suddenly, an expertly manicured hand appeared in the upstairs bedroom window, brushing back happy Brunswig & Fils ("Morning Glory," dye lot MC6) chintz curtains. Milan stepped into frame, wearing pink silk pajamas, looking newly awakened, all perfect and dewy. Lots of southern women look dewy, but Milan was more dewy than most. It was as though her entire skeleton had been strung with skin from a baby's butt and then infused with this perpetually damp, flushed color. Wood had never seen anything like it. They exchanged a long, pleasant stare that gave nothing to the other. It didn't matter anymore how Milan looked or whether he even still wanted her. He wasn't going to stir the waters. He knew what he had, knew what he was going to do. He was going to lay low, keep his head down, and stay on the ride.

CHAPTER 2

Earl Brundidge was in his kitchen, watching the toaster and talking on his cell phone. "Look, we're trying to raise little girls down here and you've got a show on national television sayin' that we're ignorant and sleepin' with our relatives."

An officious male voice responded, "I think you're overparaphrasing."

"Do you? Well, I'll have to watch that. In the meantime, what they said was that everybody in Arkansas has big eye–little eye syndrome, ha, ha, ha—which I'm pretty sure means what I said it means. And when you say that we have one book and it's called the State Book, that implies that we're all illiterate." Two pieces of toast popped up and he began buttering them. "Do you know how many books my seven-year-old daughter has already read? A thousand. You got a little seven-year-old girl out there in Hollywood who's read a thousand books? C'mon, bring her down here. My little girl will whip her ass."

The voice on the other end was growing impatient. "Mr. Brundidge, we try to be politically sensitive in our portrayal of all groups of people, regardless of ethnicity, religion, geography—"

"No, you don't. I've called you a bunch of times. You're sensitive to ever'body else, 'cause you know if you said this kinda shit about them, they'd be so far up your ass you could deduct 'em. But you're not sensitive to hicks 'cause you figure we're too dumb and disorganized to do anything about it. Now that's just the truth of it, isn't it?"

Two little girls came in and began to set the table. Their daddy smiled at them as he unscrewed the jelly jar. The voice on the other end was done with him.

"Well, sir, I don't know what else to tell you. I'll certainly make the network aware of your complaint."

Brundidge winked at his daughters and continued his conversation. "Right, you do that. I just have one more question."

He crossed to the refrigerator and removed a carton of juice.

"Seriously, now, just between you and me.

Do you ever feel silly lookin' down on us
when you live in a place where people say
stuff like 'Happy Wednesday' and 'Watch out
for the rain'?"

There was a long pause and then a beep.
Brundidge said, "I've got another call. Gotta
go." He pressed a button while pouring the
juice. "Hello?" There was a pause, then, "Oh,
God. Oh, no. When? . . . All right. I'll let
everybody know. I'm on my way."

The man who was lying down with shards of
colored sunlight dancing around him was by
all accounts an excellent man. Babies loved
him. Their mothers swore by him. Their daddies wanted to be his friend. And now that
he was gone, there was so much crying in
the air, one could scarcely hear the Blue
Notes Jazz Ensemble, which had driven all
the way from Memphis, Tennessee, just to
play his favorite hymns.

Somehow it had seemed unthinkable that
Wood's dad might fall victim to the same end
as ordinary mortals. His heart was so good,
no one imagined that it could go bad. But
that's exactly what had happened. And now
his fine deeds would become the stuff of legend. It had already begun as each speaker,

black and white, mounted the pulpit carrying a little piece of the picture that was Woodrow Phineas McIlmore Jr. No patient turned down *ever* for lack of payment. For him and his father before him, being a physician was not a profession. It was a ministry. He treated people, not just symptoms. He listened to their stories without arrogance, accepting whatever payment they could muster. He never allowed anyone to die alone, which often meant sitting up all night. And if a patient refused to give up, he could be just as gentle in allowing them their illusions as he was ferocious in protecting them from the harshness of standardized medicine. He would have been an important doctor anywhere. But he had chosen to be one here in Paris. He had put his arms around his little town and cared for just about everyone in it.

And now, it would not be easy for them to put him in the ground on such a splendid fall day. A day that seemed cruel in its promise compared to the reality at hand, with velvet geese floating across the tops of red-copper trees, their serene formations rising in unison and disappearing into wavy black streamers on the horizon. People knew they would not see the likes of this man again. But that didn't stop them, even today, from beginning to look toward the son.

Wood tilted his head down with eyes cast upward, a habit he had inherited from his mother. He had planned not to cry, but when he entered the church doors and heard the jazzy exultations of "Just a Closer Walk with Thee"—a sophisticated, emotional rendering that would've brought his own father to his feet, it had knocked all the air out of him and sent him struggling toward his seat. Milan had tried to hold his hand but he had quietly taken it back. This was one day he was not willing to be a part of her show.

He stared at her as she scanned the memorial service program, no doubt making sure that everything was unfolding according to her plan. Even though all the beauty of her youth was still on her, he marveled that her black Escada suit and perfectly arranged hair somehow diminished it. He knew it was an Escada because she had asked which black suit she should wear and he had chosen the wrong one—the one that wasn't an Escada. There was no question that Milan was even more striking without her clothes on. When the sermon was bad, he had often spent time thinking about her underneath her suit. But this would be the first time he had done so while weeping.

He had to stop thinking about the man in the coffin. The man who had delivered him from his own mother's womb and taught him how to make fire; who could recite every word of Tennyson by heart and who would put his highball down just so he could applaud the sunset. He could not think about him right now. Instead, he would steel himself by concentrating on Milan's body. It didn't matter that his desire for her had diminished. He could still stand in awe and even clinical appreciation of her abundant gifts. Even though she, like him, had turned forty, her figure had acquired none of the encroaching thickness that often accompanies such a milestone. Milan was only five feet, four inches, but well proportioned. It was almost unfair that just below the perfect symmetry of her face, she should have been blessed with wonderfully fashioned, slightly swingy, teenage-boy-fantasy breasts—the kind that could command a man's attention after years of professionally probing an endless parade of others.

Milan reached out and put her hand again in Wood's. This time, he let it stay, mostly as

a thanks for the imaginary use of her
breasts. In spite of how much she could de-
plete him, there was something reassuring
about the sameness of her. She was the
most continuously unchanged person he
had ever known and today, the last day his
father would spend above the ground, her
sameness was something he needed.

Another speaker was telling of Woodrow
Phineas McIlmore Jr.'s heroism in World
War II. How he was a medic who volunteered for a dangerous mission that apparently medics didn't have to go on at all. How
he was shot at Malmedy while defending his
battalion and even dug a bullet out of his
own leg. He did this without anesthetic,
which he saved for men who were more severely injured. All this had been taken down
by people who were there and sent to the
War Department. (Later, when Dr. Mac and
his wife, Slim, compared notes, they realized that at the exact moment he was shot,
she had set bolt upright in her bed, already
knowing what was in the telegram that
came days later.) Afterward, he spent another year in the European theater, declin-
ing to be sent stateside for rehabilitation.
This caused permanent injury to his leg and

later some comments that he walked a lot like Chester on *Gunsmoke.*

Wood was thinking how much Dr. Mac would hate all this—people making him sound like some kind of saint and surely better than he really was. Maybe he should stand up and remind everybody how mad they all got when his dad made speeches against the Vietnam War. How the local barbershop even refused to cut his hair. And maybe he should also remind them just how much his old man could drink. But truthfully, even that wasn't much of a criticism. Mae Ethel said it only made him sweeter and not mean, the way it did some men. Once while waiting for Slim to get dressed and after several libations, Dr. Mac had put on a record and jitterbugged with Mae Ethel all over the house. Wood remembered how surprised he had been to see that she was so light on her feet. And how, in spite of Mae Ethel's pretending to act embarrassed, she and Slim thought it was all pretty funny. He also remembered how his elementary school principal called Slim the next day to tell her that her son was saying Dr. Mac had been "waltzing around with the McIlmores' colored maid." And Slim had said, "Oh, that boy, he never gets anything right! They were not waltzing at all. They were doing the jitterbug. If you need to straighten anything else out, please don't hesitate to call." Click.

The World War II speaker was finished. Wood could see, on the other side of his wife, that their fifteen-year-old son, Charlie, had slumped beneath the weight of the day's testimonials. Charlie wept until his shoulders shook. Wood was filled near to bursting by the sight of his son grieving so unashamedly for his father. He reached across Milan's back and squeezed Charlie's neck, offering a reassuring smile. Almost everything about his son made him smile—including the Indian name he had given him, Charlie-Sleeps-All-Day, a nickname derived from the son's inability to arise in the morning. Charlie was a dream of a boy, so easygoing and affable. He was the physical image of his mother, quiet and shy in temperament, but he had Wood's lowered eyelids and a half-baked smile that made teenage girls, as well as their mothers, fall in love with him. He had never given his parents one day of worry, nor had he excelled at any particular thing, either. He was just Charlie, the beautiful boy whose curly hair people wanted to tousle and whose cheeks they wanted to pinch, probably because they knew they could. Even though Charlie was a teenager, Wood sometimes still picked him up and swung him around and kissed him, without giving a damn what anybody thought. Charlie would scream and holler like he hated it, then afterward stalk off in protest, tucking his shirt in, trying unsuccessfully to repress his trademark loopy grin.

Charlie's sister, Elizabeth, sat next to him, mindlessly folding her program into an accordion. At twenty-two, she was sure of herself and fearless. Elizabeth could be loud and even a show-off, but these qualities came more from a boundless spirit than ego. In fact, her effortless ability to be happy was her most attractive and enduring trait. But today, no measure of joy, even the kind she had recently discovered and hadn't yet told her family about, could diminish the sense that she had lost something of greater value than all the other things she would gather in her life. She was her grandfather's first grandchild. The one he called a pistol. The one he gave his own canoe to when she was only nine years old, telling her that the Champanelle River was her river and that she could go anywhere on it. He had taught her how to paddle, too, as he had once taught his son, showing her things like how one never puts one's oar in the water while in the middle of a glide. And when she got older, he insisted that she come by and dance with him before every prom, loudly warning her embarrassed escorts that he pitied the poor boy who would try and boss her. Elizabeth had poured her tears into the skirts of Sadie, a French rag doll her grandparents had brought her many years ago on a ship from Le Havre. Like her mother, she preferred not to cry in front of people. If anyone criticized her dry eyes, well, that was fine with her. Her grandpa knew that Sadie's skirts were wet, and that was all that mattered.

The minister was saying the closing prayer. Wood's mother stirred next to him. Slim McIlmore, whose given name was Evangeline, was tall, sparingly proportioned, with sleek black hair and olive skin. But today she appeared much smaller than Wood remembered. The slender parchment hands wound tightly in her lap, had begun to tremble. Wood saw this and put his free arm around her, without his mother seeming to notice.

Slim's marriage had been the envy of everyone in Paris. Try as he might, her only son had been unable to assemble a comparable union with Milan, one in which each person allowed the other such exquisite consideration, where shared observations and jokes went back and forth like a new box of chocolates and even discussing the parameters of fidelity would have been an insult to their devotion. Perhaps after having the good fortune to be the product of such a union, it would have been too much for Wood to have also received the gift of duplicating it in his own life.

Suddenly, there were feet shuffling all round and a symphony of cleared throats. The sun had now climbed the stained-glass window near the front of the church. The purple cast of an angel's fallen robe lit up the entire McIlmore family as they rose to sing their patriarch's final hymn. As Wood joined in, it seemed to him that people were singing louder than they had ever sung before. The wildly beautiful instrumentation was ricocheting off the rafters and out the open doors. The air had turned a golden yellow. Even the ink in the hymnals smelled musty and familiar and good. It was the sort of moment one wishes all the moments of life could be like—when the most profound sadness transforms inexplicably into joy—and ordinary happiness gives way to some new kind of glory.

And then it was over. Everyone headed for their cars in order to form the long funereal snake that would wind its way through the heart of Paris. Or what was left of it. It was mostly abandoned now, a place where hardly anything happened anymore. It had been a long time since a procession this large had passed along the Main Street. Somehow, it seemed fitting to Wood that this one would be carrying the simple pine coffin of his father.

CHAPTER 3

Milan stretched her newly waxed, artificially tanned legs inside the solemn El Presidente limo, thankful that it was black. She had hated the cheap, white Continental pimp-mobile that Victor Lee Sayres had rented for their senior prom—hated the mossy carpet and maroon velour seats that smelled like vanilla car-wash cologne on top of old sex and cigarettes. She didn't care for Victor Lee much either, but what choice did she have since she and Wood were broken up at the time?

Right now, she was looking at her husband for some sign of whatever he was feeling inside, knowing full well he was not about to surrender this kind of information to her, especially not today. Wood continued staring out the limousine window. That was all right. Milan had enough love and resourcefulness to keep this marriage running for both of them. She brushed the hair out of her son's eyes and gave him a long, sweet pat. He continued weeping and Wood handed him his handkerchief.

"Here you go, son."

Charlie accepted it. "Thanks."

So far, this was all that had been said on the ride from the church to the cemetery.

Elizabeth rested her head on her grandmother's shoulder, the older woman and the girl lost in their own thoughts. That was all right with Milan, too. She liked to get lost in thoughts herself. She had been doing it for as long as she could remember. And right now, in spite of the sadness of the occasion, she was thinking that she bet her family looked good riding in this car. And that no one today would be wondering, "What's wrong with this picture?" The way people had once wondered about the little girl sitting in front of her parents' cinder-block house, a stunning blonde child with impossibly chiseled cheekbones and eyes the color of swimming pools—a girl who looked completely out of place next to a wrung-out old gas-station dog, rusted refrigerators, and mountains of used-up tires.

If it hadn't been for Woodrow Phineas McIlmore III, she might still be there, living in Hayti (long i), on the outskirts of Paris. Milan had made it her life's work to put the best face on everything and so far it had worked handsomely. Her siblings, Rachel, Roma, Tom Jr., Frank, and Delilah, had all managed to move no farther than two blocks from their mother—Milan never said "Mama"— that was hick-*Coal-Miner's-Daughter* talk— settling into various replications of their childhood environment, each moving his or her family into a discounted mobile home, all of which had become available after the

killer tornado of '89 wiped out everybody living at the Our Lady of Perpetual Grace
Trailer Park.

Wood and Milan had turned her mother's
house into a showplace, bricking the outside
and filling it with antique lamps and overstuffed sofas that were so beautiful Mrs.
Lanier wept and tried to cover them with
plastic until Milan reminded her that's the
sort of thing hip Hollywood people make fun
of on television. Milan's mother's house, with
its elaborate eighteenth-century reproduc-
tion porch light, now glowed like an eternally
burning candle on the altar of her daughter's
success. Othelia Lanier lived there, surrounded by five of her children in their satel-
lite trailers, forming a sort of "Osmonds of
the Ozarks" compound. The Laniers didn't
have money or fame, but they did have a
shining star and that star was Milan, as exotic and different from them as the travel
brochure that inspired her name.

Unlike a lot of people who manage to rise
above their raising, Milan often came home
again, driving the sixteen miles to Hayti in
her kid-glove-upholstered, cream-colored
Mercedes roadster. And when she arrived
with Faith Hill blaring on the stereo, her arms

were always full. There were designer clothes, vitamins, exercise equipment. And it wasn't just stuff she gave them either. She also tended to their psychological needs, selecting individual self-help books to fit any problem. After Rachel's husband, Donny, called his wife a fat bitch at a family gathering, they received a copy of *Men Are from Mars, Women Are from Venus.* When Delilah decided to have a surrogate child for her boyfriend and his wife, she was FedExed the hardcover edition of *Ten Stupid Things Women Do to Mess Up Their Lives.* Each sibling also got copies of the *Encyclopaedia Britannica, A Thousand and One Toasts for Special Occasions,* and *Emily Post: Etiquette Made Simple.* Milan was undeterred when her brother Frank advertised his books as "Never Before Read" in the local *Recycler*—throwing in *Chicken Soup for the Soul* as a bonus. No problem, real or potential, was too small for her to turn the white-hot light of her can-do ingenuity on it. Even the bouquets she sent on family birthdays were accompanied by little bootleg packets of Viagra, which she had learned could make cut flowers stand up for at least a week longer than normal.

Some, who were no doubt jealous, said Milan was just showing off or, even more darkly, making sure that her relatives were respectable enough to be related to her. But her family knew better. Yes, she cared about appearances, but that was only because Milan wanted the best for herself and everyone around her. She had always been like that, taking the old dresses she had sewn for school dances and reinventing them for her younger sisters, gluing sequins and pearls on a funky thrift-store cardigan or cutting the back out of her mother's navy shirtwaist and transforming it into the daring cocktail dress Delilah had turned heads with at the Holiday Inn Tap Room.

Once, she had even taken two strands of plastic pop-beads and spray-painted them silver, creating a magnificent Indian necklace. That was the beginning of the spray paint epidemic, which culminated in Milan's discovery of the color "celadon." She liked the idea of pushing a button and watching all the dirt and grime of your life evaporate into a clean, happy, brightly colored cloud. It required forty-one cans of "celadon" to cover the exterior of the Laniers' house, and even though people of lesser vision criticized it, her parents never said a word. When it came to taste, Milan was king.

The walls of the bedroom she shared with her three sisters were covered with tear-outs from all the latest fashion magazines, which had been donated by Claire Cutsinger, the woman for whom Milan babysat. Claire was one of the most sophisticated women in Paris. She drank martinis with little onions in them before dinner, had her own Neiman Marcus credit card, and ordered individual false eyelashes from a beauty supply house in New York City. She even showed Milan how to hike up her breasts with full-strength packaging tape, as well as how to lower her voice by yawning with her mouth closed ("Tits up, voice down" was one of Claire's mantras).

From the magazines and Claire's tutelage, Milan absorbed all the latest cutting-edge makeup techniques until she was good enough, at age sixteen, to get a job at Cotrell's Funeral Home. It wasn't long before she was wowing mourners with her ability to make the dead women of Paris appear far more sexy and come-hither than they ever had in life. Everyone said Naomi Kimble, a bony, pale-faced spinster, went to her reward looking a lot like Cher-when-she-was-still-with-Sonny. Other patrons favored, at least in hairstyle, the Charlie's Angels, a popular TV show at the time. Some thought Wanda Tarkington resembled a very old Raquel Welch, including Wanda's breasts, which looked enormous from the panty hose Milan had stuffed inside her suit jacket to give it just the right shape. Pretty soon the general complaint was that all the female corpses at Cotrell's Funeral Home had been made up to look like a bunch of chesty hookers with raccoon eyes. And when business began to fall off, Milan received her first warning from Mr. Cotrell. Small towns were like that. What initially seemed new and exciting almost always gave way to whatever the consensus opinion had been that brought about the original status quo in the first place.

It was around this time that the movie *Annie Hall* came out and all of a sudden the bodies at Cotrell's began appearing at visitation with no makeup at all. Mrs. Viola Belford, an eighty-year-old grandmother of twelve, had to be quickly whisked away after family members questioned why she was wearing a man's oversized shirt, vest, and tie. As soon as visitation was over, Milan was fired.

Her tenure at Cotrell's was the only time in her life that she had ever lost control of herself—becoming completely intoxicated with the notion that she had the power to transform people into something genuinely, permanently, better. She delighted in the thought that not a single one of her clients would ever again be made to feel insecure by the unimaginative opinion of small-town relatives and friends. She knew she had sent them on their way looking the best that they would ever be, each frozen visage providing that final, pinnacle Kodak moment for loved ones to cherish forever. Or not.

Lots of folks thought that working with dead people was depressing, but Milan, who disliked surprises, found it downright reassuring. It was completely unlike being at home where her daddy, who, after hauling other people's garbage and firewood all day, often got drunk and howled incoherently into the dark Ozark night.

If Tom Lanier had any dreams at all, he had long ago surrendered them to liquor. But every so often, when Milan entered the room, he would lift his head and narrow his eyes in an attempt to squint his firstborn daughter into focus. For a brief moment, it always seemed there was something he had to say, something uncertain and vague, that would then just as quickly recede into the evening haze of tobacco and whiskey.

Of all his children, Milan was his favorite. When he was sober, he laid before her the finest treasures culled from the residue of his head-down, low-dog life. While all the Lanier children had received some kind of toy or scrap from the Paris dump, it was Milan who was given the two cracked but genuine tortoiseshell hair combs, an apple red faux-leather belt, a cherub pin, a mirror framed in seashells, because, as Tom said, they "went with her." He could see, even for a man of his humble station, that his eldest daughter had not only beauty, but a certain presence that was lacking in his other offspring.

That was why everything fell to Milan after Tom died, well, to tell the truth, put a gun under his chin and blew his brains all over the celadon-colored wall of the Lanier front porch. After that, Milan had to redouble her efforts toward excellence and self-improvement, not only because she had been the sole star of

her father's ragged dreams, but also because
the shame of his suicide, the sheer overwhelming weakness of it all, set against the
landscape of a family living among other people's garbage—well it was just too much—and
since no one else in the Lanier family ever
seemed to have a plan about much of anything (Tom Jr. and Frank regularly said "I
dunno" even to questions like "How are
you?")—Milan knew it would be up to her to
remove the stigma.

She was suddenly jolted back to the present by the worrisome thought of her two
brothers being a part of this funeral procession. She had seen them along with the
rest of her family at the church and had
specifically instructed them not to drive in
their souped-up, rusted-out 1977 Trans Am
with fire painted on the hood. They had said
they would try to ride with someone else. Milan turned around and peered out the rear
window of the limo. Sure enough, about four
cars back were Tom Jr. and Frank, sitting in
the front seat, their heads framed in giant
metal flames. Plastered across the bumper
was a long row of stickers, all with the same
dated message: "Honk if you're horny."
Sometimes she just wanted to strangle

them, like she had when she was only fourteen and they sold tickets to their friends to
peek at her naked in the shower. Milan constantly had to remind herself that they were
never taught any better and that it was up to
her to fill the space where Tom Lanier had
never stood.

Wood had seen right away that she was a
victim of mistaken identity, that none of the
stuff surrounding her fit with who she really
was. Not the toile hunting-scene curtain she
had sewn for the back window of her father's
garbage truck, or the carefully crafted sec-
ondhand clothes or the repainted celadon
cinder-block house or any of the people in it.
He had been her shining knight on horse-
back, the person who had finally provided
her with her real identity, the one that
matched the imaginary driver's license Milan
carried around in her head. Screw the femi-
nists if they didn't like it, she was not Milan
Lanier—she was Mrs. Dr. Wood McIlmore,
wife, mother, professional shopper, and
Paris socialite.

The limo came to a halt, then lurched forward again, turning right toward the Main
Street of Paris. Milan reminded herself there
was no need to think about these things

right now. This was a time for mourning the man who had made all things possible—had given her her husband and even her nickname, calling it out wherever she arrived: "Well, look who's here! How you doin', Italy?" Dr. Mac had been nothing but kind to her and she had reveled in this chance to have a real father. He had even bought her a horse and taught her how to jump. And when she got thrown off, he had come running and lifted her up and held her tight against his barrel chest, like she was his own little girl— all the while cussing the horse a blue streak. And Slim was good to her, too, passing along some beautiful winter coats and showing her how to set a proper table. Amazingly, neither of Wood's parents had ever spoken a harsh word about where she came from. For her sixteenth birthday, they had all gone to Little Rock in Slim's station wagon with Milan at the wheel. When Wood hollered that she was missing the exit, she brazenly shot across four lanes, barely making the off ramp. Dr. Mac had turned to Slim in the backseat and said, "Well, looks like ol' Wood's got his hands full." He said it like she was really somethin'. Like the McIlmores were darn lucky to get her. And now she was determined to repay that acceptance by giving him the greatest funeral Paris had ever seen.

She pulled out her compact and began checking her face. She had cried alone in the church vestry and now needed a touch-up. People stared as the procession passed, some bowing their heads, others removing hats. Now Milan saw the reflection of the slick black car in the empty store windows and was pleased to see that her family did indeed look important sitting inside. For a moment, she wished she could have a picture of it. She loved to get pictures of things when they were at their absolute peak best because you just never knew what might happen next. The only thing you could really be sure of was that something would happen and whatever it was, Milan was going to be ready.

"Well, that was a beautiful service. Just beautiful." She could stand the silence no longer. "And some of those floral sprays from Dwight and Denny's Secret Garden were incredible. I think your dad would've loved it, don't you, Wood?"

"What?"

"The funeral, the flowers, everything."

Wood appeared to think for a while, then said, "Right."

Elizabeth threw an arm around her brother. "Charlie-horse, you need to get hold of yourself." She turned to the others, "He's been crying nonstop for two whole days."

"I can't help it."

"I could hypnotize you and make you stop. I learned that in my college psych class." She nudged him playfully, getting in his face. "I can also make you think you're a chicken who can really dance."

Slim laughed a little in spite of herself.

Milan admonished, "Well, don't do it here."

Elizabeth answered, "It was just a joke, Mims. Thank you, Grand-mère. At least you get me."

Wood gave his daughter a wink.

Milan studied Elizabeth's face. "Elizabeth, what is that on your—come here." Milan opened her purse and removed a Kleenex. "You know, people should have the common decency to air kiss so they don't leave one of those awful imprints." Milan moistened the Kleenex with her own saliva and began scrubbing Elizabeth's face.

Elizabeth protested, "Mother, I wish you wouldn't do that."

"Oh, hush, I gave birth to you." Milan said hush so sweetly and so often that her children called her "the Husher."

"I'm not sure that gives you the right to spit on me."

Milan was pleased. "There, I got it."

The air in the limo was growing stale. She attempted to fill it. "Well, I just think everything's gone really well, don't you, Wood?"

There was a long pause as Wood decided not to answer.

CHAPTER 4

Somewhere between the El Presidente limo and the Lanier brothers' flaming Trans Am was a van carrying the three best friends Wood and Milan McIlmore would ever have. It wasn't just any old van. It was a late model, immaculately detailed, commercial vehicle with Olde English–style calligraphy on each side, spelling out the words "Brundidge Beer and Beverage Company." The company's founder and CEO, Earl Brun-

didge Jr., was driving. He was of average
height and build with a round, pleasant face
and thinning hair. Today Brundidge was
wearing his two-button Armani suit and his
soft black loafers, the ones without tassels.
In spite of his pronounced redneck accent,
he had been voted best dressed in high
school and college, a title he accepted as
seriously as if it had been bestowed by an
international panel of fashion arbiters.

Sitting across from him in the passenger
seat was Mavis Pinkerton. She was red-
headed, overweight, and as unkempt as
Brundidge was impeccable—the kind of
woman who lets her arm fat flap in the
breeze out a car window. An accomplished
cook, Mavis owned Doe's Bakery and Cater-
ing Service, which had evolved from a once-
popular diner on Main Street. She was
known not only for keeping up with the edgi-
est ideas in gourmet cooking, but for adding
her own unique artistry to the latest craze.
For example, when southwestern became
all the rage, she knocked everyone's socks
off by marrying buffalo tamales with Asian
spices. And for dessert, she was a master at
turning American classics like bananas Foster into homemade bananas Foster ice

cream. Best of all, Mavis wasn't a snob about food, either. She still maintained that someone named "Little Debbie" made one of the finest cupcakes in America (with Milan concurring in this). For Mavis, there was no specific comfort food. All food was a comfort. That's why today she was eating a package of corn nuts as tears ran down her cheeks.

Behind Mavis and Brundidge, strapped to a wheelchair in the rear section of the van, was Carl Jeter. Right now he was sitting in the middle of stacks of liquor cases and a perfectly arranged CD collection. In spite of the fact that all three friends, like Wood and Milan, had been out of high school for over two decades, Jeter still looked like a kid. A quadriplegic since he was seventeen, he was miraculously still able to move the little finger on his right hand, a feat he saved for special occasions. Despite many years of physical therapy, his body had gradually at-rophied, giving his head an abnormally sized "Mr. Potato Head" look. And somehow, the once boyishly handsome face, made large, had translated into an even more lovable ap-pearance, an advantage that Jeter neither used nor appreciated. He especially hated it when Mavis said in front of people that he looked just like a big ol' baby, so cute that all his pants should have feet in them. Because Jeter's parents had passed away, he lived at the local nursing home. Most of his time was spent writing poetry and short stories on the computer Wood had bought for him. The fact that he typed with a stick in his mouth had not stopped him from turning out a considerable volume of work, including several poems that had been published in the *Oxford American.*

Wood, Milan, Brundidge, Jeter, and Mavis had been friends for as long as anyone could remember. Wood and Milan had married and provided the house where everyone liked to gather. Brundidge was the divorced slave of two preschool angels named Cake and Lily, of whom he had custody. But Mavis and Jeter had remained single. Throughout all their friendships, there had been variations of emotional intimacy between one and the other, depending on the year and the circumstance. But the basic dynamic of the quintet went like this: Wood was to the group what Frank Sinatra was to the Rat Pack. In fact, it was not unusual when they had a party and everyone was drunk—except for Milan, who never got drunk—for Brundidge to throw on "Here's to the Winners." Then he and Wood and Jeter would sing it over and over, their voices cracking and their tears falling as people left in droves, while the men only increased their volume, especially on the part that said, "Here's to all brothers, here's to the battle whatever it may be."

Once there had been six friends, but no one talked about that anymore. In fact, no one had spoken of *her* in years. At least not in front of Milan. The few times it had happened, Milan had given the offending person a look that was almost comical in its attempt at evilness—the kind mothers give when they want to discipline their children, but lack the ability to pull off. But the feeling behind it—that was enough to discourage anyone in the group from ever mentioning her name again. And then after she moved away, in spite of the fact that some in the group missed her, not talking about her became a lot easier.

Brundidge removed "What Becomes of the Brokenhearted" from the CD player and punched in Placido Domingo's rendition of "Ave Maria." He was the proud owner of the largest, most eclectic music collection in west Arkansas. And he instinctively knew

that today, following on the heels of the
jazzed-up church hymns, a religious classic
would be right on the money. Brundidge was
a stickler for matching just the right song
with the right occasion. That's why he had
convinced Milan to hire the Blue Notes Jazz
Ensemble as a surprise for Wood and Evangeline. Because Dr. Mac loved jazz and
nothing else would have been as right.
Frankly, he was a little disappointed that
Mavis and Jeter had not even mentioned it,
despite the several openings he had given
them to do so.

Brundidge decided to try once more. "I'm
glad I suggested that band. Hell, they made
the service!" Mavis wiped her nose on the
hem of her dress. "I'm really gonna miss that
man." Brundidge looked at her, disgusted,
then forged on, "I mean, the youth choir's
fine for regular stuff, but not for Dr. Mac—"

Mavis grew impatient. "Would you please
stop bragging about the damned band? The
man's dead. Who cares about the music?"

Brundidge reacted, "I care. And just for the
record, when I die, I expect some really boffo
tunes." He gestured toward the back of the
van. "Not that stuff back there. I'm talkin'

about some of the mint vinyls I keep under lock and key in my closet."

Mavis put in another mouthful of nuts. "When you die, we'll probably just throw you in my pond."

Brundidge leaned toward Mavis, scanning all the bare storefront windows. "Would you look at that? Damn Fed-Mart vultures drove another one out."

Jeter's voice, coming from the back, was worried. "Who is it this time?"

Brundidge replied, "Tillman Electric. They must've been there fifty years."

There was a long pause before Jeter said softly, "Longer."

Just thinking about everything being gone made him tired.

Brundidge was wondering whether this news might have upset Jeter, whose family grocery store had been next door to Tillman's. He said, looking in the rearview mirror, "I'm sorry, buddy. That's rough." Then, unable to stand the crunching any longer, he finally turned to Mavis, "Do you really think now is a good time to be eating corn nuts?"

Mavis pretended to ponder. "I don't know. I don't know when corn nut eating time is."

Two fortysomething men in a Cadillac, wearing golf hats, pulled up next to the van. Smith Dunlop, whose daddy was rich and who still mentally resided on the third floor of the KA house at Ole Miss, stuck his head out the window, yelling, "Mavis Pinkerton! I hear you're lookin' for a baby. You don't have to pay some ol' boy for that. Clay here will be a direct donor for free."

Clay protested, "Shut the hell up!"

Mavis stuck her head out the van window and yelled back, "Thanks, but if I was in the market for something like that, I sure wouldn't go looking for your little overblown clitoris!"

Smith and Clay looked stricken. They rolled up the windows and the car screeched off.

Brundidge was now mortified. "What in the hell are you doing? This is supposed to be a damn funeral procession. You can't be yellin' stuff like that out my van!"

Now Mavis was fuming. She could not imagine how her personal medical information had become public. "Screw you. I happen to be very upset right now."

Brundidge said, "Hey, don't get mad at me. Who went all the way to Honduras with you, huh? Just so you could apply for a damn baby! And you still haven't even bothered to thank me."

That was the final straw. Mavis turned to Brundidge and said, clipping each word in a way that let him know she didn't mean it, "Thank you." Then she grabbed her enormous purse, stuffing it with the corn nuts. "You know, it's such a beautiful day. I think I'll just walk."

She opened the door, climbed out, and began keeping pace with the slow-moving van.

Brundidge craned his neck in disbelief. "What the hell is she doing?"

Jeter watched her for a moment. "I believe she's walking."

Brundidge began yelling at Mavis, "You're crazy! You know that? All right, that's it! I'm not ever going anywhere with you again!" Now he was yelling out the window. "Get in the damn car!"

Mavis increased her speed, never looking back.

A few minutes later, everyone was standing still with their heads bowed in the middle of Whispering Pines Memorial Cemetery. The sun lingered on the horizon, as Wood stood next to his father's casket. There was a long, wide American flag laying over it. The minister had hold of Slim's arm, even though she remained without tears and stood straight as a pin. Mavis, who had hitched a ride with the Lanier brothers, was discreetly inching away from them, while Brundidge narrowed his eyes, still chastising her. When a strong wind came up, Milan reached down and pulled Jeter's scarf, the one her mother had knitted for him, more tightly around his neck. Then, with eyes set deep in his Humpty-Dumpty head, Jeter willed Wood the reassurance he needed to begin. "Only yesterday, he was putting me on his shoulders and swimming the Champanelle River . . . what he liked best was being a doctor, the kind who would, you know," he cleared his throat and mumbled, "come to your house." Wood looked down, putting his hands in his pockets. "At any given football game, he might look down the bench and suddenly realize that he had delivered everybody on it." There was some laughter, which made him think he could finish. "Some say he delivered over three thousand babies in this town. He also held the hands of just as many . . . people leaving. . . . But you already know that. I guess there's nothing more to say, except . . ." Wood turned in the direction of his father. His voice was strong now. "I'll remember your decency. I'll remember your strength, both physical and moral. I'll remember your love for my mother. . . . Most of all, I'll remember how proud I was to be your son."

Chapter 5

Here's what Slim McIlmore knows about gardens. You can't get everything good going at the same time. You can get the foxgloves blooming with the roses, but by the time the hydrangeas are up and running, the foxgloves will be gone. Of course, you could plant only things that bloom simultaneously. But then your garden wouldn't have all your favorite flowers in it. Because all your favorite flowers would not just happen to bloom all together. That would be against nature. It's like that song by the Rolling Stones, "You Can't Always Get What You Want" (and you certainly can't get it all at

once). Slim knew something about the
Rolling Stones because they had been ar-
rested by an auxiliary deputy of the Paris
County Sheriff's Department for throwing a
Coke can out the window of their limo. Apparently, they were on their way to a concert
in Little Rock and had spoken rudely to the
officer. After that, they were the talk of the
town—even the old people, who had never
heard of them, bought their record. The general consensus was, yes sir, the Rolling
Stones understood firsthand that you can't
always get what you want. And if they had
only sung it for show before—well, now they
knew it for real, after spending a night behind bars.

Slim's garden, like the Paris County jail,
was full of hard lessons. And tending it over
the years had taught her patience and gratitude. But today she wasn't feeling any of it.
Today, it was a widow's garden and everything in it looked dead. Now she would really
let it go, let nature run its course. Let's just
see next spring who's strong enough to
come back on their own. As though she
didn't already know the answer. But that was
a secret, and right now she wasn't letting
any secrets out—not giving in to any emo-

tion. Because if she were to show her true feelings, the ones that were commensurate with her loss, then they could just go ahead and bury her beneath her flowers.

But Slim was not a woman given to histrionics. Right now, her husband was gone and her house was full of the people they had collected over a lifetime. And in a few moments she would leave this favored spot by the fireplace in his den and go out and graciously greet each and every one of them— shake their hands, hug them, "My, how your little one has grown," "Yes, I know you know how it feels," thank them for their covered dishes and good hearts and for all these years of caring about the McIlmore family— and finally, agree that yes, indeed, he was a wonderful man and this is going to take some time.

Slim would do these things because she had what people who don't have it call class. For her, it involved writing thank-you notes for things that didn't cost money and knowing who was worth being with and what was worth owning or wearing and making the people who didn't know any of it comfortable. Slim seemed to have been born knowing such things.

She had not come from wealth. Her people were merchants from the Alsace-Lorraine region of France. Her father, Charles Pinchot Longchamps, had crossed in steerage to New York, then set out for Dallas to open a dry goods business. Perhaps it was because of the name, but he stopped in Paris for a root beer and he fell almost immediately in love with Miss Emily Arnold, an auburn-haired beauty with bee-stung lips, the only daughter of an Episcopal minister. While not particularly spiritual himself, he wrote his intended long letters from Dallas, citing her religious upbringing as a reason she might not want to dance with any other beaus in Paris. He proclaimed that while he wasn't sure there was any real harm in dancing, he knew for certain there was no harm in not dancing. Emily, a strong-willed girl, wrote him back that she was an Episcopalian, not a Baptist, and that Episcopalians like to dance their heads off. The next day Charles went to a Dallas tearoom and plunked down a dollar twenty-five for his first lesson. It turned out to be a very good investment—waltzing, rumba, cha-cha, the Charleston—the Longchamps were good at all of it until the day Emily killed herself.

A few years later, Charles started a second dry goods store, making enough money to steep their three girls in good educations at boarding schools and annual trips home to Europe. Their youngest daughter, Slim, who later sat on the board of the Arkansas Ballet Company, would instill in her son her love of dance, as well as her husband's ardor for good books.

Charles Longchamps's best friend was Woodrow Phineas McIlmore the First. Wood and Belle McIlmore were rich—from each of their families they had inherited thousands of acres of black bottom-land near the Champanelle River that flowed on the outskirts of Paris. Wood was a red-faced, barrel-chested son of a Welsh farmer and a beloved physician to people all over Paris County. A man of impressive vitality and intellect, he farmed most of his land out to tenants with whom he generously shared the revenues of each year's cotton harvest. Belle, a graduate of Sophie Newcomb College, was a teacher, as well as a grand matron of the Arkansas Order of the Eastern Star and president of the Coalition of Garden Clubs of the Southern States.

The two couples got along famously, but it

was the men who held the deeper friendship, and it was Woodrow who sustained
Charles after Emily was gone. They were
well-read men, ahead of their time, who liked
to share good bourbon and argue about religion, politics, and music as well as how their
little Paris should continue to prosper and
unfold. And they were devoted to their wives,
in spite of or because of their fascination
with women in general. Each possessed a
delicious sense of humor and a keen empathy for the underdog. Wood was self-
effacing, Charles a practical joker. Older
Parisians still tell the story of how Charles
was once almost defeated in his bid to be
mayor, until he hired some lowlifes to paint
"Mrs. Charles Longchamps is a whore" on
sidewalks all over town. He then attributed
the dirty deed to his opponent and won in a
landslide sympathy vote, with Emily never
the wiser.

After Charles's daughter Slim married
Wood's son, Woodrow Phineas McIlmore
Jr., the bond between the two fathers became even stronger. And when Slim gave
birth to the only son of this prodigious union,
all hell broke loose over which grandfather
the baby would be named after. The parents

finally decided that because there had been a succession of Woodrow Phineas McIll-mores but only one Charles Pinchot Longchamps, the Woodrows would prevail. When that didn't sit well with Charles, a card game ensued in which Wood whipped him in two out of three hands of poker. Legend has it that Charles, always an emotional man, then bolted from the room, ran to the barn, and grabbed a can of kerosene, threatening to burn himself up. After Wood offered him a match, there followed a terrible row in which the two men, in spite of Belle McIlmore's protests, beat the holy hell out of each other. Everyone thought the friendship ruined until the twosome showed up on a midnight drunk, arm in arm outside Slim's hospital window, singing "If I Didn't Care." The friend-ship endured, but Charles Longchamps, un-til the day he died, referred to his grandson not by his birth name, but rather by the French word for three, "Trois."

Suddenly there was a knock at the door, forcing Slim's reverie back in the trunk. Eleanor Cahill, a well-turned-out woman, came in. She was wearing high heels and walked with a cane.

"Slim, are you all right?"

Slim looked at her for a long time. "No, Eleanor, I am not all right. And nothing will ever be all right again. You know, I'm very good at accessing these things and there is not even a shred of evidence that I'm going to be able to endure this."

"You are the strongest woman I know."

"Please don't insult us both. You're my best friend and I'm too old for pep talks." There was a pause as Slim absorbed the other woman's look of concern. "Oh, don't worry, I'm going to go through the motions. But I just need another living soul to know that I do not want to talk to people, get up tomorrow, or do good works." Then Slim turned her back on Eleanor, facing the window. "And most of all, I am so deeply ashamed that after fifty years of the gift of this man . . . I am unable to feel even a thimble of gratitude because . . ." She was whispering now. "I wanted more."

For a while, neither woman spoke. Eleanor finally crossed, put down her cane, and rested her cheek on Slim's back, holding her. They remained there for a long time, two old friends folded into one statue.

A few rooms away, as Chopin played in the background, scores of mourners were helping themselves to the generous funereal buffet. Mavis, who had earlier delivered her professionally turned out cakes and pies, was relighting the little candle under her potato timbale with horseradish cream. She was still mad that for this most auspicious funeral, she had been unable to provide her traditional mail-order Virginia ham. Mavis always kept one in the freezer in case someone died. She and her Cuban baker's assistant, Rudy, had taken to calling it the Death Ham. Incredibly, the night before Dr. Mac died, Rudy had taken the Death Ham home and eaten it. And all because of some spat with one of the town's gay florists. Now here he was, unashamedly filling his plate right in front of her.

"Hello, boss."

"Don't 'hello boss' me. You know what you did." Then, brusquely pushing past him, "Ham pig."

The Lanier brothers had already stuffed their pockets with little sandwiches, muffins, and cookies and were now in the process of ladling Mrs. Grace Hartwell's Festive Cranberry Punch into a six-quart thermos. Mavis folded her arms, giving them an ominous look. The two brothers crossed to the back door and left, their squirrelly laughter trailing behind them.

The open kitchen and den area of the house where Wood had grown up was a perfect representation of who his parents were, from the eighteenth-century American antiques that people somehow knew were there to be used, to the family photographs—an adequate amount, but not so many that one felt one was being lobbied.

Milan, who had already fed Jeter and filled the plastic container attached to his wheelchair with Dr Pepper, was now supervising in the kitchen. She watched as her husband graciously accepted another condolence. Right now, the McIlmores' middle-aged, ruddy-faced yardman, June, wearing his best cheap suit, was shaking Wood's hand. "I want you to know, Mr. Wood, just like I kept the yard all these years, I'll go every week and pull the weeds off his marker."

Wood used his other hand to squeeze June's shoulder. "Thank you, June. You're a good man."

A sixtyish gentleman with two ladies in tow was next. "Wood, we'll just get through this together. That's all. Because there's no other alternative."

"Thank you, Dr. May."

One of the ladies leaned toward Wood. "You know where we are."

"I do. I do."

The other lady spoke up. "I'm worried about your mother. She hasn't cried at all."

"I know. I'm keeping an eye on her."

Milan was interrupted by an ancient, bent-over woman who handed her a covered casserole dish and spoke loudly, "Milan, this dish needs to cook at 375 degrees for fifteen more minutes. Will you remember that?"

"I will, Miss Purtle. And you were just so sweet to bring it."

Mavis crossed to Milan and leaned into her face.

"Seriously, the twenty-six green bean casseroles—is it like a state law or something that those canned onion rings have to be on top?"

Milan admonished her, "Don't start."

Mavis fingered the lapel of Milan's black silk suit. "Very Grace Kelly."

"Neiman Marcus, fall catalogue." Now Milan had her compact and was powdering Mavis's face. "Your nose is shiny."

"Is that bad?"

Milan sighed and then added some blush,

her eyes drifting toward Wood again, who seemed to be avoiding her gaze. "Sometimes I just wish I knew what that man was thinking."

Mavis looked at Wood, too. She remembered the look on his face when he and Milan had first fallen in love. She could still picture them—Milan twirling around in her majorette skirt with the soft bunny-fur trim. Wood leaning back in a cafeteria chair with his hands behind his head, feet propped on the table and this enormous grin on his face that said, "That's my girl." It was the most happy, filled-up look Mavis had ever seen, and she had made a mental note that just once in her life, she would like to have someone give her a look like that. But unfortunately, as the years went by, the look had disappeared. And Mavis's job, as a good friend, had been not to notice.

Elizabeth and Brundidge were browsing through a box of old vinyl records at Jeter's feet. Wood had his arm around Charlie, who occasionally pretended to try and break free. Elizabeth held up an album. "Can you believe Grand-mère gave me all of Grandpa's Edith Piaf albums? Did you see them, Daddy?"

"Yeah. That's great, honey."

Brundidge pulled out several other records, "Man, this is an awesome stash, Lillabet. Don't forget your old Uncle Brundy at Christmas." Elizabeth laughed. Brundidge continued, "You still majoring in all that *parlez-vous Français* stuff?"

"Yes. Well, actually it's French literature."

Brundidge shook his head, "I don't know where you get it. That was your dad's and my worse subject."

Mavis overheard as she crossed to them. "Please. Don't get me started. At the beginning of every class we all had to say our names in French. You know, like *Je m'appelle* Mavis Pinkerton. I swear every morning, he would say, Jim's apple Earl Brundidge."

Everyone laughed. Elizabeth glanced at her watch and then impatiently tapped her fingers on one of the albums. Wood noticed, because he had seldom seen his daughter appear nervous. Elizabeth wondered whether to tell him her news now or wait. She decided to wait.

Slim appeared carrying an armload. Wood jumped up. "Here, Mother, let me get that." She waved toward some more of boxes. "No,

you just make sure that you all take some of
these tapes home. Your father loved his music, and I want everyone to have these to remember him by." Then she knelt in front of
Jeter and took out a weathered old cloth hat
with fishing lures on it. "Mac would want you
to have this, Carl—he said you were the only
person who appreciated his hat." She placed
it on his head and then began removing
some of the tapes and albums from the box.
"There's the two Louies, Prima and Arm-
strong, and some of that old blues stuff you
two liked." She dipped her head a little,
meeting Jeter's eyes. "You know, you were
also a son."

He had done so well all day, but now he
was unable to speak. Dealing with funerals
was nothing new to him. He lived in the company of old people. But somehow the sight
of Dr. Mac's hat, the one he'd worn so many
afternoons when they'd gone fishing together, often with Wood, but sometimes just
the two of them, well, it had caught him off
guard. Dr. Mac had saved his life after the
accident, riding in the ambulance all the way
to Little Rock. Wood had slept by his bed
every night while the older McIlmore re-

searched and called all over the world to in-
quire about the latest cutting-edge technol-
ogy and information on paralysis. And it had
been Dr. Mac who, not all at once, but over a
period of months, gently laid in the rest of
the bad news. Like the first time, after his injury, when they had gotten the McIlmores'
old boat and gone fishing together. That was
when Wood's dad, in the middle of stringing
several good-sized perch, told him something he already figured. That he would no
longer be able to have erections. But he also
said that fact would not diminish Jeter's desire to be with girls. Dr. Mac had convinced
him that feeling such things would be better
than not feeling them and that without this
small blessing, maybe he couldn't even really become a writer.

But by then, Jeter had already known he
was a writer. That's why, in spite of being
part of the picture, he had been able to see
their silhouette from the shore. The long,
wide boat returning to land at sunset. The
boy in the wheelchair sitting ramrod-straight,
while the old man running the motor wept
quietly into his handkerchief.

Slim had stood and turned to go when

Sidney Garfinkel, a tall, serious man in his late seventies, held out his hand to her. He was handsomely dressed and spoke with a slight Dutch accent, using her given name.

"Evangeline, if you should ever become bored or lonely, I'm in the book. Perhaps we could have a coffee."

Wood suddenly went on full-scale alert. He turned to Brundidge, speaking a little too loud. "What the hell is that?"

"What?"

"Sidney Garfinkel. Asking my mother out."

"Come on, keep your voice down. Mr. G. doesn't mean anything."

Slim attempted to cover. "Sidney, I would love to, but you, of all people, understand that it's just not possible right now."

"Of course. I only wanted you to know that I'm here."

"Thank you."

Slim let go of his hand and crossed to her son, who was now standing with Milan.

She spoke softly, "He's been lonely since Esther died, son. That's all."

"You're right. I'm sorry."

She put her hand on Wood's cheek. "I know you are."

Slim moved on. Milan came over and stood next to Wood.

"You're exhausted. Why don't you go upstairs and have a nap?"

"Because I don't want a nap, Milan. Why don't you have a nap?"

"You don't have to be so hateful."

Wood waited, then said sincerely, "You know, there was a time when I believed that was true."

Milan shook her head, giving up, and returned to the kitchen. Mavis attempted to lighten the mood, cupping Charlie's chin with her hand. "Charlie McIlmore, you are just the most adorable thing I have ever seen. I should just take out my savings right now and send you to Hollywood." Then leaning closer, "By the way, anytime your mom and dad won't let you have the car, you come over and drive your Aunt Mavis's big ol' Oldsmobile Cutlass."

Brundidge said, "Oh, yeah, you're set now. That's a real babe magnet, Charlie. You might as well just douse yourself with gasoline." Charlie laughed. Mavis didn't.

A few hours later, Slim, Milan, and Wood were saying good-bye to the last of the mourners. Elizabeth and Charlie were helping Mavis and Eleanor put away the buffet. A woman in her thirties with a melodic southern accent hung on at the door.

"We love you."

Milan answered sweetly, "We love you, too."

Milan was gifted at matching the exact intent and level of emotion of whoever was speaking to her. Her mistakes in superficial social interaction were almost nonexistent. Her mother-in-law, who had no patience for such things, gently guided the woman onto the porch.

"Thank you again for coming and goodnight."

After the door was closed, it was quiet. Finally, Milan said, "Well, I just need to get my list of everybody who brought something. I think that went really well."

Charlie headed for his coat. "Dad, can I drive?"

Elizabeth intercepted him. "Not so fast, Charlie-bell. You can't leave yet; I have a very important announcement."

Milan smoothed her daughter's hair. "Lils, don't you think we've had enough excitement for one day?"

Slim said, "I told her it would be all right.

After all, she has to go back to school tomorrow and anyway, I think her grandfather would like sharing his day with her."

Charlie was growing impatient. "Well, what is it?"

Elizabeth positioned herself in the center of the room. Wood was starting to feel uneasy.

She began, "Everything has been so hectic, I haven't had a chance to tell you all, that . . . I've found someone I want to spend my life with. His name is Luke Childs and . . . I know it's kinda sudden . . ." Elizabeth strengthened her resolve, lest anyone think this was not a done deal, "but at the end of next summer, we're getting married!"

For the first time that day, Wood looked at his wife. She returned his gaze, stunned.

Mavis was in her old bathrobe, stirring pasta as it boiled on the stove. Her mongrel dog, Chester, was curled up in a chair. It had been a long day, and considering Elizabeth's news, she was pretty sure it was not over. Sure enough, she heard a car screech into the driveway, followed by a door slam. Mavis braced herself for Milan's entry, which did not disappoint. No sooner had she turned to watch the door than Milan burst through it,

throwing her coat across the sofa and digging in her purse as she headed straight toward Mavis.

"Judas H. Priest! What's next? I mean,
what are the odds that my child would go
away to college and fall in love with her
child? About the same as me getting a fucking tattoo?" Mavis stared at Milan, who
rarely swore. Milan said, "I'm sorry, I know
we were going to stop saying the f-word, but
I can't do it today, okay?"

"I wasn't gonna stop saying the f-word."

Milan, who seldom smoked, retrieved a
cigarette and lit it. "Well, I was. And I was
gonna stop smoking, too, but I can't do that
now, either."

"It *is* a state school, Milan. And she does
live in this state. That your daughter would
meet her son is not that odd."

Milan began painting the air with her ciga-
rette. "Meet? Maybe. But fall in love? It's odd!"
Suddenly she noticed the pasta. "What's that?
I thought you were gonna stop eating carbs."

"Not if you're gonna keep saying fuck."

Milan grabbed the spoon and tasted it.
"That needs sugar. It's bad enough to be losing my daughter, but to her son?"

"Have you said anything to Elizabeth?"

"Not yet."

"Good, because we're talking about a high school romance that happened over twenty years ago. Let it go."

"Let it go? Are you insane? I can't do that. He was obsessed with her. He still thinks about her. He still talks about her—"

Mavis lied, "Not to me." Milan gave her a doubtful look. Mavis relented, "Okay, maybe once in a while, when he's drunk." There was a pause, then, "I bet she doesn't even look good anymore."

"Well, why don't we drive there and see? I should've done it years ago."

"No. Trust me. That is not a good idea."

"Of course not. Because you know she looks good."

Milan began pacing. "We're just so vulnerable right now. We barely even speak."

"He's turned forty. You know, men go through changes, too."

"Oh, please! That's just a bunch of psychobabble people use to sell magazines. I'm talking about my life here, Mavis, and I am telling you, we cannot be around this woman for the next fifty years!" Milan threw herself down, almost disappearing into an overstuffed chair.

Mavis sighed, "All right, what do you want to do?"

Milan put her head in her hands and stared at her Christian Louboutin pumps. "What difference does it make? Dr. Mac's dead. Sometimes I think he was the only thing keeping brakes on Wood. Now she's coming back, and I'm losing my baby, too. I feel like Job, you know, from the Bible."

"I know where Job is from." Neither of them spoke for a moment, then Mavis said, "Do you really think it would matter that much to Elizabeth if she knew that her daddy had a . . ." Mavis searched for the right word. ". . . an affair with her fiancé's mother?"

Milan shot out of the chair. "An affair! Why do you have to call it that? You're making it sound way too important and glamorous."

"They were together for over a year."

"That's a fling. Okay? That's how we should put it."

"We?"

"Yes." Milan was pacing now. "Elizabeth has to know. I mean, we can't just pretend it isn't a problem. This boy obviously hasn't told her or he doesn't know himself. And I can't do it because she might think I have some kind of ax to grind." Milan stubbed out her cigarette and gave Mavis her sweetest smile. "It has to be you."

"Why?"

"Because you're my best friend. And this is incredibly awkward. And Elizabeth adores you." Milan loved to say "adore." Somehow it seemed more sophisticated than "love." She continued, "And you can do it in a good way. Maybe you could even, you know . . ." Her voice trailed off. ". . . make it seem funny."

Mavis stared at Milan, hating the whole idea of it. Then she picked up the last half of a key lime pie, debated for a moment, and threw it in the trash.

A few miles across town, Charlie was steering the wheel of his dad's ancient Austin-Healy as Wood, in the passenger seat, wept softly.

"She's just getting married, Dad. It's not like you'll never see her again."

"It's been a helluva day, Charlie. A helluva day. You still have that handkerchief I gave you at your grandpa's funeral?"

Charlie dug in his pocket. "Sorry. Guess I lost it."

Wood picked up a scarf from the center

console, wiped his eyes, and blew his nose on it.

Charlie said, "I think that was Elizabeth's scarf."

"That's okay. I'll have it dry-cleaned."

"It seems like the men in this family sure do cry a lot."

"Nah. That's just because the women never cry. They make us look bad." Charlie grinned, keeping his eyes on the road.

Chapter 6

Earl Brundidge Jr. had himself a "situation"—his favorite term for whatever happened to be the problem of the moment. Well, actually, it was more of a problem for Paris—but anything that affected his town affected him. He hadn't been able to sleep all night. Just thinking about yesterday's depressing, funereal ride through the downtown had left him tossing and fuming. To Brundidge, it was no coincidence that Dr. Mac and so many other Parisiennes of his

generation were dying at the same time as
the stores on Main Street. No accident at all
that the people most worth knowing, maybe
of all the people who ever lived, were disappearing right alongside the stuff most worth
keeping. Now maybe nobody else cared
about that, but Earl Brundidge sure as hell
did. That's why he had picked up his first cup
of coffee of the day at Digger's Truck Stop &
Autel, a morning ritual, and was now circling
the Monster that seemed to be destroying
everything in its path. While the remodel was
under construction, he had refused to even
look in its direction. But now he had decided
to "know thy enemy," to meet head-on the
Massive Structure that had just become one
of the largest Fed-Mart stores in America. It
was even more butt-ugly than he had feared
(breathing new optimism into the maxim, "If
you build it, they will come"), with its cinder-
block walls, tar/gravel composition roof, and
parking lot that was so humongous, it was
rumored they might have to install a tram. Of
course, you couldn't put a lot of stock in
small-town rumors. At one time, there was a
rumor that he had died from botched hair-
plug surgery. He attributed that one to his
ex-wife, Darlene, who would certainly want

to remind people that on top of his being dead, he was also bald. He wasn't bald, really. He just had a receding hairline.

Brundidge exited the parking lot and drove up an adjacent hill, where he stopped his van and looked down on the sea of people, who were now flowing from every car-lined tributary toward the two-hundred-thousand-square-foot superstore. No question about it, this was a Disneyland kinda deal. Just like he knew it would be.

Years ago, he had done everything in his power to prevent the Mammoth Retailer from encroaching even on the perimeter of his beloved hometown. Though Paris itself was relatively small, it was the county seat to scores of even tinier communities populated by an approximate quarter million people, thereby constituting an "ideal trade area" for the Fed-Mart Corporation of America. Brundidge and Jeter had attempted to rouse the citizenry through letters to the editor, but in the end Fed-Mart purchased land just outside the city limits where the townspeople had no jurisdiction. Not that the townspeople seemed to care. They liked the easy, one-stop shopping, competitive prices, and miles and miles of product choices. And now, except for the local merchants, most people were proud that their city had been selected by Fed-Mart as a place deserving of one of its superstores.

Brundidge already knew the drill. As soon as Fed-Mart moved in, the Main Street died. Family businesses that had been there for more than a hundred years, entire blocks of merchants who specialized in, not thousands of products, but "specific" products, and knew everything there was to know about them, were edged out. It didn't seem to matter that Main Street, the very heart and soul of a town's business and social life, and the place where millions of veterans had been cheered when they returned home from war, was disappearing—this avenue of dreams, where little kids pressed their noses against snowy Christmas windows decorated with gleaming bicycles and mechanical Santas, the boulevard of beauty queens and marching bands who were handed their Andy Warhol fifteen minutes of fame by passing briefly through that magical spotlight on the most important street in their lives, the street that Jimmy Stewart, for crying out loud, had run down on his way to getting his family back in *It's a Wonderful*

Life—apparently, it didn't matter to the people of Paris, Arkansas, or anywhere else that these things were going to be gone.

But it mattered to Earl Brundidge Jr. Oh, he wasn't worried about himself. He was in the liquor business and luckily Fed-Mart didn't sell liquor. This was much larger than him or his little enterprise. He savored the steaming, pungent aroma of Digger's coffee, then sipped gingerly at the edge of the Styrofoam cup, careful not to spill any on his blue Zegna shirt. No, this was about America, and America was something Brundidge cared about deeply. That's why he flew the flag every day outside his house and beverage office (he figured that was the least he could do since he'd been born too late for World War II, Korea, and Vietnam). That's why he put his hand over his heart and sang every word of the national anthem at sporting events and why it always made him tear up (like the fourteen times he had watched *The Lion King* with his two little girls). That's why he provided discounts on liquor to the local VFW and other veteran's organizations and had almost single-handedly raised the money for a Vietnam Memorial statue. But it was his Fourth of July spectaculars that re-

ally put him on the map—not just with veterans, but with everybody who knew the place
to be was Earl Brundidge's cabin on the
Champanelle River for the greatest fireworks
display in Paris County. His was no cheap
roadside stand show. Brundidge had actually contacted a member of the famous Italian fireworks family, the Gruccis, and
received not only cases of their finest stuff
but also advice and tips on the latest tech-
nology. Brundidge had a "man" for everything and Mr. Grucci was his man for
fireworks; Digger Oliver, for gas and coffee;
Wood, for free medical advice—yes, he was
a hypochondriac; and Frank Lanier, Milan's
brother, for any stupid odd job nobody else
would do.

People said Brundidge was never happier
than when he was cooking for the masses. It
didn't matter if it was a catfish, dove, or quail
feed, as long as the word *feed* was involved
and hundreds of people showed up. He was
like a redneck Martha Stewart, fussing over
the jalapeño bean dip, making just the right
selection of manly apron, smoking turkeys,
roasting pigs, and dispensing free beer. He
pulled out all the stops on entertainment,
too, one year even getting Jimmy Buffett's

band. Jimmy himself would've been an additional fifteen thousand and that was the summer Darlene had left him and cleaned out his bank account.

Maybe women had not been good to Brundidge, but liquor had, and that's why at Christmas, he and his two little girls made the rounds of the poorest houses in Paris, trying to give back, delivering toys, clothes, and groceries. He personally manned the soft drink stand for all the Paris home football games and had served as president of the Chamber of Commerce and the local Rotarians, as well as the Twentieth-Century Millennium Time Capsule Committee, and just about any other community organization you could name (the Millennium Committee had been his toughest challenge, because everybody had something they thought deserved to go in the capsule).

There was no one more civic-minded, more *America*-minded than Earl Brundidge Jr. And he deeply resented the Giant, Greedy Monster that had come to eat up his town and possibly his country. Deeply resented that the best things about Main Street, and maybe the best things about America, were slowly dying. Deeply resented that Falkoff's Drugstore and its red Naugahyde booths and cranky Mrs. Falkoff, with her crisp handkerchief, old-lady hairnet, and rouge-balled cheeks had already been replaced by strange "Stepford" people who wore loud purple vests and greeted arriving Fed-Mart shoppers with their phony, exaggerated smiles. He was particularly offended that Ione Falkoff's cherry Cokes and ham sandwiches, individually grilled on a waffle iron, had been thrown over for a contraption that produced melted Cheez Whiz and Fritos. And he deeply resented that Mr. Elmer Tillman, possibly the finest appliance sales and repair person in all of Arkansas, a man who gave lifetime guarantees and would come to your house faster than paramedics to fix something, was now gone.

But most of all, Brundidge resented that Mr. Sidney Garfinkel, expert clothier and tailor extraordinaire, had been driven out—the tireless showman who featured each year in his window the most memorable ensembles of the season for men and women, painstakingly put together, not because they represented the latest fad knockoffs, but because they represented Sidney Garfinkel's unimpeachable old-world taste. Here was a man who had served a youthful apprenticeship with Turnbull & Asser in London as well as been a procurer of fine fabrics for many of the top European clothiers, before returning to his native Brussels and being imprisoned by the Nazis. After the war, Sidney had arrived in America and taken a job with the Dillard's department store chain and was assigned to Arkansas. On his drives between stores he became so enamored with the town of Paris and the plum blue hills around it, he and his wife eventually settled there.

Over the years, he had provided the everyday and formal attire needs for two generations of "Parisians" and had taught Brundidge as early as tenth grade, that one never, ever tampers with the basic concept of the formal tuxedo—no Nehru collars, no pastels, no ruffles. Try learning something like that from some bozo wearing a name tag and a purple vest. Where else could an old Jew from Europe with a concentration camp number on his arm help a young Arkansas boy get "spiffy" for his first prom? It could and did happen on Main Street. Brundidge knew it would never happen at Fed-Mart.

Thank goodness the Killer Store had not slain Sidney Garfinkel before he could special order Brundidge's Oscar de la Renta tuxedo, the one that hangs in his closet to this day, the one he wears to all formal occasions and has already left explicit instructions to be buried in. Thank goodness he was given a chance to see Mr. Garfinkel on his knees, in his immaculate suit and tie, his expert hands pinning hundreds of people into their clothes, literally reshaping them in some new way they had not imagined before. Without that, Brundidge would never have known that the secret to dressing well is in the tailoring or, as Mr. Garfinkel put it, in his soft clipped accent, "It is not important how the clothes move, only how the person is moving inside them."

He was grateful to have lived in the pre-Fed-Mart era, when a man of Mr. Garfinkel's caliber could help him establish his own style. Any fool could tell that clogs make a man look like a male nurse, but without Sidney Garfinkel, Brundidge might never have understood the inviolable rightness of simple Italian loafers and the incredible wrongness of flip-flops with socks. Might never have known that Doc Martens were too clichéd for

him, but that his Burberry raincoat was forever. Parkas were out. His cashmere scarf
was in. And frankly, he was never going to
rip the knees out of his jeans, or stop wearing button-down shirts simply because they
had fallen out of vogue. Mr. Garfinkel had
convinced him that his own good taste was
just that—and even though Wood and Jeter
(who apparently didn't give a damn about
how they looked and it showed) ridiculed
him unmercifully, he was proud of the meticulous, well-groomed image he presented to
the world. Milan was the only one of all his
friends who felt the way he did about "personal presentation," and he liked her for that.
It was the main thing, besides Wood, that
they had in common.

Brundidge gave his daughters' wardrobe
as much attention as his own. People said
they looked like the Morton salt girl in their
yellow rain slickers, that they were adorable
in their Little Slugger overalls and matching
baseball hats, and that Cake, in her white
faux-bunny jacket, had been the best-
dressed Mary in the history of the Lutheran
Church Christmas Pageant. It was hard
enough to maintain a standard of excellence
in a small town. Now Fed-Mart was destroy-

ing any chance of obtaining *real quality* things locally. Oh sure, you could shop the Internet, but you never knew if some store in Vermont's size 5T was going to fit. Now he would have to be even more diligent in his search for excellence for himself and his girls.

In the meantime, he would do everything in his power to bring down this King Kong of bad taste, where, in spite of the slogan "If You Can't Find It at Fed-Mart, You Can't Find It" you could seldom find anyone to wait on you, and if you did, they didn't know squat about what they were selling or they would tell you, "Oh, that's Larry's department. He's on break." Not that Brundidge had gone inside. No sir, he had not and would not. He and Jeter had a pact. And Wood, who was always reluctant to rock the boat unless it was actually sinking, had eventually joined them, too. They agreed to stick together, like the three musketeers they had been since they were boys, even if they were the last ones in the whole damn town to never set foot inside the Paris County Fed-Mart Superstore. And they were not alone either. Miss Phipps, who resided at the nursing home with Jeter and who had taught them all in first grade, had said it best in her letter to the *Paris Beacon:* "This is everything we don't wish our little town to be—ugly, impersonal, and, frankly, based on the Communist assumption that larger and undistinguished is better. I personally do not care to join the hoards of slack-jawed strangers overflowing their rubber thongs while steering pushcarts filled with T-shirts, plastic junk, and babies who sneeze Popsicle juice on you." Hey, Fed-Mart, how's that for a polite "Screw you"? And from a teacher, no less! Brundidge had immediately had it laminated and had taken it by to give to Miss Phipps. That was something he liked to do for people. Anytime somebody he knew got in the paper, he laminated it and gave it to them as a memento for posterity. He was not a man who lived in the past, but he knew what the past was worth.

Brundidge hated the stereotypical redneck image so often assigned to small-town people, though he was proud to be one himself—a well-dressed, nonbigoted, gooddaddy kind of redneck, not the kind you see on TV. That was why he hated the name Earl. Why he insisted that everyone call him Brundidge. If he was in Little Rock or Fort

Belvedere on business, and a woman didn't
know him, he would never reveal his first
name. "Earl" was just a killer with women—
the quintessential good ol' boy nom de
plume. Darlene had used it when she
wanted to get under his skin. The truth was,
he had never known anyone named Darlene
who had been worth a damn. They were invariably the kind of girls who wore cheap se-
quined evening gowns with toothpicks
hanging out of their mouths, who went to the
bathroom together in the middle of dinner
and, while fixing their lipstick and rearranging their overperoxided hair, asked each
other, "How was your meat?" Of course, being sort of a public person, he would never
say that. You couldn't be too careful these
days. People would sue you for looking at
them funny. Sure enough, as soon as he
slandered the name Darlene, he would hear
from something called "The Darlene Society" and he would be in a lot of trouble—
even though she was the one who'd had
affairs all over the tristate area, and then
abandoned her two little girls for the backup
guitarist at the El Rondo Motor Harbor and
Lounge.
    That was why he disliked Frank Lanier so

much—because Frank had sued him after being fired as a deliveryman for the Brundidge Beer and Beverage Company, a job he had been given as a favor to Milan. Frank, like Darlene, fell into the last category on the scale of Earl Brundidge Humanitarian Aid—people who "just can't be helped." They were both real bottom-feeders, the kind who drag a man and a town down. But fortunately, since Frank didn't have size 36D breasts, it had taken Brundidge less time to find him out. Believe it or not, and Brundidge swears it's not a joke, Frank actually printed the words "Whee Doggies" under "Sex" on his job application. Brundidge was finally forced to fire him when Frank and his brother, Tom Jr., started pretending to be part of backstage security at local music concerts. They used Frank's old defunct auxiliary deputy sheriff's badge (he'd gotten hired before a written test was implemented) and a couple of plastic toy walkie-talkies to make people think they were somebody. Brundidge had been part of the welcoming committee for The Dixie Chicks—had been dressed in his Brooks Brothers khakis with pin-striped cotton shirt and three-button navy blazer—had been actually speaking to Natalie Maines and by the way, no flies on her, when Frank, reeking of liquor, had walked up carrying his stupid plastic-shit, lavender walkie-talkie with Hello Kitty painted on it, for crying out loud, and called him "Boss!" It was the most humiliating moment of Brundidge's life, and Frank was fired on the spot. They later resolved Frank's lawsuit by Brundidge's agreeing to rehire him as his man for "odd jobs."

There was no denying it was people like Frank and Darlene who gave hicks a bad name. They were the reason words like *hee-haw* and *honky-tonk* got started—the kind of people the media always interview after a tornado. It burned Brundidge up that reporters, especially northern ones, seemed to intentionally pick people who sounded ignorant and dressed like white trash off-the-rack. "Well, we's all in our double-wide when we seen it a comin'. It lacked to scared Momma 'n 'em to death." Brundidge had a fantasy that if a tornado ever hit Paris, he would be talking to Dan Rather in his black cashmere overcoat and burgundy scarf (yes, it would probably be in the spring, but that was his best coat, and he was going to wear it), saying something like, "I had just sat down for bit of backgammon in the conser-

vatory, Dan, when the terrible twister struck."
Brundidge had never actually known anyone
with a conservatory, but ever since he was a
boy, he had liked the looks of it on his Clue
board.

Anyway, people could think what they
wanted to about hicks. Maybe some hicks
even deserved it, if they could fall for a place
like the Paris County Fed-Mart Superstore.
Brundidge replaced his coffee cup in the little car tray and punched in Tim McGraw. He
started the van, steering it away from his
New Nemesis, as Tim began softly crooning,
"I may be a real bad boy, but I can be a real
good man . . ." Ah, *now we're in business*.
The mellow strains of the music put Brundidge in a more relaxed state of mind, making it just the right song for the right
occasion. *You tell 'em, Tim. Tell 'em who we
are*. In a few minutes, he would be back on
the highway and heading toward the city limits of Paris, where soon he would be sitting
at his desk, fielding phone calls, sharing the
day's jokes and handing out encouragement
as easily as if it were sticks of gum.

He already knew what he thought. He
thought living in a small town was just about
the greatest thing that could ever happen to

anyone. But mostly, he was just glad it had happened to him. And now he was going to spend the rest of his life trying to pay that back.

Chapter 7

Mavis put another log in the little fireplace in her kitchen. Then she picked up a small strainer and placed it across the rim of a porcelain cup with bluebirds painted on it— the one that she had purchased from a hundred-year-old woman at a garage sale. After a time, she lifted a teapot and poured something called British Colonial Tea, "the preferred morning drink of aristocrats," through the strainer. Mavis enjoyed the idea that the old Arkansas woman and the mus- tachioed Englishman on the British Colonial can had somehow joined forces to provide her with the nicest cup of tea in Paris. Not having much family of her own, she liked bringing people together like that. It was something she was good at, making small bonds and little families where before there had been none. That's why, after last night's conversation with Milan, she had called Elizabeth and arranged to meet her for breakfast. Because friends were important to Mavis. Friends were family. But right now she was going to enjoy her tea, read the newest magazine arrivals (a lifetime addiction), and try not to think about the odious task ahead.

Mavis smeared apple jelly on a scone and studied the latest seriously acclaimed Hollywood actress to pose with her scrawny cheeks hanging out of her underpants while wearing a smile that begged the seemingly incongruent question, "Hi, I just won the Oscar, wouldn't you like to do the dirty with me?" Inside, it was always the same spiel, how this girl's never had any self-esteem because she's only been valued only for her beauty. (Yeah. Yeah. Don't people know that sometimes there's a good reason for low self-esteem?) Anyway now she's never felt more in tune with her own sexuality, and after some custom-designed Taebo, a fearless, chance-taking director, and daily sessions with her herbal supplement guru (strict, but loving), it looks like everything's gonna be okay. Next were the obligatory articles on "How to Have Better and Better and Better and Better and Better and Better and Better and Better Sex" (as though there were no other reason to be alive, really) or how some famous model or TV personality has decided to try to be happy at a size eight. For Mavis that was as twisted as when they presented plus-size models on daytime talk shows with the promise "We want to show the world what real women look like," when the plus-size models never even looked very overweight. What Mavis wanted to see waddling down the catwalk was a huge, happy, honking three-hundred-pound "you can kiss my fat ass" kind of gal, with cellulite forearms and hamhock thighs draped in some fabulous designer togs. Even just one woman like that pitted against the scores of skeletal chic chicks would go a long way toward making up for all the size-zero clothes in department stores. Tank tops so small Mavis wouldn't even bother to blow her nose on them. Well, maybe she had bothered, once. Anyway, she knew that fat girl was never going to float across her TV screen, anymore than all the experts who make a living telling people like Mavis that "beauty comes from within" wanted her to.

Mavis knew all too well where beauty came from—it came from having a long, thin body with a perfectly symmetrical face, large wide-set eyes, and Halloween-style paraffin lips with humongous Chiclet teeth. It did not come from being yourself and weighing two hundred and forty-eight pounds and wearing a muumuu. So just stop it! She's not fat and stupid. Okay?

Mavis was polishing off her scone, now. After years of trying to spin fatness as a state of independence, she had settled into the art of eating without apology. So maybe she would die five or ten years early—we all make our deal with the devil. In the meantime, she was going to enjoy herself. She loved her kitchen and the way things she made in it smelled and tasted. It was like the residue of everything she had ever made before was still just a little bit in the next thing. The way it was with generations of families. (Not that she knew much about that. It had mostly been just her mom and her.)

Mavis tossed the magazine onto the sofa and gave Chester her last bite. She would have to hurry. It was almost 8:30 and her breakfast with Elizabeth was set for nine. She also had to go by Wood's office and give them a piece of her mind over the infuriating thing that had happened to her in yesterday's funeral procession. For Mavis, the worst part about living in a small town was that everybody knew your personal business. On the other hand, she liked the wide berth people gave each other—how Tommy Epps, a long-haired apparition from the sixties, slept in the maintenance room at the nursing home, but not only did they not make a fuss, they left the window unlocked for him. Or how Milan wore totally coordinated outfits and full makeup to the Kroger, but Mavis could still go in her pajamas and everyone would say, "Well, that's just ol' Mavis. She likes to shop in her PJs." And even though Paris was often the butt of her jokes and almost every time she left, she threatened not to come back, for some reason, she always did.

Oh sure, the goobers and rednecks, the sheer provincialism of it all, drove her nuts—the having to greet each person like at least one of you has been in a foreign prison for the last twenty-five years, the overniceness—having to write a damn thank-you note every time somebody threw a rock at you, the taking of fifteen minutes to say *any-*

thing—you couldn't even ask someone to perform the Heimlich without first inquiring as to how they were, the oversolicitousness—you all come back now, you hear? You must spend the night, stay for dinner, eat our food, sleep in our bed, smell this, wear this, use this, and please just let us know if we can do anything else for you in any way. And then you had to figure out the difference between which invitations were sincere and which were simply being polite—something northerners were invariably confused about but southerners understood implicitly. Mavis, who was not a "real Parisian," finally decided that the first invitation is generally extended purely out of social graciousness. The second one means you could stay and it would be okay. The third one means they really want you. But phew! Isn't everyone just exhausted by now?

Mavis and her mom had moved to Paris from St. Louis when Mavis was six. At first they came to look after her mother's Aunt Nell. Then after Nell died and left them her house, they decided to stay.

Mavis's father, Laddie Pinkerton, had been a school-supply salesman for the Red Chief Paper Company. He covered Missouri,

Illinois, and Iowa and was on his way home
for Thanksgiving when he stopped to fix a
flat tire and was struck by lightning. Everybody always said the rubber on tires would
keep you safe from lightning but evidently
you had to be *inside* your car, not outside,
under a tree. Anyway, the coroner told
Mavis's mother it wasn't the lightning that
killed him. It was lying facedown in a one-
inch puddle of water. *One inch.* Mavis had
studied, no, become obsessed with that particular measurement on the wooden ruler
her dad had given her. All through elementary school, the teachers could be talking
about multiplication, the fifty states, even the
basic food groups, but most of the time
Mavis found that one-inch mark on her ruler
emblazoned with Red Chief Paper Company
much more fascinating. *One inch?* Were
they kidding? How could anybody have such
bad luck? I mean, first to be struck by lightning, then to survive that but die because
you also happen to land in *one inch* of water.
Well, it was too much. How could a child ever
have confidence in anything again? To a kid,
that's got to feel, well, personal. Was it because she had forgotten to kiss him good-
bye? Or that she had left her little bicycle in

the rain when he had told her to bring it in?
She had been alive for six years when it happened and she did not have one single play-
mate whose parent had been struck by
lightning and then died in one inch of water.
To this day, she did not know one other person it had happened to. Even now, when
Mavis is filling a measuring cup, she is always exquisitely aware of when the liquid
hits the one-inch mark—a reminder of how
little it takes to change your life forever.

Right after "the accident," when people began arriving with cakes, cookies, and hams,
Mavis stayed up late and ate some of it.
Well, actually, she ate almost all of it. And
since she was a hefty kid but not large
enough to accommodate that much food, a
doctor had to be called and she was pretty
sure they eventually pumped her stomach.
She knew she had been taken to an all-
white room when they first thought it might
be appendicitis. And then she remembered
leaving the hospital with her mother, who
was crying and holding her hand while
Mavis clung to the little chalk figurine she
had been given for being such a good girl.
She guessed they had chosen a chalk figurine for her instead of a sucker because

she couldn't eat that—which she later did anyway.

Only six years with maybe the most important person in your life and for two of those you're barely able to walk and talk—it wasn't fair. Mavis closed her eyes, the way she had all through her childhood and tried to picture him. But too often, she knew she was picturing *snapshots* of him, instead of the real, warm, flesh-and-blood him—bending down with his arms around her at Busch Gardens—no, that must be a photograph, because he's *posing*—here's one! Daddy clapping as she wobbles toward him on her bike. No, that's a movie her mother made— how about leaning over her bed and saying, "Goodnight, Miss America. Sweet dreams." Wait! Stop! That's a real one! Nobody ever made a picture of that! Stay right there! Wait! Daddy, please, don't go. You're getting fuzzy. This is the part where Mavis squints her eyes tighter and tighter trying to keep the picture inside. But, eventually, he always leaves.

That was another reason Mavis wanted a baby more than anything. She liked the idea of another person in this world who would share her father's genes and characteristics

and who might even help bring him into focus. Maybe that wasn't a very good reason
for wanting a baby. She had some others
that were better. But that was the one that
made her fall asleep feeling easy.

She was upstairs trying to find something
to wear—not the paisley skirt. Mavis always
felt she had to back out of the room in that.
Anyway, now all she needed was a sperm
daddy. After two years of trying to adopt, after all the near misses—"I'm sorry, but two-
parent families take precedence"; "If only
you could get your congressman to call our
embassy"—she and Dr. Mac had decided
sperm banks were definitely the way to go.
And she sure as hell wasn't going to wait until she found the right partner. That was
about as likely to happen as her mixing
Velveeta cheese with canned chili for a party
dip. The truth was, Mavis was no longer
looking for nor believed in the ridiculous notion of a soul mate who miraculously fills all
your empty places. She didn't need "Mr. I'm
the Other Half of You" to finish her off. And
she was sick and tired of townspeople asking when she was going to find someone
and settle down. Were they kidding? Were
they insane? She was as big as a barn and

forty years old. What did it take to discourage these people? But what really rankled
were all the women who complained about
their own husbands. How this one or that
one was cheating on them or never paid any
attention to them. Then they would turn right
around and tell Mavis that she needed to
hurry up and get her one. "Better stop playing hard to get and let one of these men
around here catch you. Ha-ha." Oddly, almost no one seemed to think Mavis was too
old or too fat to get married. The general
opinion was that she was too uppity and too
set in her own ways.

Okay, how about long denim skirt with
light blue shirt hanging loose? Yes. When in
doubt, always go with your fat-girl uniform.
Anyway, right now, she had to get her story
together for Elizabeth—how to tell her about
whatever it was that had gone on between
her fiancé's mother and her dad. It was just
like Milan to stick her with this. And then
have the flat-out balls to suggest that she
also make it funny! "Hey, kid! Congratulations on getting married! And here's some
more good news. You don't have to worry
about all the in-laws liking each other.
They've already slept together!"

Maybe Elizabeth wouldn't even care. Mavis was in her car and wishing she didn't feel so nauseated from all the fertility hormones. Anyway, who even knew what the deal was between Wood and Duff? I mean, in high school it had seemed pretty damn steamy, but everything feels steamy in high school. Not that Mavis would have any first hand knowledge about that. She'd had a couple of boyfriends, like Ricky Starkweather, but he actually had seemed more dirty than steamy.

Anyway, here's how it happened. After several years of going together, Wood and Milan broke up because Kathleen Duffer had finally managed to turn Wood's head. The date was February 12, 1979. Mavis remembers, because that was the day senior pictures were being made and she and Milan had locked themselves in the largest stall of the girls' bathroom while Milan, who almost never cried, sobbed barrels of Maybelline mascara all over Mavis's shirt and sweater. You can see the black on Mavis's collar in the yearbook. The second thing Mavis remembers about the breakup is that there is no sadder picture in all of human history, well, at least not human *social* history, than

the one of Milan standing next to Victor Lee
Sayres at that year's prom. By the time
Wood and Milan had broken up, the best
people had already been taken and Milan
had been left with Victor Lee and his cheesy
string tie and Hitler mustache. Of course,
Mavis's own prom picture with Ricky Starkweather, wearing his Elvis sneer and pink
ruffled shirt, was not something you would
save for the mantel, either. Especially not after Ricky, having failed to graduate, robbed
the prom the following year. But poor Milan!
Mavis had seen happier looks on the faces
of POWs. And all the while, Duff and Wood,
who were too cool to have their own picture
made, had danced circles around her. Mavis
remembered how those two were always in
their own little world, reading each other
passages from Thoreau, feeding each other
french fries, riding for miles in Wood's
Austin-Healy with the top down—unlike Milan, Duff loved getting her hair mussed. The
"I just fell out of bed" look and wearing
Wood's shirts became her trademarks. You
might think because he fell so hard and so
fast that Wood was a young man who liked
to play around. But Mavis couldn't remember
him having any other serious girlfriends,

ever, besides Duff and Milan, in spite of the fact that there were plenty waiting in line for their crack at the town prince.

After graduation, Wood burned up the interstate between Duke (where he was in premed) and Atlanta, where Duff had gone to study art. Milan was on scholarship at Arkansas State Teachers College but spent most of her time putting her broken heart on paper in letters home to Mavis. Then one day, only a few months after Tom Lanier shot himself, a breathless phone call from Milan—she and Wood were getting married! Apparently, he had been burning up more interstates than anyone knew. "We're going to have a baby, Mave! We're on our way to New Orleans and this is the happiest day of our lives!" That was pure Milan. Putting the best face on everything, including the very baby that Mavis was now on her way to try to explain all this mess to—What mess? Was there already a mess? She turned on her blinker and began changing lanes, getting ready to make her turn at the new Fed-Mart Superstore exit. A short distance beyond would be the Motor Harbor. She hated driving all the way out to a truck stop for breakfast, but Elizabeth liked to "go slumming" when she was home from college.

Suddenly, Mavis was seized with a real sense of dread. Wasn't living in the present hard enough without digging up all this cargo from the past? That's why Mavis had not even bothered to tell Milan what Wood had said about Duff when he was drunk—how she was the only girl he had ever felt he could be himself with, how after all these years he could still smell her hair—yeah, yeah, yeah, you don't need to relive every word, Mavis; anyway, how he knew that was wrong, but there it was—things Wood would never say if he were sober. And it had shocked her to see that kind of pain could be caused by someone who was essentially a stranger to all of them now.

Mavis circled the gigantic parking lot and finally pulled into a space about a half-acre of cars from the restaurant. As she spilled out of the Cutlass, gathering her coat and overflowing purse, she reminded herself that people do and say all sorts of stupid things when they're drunk. Mavis struggled into her coat as she headed out, her purse leaking Kleenex. Hell, she had almost married her

Cuban baker's assistant in order to get him a green card. But fortunately they had both sobered up in the backseat of a cab on the way to Hot Springs.

Now Mavis was walking just ahead of two truckers, moving toward the entrance. She tried to appear businesslike, lest they mistake her for some easy loser fat girl who was looking for a ride somewhere. Mavis always assumed men thought overweight women were desperate for sex. She could feel their eyes on her backside. They were probably thinking the best sex she'd ever had had been with herself. Anyway, despite numerous warnings, Mavis had dismissed the whole Duff-Wood affair from her mind until Elizabeth announced her bombshell and Milan had shown up last night to pitch a hissy fit in her kitchen. Mavis had tried her best to act nonchalant, but the truth was, by then, the high piercing violin stabs that dominate the sound track of *Psycho* were already going off in her head. She and Milan had seen it on cable TV at Claire Cutsinger's house when they were eleven and it had scared the hell out of them—so much so that it became the music Mavis always hears as the accompaniment for any dramatically bad news. Or news that seems on its way to becoming bad. And this latest news seemed to have that kind of potential. Yes, now there were just too many coincidences (not unlike the unbelievable happenstance in her own life involving lightning, a flat tire, and one inch of water). A married man yearns for his lost love. His daughter goes away to college and, out of twenty thousand students, falls in love with the woman's son. Can romantic chemistry be inherited or, even more incredibly, seek itself out? Yearning married man and lost love are reunited. Oh, yeah. This will have a happy ending. The violin strings of *Psycho* began pounding Mavis's brain again at the exact moment she saw Elizabeth, smiling and waving in the truck-stop window. Mavis smiled and waved back, something that was not easy to do in the middle of so much noise and confusion. As she entered the door, the violin stabs were slowly swallowed up by Tracy Byrd lamenting, "Ten Rounds with Jose Cuervo." Mavis gathered herself and crossed toward Elizabeth, feeling grateful for the first time in her life for country music.

CHAPTER 8

All the breakfast dishes had been cleared at the Pleasant Valley Retirement Villa, and most of the residents had assumed their stagnant positions for the day. A canned instrumental version of "Knock Three Times" played over and over on the loudspeaker. People who had once been loving, talkative, vibrant, annoying, dazzling, deceitful, and sexy were now, for the most part, quiet. Except for two or three holdouts, they had no more battles to fight, no hearts to win over. And at night, they lay in their assigned beds facing heaven, as though waiting for the final note of an old movie score that now hung expectantly over their rooftop.

Mr. Henry Dill, who was a hundred and two years old, had been wheeled to his spot by the window, where he would spend most of the day, head down, like an old blue-rooted tree, occasionally drooling sap. Mr. and Mrs. Harold Chapman, dressed as always in their Sunday best, held hands on the sofa, neither quite sure of who the other was anymore, but somehow still knowing they belonged to each other.

A few feet away, Jeter was being spoon-fed his morning Rice Krispies by Rudy Cas-tenera, a sharp-talking, fast-moving Cuban man in his twenties. Jeter often got up late. At first, the staff had tried to enforce a cur-few, but after learning that he would not be as pliable as some of their more elderly charges, they had given up—sometimes even allowing him to sit up all night sleeping in his wheelchair. On the evenings when Rudy worked until midnight, he would find extra chores to do, so he could be there to put Jeter to bed when Jeter was ready. As repayment for this kindness, Jeter had been responsible for teaching Rudy, a Cuban refugee, English. Rudy's parents still ran a dance school in Havana. The rest of his story involved a rickety fishing boat and a cousin in Little Rock whose medical-supply company went belly-up. Rudy had embraced all things American, including the belief that anyone who works hard can achieve some-thing called The American Dream. That's why he almost never slept and why he held down two jobs, the other as a baker for Mavis at Doe's.

Not far from Jeter, Miss Lodusky Phipps, ancient and tiny, sat playing canasta. A retired first-grade teacher, she suffered from dementia as well as inexplicable bouts of blinding coherence. Miss Phipps had recently had a long, interesting conversation with Rudy. Then a few minutes later, she had asked him who he was. He had reacted, confused, until she had clapped her hands and exclaimed delightedly, "Oh, I know you! You're from America, aren't you?" Rudy, being both tickled and flattered, had repeated this story to everyone.

The worst moment of Miss Phipps's life had occurred when her husband and little boy had been killed on their way to buy a package of walnuts. If she had made a different cake that day, they would probably still be here. Even now, within minutes of meeting someone new, she will have her old tattered wallet out showing their pictures, telling the story. She always tells it flatly, without emotion, as though she knows to tell it any other way would be the end of her.

Miss Phipps was a stickler for perfect social behavior. She wrote flawlessly in the old-style Palmer script. And she cared deeply about each of her students, having once even given a month's pay to have a little boy's enormous ears surgically pinned back. She had also kept a snapshot of each of her first-grade classes. Milan, Jeter, Wood, and Brundidge had all been in her class together. In the picture that showed the class of 1968, Jeter and Milan have their arms around each other.

Miss Phipps had often recalled to Jeter that Milan was one of the loveliest children she had ever taught—how Milan had given her a gold cherub pin with blue sequins glued where the eyes might have been and a childishly scrawled note that said, "To Miss Phipps. So cool. So in the groove. I love you. Milan." It had touched Miss Phipps because she knew the family had no money. There was even a winter when Frank Lanier had to attend school wearing his sister's shoes.

She also remembered that Earl Brundidge had been a very nervous little boy. He got upset and cried when the other children wouldn't form a straight line or someone stole his pencils. And he refused to leave at the end of a school day until Miss Phipps had given him a kiss.

Miss Phipps was never shy about reminding Jeter that he and Wood had been a
handful, first graders who read on a fifth-
grade level and were overly curious about
everything. She had decided early on
against sending them off to the library to
read alone, where they might have come up
with the unfortunate notion that they were
gifted. Instead, she had discreetly provided
them with more difficult books, while giving
them the responsibility of reading stories to
the other children every day. To Miss Phipps,
the life lessons involving volunteerism, self-
lessness, and courtesy were every bit as important as test scores.

As her memories faded, Jeter had become the chief reservoir for all her knowledge and insights regarding the one
thousand nine hundred and fifty students
she had taught over a period of forty-eight
years. He also happened to know the sort of
people most of these children had become.
It was useful information, one of the few ad-
vantages settled on a writer who ends up living in a nursing home with his first-grade
teacher.

Miss Phipps's card partner was Margaret
Delaney, a renowned teacher of literature.

Miss Delaney had never married, but had instead devoted her life to putting words and scenery inside of young people and changing them forever. For her trouble, she was now a legend to several generations of Parisians. And she considered the class of 1980, the last one she presided over before retiring, the one that included Wood, Milan, Jeter, Brundidge, Mavis, and the unspeakable her, to be one of the finest of her career. Miss Delaney's body may have grown old but her mind had remained as bright and independent as when she was teaching. And that was why she deeply resented the new owners of the Pleasant Valley Retirement Villa. The first thing they had done was change their name from the Old Folks Home of Paris. Miss Delaney felt it was the business of language to reflect reality, not manipulate it. Perhaps that was why she had gotten off on the wrong foot the very first day the supremely confident Ms. Judith Nutter had arrived from Los Angeles, California, and begun to oversee things. Ms. Nutter had made the mistake of saying that Miss Phipps's loss had occurred so long ago, she should surely have experienced closure by now. And Miss Delaney had told her, "Just so you know, we don't have closure here in Paris. People die. Some people get over it. Some people don't. Some people don't want to. And that's all we have. Just so you know."

After that, Judith Nutter, undeterred, had decided to change the names of meals. The noon meal, which had been called dinner for as long as anyone could remember, was changed to lunch. And supper, which had always been the final meal of the day, turned into dinner. Residents immediately became confused. Some thought if they were eating dinner, it must be noon. Others didn't show up for dinner at all because they insisted on waiting for supper. Then Judith Nutter, on a roll, began eliminating favorite menu items like chicken and dumplings and replacing them with healthful but idiotic entrées like Vegetable Burrito Olé and Tofu Surprise. A majority of the residents at Pleasant Valley had already lost their spouses, their jobs, and many of their friends. For the most part, they were through with life. At this late stage, they did not want to be surprised by tofu or anything else. The one thing they had to look forward to each day was supper or dinner or whatever it was called. And now that had been taken away by Judith Nutter—a person who somehow was allowed to boss people around who had been alive for eight or nine decades, people who in all those years had never even heard of her.

Even worse, Judith Nutter and her associates had affected a phony cordiality with the old folks. Miss Delaney especially hated the way they had hooted and hollered when the Chapmans kissed, making inappropriate insinuations, pretending the old couple was still in the game. It was all so condescending, a mockery of the genuine affection that existed between them. So this is how it ends, with some cheesy California cheerleader acting as though they're hot? It was even worse than people saying elderly people having sex was repulsive. Anyway, Miss Delaney knew something about that. Not only did she get cable, but she'd had two lovers in her lifetime and had enjoyed them both. It had not been as romantic as poetry had led her to believe it might be, but it was still more than satisfactory. And now that she was old, she wondered what was so offensive about a couple with sagging skin and wrinkles making love? Did these fornicating youngsters on her TV set really not know that sex is in the brain? Had they never read the passages where Heathcliff makes love to Cathy without ever touching her? It genuinely puzzled Miss Delaney that twenty-year-olds who had known each other for less than ten minutes and who were on all fours exchanging bodily fluids with their legs apart and their tongues hanging out and nothing more interesting to say than "Fuck me. Fuck me hard" had the gall to think that old people were repulsive.

Then, the final indignity occurred when Judith Nutter decreed that Muzak would be played over the public address system every day from 8 A.M. to 8 P.M., providing "a positive and cheerful environment for visitors as well as staff and residents." For Margaret Delaney, that was it. She had been willing to overlook the condescending attitude, the silly menus, marginal health care, and confusing meal names. But for someone who had once set her students on fire by teaching James Joyce to the accompaniment of Mozart, this was simply too much!

That was why, just as Rudy was putting in Jeter's last mouthful of cereal, Miss Delaney had leapt to her feet, climbed up on a folding chair, and shouted at the top of her lungs, "I cannot endure another minute of this insuf-

ferable, mind-numbing Muzak! Someone
has got to stop management from killing us
with this . . . this artificial sweetener for the
soul! Pleasant Valley Corporation of America and all of its subsidiaries, rot in hell!"

Mr. Henry Dill woke up.

Mr. and Mrs. Harold Chapman moved
closer together, frightened.

Miss Phipps clapped her hands with glee.

Jeter and Rudy looked at each other and
smiled.

Miss Delaney sat back down.

Elizabeth was resplendent in no makeup, a
winter-white turtleneck sweater, and jeans.
She and Mavis had just filled their plates at
the Motor Harbor's $5.95 all-you-can-eat
buffet and were now seated.

Mavis said, "That's what I love about this
town. No pesky maître d's, no specials du
jour; just come on in and troll the pig trough."

Elizabeth laughed. Then, even though it
was still breakfast, Mavis fortified herself
with some wine. After several glasses, she
said, "So, you poor little ol' homely girl,
you're gonna beat me to the altar, huh?"

"Well, I, I—"

"That's a joke, darlin'. I'm not even in the

race anymore." "Darlin'" was the one southern word Mavis had allowed herself to appropriate, but she still felt odd saying it.

Elizabeth took her hand, "Aunt Mavis, I
never expected this to happen. It's like,
there's this *chimie mysterieuse* between us."

Mavis attempted nonchalance. "Mysterious chemistry? That does sound serious."
There was a long pause as she stared at
Elizabeth, then, "Listen, jelly bean, I've got
something to tell you. I don't believe it's
gonna make any difference, but I think you
should know." Mavis steeled herself. "Your
father dated, and that's 'dated' with a hard
'D,' Luke's mother, you know, in high school
and," her voice trailed off, "maybe a little of
college."

Elizabeth was taken aback. "You're kidding. I knew she was from around here,
but . . . why didn't Luke say something?

"My guess is, he probably doesn't know.
You haven't met her yet?"

"No, just on the phone." Elizabeth was
quiet for a moment, then, "I can't believe this.
I just don't get why nobody mentioned it."

Mavis stumbled. "Probably . . . not sure
how you would . . . feel."

"Well, I don't know how I feel. It's okay, I

guess, I mean, it's kind of weird." Elizabeth searched Mavis's face, then, "How serious were they?"

Mavis told Elizabeth the answer with her eyes.

"Okay. Don't wanna know." Elizabeth sat absorbing this. Then, using her grandfather's pet name for Milan, "So what does Italy think?"

"She just wants you to be happy."

"Italy wants me to be happy with the son of my dad's ex-girlfriend?"

"Absolutely."

"Are we talking about the same country here?"

"Look, Lils, I'm not gonna lie to you. It's gonna take some getting used to. But the important thing is what you and . . ." Mavis searched for the name.

"Luke."

"Right. What the two of you want." Then Mavis added, "You know you're my baby, too. And I do just have to throw in here that I think this is a little fast."

"I know!" Elizabeth let out her breath. "Can you believe it? It's outrageous. I'm surprised more people aren't trying to stop it."

"Do you want us to?"

"No. I wouldn't listen. I'm much too in love"

"Well, I, for one, can't wait to meet this person."

"Okay, but if you don't like him, you'll just have to pretend, because I can't give him up now. And don't worry, I'm not gonna make you give me a bridal shower and find out how many words people can make out of Mrs. Luke Childs."

"Thank you. You'll be in my will."

Then, regarding her empty glass, "God, this truck stop wine is brutal."

Elizabeth lit up. "No wonder we were so attracted. It's in our genes, like fate! Is that possible?"

"No."

"I just love you so much. This is going to be the coolest summer. It won't just be a wedding, it'll be like a reunion, too!"

Mavis worked hard to keep the pain out of her smile. "Yeah. Kind of."

Charlie was firing baskets through a hoop in the McIlmores' driveway as Wood finished loading Elizabeth's suitcase into the back of her Mustang. P. Diddy's "You Gets No Love" was playing on Charlie's jambox. Wood followed his daughter to the driver's side and hugged her hard. Then he held Elizabeth away from him.

"I want to meet this boy, now."

"You will. He says he takes after his mother . . ." Elizabeth decided to fish. "Kinda like I take after you."

"Well, he must be a very fine fella." Wood opened the car door.

She decided to try again, "Did you love her?"

There was a brief moment as father and daughter understood each other.

"Elizabeth, that was a long time ago. Who told you that?"

"It doesn't matter." Then studying her father's face, "You did! Does Mother know?"

Wood's voice became more firm. "Go on now. Get in the car."

Elizabeth spoke as she did so, "Why does everyone act so weird about this? I thought it was a long time ago."

Wood closed the door and leaned his head in a little. "Listen, Ace, these next few years—it's the most alive you're ever gonna feel. Don't waste one minute worrying about some silly thing like that." He kissed her cheek, then, "All you need to know is how stuck your mom and I are on you."

Swish. Charlie made a basket from far away. Wood smiled, pleased, then returned to Elizabeth. "And ol' Charlie-boy over there. Remember when you tried to sell him to June for a quarter?"

Elizabeth smiled a little in spite of herself. She knew better than to push Wood once he had decided not to talk about something. "I love you, Daddy."

Wood looked straight at her. "You're it for me, kid. You and Charlie. You're the whole deal." He stepped away from the car. "Drive careful now."

"I will." Elizabeth backed the Mustang out of the driveway a little too fast and screeched the tires as she pulled away. "Bye, Charlie-horse. Stay out of my clothes and makeup!"

Charlie rolled his eyes as Elizabeth's car disappeared. Then he turned to Wood and began dribbling the basketball all around him. "Hey, Dad, go for it."

Wood grabbed the ball and went in for a jump shot. He missed. Charlie grinned, shaking his head. "Oh, man, you're gettin' old."

"You got that right, son." Wood headed toward the house. "You got that right."

Charlie's eyes followed his dad through the front door, a little puzzled. P. Diddy droned on, *". . . whatever you do will come back to you . . ."*

Twelve patients were waiting to see Dr. Wood McIlmore as he stood in the middle of his reception area handing a bottle of pills to one of them.

"This ought to bring the fever down. But if it doesn't, you call me at home tonight."

"Thanks, Dr. McIlmore."

Wood crossed to a man in his seventies. "How you doing there, Mr. Tibb? Is that hip bothering you again?

"It ain't just my hip, Doc. Ever'thing hurts."

"It's a heckuva way to live, isn't it? You just give me a few minutes, and then we're gonna sit down and figure out how we can make things better for you."

"All right."

Wood steered another patient toward a nurse, "Joanne, you want to go with Mike there?" Then, turning to Mike, "Get her vitals and current meds." He picked up a little girl who was waiting with her mother. Mae Ethel had passed more than ten years ago, but

Wood still saw all her children and grandchildren gratis. "Okay, who ate all my little peanut butter cups? Was that you, Elizabeth Brown?"

She nodded.

Wood said, "Well, all right, as long as it was you. I just wanted to make sure it was somebody I like and admire."

Just as Wood, the child, and her mother disappeared into an adjacent office, Mavis burst through the front door.

"I just came by to tell you all that while I was riding in the procession yesterday, I was accosted in an incredibly ugly manner by Smith Dunlop, who against all odds, continues to operate full tilt on that one defective brain cell. Now, my question for you is, how the hell did he find out that I am even interested in having a baby, much less looking for a sperm donor?" Suddenly, Mavis noticed the other patients staring. "Do you mind? We're trying to have a private conversation here!"

Wood's nurse said, "Mavis, we haven't told anyone—"

"Well, then, how else did it get out?"

The receptionist offered, "I heard you

telling two people in the Piggly Wiggly myself."

It was impossible to know whether it was the cheap wine or the receptionist's tone, but now Mavis was even madder. "That is so absurd. I never socialize in the Piggly Wiggly. I hate that damn name and I don't even go there unless Kroger is out of something. Just give me my file."

Mavis sailed around the reception area, upsetting everyone. One of the nurses tried to block her.

"You can't come in here! Anyway, that isn't even where we keep patient files."

Mavis headed for a cabinet. "I know. It's the 'Looking for Mr. Sperm Donor' drawer." She opened it and began rifling through the folders. "And I want my name out before anyone else sees it!" Mavis grabbed a file and then, for a moment, appeared startled. "Carl Jeter? What the hell's he doing in here?"

One of the nurses threw up her arms. "I don't believe this. You worry about your own privacy but you don't respect anyone else's. Get out!"

Wood emerged from the inner office. "What's going on?"

Mavis planted her feet firmly in his carpet, waving her file in the air. "I'll tell you what's going on! No matter how hard you try, nothing in this damn town is ever confidential! Which is why I'm getting my records and keeping them myself. And if one more word gets out about my personal reproductive information, I will hold everyone in this office responsible." She turned to the waiting patients, "And that goes for all of you, too!"

Mavis stomped her size-ten feet across the reception area and out the door, slamming it. There was a long pause while nobody said anything. Then, an elderly man, who was hard of hearing, yelled, "What's her problem?"

His wife answered sincerely, "Reproductive inflammation."

Wood shook his head and went back in his office.

A long silence was now in progress, the kind that comes from having a conversation that keeps hitting the same old snag. Mavis had her back to Jeter, arms stubbornly folded, staring out the window of his tiny room. Jeter pretended to watch a rerun of *Bewitched* as he sipped Dr Pepper through a long, clear straw.

Mavis tried again. "I just don't understand. Why would you keep something like that from me?"

"I wasn't keeping it from you. I never thought about it," Jeter said, his eyes fixed on the TV.

"All these months, I've been looking through these sperm donor catalogs, and you never once thought to mention that you yourself had some 'on file'?"

"No."

"Why?"

"Because I told you, it was a hundred years ago. Anyway, I'm sure they threw it out by now." Then, trying to make her smile, "Or maybe they sent it to the genius sperm bank. You should check there."

"You didn't mention it because you thought I would be interested."

He looked at her a good while, then, "Well, you are, aren't you?"

"No. Not anymore."

"Yes, you are. Because it's logical. I was reasonably good-looking in my original state. I had the highest SAT scores in our class and there's no hair on my back."

Mavis did not smile. Then she said evenly, "That stuff has a very long shelf life."

Jeter matched her resolve, measuring each word for effect, "I don't want kids."

"Why not?"

"Because when we play ball, I would have trouble sliding into home plate."

"I want a real answer."

Jeter was getting impatient. "It wasn't my idea, okay? It was way after I got hurt. Dr. Mac had a friend at some sperm bank, so I said, 'Hey, what the hell, maybe someday I'll want a couple of little hockey pucks.' But as it turns out, I don't."

Neither of them said anything. Then he added, "Why do you want to be a mother anyway? Have you forgotten that you didn't have a single doll with a head on it?"

Mavis glared at him. Then she gathered her giant, carpetbag purse and crossed to the door. "Don't worry about it . . . It's just as well. I think we already have all the little ass-holes we need in this world."

Jeter smiled. "Yeah. That, too."

She left without saying good-bye or closing the door. An old man was groaning down the hall. Jeter went back to his long straw and the TV.

CHAPTER 9

Several pages of the *Paris Beacon* drifted like tumbleweed along the sidewalk nobody walked down anymore. Tommy Epps, wearing one of Brundidge's good raincoats with some old sweatpants and raggedy tennis shoes, was busy painting graffiti on the side of Falkoff's.

Tommy was a Vietnam veteran. But unlike the stereotype, he did not become homeless or mentally unbalanced because of his service. He had mental disorders before he was drafted and people said he should never have been in the army at all. Dr. Mac even wrote a letter to that effect, but Tommy's parents were poor and he somehow fell through the cracks. He endured two full years in Southeast Asia, and managed to return home upright, without distinguishing himself by being either wounded or decorated. Marcus West's older brother, Lionel, who served with Tommy, said that already being crazy before he went is probably what saved him.

A talented artist, Tommy now spent his days painting murals on Main Street. At night, he slept in the maintenance room of the nursing home. He loved to paint buildings on top of buildings, and doors and windows and curtains where there were none. And he often mixed the real live residents of Paris with his favorite car models and cartoon characters. There was considerable controversy about letting Tommy paint over all the abandoned stores downtown. Purists said they should be left just as they were. Others felt that Tommy's art made it all seem less depressing. And the more literary types said there was authentic symbolism at work here—that as the town slowly disappeared, Tommy was putting the people back in. But that was only partially true. While he did paint large portraits of Main Street's notables, they were rarely depicted on their own stores and they were almost never doing anything that made sense. For example, there was a wonderful twelve-foot likeness of Lena Farnham Stokes, the former haberdasher, painted on the side of Arkansas Tire and Supply. But she was sitting hatless, on a

Pontiac GTO with her legs crossed, talking to Spiderman.

Tommy stepped back from his painting and nodded, as though he were agreeing with himself about something. Almost every storefront in his immediate vicinity and across the street was now in some stage of neglect and disrepair. Gone was any discussion of heroic measures to save them, any chance of unexpected angels stepping in on their behalf. There were still a few death rattles here and there, some final gasps of "Everything Must Go," but for the most part, large sections of the street were quiet now. Unlike houses, where all sorts of depressing and harsh words were sometimes exchanged, these buildings had been inhabited by people bent on showing their most amiable natures, on putting their finest selves forward in the marketplace of ideas and personalities. But, except for Mavis Pinkerton and Earl Brundidge and a precious few others, those people had disappeared. And the walls of their stores now stood like lovely old frames—the pictures they once encased forever lost—moving pictures that testified to the truths of Main Street. People could be cruel and petty and even deadly—but here, they had mostly been the best that human beings can ever be.

Perhaps those who never set foot in such a place didn't understand its value. But for those who had once been a part of it, and for some in the little town of Paris, nothing would erase from their minds the blazing goodness and optimism that had once flourished here.

Wood, Brundidge, and Jeter were now coming down the sidewalk, not far from where Tommy was working. When Brundidge saw what he was wearing, he cussed under his breath and shook his head. "Look at that! Do you believe that? I'm not giving him another one of my shirts if he's gonna wear it with sorry shit like that." Brundidge had given Tommy numerous articles of designer clothing over the years. And the fact that the eccentric street artist mixed them haphazardly made Brundidge crazy.

When they got close, Brundidge said, "Tommy, what the hell have you got on? Where's those brown corduroy pants I gave you? That's what you should have on with that raincoat."

"I don't like those pants," Tommy said matter-of-factly.

Brundidge straightened Tommy's collar. "I've told you fifty times, you don't wear a dress shirt with sweatpants, damnit! At least put on a decent pair of jeans. You've got all kinds of nice jeans." Tommy said, "Okay, okay. Just follow the sparrow, man. Just follow the sparrow." Brundidge frowned. "Don't follow the sparrow me. You need to get with the damn program! Tommy turned his back on Brundidge, letting him know that he was done with him.

The three men moved on. At the corner, they stopped again, sizing up the long row of devastation.

Across the street was where Jeter's Market had once been and where Jeter had lived upstairs with his parents. This had been the boys' headquarters. During the summer, the threesome had all worked in the little market waiting on customers and helping them out to their cars. They loved that they could reach in the old meat case anytime they wanted and cut themselves a huge slice of bologna. And they were consumed with the supervision and mainte-nance of the candy counter, worrying constantly that Jeter's mom was running out of necessary items like chocolate Milk Duds, red-hot jawbreakers, and black licorice. But the chore that thrilled them occurred only sporadically when either of the two klepto- maniacs in Paris came in to browse. The boys would then follow that person around, writing down what they took, so that a bill could be sent later.

By age eleven, they were promoted to helping Mervin Ritchie, a slightly retarded man who worked in the back, deliver gro- ceries. When they weren't in a hurry, Mervin would sometimes let them drive Hank's truck. Townspeople knew they could call Jeter's Market and order what they wanted, leave a key under the mat, and find it all put away by the time they got home. And there were perks here, too. The three youngsters and Mervin often returned to the store breathless with news of a new man in his un- dershirt at Miss So-and-So's house. Hank Jeter pegged his son's friends just right when he said, "Little Brundidge, he likes to tell everything he knows. Now Wood, he likes to have it told, but he don't like to do the tellin'."

After their chores were done, the boys had the run of a two-mile stretch if you counted both sides. They were the little princes of Main Street (and the last generation to flourish here), riding their horses downtown, tying them to parking meters, patrolling the stores, and protecting the merchandise with the water pistols they kept tucked in their Levi's. They could go to the drugstore and, if Ione Falkoff was busy, look at dirty magazines in the back. *Playboy* was the only thing they had ever seen that could beat Dr. Mac's medical books. Most of the women in there were old or sick looking and they weren't even posed good. But these *Playboy* women were young and naked and all pink colored, the kind who looked like their pubic hair would be soft as a teddy bear. It was wonderful. Sometimes they tore the pages out and took them back to their tree house.

They also liked it at Sam's Shoes, where Sam Gambelluca allowed them to witness firsthand the vast array of public feet in all their glorious stages of deterioration and pathology: the corns, the calluses, the misshapen arches, the blackened ingrown toenails, even the ravages left by gangrene. The boys were amazed that Sam wanted to handle anyone's feet at all, much less the bad ones. But he acted as though each foot was a little treasure and he was looking for just the right case to keep it in.

Then there was Lena Farnham Stokes, the first woman in Paris to use three names. Lena, who never married, lived in a grand old house that almost no one ever went to. But the few who did said that "it looked like a fancy movie set, like it was just waitin' for somethin' to happen there." She also had an enormous picture of Queen Elizabeth in her storefront window. Lena had actually visited London during the coronation and had personally snapped this photograph of the monarch waving ever so slightly from inside her coach. Lots of people said it looked like the queen was waving directly at Lena Farnham Stokes.

She paid each of the boys a dollar a week to keep the sidewalk clean in front of her store. They did this begrudgingly because in order to collect your money, you had to have a conversation with her dog. It was always "Go ahead, Sweetie Pie, did you thank the nice young men for cleaning up the walk? Did you?" And Brundidge would say, "That's okay, ma'am. He already did." And then, before they could get away, there would be the strange advice on the opposite sex. This was delivered by Lena herself, and made more dramatic by the fact that she'd had a stroke, causing her to hold up one side of her face so that it matched the other. With her hand flattened against her cheek and her eye pulled tight, she would sigh flirtatiously and say, "Remember, boys, you must never smile at a girl, it gives away all your power" or "Always keep a faraway look in your eye, boys, it causes charisma."

They didn't know what charisma was, but they were pretty sure Sidney Garfinkel had it because he always had a faraway look. Even when he smiled, he seemed sad, and not just because a tornado had once damaged his store the worst of anyone's on Main Street. Mr. Garfinkel had been out of town and the other merchants had taken up a collection to repair things before he even got home. But the boys felt sure he was sad about something else. They just didn't know what. It bothered them because they liked him. They especially liked that he gave them all his shipping crates for the fort they were constantly expanding in the woods behind his store. And also that each morning he made something called "strong European coffee," always letting them have some with lots of cream. On the days he changed his window display, they stood outside, sipping the fragrant brew and watching Mr. Garfinkel dress and undress the mannequins. They noticed how good he treated the girl ones, putting a little drape over them until he was ready with their outfits. And how he always touched each one gently and never in the wrong places, as though he knew them. Then one day, when he was trying on a shirt that had just arrived, they had seen a number on his arm. Brundidge had asked him where he got it. And Mr. Garfinkel had said when he lived in Europe, some people had thought he was special, so they had him numbered, in case he ever got lost. It wasn't until they were nine or ten that Wood's dad had told them how the Nazis had killed Mr. Garfinkel's entire family and almost starved him to death.

This new information set the three boys on fire. The Vietnam War was in full swing, but they now spent their afternoons at the library reading about Nazis. When they went hunting, they pretended whatever they were after was a Nazi. They even wrote their birthdays in digits on their left arms so they could be like Sidney Garfinkel. Then one day they informed him that if a Nazi ever did come through Paris, they would get Dr. Mac's twelve-gauge shotgun and put a hole in him. After that, they planned to take him to the woods in a wheelbarrow and let wild animals eat him. They had expected Sidney to be pleased. But instead, he had gotten that faraway look again. And then he told them that nothing would please Hitler more than knowing he could make little boys in Arkansas do such things. He said this with straight pins in his mouth, while taking in the seat of a man's pants. Now they felt confused. After a while, they washed the numbers off their arms. Eventually, they stopped mentioning the Nazis to Mr. Garfinkel. And he never changed his shirt in front of them again.

A few doors down from Garfinkel's was Case Hardware, a virtual paradise of short, narrow aisles filled with fishing poles, tent stakes, tackle boxes, bicycles, and BB guns. You name it and Lloyd Case either had it, could get it, or could tell you about it. A reticent man, he was also known as a master of paint mixing. If someone wanted her living room to be the color of a certain lipstick, or if the florists, Dwight and Denny, were looking for a faded terra-cotta, Lloyd Case could pretty much hit it on the head the first time. And do it with a Pall Mall cigarette hanging from his mouth, without ever losing an ash.

Then one day Claire Cutsinger, who drank, decided to paint her den the color of the Champanelle River. The boys assured her this would be easy and since Mr. Case was busy, they started pulling out the chips themselves. Pretty soon, no one could agree on what the color of the Champanelle River was. Or what the color of any river was for that matter. Finally, Lloyd came over and stated matter-of-factly that the color of a river cannot be mixed in a bowl in a hardware store. Then he went back to his Pall Mall cigarettes and his cash register as though he had said nothing important at all.

That was how it was on Main Street. It wasn't like school, where you knew you were learning something. It was a place like your daddy's lap, where permanent ideas and notions got inside of you and you never even felt them being put there.

And now, all that was being cast aside. For what? Didn't progress dictate that one thing is replaced with something better? What new, improved arena had emerged to replace this one? The Fed-Mart Corporation of America? An assortment of strip malls filled with strangers? The Internet? So far, no one seemed to have come up with an answer.

Brundidge, Jeter, and Wood walked toward the entrance of Case Hardware, one of the few remaining stores. Just a block away was Doe's, which, though struggling, had been granted a dispensation due to the fact that Mavis could bake things Fed-Mart had no interest in duplicating—like her Three-Cheese Prosciutto Onion Quiche and fresh-from-the-garden Sun-Dried Tomato Bread. Most of the cars on the street were parked in front of her business.

Jeter, who was wearing Dr. Mac's hat, said, "Well, looks like ol' Mavis is holding her own."

Brundidge answered, "Yeah, she's too ornery to be run out. They'll have to drive a stake through her heart."

Wood had tried his best to keep his mind on the business at hand, but Elizabeth, wearing a long veil and wedding gown, had wandered disturbingly across his mind while *she* watched smiling from a distance. He hadn't told Brundidge and Jeter the incredible news Elizabeth had delivered after the

funeral. He was still trying to sort it out himself, trying to make sense of it. Just as *she*
opened her arms to embrace his daughter,
Wood resurfaced on Main Street.

"Wonder what they're gonna do with your
old place?" Brundidge was speaking to
Jeter.

Jeter answered, "If there's any justice,
they'll turn it into a national historical site
and you two will be docents."

Wood and Brundidge headed inside the
store. Jeter followed, the motor of his electric
wheelchair whirring.

Lloyd Case, now in his eighties, was on
his knees taking inventory of the sparsely
stocked shelves.

Jeter spoke first, "Hey, Mr. Case, how's it
going?"

Lloyd coughed, causing his dangling cigarette to shake a little. "It's goin'. What can I
do for you boys?" He had been calling them
boys for almost forty years now.

"Well, we thought we might get lucky tomorrow and kill us a couple of careless
ducks," Wood said, half-smiling. "You got
anything for that?"

"I've got two cartons of Remington and

one carton of Winchester," he said, in a voice that was much stronger than he looked.

Brundidge offered, "We'll take 'em."

Lloyd turned to Jeter. "How about you, Carl? You need anything?" A lot of the older people in Paris used Jeter's first name.

Jeter said, "Do you have the new Nordic-Track?"

Lloyd shot Jeter an ever-so-slightly be-mused look.

Wood said, "Seriously, he needs some gloves." Then, turning to Jeter, "I'm not going to spend two hours rubbing your hands again."

"Okay, but it won't be the same for me," answered Jeter. "You know how much I look forward to that."

Wood narrowed his eyes, studying his old-est friend. "Remind me to cut down on your Perconal. You're becoming way too chatty."

All the men crossed to the cash register.

Lloyd said, "I'm sorry, Woodrow. We don't carry gloves anymore. You might try Fed-Mart."

The three younger men gave one another a look, then Brundidge spoke solemnly. "I'm afraid that won't be possible."

Wood backed him up, "That's right. We don't buy anything from anybody who's wearing a name tag."

Jeter added, "It's just a rule we have."

"I appreciate the sentiment." Lloyd put the ammo on the counter next to the cash register. "What the heck? I'll give you these half-off. We're going out of business anyway."

Wood, Brundidge, and Jeter were quiet as the old man rang up the sale. Then Brundidge said, "Hell, that's just about the end of downtown."

Lloyd said matter-of-factly, "We can't compete, Earl. You know that. They've got the volume."

Wood got out his wallet and paid. "We're real sorry to hear that, Mr. Case."

Lloyd gave Wood his change. Then he seemed to get an idea. "I do have one thing they don't have, though."

He removed a small wooden box from beneath the counter and opened it proudly, revealing a four-inch tubelike object set against a blue velvet lining. "This expertly handcrafted, limited-edition duck caller, carved in the finest African blackwood." He inclined himself toward them, speaking discreetly, "Let's see Fed-Mart try to mass-produce these." The men studied it, in-trigued. "They say in the right hands it car-ries the perfect pitch of a mating call."

They all stood admiring the little master-piece. Then, Brundidge, who could stand it no longer, took it in his well-manicured hand. "Little darlin'. Come to Papa."

It was evening and Lena Horne, courtesy of Dr. Mac, was helping Wood clean the two disassembled shotguns lying on his desk. He stopped every once in a while to savor the way she hugged a certain phrase. He was thinking how much he enjoyed being in his den by himself. He actually liked the way Milan had put this room together—the worn leather furniture, tapestried pillows, and needlepoint rug—the fact that it was a little *too* perfect, like a corner of some decorator showroom, did not diminish his pleasure in being among his favorite family photographs and books. When he looked up, Milan was standing in the doorway wearing something that looked like a mother-of-the-bride peignoir.

"We have to talk."

Wood rubbed a felt rag back and forth a few more times, then said, "Talk."

She crossed to him and sat on the plush ottoman next to his desk. "Do you think Elizabeth's known this boy long enough to be getting married?"

"No."

"Well, what are we going to do about it?"

"I don't think there's anything we can do."

"Wood, if there is going to be a wedding, I need to know. The church hall is sometimes booked even a year in advance. There's the invitations, the flowers, the dress, she can't wear mine because we eloped." Milan let a little time pass before she ventured, "Of course, I know it's going to be hard on you. Seeing her again."

Wood stopped his cleaning. "That's good, Milan. This is not really about Elizabeth. It's about you."

Milan stood up, "No, it's about us. All of us. I just ask, if this wedding does come off, that you please not humiliate me in front of our family and friends." Milan walked the door and assumed the most flattering pose she could muster, backlit with the light from the kitchen, "You know, anybody can seem fascinating when you haven't been lying next to them for the past twenty years."

Milan disappeared in a huff of silk. Wood returned to his guns.

Ms. Judith Nutter had gone home for the day and only a handful of visitors still lingered at the Pleasant Valley Retirement Villa. A good number of leathery souls had already settled into their chairs for the evening. Miss Delaney and Miss Phipps and Serious West, the ex-sheriff of Paris County, were engaged in yet another game of canasta. Sometimes Serious studied his hand so long that Miss Delaney stepped outside to get some air, while Miss Phipps fell asleep. Serious was a large man with a massive dignity. He did not like to lose at cards or anything else and though gentlemanly, he was not above whipping old women.

A few feet away, Jeter was reading an old edition of the *Oxford American*. He turned the pages with the pointer held in his mouth, trying not to notice that Rudy had spilled Hawaiian Punch on some of them. On the TV, a newscaster in Little Rock was saying that the Sunday School Stalker had struck again—that two little girls had been raped and murdered on Sunday morning while using the bathroom at their respective churches. Serious West discarded a low card with a growl. He hated the way the news media glorified criminal, like they were movie stars or something. "The Sunday School Stalker. Idn't that pitiful? Why don't they call him the Sissy Boy Bed Wettin' Still Lives With His Mama Killer? That's who he really is. That'll get him callin' the newspapers to complain." All the old people chimed in their agreement. Besides the high price of medicine, nothing electrified these old folks more than tails of crime and mayhem. They felt sure that America had lost its way. That the criminals were laughing at the law-abiding people. And it seemed to them that people didn't used to be so mean, like during the twenty-nine years that Serious West had been sheriff—an almost unprecedented run for a lawman anywhere. But when you stirred in the fact that he was black, people said it was a damn miracle.

Serious had a bad case of palsy, causing his left arm to shake like the dickens. But he still seemed like a man you might not want to mess with. His greatest achievement was shutting down a crystal meth lab over in Lodi, the most prosperous one being run west of the Mississippi. But some lawyers from St. Louis had gotten the dealers off on a technicality. People said that Serious had a way with wife beaters, too, making personal time for each one of them in his private office. No one ever knew exactly what he said or did, but when the men left, they were often in tears. His son Marcus was now the new sheriff and the word around town was that he was a star, just like his daddy.

The newscaster was winding up with information about a candlelight vigil where people could light a candle for "Little Jessica." Serious scooted his chair back in disgust. Miss Phipps, picking up on his ire, suddenly blurted out, "Oh, pooh. Forget candles; I say put a bullet in somebody's head for Little Jessica." Miss Delaney and Serious looked at each other, shocked. Then she grabbed his arm, as they both burst out laughing. A good hearty laugh that went on long enough for Miss Phipps, now a little embarrassed, to join them. When they were done, Miss Delaney moved her hand, but not before Serious squeezed it and a look passed between them. He cleared his throat and discarded.

Miss Phipps picked up the deck and let out a girlish squeal. Serious had been so distracted by the Sunday School Stalker and Miss Delaney's unexpected gesture that he had accidentally wasted his queen. He took it good-naturedly, patting Miss Phipps on the back, glad to see her enjoying a moment of pure happiness.

Miss Lena Farnham Stokes, a woman of delicate sensibilities, had changed the channel to a groundbreaking show about four gorgeous single women living in New York. Miss Delaney crossed and gently took the remote, reminding her, "Lena, this is the show you saw before, remember?"

Lena said, "Oh, that's right. Those pictures they put at the start are always so enticing. I forget." Since arriving at Pleasant Valley, the best of Lena's grand décor had been squeezed into her assisted-living apartment and she had, for some reason, finally begun to entertain. Having heard or read that this program was racy and naughty, she had invited a half-dozen other female residents to watch it with her. Someone brought a cake and Miss Grace Hartwell made her festive punch. Everyone gathered around the TV with wicked anticipation. Then, halfway through the episode, there was some sort of social gathering at which a naked man was manually masturbated until he finally ejaculated all over the faces and party dresses of the four dynamic female stars. For years, nothing had happened within the confines of Lena Farnham Stokes's grandiose movie set, but now something had and the women who were there would never forget it. Lena herself was so taken aback, her hand fell from her cheek, causing the sides of the face not to match. The other attendees were so stunned, some had to be helped back to their rooms. After word got around, when any program came on that was said to be "groundbreaking," all the female residents of Pleasant Valley who were able scrambled for the remote in order to turn the thing off.

By now most of the elderly people had fallen asleep on the sofa or in their chairs. Almost no one noticed when Rudy entered carrying a boom box, setting it against the far wall and inserting one of Dr. Mac's old tapes. Jeter gave Rudy a conspiratorial look, then pretended to read his magazine while keeping his eyes just above the page. Rudy began sweeping the floor nonchalantly with a large industrial broom. Miss Delaney shuffled the cards in preparation for another hand. It wasn't long before a glorious sound began to drift over and around them, adding color to the lifeless beige walls and making the overhead fluorescent lights seem a little dazzling. Even the all-too-familiar urine smell had suddenly become sweeter. It was more than just music. The individual notes, the instrumentation, the unique phrasing were simultaneously vibrant, hopeful, naughty, and fun. And it washed over Pleasant Valley's wintry boarders like sun being lapped up by old sea lions. Miss Delaney smiled at Jeter. Mr. Henry Dill, who never looked up, seemed to tap his foot. And Jeter was sure he heard Mrs. Evelyn Poole try to snap her fingers as Rudy's hips began to sway with the beat. *"A woman is a woman and a man ain't nothin' but a male."* Pretty soon a good number of arthritic hands were clapping to the strains of Louis Prima singing "Jump, Jive an' Wail." Serious was now on his feet keeping time with the beat. Lena Farnham Stokes was bobbing her head with all the sauciness of a chanteuse posed on a barstool. And when the music paused just so Louis could say, *"Momma's in the backyard learnin' how to jive an' wail,"* Rudy tossed the broom handle to Serious, who threw it back in time for Rudy to catapult himself over the

coffee table and into a whirling human gyra-
tion, ending in a perfect legs-to-the-floor
split, his arms extended toward heaven.
Several female residents who had not heard
their own voices in years shrieked with de-
light. Mr. Henry Dill, who was now confused,
held his ears and howled. Then Rudy leapt
to his feet and accelerated the hip-swiveling
motion as he traveled back across the room,
matching each suggestive movement to the
sound of newly awakened hands. In keeping with the idea that at the end of life there
are no small victories, Miss Margaret Delaney blew Jeter a kiss from across the
room. In return, he wiggled the only finger
that worked.

CHAPTER 10

The little clock on Jeter's nightstand glowed
11 P.M. A lonesome truck out on the interstate struggled to climb a hill. As the driver
changed gears, Jeter willed him the strength
to make it. Then it was quiet again. He hated

nights like this, when he couldn't sleep. It
wasn't as though he could get up and go for
a walk or run to the Quick Stop. On the con-
trary, he was stuck. And when morning
came, he'd still be stuck, but at least there'd
be light. And hope. He didn't know why people couldn't feel more hopeful in the dark,
but it was harder.

He wished he could turn over on his stomach. Now he would have to wait till Rudy
came back in the morning. In the meantime,
he would do his best to forget about the fight
with Mavis. What the hell was wrong with her
anyway? She must really be getting desperate to come sniffing around a cripple for
sperm.

He stared at the images in the plaster ceiling. In the corner was Abraham Lincoln in a
stovepipe hat. It used to be an ape with a
huge knot on his head, but he had changed
it. Directly opposite was the profile of a wonderfully pert breast. He knew who that belonged to and he wasn't going to mess with
it. In between, there was a Coke bottle,
some pointy mountains, the state of Texas,
and a lot of other stuff that faded or returned
according to his mood.

Since the accident he often lived inside

his head. For the most part, life on the outside was hardly worth noticing. It was much
nicer somewhere else, making love with the
best-looking women in Paris, and yes, they
were all babes. In his sparse existence,
there was no room for imaginary homely
girls with good personalities. Sometimes,
when he got tired of the women, he could be
found pulling small children out of burning
houses or riding down Main Street on a float
emblazoned with the words, "Carl Jeter,
Pulitzer Prize–Winning Poet, Gold Medal
Triathalon Man, and Paris County King of
Cunnilingus." Normally, he wasn't rowdy or
boastful, but that's what could happen if the
right combination of scotch and morphine
got together. Anyway, he was thinking of
phasing out the float because it always
came with the sound of people cheering.
And once people started cheering, that ball
would not be far behind. It would, in fact,
start coming toward him and then he would
have to jump higher than he had ever
jumped before, twisting himself in some
strange new way.

It happened his senior year, when Paris
was playing (for only the second time in half
a century) for the Arkansas Class AAA State

Championship. The score was 28–7. Wood, who was quarterback, could have run out the clock, but as people said later, he just wasn't a run-out-the-clock kind of guy. In the final seconds, Wood threw an unbelievable fifty-three-yard pass. And Jeter, though nothing important was at stake, and though he knew the goalpost was coming up dangerously close, had made an almost Herculean effort to catch it.

Later, when he felt cold from the neck down, all he could think was how he never knew you could play the radio in an ambulance. It must have been an oldies station, because the words that he remembered went something like this: "Boogity-boogity, woogity-woogity-shoo." How he hated that song. To this day, he didn't know the name of it. Only that it had marked the end of him. Yes, he would go on and live inside the dead boy's body. But it was over as sure as if a referee had fired his starter pistol, signaling the end of the game.

He and Wood had been magic together. Like their heroes Unitas and Berry, they had stayed for hours every night after practice, perfecting each move and play and possibility. During games, they regularly brought townspeople to their feet. If Wood faked left, Jeter was already twenty yards to the right and waiting. If Jeter were covered, he could break route and Wood would still know where to throw. They were a miraculously timed, two-man symphony of thought, antici-pation, and action.

In a way, Wood had been his hero, too. When they were little and knocked a ball through a window, Wood was the one who always rang the doorbell and told. As they got older and Wood could have any girl he wanted, Jeter liked it that he never bragged about the ones he got. And then there was the way Wood left the football field, after throwing a spectacular touchdown pass, never dancing or thrusting his fist into the air, but rather, moving fast, head down, with-out acknowledging the cheering crowd. Jeter liked that, too.

After his accident, he remembers Wood standing at the end of his bed. He had a look that Jeter had seen before. It was after a truck had run over Wood's dog, Ted. Some-how, the bumper had torn Ted open and Wood had tried to stick his heart back in. That was the look Wood had in Jeter's hospi-tal room. It's still there sometimes, when he wakes up and Wood is staring at him. The same look, after all these years, still there.

When Jeter came home, his parents' living room became his room, so he could sit in his wheelchair and look out the picture window onto Main Street. Strangely, he had never cried over what happened. Even today, the only thing that could make him weep was the goodness of his own mother and father. People so hardworking and earnest, even in pictures when they were young, they still looked worn-out. If he closed his eyes, he could see them now, pulling away from the house, the backs of their heads framed by their old Buick. Hank, in his beat-up canvas hat and nylon jacket. And Pauline with her pocketbook in her lap. On their way to make a payment on a note or maybe to buy him some new pajamas or a birthday card. They could spend twenty minutes at the drugstore looking for just the right one. The one that had to have the word "Son" on it, like "For a Fine Son" or "Happy Birthday, Son." And then it had to say something about Carl that was true. Something that if they could, they would have said themselves.

Sometimes, Jeter wished he could crawl

into their old backseat again. That the three of them were still riding around like they used to. Maybe they'd just had dinner at the truck stop and were on their way home. It would probably have been chicken-fried steak with mashed potatoes and the salad bar with those little packages of crackers that he had to open for his mother on account of her arthritis. Afterward his parents would worry if they'd left enough for a tip. Then Hank would pay the bill and put his arm around his son as they talked their way out.

"How are you tonight, Mr. Malvern? Yes, sir, it sure is. Boy, they grow up fast, don't they? They sure do."

After Hank had spun the little toothpick dispenser, getting one for himself and buying a York peppermint patty for his wife, they were off again, driving through the streets of Paris. By now, Carl would probably be lying on his back in the rear window, eating a cone from the Dairy Queen and looking up at the stars. The old Buick would stop and start again at the end of every block, keeping a soft rhythm with his parents' conversation.

"Looks like old Virgil's really got the business tonight."

"Wonder what they're buildin' there?"

"Miss Minnie Ritchie's yard sure does have the roses, don't it?" And so on. And so on. Until the mother and father's quiet, melodic words lulled their boy to sleep, like the sound of the Champanelle River when they all went camping.

There had been another boy once, but he had died before Jeter was born. Dr. Mac called it some kind of meningitis. But others claimed he was the last baby in Arkansas to die of polio. Whatever it was, Hank said his and Pauline's hearts "stayed near broke till ten years later when Carl come."

As Jeter grew, he worked right alongside them in the little grocery store below their apartment, at first stocking shelves and later manning the cash register while standing on a box. Over the years, Hank Jeter gave away so much credit that the store was near going under. Luckily, Mervin Ritchie, when he wasn't delivering groceries for Hank, had made a tidy sum of money buying repossessed land at auctions. Enough, in fact, to become a full partner in the store. The deal was made on a small white envelope, the kind with a window in it where a name could go. On the back were the words, "Hank Jeter and Mervin Ritchie now own Jeter's Market, fifty-fifty." That was it. No lawyers. Nothing to file. Just a good hard handshake that lasted for thirty years.

Hank and Pauline were gone now. And Mervin Ritchie slept away his days at the nursing home, a few rooms down the hall from their son. When Hank died, people came from all around to tell Jeter how his dad had helped them out during this one year or that, when their kids never had enough to eat. Milan's mother told him flat out that when Tom Lanier was in the mental ward, their family would have starved to death if it had not been for Hank and Pauline Jeter. How she had tried to trade the only thing she had of value, an old silver-plated punch bowl, for a Christmas turkey. And how Hank would not hear of it. Later, when Mervin had delivered the box of free groceries, stuffed in the bottom were twelve pairs of new socks. Mrs. Lanier knew Jeter's did not sell socks, which caused her to have to wipe her eyes with a pair of them. Jeter had attempted to remind Mervin of this story, but the older man just stared at him and finally yelled without his teeth, "Are you Hank's boy? You better tell him I can't open up tomorrow. Now don't ask me no more."

Strangely, Jeter felt most comfortable with
the old people who lived with him. It wasn't
that he enjoyed their company so much as
he appreciated their lack of judgment. Their
struggle each morning was to stay one more
day in this world or to sleep until they were
called to the next one. Most of them had neither the interest nor the ability to notice that
his wheelchair was sometimes dirty or that
his body was shrinking. The fact was, they
were all shrinking. He repaid their acceptance in little ways. Like reminding Miss
Phipps when the first day of autumn was so
that she could make the appropriate
wardrobe adjustments. Or telling others
when it was time to deposit their Social Security checks or take their medicine.

After his parents passed away, Jeter had
made one vain attempt to start a new life.
Despite everyone's protest, he had paid a
young couple whom he met at the truck stop
to drive him to California. Sixteen hours
later, a highway patrolman found him lying
belly-up in the hot Amarillo sun, with his
pockets hanging out of his pants. Wood and
Brundidge had come to get him. As they had
so often, Wood and Milan begged him to live
with them, but he declined. A few days later,

he moved into the nursing home and the Paris Jaycees bought him a new wheelchair. Since then he had spent most of his time writing poetry and tutoring high school students.

But his deepest passion was reserved for the Literary Society of Paris, of which he and Miss Delaney were the founders. The society had over forty members. Their simple stated goal was to honor, enjoy, and make available to others the superbly written word. By others, they especially meant people like Wanda Faye Marlin, a tenth-grade dropout who in spite of being warned that Hemingway was a man's writer, fell so in love with Lieutenant Frederick Henry in *A Farewell to Arms* that she later broke up with her boyfriend for being uninteresting. The society still gets hate mail from him to this day. And there was Dub Wilkerson, who was one of the last people in town still willing to pump your gas for you. When Jeter had been getting his wheelchair tires filled at the Texaco, he swore he heard Dub say to another attendant, in his sweet twang, "Hey, Virgil, how'd you like that *Pride and Prejudice*? I toldja it was good, did'n I?"

Teachers and college graduates belonged to the society, too. But, over the years, it was the unsparing literary critiques of ordinary folks that delighted Jeter and filled his journals. Things like "Well, you know, he built that big house and threw all them parties to put on the dog for her, but she was just sorry. And the people around her was sorry, too, 'cept for the one that told the story." Or "He let that fish just eat him up. You know, it's never a good idea to let a fish get to thinkin' it's smarter than you are." Or "When that Negro preacher got the little girl by the arm and said, 'Stand up, Scout, your daddy's passin'.' Well, it just went right through me. In the whole history of talkin', has there ever been any words said better than that?"

But the Literary Society meeting that changed Jeter's life was the one that occurred on a clear December night, just after they had finished the annual reading of Truman Capote's "A Christmas Memory." Miss Delaney stood up and announced that she had a most special treat. She said she had been going through some old boxes filled with the work of her most prized students and had come across a poem. She also said that she had asked for and received the author's permission to read it. Jeter, who had been only seventeen when it was written, felt that it was much too amateurish for public consumption. Also, time and distance had since muted the raw moment in the poem, which could now only serve to embarrass him. But Miss Delaney was so sure of its value, he hadn't had the heart to turn her down. And here she was standing, holding it in her hand.

Jeter stared at the floor as the room went quiet.

"Many of you are familiar with this author's work," Miss Delaney said. "But it is always interesting to see the beginning. It is a young man's poem, written right after his injury in a high school football game." No one looked at Jeter as Miss Delaney began.

I wonder how my nights would fare
Had I been spared
The time when young men
Singe at a woman's touch,
Had I been disdainful of the warmth of
* womanhood*
By a sort of coolant added to my blood.
But instead my blood boiled high
At the slightest stroke, and I, a devil
* Romeo*
With a fresh haircut and a wild heart

Went off to play my part.
Till stalled in a field, out of the game
I cursed that my wick should flicker here,
my fellow-lame
As young girls I have never known
Danced round my head without a care
Tonight the boy stalled in a field
Will sleep like an old man dozing in a
chair
And dream of woman, burning in the air.

At first, no one made a sound. Then there was polite applause. Milan, who had come along only to impress Wood, got up and left. A moment later, she was holed up in a stall of the ladies room, her face buried in a handful of paper toilet-seat covers. It had been the same way in high school when Wood had broken up with her. There was never any toilet paper when she needed to cry.

Now she knew what she had always suspected was true. Jeter had not told her himself, but his poem had done it for him. He had been a virgin when he was injured. She'd asked Wood this question many times and he always told her he didn't know for sure, and she had never believed him. She knew a few of the girls Jeter dated in high school. There had probably been the quick brush of a thigh or the made-to-look-accidental caress of a breast, but there it was. He had never and would never know the joy of holding a woman against his own heart after making love to her. Milan could hardly bear the thought of it. Of all their friends, Jeter was the one she loved without thinking about it. She couldn't say why really. He had told her once that poverty is a kind of paralysis, too. And how maybe that was the bond they shared. But that wasn't talk that interested Milan. She couldn't have cared less why things are the way they are. Which is why the very next morning she got in her Mercedes and drove sixty miles to the town of Gunther, where she proceeded to hire a thirty-eight-year-old hooker named Cherry Smoke, who was thereafter to be paid a hundred dollars for every visit made to a Mr. Carl Jeter.

Wood worried about Jeter's health and Mavis cooked for him and Brundidge gave him his old clothes, which Sidney Garfinkel discreetly altered without ever saying a word about his shrinkage. But it was Milan who always knew, without being told, what he really needed. Even during their graduation

night party, when his colostomy bag had
started to leak, and everyone else had tried
to cover their horror with frantic words, and
Duff had held his hand while regaling everyone with the day she got her period all over
her white, cashmere wool pants, it was Milan
who was on her knees cleaning up the mess
and acting as though he had just spilled a little champagne on her skirt.

Over the years, she had taken good care
of Jeter. Much to Wood's dismay, she found
a special homeopathic cream for his bed-
sores that worked. She got him the reading
stand and a stick for turning pages that he
could hold in his mouth. She kept a jar in his
room filled with his favorite hard candy. She
bought him lamps and painted all his light-
bulbs a soft beige to diffuse the harsh lighting around his bed. And best of all, she had
used her childhood sewing skills to make
him a beautiful quilt of brightly colored, velvet squares. Jeter liked the way the lush fabric felt next to his face. Nothing in recent
years had soothed him more than Milan's
hand-stitched comforter. Well, at least nothing had until Cherry Smoke came along.
Jeter could hardly believe it when she just
appeared one day in his doorway, like an

adolescent fantasy sprung to life. In spite of being fifteen years older than him, she was splendid and leggy with huge bosoms and not an ounce of silicone. Not that he was picky or an expert, but anyone could tell, once she got her clothes off, that she was as fine as any girl in his and Wood and Brundidge's old tree-house *Playboys*. Leave it to Milan to even be good at picking whores.

Cherry, who was given the official title of "massage therapist," came to see him twice a month. If the old people at the nursing home suspected her real purpose, no one ever said so. Once Judith Nutter had stopped Cherry in the hall and asked to see her credentials. Cherry had politely told her in a voice toasted by cigarettes, "If you want to see my pussy, you'll have to pay for it."

Over the years, Cherry gave Jeter the physical pleasures he had never known. In return, he put her in mind of some long-ago romantic feeling she had almost forgotten. After retiring at forty-five, Cherry kept Jeter as her only client. She said she was afraid no one else would know how to treat him. But it might have also been that he recited long passages of poetry to her and each time she left kissed her good-bye like a young boy going off to war. Jeter's face was his sole erogenous zone. And there wasn't an inch of Cherry that hadn't been pressed up against it. He had smelled and tasted and licked all of her. And when she dangled her big ol' bosoms over his eyes and nose and forehead, well, it was like getting lost in a silky pink ether. Then one night after a visit with Jeter, Cherry's car skidded on some ice and crashed into a light pole. It happened on Main Street, not more than thirty yards from the picture window where Jeter had sat for years, collecting dust along with his mother's porcelain knickknacks.

It was Milan who came and held him in her arms all night while hot silent tears drifted down their cheeks. He thought when the sun came up, he might feel more hopeful, but that hadn't been the case. Just like Wood and Brundidge thought they could patch things up when only a week later they hired a younger and more beautiful "therapist" to service him. When the girl showed up in Jeter's room, he went crazy, screeching at her to get the hell out. By the time Wood and Brundidge stopped by to collect their friend's gratitude, the whole nursing home was in an uproar and Jeter was lying in bed facing the wall. His voice was a raw whisper.

"She was my girl. Didn't you know? I thought you knew."

It was a long time before Milan told him that Cherry hadn't cashed any of her checks in years. And that finally Milan had quit sending them. She had promised not to tell Jeter this, but now she felt he should know. For weeks after Cherry's death, this single piece of information became the bedrock of Jeter's meager optimism. It was knowledge that lifted him from the darkness and backed him away from each new 3 A.M. precipice. Cherry had loved him. His large head, his withered body, the penis that didn't work. She had embraced his ugliness as tenderly as Sam Gambelluca had caressed all the old worn-out feet on Main Street. And she hadn't been pretending either. She had done it sincerely. He grieved that she could no longer lie on top of him, but it was glorious that she had once been there. Just glorious. That's how it all seemed for a while. Then Jeter began to feel utterly desolate and inconsolable. The fact that Cherry loved him meant that he had lost even more than he realized. And even worse, he had loved her, too. All those years of caring for each other and never saying so, because they thought they were a whore and an invalid in a business deal. And now she was gone.

He had been a good sport about almost everything. Being removed from the game at seventeen. Losing his parents. Losing his home. He hadn't even said very much about having to lie down for twenty-five years. But this was too much. Too hard. It was time to go back to living inside his head, where he could keep Cherry alive, along with his other great love. The one he would never tell anyone about. The one who didn't even know herself. Yes, much safer there. A place where your girlfriend does not die on you or marry someone else. And heroes do not get carried off the field. Where beautiful pigskin missiles always arrive safely in your arms, just as you carry each one across the goal line, then step from the arena, head down, as though you have never even heard the roar of the crowd. That's the place where Jeter wanted to be. Only occasionally now, on nights when he can't sleep, does he even bother to stare out the window across the long row of darkened rooftops on Main

Street, through the black, snow-covered
trees, sometimes catching the lights of the
football stadium in the distance . . . and
sometimes dreaming of woman, burning in
the air.

Chapter 11

It was Halloween. Mavis was seated at her
kitchen table, sorting through a small mountain of papers that contained the names and
biographical information of over two hundred
and fifty potential sperm daddies. She had
arranged them in stacks of "No Way in Hell,"
"Possibility, with Reservations," and "Definite
Yes." The "Definite Yes" stack had only five
donors in it and in her heart, she knew that
they were really only "Possibilities, with
Reservations." But if she didn't put somebody in the yes category, that pile would be
empty and then she would've gotten nowhere, just as she had for the last six years.
Besides, the names and backgrounds of
these two hundred and fifty men had been

culled from the files of the two top sperm-providing companies in America and it had already cost Mavis a pretty penny just to look at them.

It was after midnight now and pouring rain. There was a loud knock at the back door. Chester jumped up, howling, and Mavis demanded to know who it was.

Brundidge's voice came from the other side. "Trick or treat."

Mavis opened the door. Brundidge pushed Jeter, in his wheelchair, into the kitchen. They smelled like beer. Mavis said, "Excuse me, but I believe I filled your children's bags hours ago."

Brundidge said, "Yeah? So? Now we're trick or treating for ourselves."

Brundidge shook the water off, stomping his feet and brushing it off Jeter's coat, too.

Mavis said, "Where's your costumes?"

Brundidge removed a carton of eggs from inside his jacket. "Here. Scramble these for us. I confiscated them from errant youth." He headed toward the refrigerator. "You're lucky they're not on the side of the house."

Mavis followed him. "This is not a damn diner."

"Well, that's good, because if it was, you'd

be a damn poor hostess." Brundidge opened the door. "Whoa! Mexican lasagna! Nobody makes that better than you. That'll go great with eggs."

"Nobody makes that, period. I made it up. That's how much attention you pay."

Jeter knew Mavis had softened a little, because she was now unwrapping his scarf. Brundidge got out the lasagna. "What's all that paperwork? What the hell are you doin' over there?"

"Picking out a sperm daddy." Then, motioning toward Jeter, "Because he won't give me his." Then she added, almost to herself, "I can feed the two of you for years, but let me ask for a little cup of something . . ."

After the dirty dishes had been stacked, they were all gathered around the table. Mavis was speaking, "Okay, now, these are the fact sheets on the donors, with their race, religion, medical history, and a description of their personal appearance. There's also a little essay—"

Brundidge found a receipt in the middle of some pages. "Wait a minute. You actually paid for all this stuff with a credit card?"

"Yes. Is that a problem?"

"No. But somethin' about it doesn't seem right."

"Well, discuss it with a close friend or your clergyman, okay?"

Brundidge got up and crossed to the counter, helping himself to a cookie. "You don't have to be sarcastic."

"Listen, I'm serious. This is very important to me."

"You think we're not serious? Are we serious, Jeet?"

"Hell yes."

Brundidge was getting fired up. "Don't you worry about me. I'm a parent. I'm the treasurer of the whole damn PTA."

He gestured toward the papers. "You just get it all laid out there. We're not leaving till this job is done!"

Then, as he returned to the table, he acknowledged Chester by holding out his arms, slowly stomping his feet, and growling.

Jeter said, "No matter how many times you do that, it never gets old."

Brundidge gave a piece of his cookie to the dog, who licked his face. Mavis acted disgusted. "Chester, stop that! You don't know where his mouth has been."

An hour later, they were eating lemon

meringue ice cream and still at it. Mavis fed Jeter, then put another page in the reading stand that was attached to his wheelchair. He studied it for a minute, then, "What's wrong with the landscape architect again?"

Mavis answered, "Too short."

Brundidge had his glasses on now and was immersed in his own stack. Mavis handed him a different page.

"Who's that?" he asked.

She raised her eyebrows, "5158. I kind of like him."

Brundidge frowned. "No way." He tapped one of his own papers, "I'm votin' for this guy here. He's a doctor. He has a lot of hair and he speaks several languages."

Mavis took the paper in her hand, "Oh, that's a mistake. He's not even supposed to be in there."

"Why not?"

"Because he's a Hindu."

"What's wrong with being a Hindu? Hindus are fine people. What about Gandhi?"

"What about Gandhi? This is not Gandhi's sperm. Anyway, I want to immerse the baby in its own heritage and I don't know anything about Hinduism."

"Well, let me tell you. It's a hell of a lot bet-

ter than," he tapped 5158, "having an unde-
scended testicle."

Mavis narrowed her eyes at Brundidge as
he put 5158's paper on Jeter's stand. Jeter
began reading it. "My goal is to feel, respond
to, and reciprocate beauty in both verbal and
nonverbal ways." Jeter gave Mavis a dubious
look.

She responded, "So?"

Brundidge answered, "So? That's not normal. Nobody talks like that."

Jeter became more emboldened, "Oh!
And here's the real kicker." He was reading
again. "He does not have freckles, but he
does have," Jeter said it loud, "a strong facial
profile!"

Brundidge picked up his cue, "Whoa! Flag
on the field! If you're *admitting* on one of
these deals that you have a strong facial
profile, can you imagine what it really looks
like?" Brundidge pounded the table as he
and Jeter broke up laughing.

"I mean, this guy's in a world of hurt!" They
continued their merriment until Mavis
abruptly stood up and collected all the papers into one hurried stack, like a teacher
who had just caught her whole classroom
cheating. Jeter and Brundidge grew quiet.

Brundidge finally spoke. "What the hell are you doin'?"

Jeter said, "Come on, we're just kiddin' around."

"No, it's okay. I can see how it's funny. Really, I can." She put the pages back in their folders. "But you know what's even funnier?" Mavis crossed to the kitchen window again and looked out. "I don't want to have a baby with 5158. Or anybody else I've never had a conversation with. I want somebody who's tasted my lasagna . . . and been to my house. . . . Somebody who has actually had their arms around me, even if it was only when we were kids." She picked up a dish towel and dabbed her eyes, embarrassed. "Maybe I don't have a right to want that. But I do." Then she looked straight at Jeter. "And if he would just give me that chance, I swear he would never have to come around. He wouldn't even have to send a birthday card. I could just say that he ran off or . . . that he's dead."

Brundidge looked at Jeter, whose face remained as unmovable as the rest of him. Then he said to Mavis, "What the hell was that? A sales pitch? Jeez, no wonder your mother had to buy all your school candy."

*　*　*

They were on their way back to the nursing home. Brundidge punched in a CD and the mournful strains of "Desperado" drifted out through the speakers. Then, after setting the stage, he looked in the rearview mirror at Jeter.

"You know, that baby thing . . . There's nothin' like a little girl. They can tell you on a daily basis where you're makin' all your errors."

Jeter didn't say anything. Brundidge went on. "Man, I just see all these Jerry Springer people reproducing like rabbits. It's scary, you know? Who's gonna replace our parents?"

"Hey, if you want to save civilization, be my guest. I'm still learning how to make pottery with my tongue."

When they pulled up at Pleasant Valley, Rudy was waiting in the rain. Brundidge got out of the van, opened the back, and put out the ramp. Jeter came down it, just as the plaintive wail of the chorus was finishing up. "You better let somebody love you, let somebody love you, before it's too late." As his wheelchair whirred past Brundidge, Jeter shook his head, giving his old friend a look of disgust.

Then Rudy covered Jeter with an umbrella as they went toward the somber, automated entrance.

Mavis was lying in bed, depressed over the evening's lackluster results. She was no closer to getting a baby now than she had been when she first started the hormones. Which is why she was going to drown her sorrows, as she so often did, in two of the most abiding comforts for a single woman in a small town—Food and Television. She took another bite of her banana pudding and gave Chester one of the wafers. Then she picked up the remote control and began channel surfing. It was getting more and more difficult to find something she liked to watch these days. Especially since she had sworn off all the programs that were dragging her down, both mentally and spiritually.

Mavis had finally grown weary of the women on her television who had nothing on their minds but finding a man at all costs. It didn't matter how well-off or pretty or successful they were—all of it was meaningless without a man. Normally sane types, who became irresponsible and brain-dead the minute a new pair of balls rolled into town and told them to get off the phone, put on a thong, this dinner sucks and if I can't have you no one will. Women who ignored lying, cheating, drunkenness, and even getting knocked around, with the pathetic universal cry that excuses all sorry male behavior, "But I Love Him."

And she had finally decided to lay off all the "But I Love Him" networks and the hundreds of "But I Love Him" made-for-TV movies, too, which she had once compulsively watched with Milan and sometimes Rudy, wasting, she figured, a good portion of her life to date. For years, they had lost themselves in the addictive world of watching women do dog-ass stupid things, marrying men they hardly knew, giving them access to their children and all their money, and then acting stunned upon learning, after a quick middle-of-the-night wallet check, that they are really married to a world-class liar, con man, bigamist, or worse, Jimmy Del Serial Killer.

At first Mavis and Milan had thought it was all pretty funny. It made them feel good that they were so much smarter than their idiot TV sisters who, if they weren't desperate to get married, were desperate to get unmarried. They would hoot and holler every time one of these hapless women left her best friend's apartment to run up the stairs of her old house in high heels *alone* at night hoping to pack a quick bag before the abusive, insanely jealous soon-to-be-ex husband gets home. "Hey, honey, let it go! Did your Miss Phipps not tell you during fire drills that your parents can always buy a new Crayola box, but not a new you?" They personally didn't know any women who would act this lame or helpless. Mavis couldn't even remember a single woman on television who had ever successfully completed a bath, in spite of the fact that she was pretty sure if any man interrupted hers, she would beat him to death with her easy-to-remove metal towel rack. In spite of the fact that she kept a tire iron under her own car seat and a stun gun, courtesy of Serious West, under her bed— none of these television women seemed to own so much as a slingshot.

Maybe it was because Milan got busy with her committee work and Mavis was now mostly watching TV alone, but after a while, none of it seemed quite as amusing as it used to. And then it got downright scary when the women weren't fake anymore, but were real live, flesh-and-blood females on reality crime shows who were just running out to the 7-Eleven for a quick quart of milk and invariably wound up nude, in the surrender position (on their backs with legs wide apart, a final homage to male domination), and left in the woods for wild animals to clean out their skulls. It was enough to keep you from leaving your house for a quart of milk or even chemotherapy. Especially when you added all the dead hotties on cutting-edge crime series (a new addiction), where the bar seemed to be raised each week for edgier and more inventive autopsy reports. ("Are those lab results back yet, Lieutenant?" "Yes, sir. They found playing cards in her uterus and her left breast implant is missing.")

Some people on a panel Mavis watched had said these kinds of shows could not have an effect on impressionable young boys. But they did seem to be having an effect on Mavis. She had started to actually feel angry and depressed and didn't know why. It was the kind of malaise that settles on people who've had something terrible done to them and can't do anything about it. She never really connected it to her television. She just knew that there came a time when she couldn't even remember the titles of the movies anymore. They were all, *Who's in My Damn House Now?,* a very special made-for-TV drama. Or they were *The Donna Somebody Story,* with the plots getting thinner and thinner until finally one night, as she and Rudy devoured another bowl of her homemade wasabi pretzel mix and one of the faceless Donnas was being secretly videotaped by her neighbor while she sat on the toilet, even Chester had started to growl, showing his teeth and inching cautiously on his stomach toward the TV. That's when Mavis had finally stood up and said, No More. Amazingly, Chester had stood up, too, as though this were a moment he had been waiting for. Mavis picked up the remote and turned "the thing" off, telling Rudy, over his protests, to go home, write a letter to his family in Cuba, practice his verb conjugation, get a life. Mavis and Chester went to bed that night and slept like the baby they were hoping for.

After that, Mavis started to feel better. She

now realized that she was tough on the outside, but inside she could be as raw as an
old bone and had to be careful about what
she took in. But even after she beat her addiction, she was still left with an uneasy feeling about men. Not the men in her own life,
the men she knew and loved—like Rudy,
who spent almost a whole year before giving
up on teaching her to tango, and Brundidge,
who never forgot her birthday, and Wood,
who had beat the hell out of Russell Pittman
in junior high for calling her Miss Piggy, and
Jeter, who immortalized her in the *Paris
Beacon* with his "Ode to an Improbable
Soufflé." These were not the men Mavis was
mad at. It just seemed to her that men in
general caused most of the trouble in the
world. It didn't matter if news announcers
said, "Angry soccer fans rioted today" or,
"Child molesters are on the rise," or that
some "evil dictator" somewhere had started
a war, everybody knew they were really talking about men. It was men who did these
things and had been doing them for hundreds and hundreds of years. And you could
call them angry soccer fans or molesters or
evil dictators, as though men and women
were all in this together, but what they really

were, was men. And it just seemed to Mavis that, in general, women hadn't really done much of anything, except maybe look good enough to fight over and, in the end, get the blame for starting stuff.

The more Mavis thought about this, the more sure she was that she really didn't care to have a man up her own vagina one bit. She had tried it before with Ricky Stark-weather, who spilled himself all over her, and with several others, who went on way too long. (Where was Ricky Starkweather when you needed him?) She hadn't really enjoyed any of it and anyway she was often bothered by a vague feeling, which in-creased after her addiction, that nobody's penis deserved to be up there, inside of her, especially not after all the trouble and pain a mere six inches of hard flesh had caused to her own kind.

To tell the truth, she could no longer even *imagine* receiving the instrument of their kinder brothers between her own legs. Be-cause even the dear ones, who brought you flowers and candy, and held your head when you had the flu (this had never happened to Mavis), even these good men were still trying to be the top dog at the same time they were loving you, pounding you and giving it to you, while you were on the receiving end. They were the objects, you the receptacle. They were the stick, you the hole. Mavis didn't like any of it. No, thank you. Sometimes you lose the right to go somewhere, because the people who were there before you behaved badly. To Mavis, the female vagina was such a place. Maybe the most special place that has ever existed. The place where human life comes out. And as far as Mavis was concerned, men had lost the right to go there. Even the stellar ones. If other women were open for business, that was fine with her. But she was not. If she needed to pleasure herself, she would do it with her own good hand—not the hand of Jimmy Del Serial Killer or Ricky Starkweather, or Mr. I'm the Other Half of You—but her own good hand, the one she knew was well intended and she could depend on. The one the whole town of Paris trusted to make the best bread they had ever tasted. That would be more than good enough for her.

Wood was sitting at his desk, talking on the phone. "Okay, I sure appreciate your help. We'll get back to you."

He hung up and looked at Jeter and
Mavis, who were seated in front of him.

After a while, he grinned. "Well . . . They
have it."

Mavis squealed and then covered her
mouth, afraid to call attention to such unac-
customed happiness.

Brundidge, who was leaning against the
wall, crossed to Jeter and patted him. "Hey,
buddy, what did I tell you? I knew it would
still be good. You got some guerrilla fighters
out there!"

Jeter said, nonplussed, "Oh yeah. I'm a
regular samurai warrior."

Wood cautioned, "Let's not get carried
away. This is a very old sample."

Then he turned to Mavis. "And even with a
viable specimen, there's no assurance
you're going to get pregnant. Unfortunately,
the age thing is against us, too."

She nodded, overcome. Jeter said, "I think
she wants to go for it."

Wood asked, "Don't you think you all
should see an attorney first? Have him draw
up some sort of agreement?"

Jeter spoke matter-of-factly. "We already
have one. We're trading sperm for food."

Wood stared at them for a moment. "Okay.

Well, we've got a lot of tests to run. They're gonna analyze the specimen right away and then I want to get it here as soon as possible."

Brundidge said, "How do you do that?"

"FedEx."

Now Mavis found her voice, "No way."

"Yes. It's packed in liquid nitrogen."

Mavis worried, "What if it gets lost?"

"Then we're screwed. I've never heard of that happening. I've heard of a specimen that, for some reason, failed to stay below freezing."

Brundidge offered, "Well, hey, I've got a refrigerated truck. What about that, just to be safe?"

Wood said, "Fine, if you can go today. It's in Little Rock."

Brundidge was getting into his coat now, "I'm on my way. I mean, let's don't take any chances with this deal. It's too important." He pulled on his silk-lined deerskin gloves. "I could be transporting a future president."

Jeter mused, "Yeah, or a guy who makes little outhouses out of Popsicle sticks."

Wood turned to Mavis, "Right now, you need to go in there and pick yourself out a pretty little smock." Mavis stood up, facing the three men. She seemed like she was about to make a speech. But nothing came out.

Finally, Wood patted her and spoke for all of them, "We know."

CHAPTER 12

Brundidge had just paid his check and was telling Shandi with an "i," the waitress at Digger's Truck Stop & Autel, that if she got any prettier he would have to marry her. He knew it was kind of a corny thing to say, but he also knew that Shandi, who was young and fat, could use a compliment. He looked at the Coors beer clock on the wall and saw that it was just a little past 4 A.M. His two little girls were sleeping at his mother's because this was the first day of duck hunting season, an almost sacred observance for the men of Paris.

Shandi said, wanting to stretch out his offer, "If you married me, my daddy would come looking for you. He'd think you were too old for me."

Brundidge noticed Shandi didn't say she thought he was too old. Now he was confused. He had thought he was just being nice, but here Shandi was acting like she might be interested. Now he was obligated.

"Well, a good-looking girl like you might be worth getting shot over."

Shandi smiled and started to answer, then thought better of it. It was just as well. Most females confused Brundidge and he certainly didn't have time to get mixed up with one this morning. He was hunting ducks, not women.

He gave Shandi a wink, picked his coffee thermos off the counter, and spoke to several tables of men on his way out.

Don Tiller said, "Don't let them ducks get the best of you."

Brundidge answered, "If they're smart, their wills have already been written." He figured these men would have said "wrote," but bad grammar was one concession he was not willing to make just to be one of them, something he knew he already was.

Then Lee Fowler said, leaning back on the hind legs of his chair, "You know, I bee-lieve that's about the worst-lookin' outfit I've ever seen you wear. Can't you get one of them designers to whip you up a good-lookin' huntin' on-som-bull?"

Brundidge held his arms out, the thermos dangling from one hand, as he displayed his camouflage fatigues. "I feel sorry for you boys. This happens to be the latest thing for fall. Of course, no way you could know that, sittin' around here in those sorry shirts of yours that I wouldn't wear to change my oil."

Now Shelby Manis, who seldom said anything, was riled. "What are you talkin' about, you crazy fool? My shirt is made by Arrow! You can't beat a Arrow shirt!"

Bert Harwell agreed, "That's right, Arrow's the best!"

Brundidge headed for the door. "You all are just jealous 'cause you know in your hearts you'll never look as good as me." Then he paused solemnly and said, knowing they wouldn't care that it was dated, "Please don't hate me 'cause I'm beautiful."

He exited amid their jeers.

The navy blue night was still crawling with stars when Brundidge pulled out on the highway and headed back toward town. He pushed in a CD and rubbed his hands together, his breath evaporating into small winter clouds as the words began to tumble out of the speakers.

"Suckin' on chili dogs outside the Tastee-Freez . . . Diane's sittin' on Jackie's lap, he's got his hand between her knees . . ."

Brundidge rolled down the windows and turned up the volume as loud as it would go. As the cold November air struck his face, he increased his speed, feeling happy and free, like he knew he would once he got the right song going. He had to stop by his office and pick up some extra ammo. By the time he exited onto Main Street, his heart was up and racing with the promise of the day. Thank goodness for El Niño—the only worthwhile thing to come out of this year's flooding was the early, massive migration of ducks southward, pushing up the first day of duck hunting season. This was a real manly-man day, during which males were socially sanctioned to sit together in damp straw blinds for hours on end, drinking liquor, telling stories, and cursing. Nobody had to take out the garbage or apologize for being emotionally unavailable. It was just all guys, all the time, all day long. And Brundidge couldn't get enough of it. He just hoped Wood wasn't on call, and would have to bring his cell phone, which for

Brundidge ruined the ambience of the entire duck-blind experience. Brundidge was the proud owner of every technological advance known to humankind, but he knew instinctively that a cell phone has no more place in a duck blind than a girl did in their tree house when they were still boys. Of course, that hadn't stopped Mavis, who had gotten in there anyway and fouled the sanctity of their hideaway with her discarded candy wrappers and empty soda cans and then used a Magic Marker to write her name permanently over the flap of oilcloth that served as their front door. Just thinking about it even now could make Brundidge mad, but something else had drawn his attention as he slowed to a stop at the first blinking signal. In the early morning darkness, the boarded-up buildings looked gray and forgotten except for the occasional bright flash across their facades. But what caught his eye was the reflection of the stoplight continuously strafing the glass-front window of Sidney Garfinkel's vacant store. Brundidge was thinking that somebody must've broken in. The windows, which were usually empty, now featured eight or nine nude mannequins and a lone torso that was lying on the floor. The faces on the mannequins were unfazed and smiling, as if they knew a secret Brundidge would never know. He shivered as the light flickered rhythmically across the lifeless people, illuminating them like discarded stars in an old silent movie. After a moment, he accelerated too quickly, making an absurd squealing noise.

A few miles later, Wood and Charlie were a welcome sight as they lumbered down the McIlmore driveway, wearing their camouflage fatigues and carrying their shotguns. This was a drill they had been a part of many times. They got in the van without speaking and drove away.

Across town, at the Pleasant Valley Retirement Villa, Rudy Caste-nera stepped back and studied his charge with all the intensity of an artist assessing his work at midpoint. Jeter's red face shone through a mountain of winter clothing, including an insulated coat, quilted vest, wool scarf, and industrial-strength mittens.

Jeter sighed softly. "Rudy, this vest feels a little warm. Maybe we've got too much stuff on me."

Rudy fussed over him. "No, I listened to the TV. It is very cold out. Anyway, this is an official hunting vest. I asked the clerk at Fed-Mart."

Now Jeter was upset. "Rudy, I can't wear this. I don't shop at Fed-Mart."

"I am sorry, my friend, but you already have." Rudy placed a pair of furry earmuffs on Jeter's head, crowning them with Dr. Mac's hat. "There you go, Great White Hunter!" He patted Jeter on the top of his head.

Jeter caught a glimpse of himself in the dresser mirror and mumbled, "I look like a damn snowman."

The sun was edging up on a new pink horizon as Jeter's wheelchair sailed up the ramp and through the open doors of Brundidge's van. Wood then closed the doors and jumped back in on the passenger side as they sped away. Rudy stood on the curb waving good-bye like an anxious mother sending her child off to his first day of school.

The van had been moving at a good clip when out of the blue, it shot across four lanes of interstate and exited at the Fed-Mart Superstore off-ramp, turning right, sailing over the empty parking lot and arriving at the massive quarter-mile Fed-Mart Superstore entrance, at which point, without the van's ever slowing down, an orange quilted hunting vest was thrown unceremoniously out the side door and onto the pavement.

A little later, a thick gray mist was rising off the lake. Two men and a boy lowered a hammock containing the soft, plump snowman figure into the wide, flat boat below. Then Charlie untied the rope that secured the boat to the dock, and Wood and Brundidge jumped onboard behind him. Wood pulled the cord on the old seven-and-a-half horsepower Mercury, starting it up on the second try. The sun had climbed even higher now and felt warm on the men's faces. Everyone smiled, especially the snowman, as they made their way across the green porcelain lake with the little motor humming and the wheelchair on the dock becoming smaller in the distance.

Mavis was well acquainted with the scene in which Daisy Buchanan gathers up a bundle of Jay Gatsby's luxurious shirts, holding them to her cheek in wonderment and appreciation as she weeps. During Miss Delaney's twelfth-grade American Lit class, Mavis had figured Daisy for a sort of high-class phony, but now she understood the young socialite's awe over something so ordinary and beautiful. It was pretty much the way Mavis felt every time she looked around the little business she had built from scratch. There were, for example, her shiny stainless-steel bowls filled with freshly kneaded dough and her hand-carved, pine baker's racks, cracked and faded from cradling thousands of steaming loaves of bread. There were also the long French windows with their leaded panes, the high, engraved tin ceiling, and the enormous glass pastry case that came from the original Doe's. It was here that Mavis had acquired her passion for food and subsequent skill from an unlikely pair of teachers. Dauphine Doe, who was Cajun, was a master spicewoman, and her daily specials, from jambalaya to andouille sausage with black beans and rice, brought people from miles around. And her husband, Clarence, a quiet, methodical man, was a pastry chef extraordinaire whose beignets and fried pies had achieved legendary status among the locals.

It was also at Doe's that Mavis became fat and confident. She loved the brazenness of the hotheaded Dauphine (so unlike her own tepid mother, who regularly curtsied to male authority). Dauphine smoked unfiltered cigarettes and unapologetically carried an ever-present stained white dishtowel over her shoulder. But Mavis also blossomed under the paternal eye of Clarence, who spotted her talent right off and had taught her, by the age of twelve, how to turn out a slap-your-mama red velvet cake that invariably earned the prime spot in his spinning glass display case. And besides all that, Doe's was just an exciting place to hang out. Dauphine often picked fights with Clarence in front of customers, and on occasion had even thrown a knife or two. But the food was so good, people said it was worth risking your life for. And for Mavis, it was much better than going home to a house with bland food and no daddy. Not surprisingly, when the Does retired to Louisiana, they refused to entertain any offers for their business but the lowest one, which came from the person who could least afford it—Mavis Pinkerton.

She paused to blow a wisp of hair with flour specks in it off her damp forehead. Today the indoor temperature was intolerably warm, even for someone as thankful as herself. She finally put aside the dough she had been rolling and wiped the perspiration from her face with the edge of her apron. Then she removed her floundering barrette and refashioned a handful of spirited red hair into its clasp.

Rudy, who looked cool and smooth in spite of having been up since 3 A.M. to see Jeter off, was buttering a tray of freshly turned-out croissants. He gave Mavis an apologetic smile, shrugging, "I have called them. They say there is nothing they can do."

Mavis huffed, "Mr. Tillman could have fixed it. Who ever heard of a radiator that has only one temperature—the temperature of hell." She wiped her face again, "We won't make it through another winter."

Rudy and Mavis continued working a while longer.

Then Rudy ventured, "You know Denny from Dwight and Denny's Secret Garden? I am not sure he is giving Dwight my messages."

Mavis stared at him, "I believe I was laying out the idea that we won't make it through another winter."

Rudy reached for another stick of butter.

"He tells me always Dwight is in with the flowers. I think there may be something still between them."

"Well, of course there's something between them. They have a secret garden together. Where the hell have you been?"

Rudy gave her a long look that said he did not appreciate her sarcasm. He placed a hand on his hip, allowing himself to be more flamboyant with Mavis than anyone. "Perhaps I should move myself to a new place where I might be respected by, say, a Miss Sara Lee."

"Just so you know, she's not a real person. I'm a real person."

"Yes. You are a queen and I am your slave."

"Oh, so you did read your employee contract."

The lock of hair was back in her eyes, but she smiled at him anyway. Rudy cocked an eyebrow in her direction, putting a lid on this particular dish of conversation that would be served up again throughout the day, the basic ingredients varying only slightly.

Inside the duck blind, the three men and the boy were as quiet as children sleeping in a backseat. Every so often, they listened hard for any sound, however distant, that might be approaching them from the other side of a chilled, wintry silence. But so far, there had been nothing other than the grating noise of Brundidge blowing on the little duck caller that Mr. Case had said carried the perfect pitch of a mating call.

Wood had taken to giving Brundidge a look of disdain.

Brundidge finally said, "I think this thing's scarin' them off. Hell, we've been here an hour and a half and haven't attracted one damn duck." Jeter, lying on his back, said, "Maybe they don't find us . . . sexy."

Mavis was at the counter, waiting on Corinne Carlson, a woman who was so southern and nice, she often apologized just for being in your presence.

"Don't get the sun-dried tomato crois- sants. Get the blue cheese pecan bread."

No sooner had she spoken than Milan en- tered, ringing the little bell on the door, breathless, perfectly turned out, her heels clicking as she crossed to the counter.

"There you are! Thank goodness you're here!" Then, as Milan noticed Corinne, she adjusted her voice to a more dulcet tone. "Oh, hi Corinne. Could you excuse us for just a moment?"

Mavis protested, "Milan, I'm in the middle of an order, here."

Corinne smiled. "No, it's okay. It's fine, really."

Milan said winningly, "It's an emergency."

Mavis apologized, "I'm sorry, Corinne. I'll be right back. Rudy, can you cover?"

Rudy crossed to the counter. "Oh sure. Rudy can cover. I'm only in the middle of making six dozen chocolate-pistachio toile cups, which could go poof at any moment."

Mavis called back, "Give Corinne a sample of that pecan bread."

Corinne protested, "Oh no, really, that's way too much! I couldn't possibly—bless your heart! Well, at least let me pay you . . ."

Mavis and Milan huddled as Corinne's conversation played in the background.

Milan started. "She's getting a divorce."

"Who?"

"Her."

"How do you know?"

"Because she told me. I invited their whole family for Thanksgiving."

Mavis raised her eyebrows, "Why?"

"Because we have to get together, Mavis. We have to face this. You know, sometimes the church is booked a year in advance."

Mavis was incredulous, "They're staying at your house?"

"No, the Holiday Inn. But he's not coming. They're getting a divorce! Can you believe it? I really am like Job. Next I'll have sores all over my body."

"You should stop teaching Sunday school, Milan. It's making you overly dramatic."

"You're coming."

"To what?"

"Thanksgiving! Besides the food, you can help me keep the conversation going."

"You don't need me. No conversation has ever died in your presence."

Milan dug in her purse for her keys, "I have to get to the grocery store. Do I look all right?"

"You look like you're about to read some minutes. Is that all right?"

"Just forget it." Milan prissed toward the door. "I get so tired of you saying what I look like." Then, as she turned back, "By the way, did Brundidge and Jeter go duck hunting today?

"I don't know. Why?"

"Because Wood was up at four and now Charlie's missing too."

Rudy overheard and answered, "Everybody went. They were wearing combat outfits and carrying guns. It was all very Hemingway."

Milan said cheerfully, "Oh. Well, good. Now we can have ducks for Thanksgiving."

Milan left, ringing the little bell again on her way out.

Corinne spoke with her mouth full, "Mavis, this bread is simply delicious."

"That's the last of it. You can have it."

"Oh, my gracious. You are just too kind. Really, I can't thank you—"

Mavis cut her off. "You're welcome. Just don't send me a damn note."

Mavis was watching Milan through the window, struck for the first time by how small her friend seemed. From the front, Milan was all confidence and bravado, but from behind she looked like a little girl sashaying around in her mother's high heels. Suddenly, Mavis hugged herself and felt cold for the first time all day.

In the duck blind, Brundidge was refilling his and Wood's coffee mugs as well as the bottle from Jeter's wheelchair. Charlie nursed a soft drink as Jeter, who was still lying with his face to the sky, completed the recitation of a poem.

> *. . . Where rivulets danced their wayward round*
> *And beauty born of murmuring sound*
> *Shall pass into her face.*

Brundidge attempted to run a straw to Jeter's mouth as Wood joined in a manly, deep-voiced duet.

> *Thus nature spake—The work was done,*
> *She died and left to me*
> *This heath, this calm and quiet scene;*
> *The memory of what has been.*
> *And never more will be.*

Brundidge spoke as he picked up his own drink. "Now that's a damn good poem! Of course, iambic pentameter is always better when enhanced with a little early morning screw-damn-driver."

Jeter smiled. "Mr. Wordsworth from 'Three Years She Grew in Sun and Shower.' Or, as it is better known today, 'Four Guys Doing Diddly-shit in a Duck Blind.'"

Charlie was impressed. "How do you re-member all that stuff?"

Brundidge said, "Are you kidding? Look at him. If your head was that big, you'd remem-ber everything, too."

Wood turned to Jeter. "So, you written any masterpieces lately?"

"Nah. I sent something out a few weeks ago. Still waiting to hear."

Some birds passed overhead, but they turned out to be cranes. Brundidge was get-ting wound up. "You know what your problem is? You're not commercial. Poetry doesn't sell for shit. You need to write one of those deals like a screenplay. We'd be so rich! I can tell you the exact title right now."

Intrigued, Charlie asked, "What?"

Brundidge milked the silence, then said grandly, "Three words. *Barbie, the Movie.*"

There was a long pause as the others pondered this. Then Wood said, "You mean, like a cartoon?"

"Hell, no. Real people."

Jeter used a smile you would give to a drunk. "I think it's been done."

"No. It hasn't been done! I've been think-ing about it for years! We should put together a financial cartel—ordinary men bringing

Barbie to life. You copy her little car, her little wardrobe, her little shoes . . ."

Wood asked, "What time did you start drinking?"

"There isn't a person in America who wouldn't go see that movie. Am I right, Charlie?"

"I don't know."

"Well, why the hell not?"

Wood spoke up, "Because he's never thought about it. Who the hell thinks about shit like that?"

"I do. It's a damn genius idea! And think of the sequels. You put Ken in there—whoa! Now you've got Barbie and Ken in a real-life love scene!"

Jeter said, "Mattel's not gonna let their dolls screw."

Wood added, "That's right. Anyway, Ken hasn't got anything."

Brundidge was out of patience. "What do you mean?"

"Look inside his pants."

"Oh, I see. You don't think about shit like this. But you have time to look inside Ken's pants."

"I'm a doctor. Anyway, ask Charlie. He knows about Ken."

"It's true. He hasn't got much."

Now Brundidge was apoplectic. "We're not talking about dolls, damn it! We're talking about people playing dolls that screw! Have you never heard of an independent film! What the hell's wrong with you people?"

The ducks would probably have shown up anyway, but the point is they didn't until Brundidge started yelling and Wood, exasperated, had grabbed the little masterpiece duck caller out of his hands and begun blowing loud enough to drown him out. The response was immediate—at first, just a few distant calls coming from the north, but little by little, the sound and the number of ducks grew until the sky had grown almost dark. Charlie, Brundidge, and Wood picked up their rifles and began firing.

Between shots, Brundidge shouted, "Holy shit! What did you do?"

Wood answered, "It's not the equipment. It's how you use it."

Charlie smiled, content.

People don't spend much time picturing game wardens, but if they did, Linus Felker would be who they had in mind. He was a tall, beefy, red-cheeked farm boy—the kind who looks like he's been well loved by someone, probably his mama. Right now, he had everyone pulled out of the van and was contemplating the extremely puffy nature of Jeter's hunting jacket. Linus set his jaw and made his eyes narrow.

Finally, he said it. "Unzip his coat."

Brundidge was not happy. "Oh, man, come on. He's an invalid."

Linus fixed his gaze on Brundidge, like a father saying, "Don't make me get my belt." Brundidge crossed to Jeter and unzipped the jacket. There was almost no sound as a half dozen ducks tumbled to the ground beside Jeter's wheelchair.

Linus spoke without a trace of sarcasm. "I guess you boys are aware that puts you over the limit."

There was more silence, then Wood sidled over to Linus and whispered, "I know this looks bad, but I'm his doctor. You see, lately he's been getting just the tiniest bit of mobility back in one of his arms. It's like a miracle, really. He hasn't fired a gun in twenty years. When he saw the ducks coming, he just went crazy." Wood paused and looked at the ground. "I'm sorry. I just didn't have the heart to stop him."

Jeter picked up the story, milking it. "Hey, it's not your fault. I'm always pushing. Stupid, stupid, stupid." Then, to Linus, "Give me the ticket."

Linus looked at each one of the men's faces, sure that he could tell if they were lying. Finally he smiled, satisfied, "No, that's okay. We'll let it slide this one time." Then he put a hand on Jeter's shoulder, "Just keep on gettin' better, buddy."

Brundidge had tears in his eyes from the day's drinking and the decency of the boy.

Jeter said, "Thank you, sir. Thank you very much."

The newly emboldened van was blazing down the interstate, The Eagles blasting from the stereo. Wood, Brundidge, and Jeter joined in on the chorus.

"You can't hide your lyin' eyes, and your smile is a thin disguise . . ."

As the song continued, Brundidge lowered the volume, "Now that's music, Charlie-boy! That's what your old man and Uncle Jeet and I grew up on. What are y'all gonna talk about at your reunion? 'Hey, baby, re-member when we danced to'"—affecting a rapper—"'I kick yo ass, bitch, to the window, to the flo, 'cause you is my ho.'"

Charlie said, "C'mon, there's all kinds of rap—"

Brundidge glanced at Wood.

"See? It's too late."

Wood looked back at his son, "Yeah, it's always the quiet ones you gotta watch."

Charlie stared out the window, pleased at the thought that he might be evil.

Jeter said, "Hey, pit stop. Ernest is gonna blow."

A half mile later, the van was parked on a country road with the doors open. Jeter, in his wheelchair, and Charlie and Brundidge were perfectly lined up next to each other. The Ea-gles continued singing as Wood pulled the stopper on the opaque plastic urine pouch at-tached to Jeter's rolled-up pant leg. Then Wood stepped quickly back into formation. As Jeter's pouch emptied onto the ground, the three men and the boy rejoined the Ea-gles, while taking a manly leak in unison.

"I thought by now you'd realize, there ain't no way to hide your lyin' eyes."

CHAPTER 13

Mary Kathleen Duffer—that was her full name—was on her way home for Thanksgiving and feeling more hopeful than she had in years. And she was especially pleased that her son, riding next to her in their little Toyota, was sound asleep. Because it would have required too much effort to keep this new smile off her face. Her only child had found someone worthy of his gifts, and she herself was about to be reunited with an old love. How improbable and fitting that their children had discovered each other when they were not much older than Wood and Duff had been when they first fell in love. For years, Wood had never been far from her thoughts. However, she was not allowing herself to imagine that he might still be thinking of her. In her younger days, she would have had the arrogance to know that he was. But since then life had dealt her enough wrong men that she had lost all her confidence. All she knew at this moment was this: whatever had once gone on between Elizabeth McIlmore's dad and herself, that crazy high school red convertible kind of ether—well, she had never known anything like it again. Of course, she wasn't going to do anything about that. But just seeing the man who had once made her heart race as fast as his old Austin-Healy sailing toward the Champanelle River with the top down—that would be more than enough for her. Surely she was entitled to these few pleasant memories on a Sunday afternoon without feeling as though she was betraying her own son.

Anyway, it wasn't just Wood she was excited about seeing again. It was all of them. Jeter with his sweet open smile, the kind most people saved for a child, but he gave easily to everyone. And dear, tougher-than-boots Mavis, always willing to take on whatever needed whipping. Even Brundidge, whose bourgeois, and, yes, that was a word she used even in high school, sentiments used to so annoy her, she was now looking forward to catching up with. The truth was, she had missed them all. Except, of course, for Milan, in whom she had never found any redeeming traits. Her perfect hair and man-

ners, her tireless committee work, the doe-
eyed way she regarded Wood. How had he
stood it all these years—the sheer mud-thick
banality of her?

Duff had to admit that she had liked Elizabeth's forthright manner and unembar-
rassed enthusiasm on the phone. She
actually already reminded Duff more of herself than of Milan. From Luke's description,
Elizabeth seemed like the sort of girl who
was going to make the world her home—the
sort of girl Duff had once been, back when
things were going mostly her way.

She couldn't remember anymore the exact moment when she had realized her own
dreams were not going to come true. It was
a gradual thing really, like watching someone who is terminally ill lose a little more
ground each day. It had been a surprise to
find out that dreams, like people, can simply
rot away. Not that she would have worried
about it much. Hers was a mellow personality. Unlike Milan, who insisted on making
things happen, Duff was someone who
things happened to. Part of her charm was
her willingness to go where life led her. If
Duff had been born a decade earlier, she
would have been a highly successful hippie.

In the late seventies, there was no one in Paris like her. She smoked Turkish cigarettes and openly cursed in front of the teachers. She never wore makeup or underwear and went around calling Wood her lover. She brooded and wrote poems about menstrual blood and depression. But the thing people still talk about were those riding pants. The ones she started wearing with high, lace-up leather boots before she even owned a horse. When she and Wood were dating, she would show up at school events wearing "the pants" with a white, see-through peasant blouse and a thin layer of perspiration on her upper lip. It had the desired effect of making Milan, strapped into the drum majorette uniform she had worked all summer to buy, feel unsophisticated and silly.

Duff liked to ride for hours with Wood in the pasture behind his house. There was a little creek beside a cluster of persimmon trees where they always made love while their horses looked on. They had laughed about how, when people made love in old movies, the camera always cut to horses running through a field. But their horses had actually watched them have sex. When she and Wood were done, they would lie on their

backs and drink Dr. Mac's brandy after
warming the flask with their cigarette
lighters. They loved lying around on the McIlmores' back porch, reading their favorite
books out loud, or going to the movies and
discussing the characters afterward. They
especially liked foreign films and many of the
darker cinematic offerings, like *A Clockwork
Orange* and *Satyricon,* which the others in
the group had failed to appreciate. Brundidge had called them two of the worst damn
movies he ever saw. And Milan had chimed
in with her usual annoying bromide, "If you
pay six-fifty for something, I just think it
should make you feel good."

Duff wasn't an excitable person, but if she
had been, Milan's was the kind of cheerful
idiocy that could drive her straight up the
wall. That's why Duff refused to join something called "the Pep Club." Before Wood,
Duff had never even attended a football
game. Then she and Milan had both been
nominated for homecoming royalty. And Duff
had taken herself out of the running because
she didn't believe in competition. It wasn't in
Duff's nature to be jealous or competitive.
Even after her selfless gesture was widely
misunderstood, Duff had never questioned

the value of her own noble ideas. It wasn't until much later, after years of disappointing returns, that she had finally begun to wonder if people don't indeed have a competitive other, someone who spends a lifetime trying to edge them out, wishing them ill, rejoicing in their defeat. In Duff's life, it looked like that person was and always would be Milan Lanier McIlmore.

Once, while waiting to be disciplined in the vice principal's office, she had looked up Milan's SAT scores. And what she found had shocked her. Milan's scores were in the top twenty percent of the senior class. They were, in fact, just a few points lower than her own. It was unbelievable. Sure Milan made good grades, but that was just because she worked hard. The fact that she could spout such moronic drivel and still test almost as good as Duff—well, it didn't make any more sense than Wood's finally ending up with her.

Certainly, Milan had not been careless. She was the single most calculating person Duff had ever known. And forgetting to take birth control pills? Well, that was about as likely as Milan forgetting to put on her makeup. The actual act of not taking the pills, of trapping Wood into marrying her,

was so clichéd and predictable only Milan
would have failed to be embarrassed by it. It
was like something out of one of her soap
operas, whose characters she discussed
with awe and reverence, as though they had
sprung from novels. In Miss Delaney's class,
Milan had even written a term paper arguing
that someone named Lisa Miller Hughes on
As the World Turns was every bit as layered
and worthy of literary recognition as Madame Bovary. Imagine such a person pretending to be Wood's soul mate. Seducer
was more like it. Always ready to be on her
knees, with her perpetually moist eyes,
which of course put a man in mind of the rest
of her. Duff certainly understood Wood's being vulnerable to all that. After all, she was a
man's woman herself. But the fact that Wood
had entrusted his and Duff's future to Milan's
integrity, that's what was so unforgivable.
How carelessly he had given away a mind
so in tune with his own, along with the two
long legs that wrapped around him with such
ease and the silky voice that spoke of interesting things.

Yes, there had been a breakup. Wood had
said some things he didn't mean—words
that could have been put right if Milan had

played fair and a certain wild-ass sperm had been stopped at the circle that became the girl that the sleeping boy next to her was now going to marry. The same person who in all innocence had ruined his mother's life. A soap opera of more tragic proportion than any of those Milan had succumbed to. It was, in fact, more akin to the Greek tragedies that filled the bottom right shelf of Wood's parents' den. She knew that shelf well because she had seen it from upside down when she and Wood had made love in there, too.

Duff pulled the little Toyota into a gas station and got out. Luke continued to sleep as she filled the car and went inside to pay. A little later, as they pulled away, she tossed a Stuckey's pecan log in his lap. He woke up just long enough to eat his half and fell asleep again, exhausted from studying for exams. It was a ritual they had shared many times, driving on southern highways, eating the rich marshmallow and caramel-filled bar, playing the radio with their shoes off, one or the other asleep, never having to talk unless they felt like it. That's the way it had always been between them.

When Luke was a baby, she had taken

him everywhere. To dinner, to class, to California. She had carried him on her back and in her arms. And when she couldn't afford a new baby carrier, she had lugged him around in her purse. Duff looked again at her boy for as long as the road would allow. In the late afternoon light, he looked even younger than his years. The way he looked sometimes when she stood beside his bed, having just come home between waitress shifts, to turn his lamp out or put the quilt back over him. Whatever had gone wrong in her life, he was the one good thing she could point to and say, "There. How 'bout that now? How about that?" No, she could never do anything to hurt him. This one good boy would be more than enough for a woman who's made her share of bad calls. To have been young once herself, to have felt the promise of happiness, maybe that was almost as good as actually getting it. Anyway, she was sure her memories were better than anything she was going to come up with now.

Her parents, Dr. Jim and Susan Duffer, had doted on their only daughter, nicknaming her "Katrina." "Duff" came later, as her own idea. The Duffers were as climbing and

pretentious as the McIlmores were their relaxed, unassuming selves. They built a
French château on the edge of town and
then spent a fortune trying to make it look
old. They imported a maid from El Salvador
and insisted that she wear a uniform, something that was virtually unheard of in a small
town, except maybe at Christmas.

Jim Duffer was a podiatrist, but when people came to the house, Susan always spoke
in hushed, reverential tones about whether or
not "Doctor is in" or "Please be quiet, Doctor
is sleeping." Wood's dad had said, "The man
scrapes feet for a living. You'd think he was
upstairs discovering penicillin." The Duffers
were joiners, the king and queen of the country club, the first ones to have a theme party,
be it hobo night, which involved dressing up
like homeless people, or a Hawaiian luau,
which involved Susan Duffer demonstrating
the hula, which she had learned from her
Polynesian massage therapist. For the Duffers, every day was an excuse to mix up a
batch of dirty martinis and throw some two-
inch steaks on the grill. On football weekends,
they presided over twenty-five-hundred-dollar
tailgate parties. By January, they were in
Florida playing all the signature golf courses.

They were, in fact, having such a good time, one can only imagine their surprise when they learned that little Kathleen had stolen money from her father's wallet and liberated the El Salvadoran maid, who used it to buy a bus ticket to Las Vegas. This was especially sticky for Dr. Jim, who had forgotten to pay the taxes on Martita's wages. Then, as a teenager, Kathleen had eschewed her parents' country-club membership, where she had been the first girl to lie around topless, in favor of hanging out at the municipal pool—where Wood and Brundidge and Jeter had made a point to swim on "Colored Day." Duff passionately admired the McIlmores. She especially loved that Slim McIlmore had herded Wood and Brundidge and Jeter into her station wagon and driven them all the way to the Lorraine Motel in Memphis, Tennessee, just to see the exact spot where Martin Luther King had been killed. She was ashamed that her own parents did not have that kind of social consciousness. Social consciousness? Hell, they were brain-dead. Hobo Night? If the Duffers had stopped to believe in anything, it would probably have been the notion that if you're not doing well, it's your own damn fault. That's why Jim had so much trouble understanding why his daughter enjoyed hanging out at the old train station and playing her guitar for the winos. Even at fifteen, she had joined the line of cashiers and box boys picketing the Piggly Wiggly for higher wages. This caused a question to develop in Susan Duffer's mind that she asked over and over again to anyone who would listen. "If you don't work at the Piggly Wiggly, what business is it of yours what the employees are doing there?"

And that's pretty much how it went for most of Kathleen's adolescence. There was the time she invited migrant farm workers to the house when the Duffers were out of town. Miraculously, nothing had been stolen, but Jim Duffer was incensed that they had roasted a goat on his ten-thousand-dollar Jenn-Air grill. There was also an ugly pen-pal incident in which Kathleen's parents hadn't even known that she was writing to a man in prison, much less that she was up half the night reading his letters by candle-light in her closet. Kathleen had thought she might actually be in love with this person until the day he wrote that he was getting paroled in a few weeks and could not wait to see the smile on her face when he shoved his old army bayonet up her sweet ass. That was when she had been forced to tell her parents, who surprised her by acting just as scared as she was. This was the first time Kathleen had realized that mothers and fathers are no more brave than children, but are simply better actors.

Finally, mercifully, at seventeen, Wood had entered her life and Kathleen had become "Duff"—a mature, lighthearted, reasonable young woman. After seeing the relationship Wood had with his own parents, she desperately tried to emulate it with Jim and Susan. For their part, the Duffers bought their daughter an Arabian horse and English saddle so that she could ride over to the McIlmores in style. As far as they were concerned, Wood was as welcome in their home as Tom Collins. He was the prodigal son of a family that was at least as good as their own. Sure, as a kid, he had tried to integrate the city pool, but that was just his parents talking. The Duffers didn't understand why the McIlmores didn't drive better cars or why they refused to join the country club. Jim Duffer wasn't buying that old excuse about them not joining because blacks and Jews were not admitted. He said Dr. Mac was just too cheap to pay the dues. Look how they put masking tape on an old clock radio instead of buying a new one. But the real mystery was all those books in every room of the McIlmore house. Hell, their whole house smelled like old books! Like a damn library! Susan Duffer had paid a small fortune for an expert artist to paint the classics on their own den wall—books that looked so real, you felt you could almost reach out and read one.

But overall, the Duffers would have laid down their own lives for the boy who had given them the daughter they always wanted. Sure, Kathleen had grown up some on her own, but it was Wood's influence, his unerring steadiness and good sense that had finally overtaken their Katrina. It also didn't hurt that on good days he could throw a football over fifty yards. They were already planning a hundred-thousand-dollar wedding in their minds when they heard of Wood's betrothal to the brazen white-trash daughter of their garbage man—Florence or Rome or Milan or whatever the hell her name was. Jim and Susan were almost as inconsolable as Duff.

That's why they decided not to say anything when she showed up from college a few weeks later with a young black man in tow. His name was Keith Walters and he was a talented assistant professor in the Graphic Arts Department at Emory. Duff was pleasantly surprised that she did not have to make the speech about racial acceptance she'd been rehearsing for days. And she was also puzzled to learn that he thought her parents were mildly amusing. Especially when Jim kept asking Keith how he had enjoyed that television program *Roots*. Keith's inability to take offense at things mystified Duff. Even when they made love, and she insisted on always being on the bottom, he never got the significance or symbolism of her sacrifice. Duff had been thinking of ending their relationship on the day Elizabeth Marie McIlmore was born. Up until then, she had survived in a sort of dreamlike state where unwanted babies are never born. They are always on the way. A few days later, at Duff's insistence, she and Keith eloped to Vermont, where interracial couples were treated with dignity and respect. That was when Jim and Susan Duffer made the painful decision to disown their only child. They had put up with a lot over the years. They had lost their maid, paid excessive taxes, posted bail, and obtained a restraining order against some Rastafarian convict pedophile. But they were not about to also end up with grandchildren the color of fried chicken. Now Kathleen was screwing with the purity of the Duffer family gene pool and this they would not allow.

They needn't have worried. A few weeks later, Keith, who was homesick, had the marriage annulled and returned to Arkansas. Duff gathered her guitar and her paints and caught a ride with several artist friends to California. Over the next year, people in Paris told different stories about what she was up to. Someone had seen her selling her watercolors on the beach in Venice. Mavis got a card that she was a hostess at the Hard Rock Café. A friend in Santa Barbara sent Jim and Susan a picture of Duff from a national magazine. The caption read, "Record producer Ron Hurley and date attend a party for Billy Joel." It wasn't long be-

fore word got around Paris that Duff was living in an artist colony in Excelsior Springs,
Arkansas, and dating a used-car salesman.
People who heard this and knew Duff
thought it sounded about right. Especially
the part about her giving birth to this man's
son out of wedlock. The Duffers, who had
moved to Florida, no longer supported their
daughter. However, they did send a small
check and some baby clothes for their
grandson.

The new man in Duff's life was Dennis
Childs. Like his wife, Dennis was a dreamer.
And an idea man. He had an idea for chocolate cola. And a bleacher cushion that un-
folds into a rain tarp. And a CD containing all
the birthday songs ever written. He also had
the idea that no one should question his authority. Ever. He was the first male Duff had
known since Wood who made her feel safe
and protected. And he was adventurous like
Wood, too. Especially the way he liked to
have sex in strange places. Moments after
they applied for their marriage license, he
had stopped the elevator between floors at
the Cabe County Courthouse, taken her
panties off right there, turned her on her

stomach and pounded her for a good long twenty minutes while everyone else cooled their heels. It was one of the most thrilling things Duff had ever had a man do. No one else had made her feel that way except Wood. And Wood could do it without stopping elevators. Wood, with his knee-wobbling charisma, could do it with just a look. Like the first time he had put his own dark eyes level with hers and said sincerely, "Kathleen, can I kiss you?" Of course, she wasn't about to tell Dennis who his best side put her in mind of. She had already begun to notice that what had once seemed like strong male leadership was starting to look more like garden-variety bulliness. Like a lot of women, she had mistaken meanness for manliness.

It was around this time that Dennis hit Duff. Just a little at first. Then it got harder and more regular. Sometimes she gave as good as she got. But mostly the one who weighed two hundred pounds came out on top. It didn't happen every day really, but over the years, as the money dwindled and tempers frayed, Duff had checked into various emergency rooms with a broken nose, a fractured wrist, and several cracked ribs. When Luke got old enough, he had stood up to his father, several times exchanging blows, which had further increased their estrangement. That and the fact that Luke now spent his summers with Jim and Susan Duffer, who lavished all the love they held in reserve for their daughter on their grandson.

By the time Luke left for college, Duff remembered just enough of the high-spirited girl she used to be that she decided to file for divorce. After that, Dennis Childs had only one idea left. And that was to get his wife back. He begged. He cried. He bought her gifts. He beat her up and bought her more gifts. But nothing seemed to work. By this time, Duff no longer believed in even the redemption of herself, much less anyone else. After Dennis left town with what little money they had, Duff took a job as a waitress at IHOP. Then she changed all the locks on her doors and waited to see where life would lead her next. The next morning, her boy came home from college and announced he had met a girl from Paris—a girl he had fallen in love with and wanted to marry.

Chapter 14

It was Thanksgiving morning and Milan had already whipped through six outfits before deciding to go with her red Valentino sweater and matching pants. She was now standing in the middle of her country French farm kitchen, worrying that the calligraphy on the place cards wasn't dark enough, and wondering if they had enough food. She remembered another Thanksgiving right after she and Wood were first married, when she had bought so many groceries, they ran out of places to put them all away. And Wood had stood behind her, holding her, and whispered in her ear, "You have to stop this. I promise, we're never going to run out."

Mavis was brushing her hot-pepper-jelly-and-bourbon marinade on two ducks roasting over a hearth rotisserie as Rudy presided over several other dishes. Milan slipped one of her newly manicured hands into a quilted mitt and opened one of the oven doors.

"Rudy, these rolls are just sitting there."

Rudy pushed the door shut. "Trust me, they will rise."

Mavis looked toward Milan. "Especially if you keep the damn door closed."

Milan said, "Please don't cuss. It's Thanksgiving."

Mavis spoke under her breath, "Oh, I'm sorry. I thought we were gonna stop saying fuck, but keep saying damn."

Then, noticing Milan's interest, "I'm warning you. Stay away from my ducks."

Elizabeth entered the kitchen. "They're here!" Then she flew toward the front door.

Milan nervously straightened her sweater and patted her hair. "Okay, everybody just be calm. We'll have cocktails in the den. Rudy, you circulate with the paté and bruschetta." She turned to Mavis. "Do I look all right?"

"You look like the wife of a southern governor. Is that all right?"

Milan gave Mavis a look. "Just once you could say something encouraging."

Mavis followed her as she started toward the front door. "Hey, I was just trying to lighten the mood."

"Not today, okay?"

"Okay."

As the two women arrived at the front door, the dreaded reunion was already taking place. Elizabeth and her dad had just stepped off the front porch when Duff and Luke emerged from their battered Toyota. Elizabeth rushed past her dad, literally jumping into Luke's arms. Wood stood for a moment, allowing Duff a chance to gather her things. He could see right away that her face, though still lovely, had begun to show the residue of a hard life. Her eyes looked dull and tired and there was no shine to her at all.

He spoke first, warmly. "Hello."

Duff, anxious to establish her dignity, answered him without an ounce of flirtation.

Milan and Mavis held their collective breath, just as they had when Bud and Deanie were reunited in *Splendor in the Grass*. Natalie Wood, fresh out of the mental hospital, had been radiant in a tightly fitted sheath and wide-brimmed hat. Warren Beatty, on the other hand, had stood around in some dirty overalls, digging his toe in the ground. And now, here Duff was, dressed in a modest JCPenney-type skirt and blouse, something Wood could not have known but Milan tabulated immediately. In her hands was a wilted bouquet of cheap flowers, the kind you buy at the grocery store. As far as Milan could tell, Duff was Bud. It wasn't even noon yet on Thanksgiving day and already she felt grateful.

Elizabeth grabbed her fiancé's arm and pulled him toward Wood. "Daddy, this is Luke."

The boy extended his hand, "How are you, sir?"

As Wood shook it, "Well, I'm fine, Luke. But I think a better question is, are you aware of what you've gotten yourself into?"

"Well, I've got a pretty good idea."

"And you showed up anyway? You are a brave fella." Wood saw immediately that Luke was likable and endowed with his mother's handsome, angular features. He put his arm around his future son-in-law. "Looking forward to having another doctor in the family."

"Thank you, sir."

"And we can stop this 'sir' business? I'm Wood."

"Okay, sir."

Then, as Luke caught himself, everyone laughed.

Duff turned to Wood. "Don't I get a hug?"

Wood hesitated, then opened his arms. Suddenly Milan was pulling Mavis with her down the driveway and shrieking, "You're here!"

A little later, everyone was gathered in the silky peach McIlmore dining room (Benjamin Moore #121, "Blithe Spirit"), hands held, heads bowed. A giant turkey sat in front of Wood, flanked by the two glazed ducks. The old cherrywood table was appointed with the McIlmore family silver, Limoges china, and flawlessly pressed linens. So as not to embarrass Duff, Milan had seen to it that her humble bouquet was discreetly dismantled among the two elaborate floral center-pieces. Seated around the table were Mavis and the McIlmores, Duff and Luke, Slim, Sidney Garfinkel, and Brundidge with his two little girls, who looked perfect in their eggplant-colored dresses and large white linen collars. Jeter was also there, in his wheelchair, next to the old schoolteachers, the unpredictable Miss Phipps, who was having an off day, and the ever-curious Miss

Delaney, who was grilling Charlie McIlmore about rap music.

Wood had agreed to say grace, but Milan had made so many suggestions regarding the content, he had told her to say it herself. Wood sat staring at her now as she finished. ". . . And we thank you for this food we are about to receive, for our beautiful home and acreage, for our wonderful son and daughter, and we pray that you will help us to be worthy of the important position you have given us in this community."

Mavis mumbled, without raising her head, "Lord help us."

Milan pressed on, "Also we thank you for this day that we are blessed to share with our family and friends, including Luke . . . and his mother."

Elizabeth said Amen as Milan raised her head in time to catch the smile that passed between her husband and Duff.

Wood found himself suddenly touched by his wife's childish attempt to paint an enviable face on their life together. Ironically, her assumption that others couldn't see what she was up to, her complete lack of self-awareness, was what always made him, just when he had given up, start to love her a little again—coupled with the inexplicable feeling that it was up to him to protect her.

Brundidge was giving Lily a nod. "Go ahead, honey. Say yours now. Unless the Lord is just exhausted from hearing how well we're all doing."

Everyone rebowed their heads. Lily said, "Thank you for this turkey and for our new Bibles with our names on them." Cake nudged her softly. After a pause, Lily added, "Amen."

Brundidge searched the faces of the other diners for compliments, as Rudy ladled the soup into serving bowls. Miss Delaney said good-naturedly, "Mr. Brundidge, may I say your children grow more impressive each year, a fact I could not have predicted from having attempted to teach literature to you in high school."

"Well, they take after their mother."

Cake spoke up, "Our mother and daddy are divorced."

Miss Phipps looked at her. "You're lucky. My mother and daddy are dead."

There was an awkward pause until Duff said to Cake and Lily, "I like your dresses."

Cake said, "Thank you." Then, gesturing toward Brundidge, "He had them made for us."

Duff smiled. "Is that so? Well, they're very pretty."

Brundidge was beaming now. "I've got a lady who sews for me. But I designed the collars. I thought that'd be cute, you know, to have kind of a pilgrim deal."

Miss Phipps said, in between sips of the beef consommé with bacon dumplings, "When are we going to open presents?"

Miss Delaney turned to her, "That's Christmas, Lodi. This is Thanksgiving."

"Oh, that's right. I don't know what gets into me."

Miss Delaney turned to Elizabeth and Luke. "Perhaps we should explain to your fiancé, Elizabeth, that Miss Phipps and I taught your dad and Mr. Brundidge and Mr. Jeter in school, an experience from which we have never fully recovered." Elizabeth and Luke laughed.

Jeter said, "Well, now, you taught Luke's mother and Milan and Mavis, too."

Miss Delaney winked at Duff. "Yes, but they were angels."

Suddenly, Miss Phipps became riled. "They were wild, those boys! Wild!"

Wood laughed. "Now come on, Miss Phipps, remember it's Thanksgiving."

Brundidge said, "Yeah, this is the time for forgiveness and reconciliation."

Miss Phipps pressed on, pleased to have the floor. "I never let up on them, never! If they have any manners today, it's because of me!" She lifted a spoon. "Let's show them what I taught you boys. C'mon, now, pick up your spoons! You need to show the little ones."

Jeter rolled his eyes as Wood and Brundidge picked up their spoons.

Miss Phipps continued, "Are you with me? One, two, three . . ."

All three men spoke in unison as Wood and Brundidge demonstrated the appropriate way to use a soup spoon. "Little ships go out to sea, always sail away from me."

Miss Phipps was on fire now. "Again!"

The men complied. "Little ships go out to sea, always sail away from me."

Luke and Elizabeth began to laugh. So did Duff and Wood and eventually everybody. Mavis and Milan got up and went into the kitchen where Rudy was working.

Milan said, "She doesn't look that good."

Mavis answered, "She's a waitress at IHOP."

Milan moved closer to Mavis. "She told you that?"

"Yes, she works the night shift."

Rudy was staring at Milan. "I'm sorry, but she is nothing compared to you."

Milan said, touched, "Thank you, Rudy, that is so sweet."

"Not at all. You are a goddess."

Rudy left. Then Milan turned to Mavis. "You tell him too much."

"I don't tell him anything. Every year the man is you for Halloween." She retrieved two multicolored chocolate turkeys, each in its own spun-sugar basket. "You know, she used to be so full of herself. Now she seems sort of . . . beaten down." She looked at Milan. "I know that makes you happy. But it makes me kind of sad."

"I didn't say I was happy."

Mavis headed toward the dining room. "You don't have to. By the way, very classy not giving thanks that her ass is now bigger than yours."

Milan followed Mavis out whispering, "Hey, I'm just glad her son's not as big a flake as she is."

The two women reentered the dining room, all smiles.

Miss Phipps was speaking. ". . . And may I say I am thankful once again for Mr. Jeter, who each year never fails to remind me of the cutoff date for wearing white shoes."

Mavis set the two turkey baskets in front of Cake and Lily, who drew in their breath, excited. Lily showed Brundidge her chocolate turkey. "Look, Daddy!"

He said, "That Mavis is somethin' else, isn't she?" Then, turning to Elizabeth, "Okay, Lillabet, you're up."

Elizabeth said, "Sorry. Mine's too personal."

"I don't wanna hear that. This is your Thanksgiving. Let's have it."

"Okay. But I'll have to say it in French." She turned to Luke. *"Ce jour, mon amour pour toi est illimité. Tu et moi, nous sommes en feu."*

Luke was flattered. Duff engaged Wood with her eyes. Milan was wishing she'd taken French.

Elizabeth said, "All right, Daddy, your turn."

"Sorry. Mine's personal, too."

Brundidge muttered, "Well, heck, if I'd known everybody's was gonna be personal, I would've said mine in pig latin."

Sidney Garfinkel said, "You're awfully quiet, Evangeline."

Slim answered him, warmly, "Oh, don't

mind me. I'm just along for the ride this year." Wood gave his mother a long, loving look and she returned it. Then Sidney picked up his wineglass and stood, clearing his throat. "Well, I remember a Thanksgiving that I spent on a road outside Paris, after the war. That's France, not Arkansas. I must've weighed around eighty pounds and this American G.I. shared his rations with me—it was canned beef with gravy . . . and a Hershey's chocolate bar for dessert. That was the finest Thanksgiving I ever had." He paused, then lifted his glass. "Until today. Vive le Paris, Arkansas."

The old people had gone home. Cake and Lily had been delivered to their aunt's. The rest of the holiday revelers were now at the old Criterion Palace on the corner of Main and Hyacinth. This was the last one-screen movie house in Paris. Brundidge had insisted they go there, because the Criterion was due to close its doors after Christmas, bowing finally to the sixteen-screen multiplex that had been put up next to the Fed-Mart. Most people agreed that the multiplex was a superior facility, but Brundidge had remained one of the last holdouts in support of the Criterion. He knew it was an important part of the history of Paris, with its ornate gilded doors and little rococo tower over the ticket booth. But more important, he felt sentimental about it, even though he also knew that sentimentality was now looked upon as the currency of morons.

It was here that he and Wood and Jeter and Mavis and Milan and Duff and scores of other Parisians had fallen in love with forty-foot movie stars and held hands for the first time with people they would not under any circumstances hold hands with today—gum-cracking, teenage vixens and skinny, shit-kicking heroes in cheap cowboy boots who had once seemed like, with a little imagination, small-town versions of their big-screen counterparts—who back then, for approximately one hour and forty-two minutes, could provide more breathless adventure than a whole reel of diaphanous celluloid. That was the beauty of it all—the mystery and excitement that was up there on the big screen as well as down there in the seats—where anything could happen once the humongous blue velvet curtain with the fleur-de-lis had been pulled, and the massive twelve-foot lions, which flanked the screen, stood guard with their cavernous open jaws and sharp teeth that seem to warn against anyone interfering with what was being shown. (Much more impressive than the new method of intimidation—a cartoon of a tight-ass librarian type with a finger to her lips.) Now that their long reign was coming to an end, Brundidge was thinking that these lions looked more like ordinary cats waiting to be picked up by Animal Control.

It was bad enough that Paris was losing its cinematic, as well as a good deal of its romantic, history. But now, the new multiplex would draw people from three counties. Now you could watch movies all day long and never even see anyone you knew. Brundidge hated that. For him, the best part of the entire moviegoing experience was that scores of people you knew and cared about were seeing what you were seeing. It expanded friendships and gave everyone a sense of community. Now, they might as well be living in a city.

When they emerged from the movie, snow was coming down in sheets of blinding white confetti—the kind that becomes an event of its own, almost compelling you to put your arms around whoever you were with and whoop and holler and maybe even lie on the ground and not even care if your winter coat ever looks the same again. That was the mood everyone was in as Milan caught up with Wood and grabbed his arm because she knew how much he would like the snow, and she was hoping he would view her as some offshoot of it. But Duff had come along and taken his other arm and sort of groaned with ecstasy at how enchanting it all was and ruined Milan's moment. It was astonishing. Duff had only been in their presence for less than five or six hours and she was already beginning to seem less like the tired, middle-aged woman who had emerged from a rickety old car, and more like her high-riding, putting-on-airs, girlish self. She wasn't there yet, but Milan noticed that during the movie, Duff and Wood had laughed in all the same places, and once both clapped spontaneously when this happened: one of the main characters, actually, the one who didn't like anybody, had made a joke about dogma—a little inside, ironic thing—where this man was criticizing dogma while using it himself. Ha ha ha, something like that. Milan supposed Duff and Wood thought it went right over her head, but they were wrong. Anyway, even if it had, she had figured out long ago that the most successful people were the ones who were best at hiding their own ignorance. Which is why she religiously took the *Reader's Digest* vocabulary quiz in her bathtub every month and probably knew more big words than Duff and Wood put together. But she never flaunted it, because, she thought, why show off when a smaller word can get the job done? Anyway, she was not a person who was ever going to call the snow enchanting. She would leave that to waitresses from IHOP. That was Milan's thinking on that.

Suddenly Brundidge caught up with the rest of them. He had stayed behind to ask for a refund but, as usual, had been turned down. Now it would start, as it always did, when he didn't like what he had just paid ten dollars to see.

"What the hell was that all about? Did anybody else get that?"

It was basically the same conversation that had been going on for years—just a different movie each time that started it. Like when a film that actually involved Thanksgiving had depicted young adults who hated to go home for the holidays, and Brundidge had left fuming.

"Name me one person in this whole town who hates their parents."

"Ronnie Thorpe."

"All right. His dad tried to kill him with an ax. Gimme somebody else."

Silence.

"Ah-ha! You can't. Because there aren't any. And isn't it just a little strange that in every movie and TV show you see, nobody ever likes their parents or ever wants them to come visit? And you know why? Because the assholes who make this stuff are the ones who don't like their parents!"

And then there was this, another year.

Mavis: "Boy, that was powerful, wasn't it?"

Milan: "I don't get it. Why were they all so mad at the mother? All she did was sell real estate and try to be supportive of her daughter's cheerleading."

Mavis: "She was boring and artificial. She wasn't real."

Brundidge: "Get outta here! You think a father who's screwing his little girl's best friend and doing drugs with the kid next door who sits around watching a damn plastic bag bounce off the ground is real?"

Mavis: "Yeah, in this movie, I thought it was very real. They're not saying that's everybody."

Brundidge: "Yes, they are. If there's a nice house and a picket fence, then the people inside have to be shallow and unhappy. Don't you get it? We're the fucked-up hicks out here in the boondocks, and they're the hip, artistic people taking a searing Academy Award look at us."

Wood had tried hard not to look at Milan when he said this: "In case you haven't noticed, buddy, some people *are* leading lives of quiet desperation."

Brundidge: "Bullshit. I'll tell you who's quietly desperate. People like me who want their damn money back!"

And then this:

Brundidge: "It's sick."

Jeter: "It's not sick. It's dark humor. It's camp."

Brundidge: "It's not camp. *Texas Chainsaw Massacre* is camp. This is sick."

Mavis: "I would never serve a Chianti with

liver and fava beans. I would've gone with a nice Merlot."

Brundidge: "You're all a bunch of sick bastards and I'm never going to the movies with you again!"

And later, this:

Wood: "Why the hell did you come? You knew he had to do something worse than last time."

Brundidge: "Hey, he ate the brain of a living person. That's it. I'm done."

Jeter: "Did you get your money back?"

Brundidge: "Hell, no. I never get it back. All the brain-eating assholes in Hollywood have my money."

The trees were now coated with ice. Some of them had caught the light from the streetlamps and been turned into enormous chandeliers. The group was running down the main street of Paris, which looked suddenly beautiful, as though the snow had come to cover its sadness. Even Jeter, with a flick of his good finger, had increased the speed of his wheelchair, and Milan had impulsively jumped on the back panel and ridden a short distance with her arms around his neck. Jeter thought to himself how good it felt, how he wished she would stay there and they could just keep going. Just as they were passing his parents' old store, something caught his eye and caused him to stop. The others were ahead of them now and he guided the chair closer until he and Milan could both see that several windows had been broken. He swore quietly under his breath. Milan pulled him closer and said softly, "Don't look at it. It doesn't matter."

He wished that he could put his arms around her, too. Then, she squeezed his hand, even though she knew he couldn't feel it. This was something no one but Milan ever did and it touched him like nothing else. Suddenly, he felt angry at Wood for not better understanding his wife. This improbable Aphrodite who had emerged from rubble and never seemed to grow old or tired in her quest to be worthy of the rest of them. She didn't like books and she didn't think like Wood or write like Jeter. She didn't have Mavis's sense of humor or culinary skills, but she felt things on your behalf. And it cost her to do so, too. You only had to look into her eyes to see that.

She was speaking to him now. "Does it make you sad, you know, to come here?"

He thought for a minute. "No." He looked at the stairs that went up to the old apartment where he had once lived with his mother and father. Part of the railing was missing now and the paint was hardly visible.

"This is the last place I was really alive. . . . I was coming down those stairs, on my way to the game. I was skipping some of them . . . and my dad said, 'Slow down, son, you run too fast.'"

The others were several blocks away now. The two of them stared at the broken windows a while longer and then Milan whispered, as quiet as the snow, "I love you."

He absorbed it like a kiss and then told her with his eyes what he had to leave unsaid.

By the time they caught up with everyone else, Elizabeth was out in the middle of the street, performing a short, dramatic plié. Then she lay down in the snow on her back. Elizabeth always liked to lie down where you usually couldn't—once even in the middle of an interstate for a full minute. Now Luke came and tried to pull her up but instead she yanked him into the snow with her, laughing. He then rubbed a handful of it into her hair and Charlie somehow became involved and finally almost everyone was throwing snowballs at everyone else until Wood's hit Duff in the head and shrieking, she impulsively stuffed some loose snow down the front of Wood's shirt—and suddenly everything stopped. Like at a dinner party when everyone has been laughing and then someone says completely the wrong thing and no winning comment or clever gesture can clean it up. The moment must simply be endured and then moved away from. That's what happened as they were standing near Doe's and finally someone got the idea that they should all go inside, which they did. Mavis made everyone some splendid cappuccinos—except for Brundidge, who was opposed to cappuccinos—and Charlie wolfed down a plateful of Mavis's buttermilk cinnamon rolls, while Duff went on and on, still trying to make up for the shirt, about how she just couldn't get over that Main Street was now mostly gone.

Then it was Luke, who was curious about what things used to be like here. And somehow that led back to high school and Wood telling how Milan would come high-stepping down this street, wearing her drum majorette's enormous fur hat and punctuating the air with her golden four-foot baton, and,

Wood swore, kicking her white patent leather boots about a foot over her head. Just hearing this made Milan's face hot with pride. It was true. For her, each step and every swift exhilarating kick had been a blow for her family, like when an upturned fist is thrust toward heaven on behalf of something or someone finally on the rise. Everyone was laughing now and for a few seconds it seemed to Milan that Wood had almost forgotten he wasn't in love with her anymore, at least not the way he used to be—and that he had told the story without thinking and then remembered that his emotions were no longer in it. Then Luke wanted to know what his mother had been like and no one knew what to say. With Milan present, every story seemed an unsure bet. Duff put Luke off, claiming to have just been an ordinary girl, but the way she looked down after she said this and waited, well, it was clear she wanted someone to say more. So Wood, who hadn't wanted to say anything, stepped in.

"Well, Luke, I can tell you this. I remember how the English teachers were having trouble getting some of the jocks to take poetry. But once your mother signed up, well, they had to bring in extra chairs from the cafeteria." Then there was a lull, making him finish with, "So, I guess you could say, she was the girl who put boys in mind of poetry."

Duff buried her face in Wood's sleeve and held his arm with both hands.

"Oh, Wood, that isn't true. I don't remember that."

Milan had wanted to speak up and say, I worked in the principal's office and I don't remember that either. I think my husband is completely full of crap. And if this little sideshow gets any friendlier then I'll just be telling your son that what I remember you wrote stupid poems about living in shadows and you constantly sat around on your lazy ass in PE and told the senile gym teacher that you were having your period, which apparently went on for three weeks out of every month. You bled more than Alexis, the hemophiliac son of Nicholas and Alexandra (Milan loved royal history), while everyone else ran a hundred laps and cleaned the showers. And how you were the rudest person I have ever known, always eating off other people's plates and putting your big, stupid feet in their laps. And how you were so *insipid* (this from the *Reader's Digest* vocabulary quiz) that you took your own name off the homecoming ballot and how I whipped your spoiled, *pseudo* (another quiz, don't pronounce the P) hippie butt and became the queen myself! How about we tell him that story, Miss I Stand Tall Against Piggly Wiggly *Oppression* (not from a quiz, but life experience).

This was what she wanted to say but would not, because she felt she had already revealed more of herself than she cared to when she said grace.

Suddenly Milan's head was starting to hurt. Next to her, Elizabeth was asking, "Do you really like him, Mother?"

"What?"

"Do you really like Luke?"

"Oh, I do, honey. I think he's awfully nice. And very polite, too."

Now Luke was standing with one arm around Wood and the other around his mother. And Elizabeth was grinning at the three of them and saying something about dancing. Milan gave an anemic smile, thinking, dear God, when would it all end?

The Purple Crackle nightclub was the kind of place where the live band makes such a ruckus every drink order has to be screamed in a voice that you would normally use to call for help. When Wood and the group entered, the sawdust-covered dance floor, painted by clichéd strobe lights, had become so packed, it was impossible to tell the backup singers from the sweaty patrons. The overall effect was of something that had to put up with, rather than savored and enjoyed. But Wood and Jeter and Brundidge knew this had not always been the case and they exchanged a knowing look, the same one they always gave one another when they came here now.

The Purple Crackle had been the single greatest secret pleasure of their childhood. Located several miles from downtown, it sat at the very end of Main Street like a forbidden pot of gold. Though it was now freshly painted, it once looked to be the color of burned wood. The entrance was partially hidden by trees and the structure itself resided only two or three feet from the river's levee. There wasn't a sign that said it was the Purple Crackle, it was just something people knew. In its heyday, it had been one of the best-known juke joints between Memphis and Kansas City. Only a block or two off the main highway, it became a surprising fixture for struggling talent on their way up, like Leon Redbone, or performers who by the early seventies were just trying to hold on to the last gasp of rock and roll.

As a boy, Wood had been enticed by the stories Mae Ethel told Slim about who she'd seen performing there—people like Fats Domino and Little Richard, who Mae Ethel said, while covering her mouth laughing, "had just about blown the old tar-paper roof sky high." Wood, who was only twelve at the time, had wanted to see this for himself. He and Jeter and Brundidge devised a plan that involved sneaking out of their houses around midnight and after meeting in front of Jeter's Market, riding their bicycles down to the river where they hid behind bushes at first and then eventually climbed an old sycamore tree, which provided the best vantage point from which to view things. As it turned out, there was plenty to see, especially since the Purple Crackle had a front door that in warm weather was always left open.

But the show outside was almost as good as the one in—drunk people staggering out into the night, sometimes falling down and passing out on the gravel, fancy women re-

clining in the backseats of long cars with
their dresses over their heads and well-
pressed men lying on top of them with their
feet hanging out the door and both crying
out for the Lord—men fighting and threatening each other and pulling out knives and
guns, though miraculously no one was ever
shot. The one person the boys never saw
misbehave was Mae Ethel, who always wore
a hat, with a flower pinned to her bosom and
was escorted by her brother as though she
was on her way to church. The same place
she had taken Wood to see B. B. King, when
Wood was still so small that he had to stand
up in the pew.

The boys loved to smell the fumes from
the corn mash being produced out in the
Crackle's garage, as well as the aroma of
meat that was always cooking in the old
smokehouse. But the thing that kept them
coming back—sometimes once or twice a
week and a few times till dawn—was the
music. They had become mesmerized by
one of the first songs of rock and roll when
Bill Haley, on his final reunion tour with the
Comets, sang "See you later, alligator, after
a while crocodile." For weeks, Wood, Brundidge, and Jeter went around singing these

old lyrics and looking down on their class-
mates for failing to grasp or appreciate the
coolness of it all. But nothing could have prepared them for the performers who literally
shook the walls off the old nightclub, with
songs so outrageously soothing and moving
and raucous that it was worth staying till the
last possible minute and then pedaling your
bike so fast your heart almost beat out of
your chest all the way home. From Baby
Washington and Maxine Brown to the astonishing Nellie Lutcher whose piano sounded
even bluer when you stirred in the tree frogs
outside. And sometimes there was even a
rare appearance by a giant on his way down,
like Chuck Berry duckwalking and then getting on his knees and leaning back horizontal with the floor while tearing up the strings
of his electric guitar. Afterward the boys had
watched wide-eyed as Mr. Berry held out a
brown paper bag that was filled with cash
out by the garage. And Little Richard, who
came once with the Isley Brothers, had
stomped his feet and screeched "Lucille" so
loud that he had to be carried to his Cadillac
as though he had held up a mighty weight
for as long as he could with the sheer velocity of those two syllables and was now near

death. Another one who brought the house down was Jerry Lee Lewis, who was a no-show three times before his one and only appearance, in which he sang "Whole Lotta Shakin' Goin' On" for thirty-eight minutes and then set a man's chair on fire. The boys had later tried a reenactment of this, causing Brundidge to be grounded for an entire summer after ruining his mother's dinette set.

These things had happened over three decades ago, but their occurrence had been so powerful that to this day, when Wood and Jeter and Brundidge step inside the new incarnation of the Purple Crackle, they can't help feeling a little let down—like men who once walked on the moon and are now stuck in traffic.

The others found a table, while Wood and Brundidge went off to the bar. In a little while, they returned with several pitchers of beer. Rudy, who had joined up with the group, had just finished dancing with Milan—a kind of hip-hop thing that she had struggled with, but Rudy had graciously guided her through. Milan was good at twirling, not dancing, especially if the dancing was unstructured. Anyway, strobe lights always made her feel uneasy, like something sinister was about to happen.

Duff was having no such problems. She loved to dance and had been asked by Derek Kingsley, who seemed to have stayed in a good mood since high school. Derek's family ran a fish house out on the highway and he was currently between wives, which could account for why he greeted Duff, in Milan's opinion, as though she had come to town to give him a kidney. Anyway, Milan, who was primed to calibrate the most infinitesimal change in her husband tonight, had noticed that he was uncharacteristically cool to Derek. Wood was at the bar now, getting another pitcher of beer. Mavis and Jeter and Brundidge were arguing about what to name the baby, if there ever was one.

Now Duff and Rudy were dancing next to Elizabeth and Luke. Milan turned toward Wood, who was still standing at the bar. It would have been impossible for anyone else to discern which of the four dancers he was watching with such intensity, but Milan didn't have to ask. As Wood started back toward the table, the argument that Jeter and Mavis and Brundidge were having had become more heated, until just as the music ended, Brundidge had shouted, "I get to vote, damn it! I drove the damn sperm!"

Derek Kingsley turned his drink up, pretending not to hear. Mavis looked stricken, then gathered up her ten-pound purse and waddled off to the ladies' room. Brundidge called after her, "Aw, c'mon. Lighten up. You don't have to leave." But Mavis did, anyway, accidentally forming the head of a line of waitresses who balanced their pitchers high in the air, as deftly as African women on their way to market.

Wood arrived, setting a new pitcher of beer on the table.

"What was that all about?"

Jeter answered, "Nothin'. Just a little domestic squabble."

Milan had gotten up to go check on Mavis when she noticed that Rudy and Duff were now in each other's arms, undulating to the soulful beat. And that Wood was still watching appreciatively. Then a buxom brunette who looked too tender to have gotten past the bouncer cut in, asking Rudy to dance. It was so perfect, Milan wanted to cheer. Duff had been thrown over for a younger girl. And right in front of everyone. A shamefully meager victory, but one that could sustain Milan until something more substantial came along. She turned back to make sure Wood had seen it, too. And that was when she noticed the empty chair—saw that he was no longer in it, and curiously, it had jarred her heart a little. And then she watched as he slowly made his way across the dance floor toward Duff, who was now waiting with her hands on her hips and shaking her head up and down, pleased, as though she had known all along that he would come.

Mavis emerged from the ladies' room. Milan put out her hand, smoothing her best friend's hair, "Are you okay?"

"Yeah, I'm fine." She blew her nose into a Kleenex. "I just cannot be around thoughtless, insensitive people when I'm on these hormones."

Milan put her arm on Mavis's back and rubbed it for a moment. She, too, was now worn out from the tensions and stress of the day. She looked back at the dance floor and saw that Duff had upgraded her moves to the point that other dancers had stopped to watch. Wood was only the dazzled spectator now and Duff, the show. She moved coolly and self-assuredly around him—pushing her

hips in slow, circular motions to the suggestive vibe, then humping the air with her hand
on her abdomen and swinging her head
from side to side, with her cheeks sucked in
and her hair over her eyes. Wood was thinking he hadn't seen anyone move so beautifully within the confines of the Purple
Crackle since Little Richard. Elizabeth and
Luke had burst into applause and Wood
shook his head a little, in wonderment. Milan
was shaking hers in wonderment, too. The
years seemed to have literally fallen away
from the woman with dark circles under her
eyes who when she had arrived this morning, hadn't even appeared to have good pos-
ture, but was now standing tall and filling out
every inch of her cheap clothes. Duff wasn't
Bud from *Splendor in the Grass* anymore.
She had literally transformed herself right in
front of Milan's eyes. Not only had the little
JCPenney ensemble, with its thin, fluid fabric
taken on a sensual quality, but her eyes
were fiery and bright—made even more al-
luring by the strobe lights, which were now
colored. And her lips appeared to be alternately pouty and laughing, as the ever
changing shards of light caught each move.
Pouty. Laughing. Pouty. Laughing. Pouty.

Laughing. Now Elizabeth and Luke had melted into the other dancers. As far as Milan could tell, there was no one left but Wood and Duff. And right now, Duff was dancing over to him, was actually *touching* him, grinding her hips against his, then squatting and working her way up the length of him, audaciously shaking her tits as she went. Milan looked at Mavis and was shocked that she didn't seem to think there was anything out of the ordinary going on here at all. The music had become deafening now, and the crowd was shouting the words with the band. Duff was also shouting them, and Milan thought she saw Wood singing a little, too. In all the years she had known him, Milan had never known Wood to sing while he was dancing.

"Don't you ever feel sad. Lean on me when times are bad."

She searched the faces of the spectators. What was wrong with these people? Could they not see that her husband and this ripe, grinding bitch were now in violation of the social contract under which all decent human beings operate?

"Hold on, I'm comin'! Hold on, I'm comin'!"

Suddenly, the strobe lights caught Duff

wetting her lips with her tongue. And Milan
was shocked to see that her old nemesis
had finally become the serpent she had always known lay underneath the handsome
façade. Milan put her hand to her head.
Maybe Mavis was right. Maybe teaching
Sunday school was making her too dramatic. Because she was convinced that the
serpent's head was now hideously arched—
that "the thing" was now sticking its tongue
out repeatedly, defying her, taunting her—vi-
ciously swatting its big, fat tail around for all
the world to see, like some terrible man-
eating creature out of a science-fiction horror film that would soon find its way to
Milan's house, destroying everything and
everyone in it.

CHAPTER 15

Monday morning. Milan was lying in her bed,
partially covered by her Yves Delorme du-
vet. There was a cool washrag across her
brow and a chocolate diet drink on the night-

stand that was half-gone, the half that was
her breakfast. The Sevres porcelain ashtray
was full of cigarettes, which had only been
puffed on once or twice.

Nothing had been said about the weekend. Wood had gone to work. Charlie was at
school and Elizabeth was getting ready to
go back to college. Normally, Milan would be
in her daughter's room, bringing her toast
with blackberry jelly on it, sticking a new lip
gloss in her overnight, helping her pack. But
the headache that started days ago was still
with her. The headache that waxed and
waned and throbbed and once or twice
caused her to vomit—the one that refused to
go away, even though the source of it left,
mercifully, yesterday.

Duff and her son had planned to leave on
the Saturday after Thanksgiving. But because things were going so splendidly, and
because Duff had not been home in so long,
everyone agreed that it would be insane to
stick with her original plan. So they had
played charades and Scrabble and gone
sledding and to see another movie that even
Brundidge liked. And Mavis had everyone
over for chili. And even though it had started
snowing again, Duff had wanted to go for a

trail ride. (Milan stayed home. She knew too much about Duff and Wood and horses.) And so Elizabeth and Wood and Luke and Duff had set out on their puzzled steeds, across the frozen ground, heading for the woods that flanked the north side of Fast Deer Farm. Milan had watched it all through the sheer drape of the upstairs bedroom window. This was where she loved to sit and look out on the world below her—a place of solitude and seeming omnipotence, whose existence she could not have even fathomed in her childhood. Brundidge had once joked that she stayed in that upstairs window so much, she looked like some half-witted girl on *Bonanza.* Anyway, it was here that Milan had watched Elizabeth and her dad and Duff and her son ride away together looking like a new family, with the snow falling on their backs. And in some way, it made her feel that she had already died—that she wasn't there at all anymore but was merely an unseen ghost observing events that she was powerless to change.

Elizabeth came in to say good-bye. Milan, with the washrag still covering her eyes, reached out toward her daughter, who crossed to the bed and lay down in her mother's arms. Milan removed the cloth as they embraced each other. And then, holding on to Elizabeth, she said, "I hate for you to go, Lils."

"Me, too. Tickle my back." Elizabeth pulled up her sweater as spontaneously as a little kid would. As Milan obliged, Elizabeth added, "Luke doesn't tickle backs."

"Well, then, you can't marry him. You couldn't possibly live with a boy who's not willing to do that."

"Shoulders." Elizabeth guided her mother's hand. "You can see how kind he is, can't you?"

"Yes. He has a good heart."

"Right. But he doesn't show it off. He reminds me of Daddy."

For a brief moment, Elizabeth noticed her mother's sadness.

"She was okay, wasn't she? I mean, she was nice."

"She was fine."

"Then what?"

"Nothing. Just a little mad at you for growing up so fast."

Elizabeth threw her arms around her mother, rolling her around on the bed. Milan laughed, in spite of herself.

"Mimi, I will never leave you. You and me are forever!"

"You're my girl. You know that, don't you?"

"Yes. I need a Krackel." She opened the drawer of her mother's nightstand and un-wrapped a square of chocolate and ate it.

For much of their lives, the two of them had nearly subsisted on raw cookie dough and anything else that had sugar in it. It was probably the only flaw that could be found in Milan's parenting. Even when Elizabeth was small and they took long, luxurious bubble baths together, the tub would be lined with the discarded wrappers from their feast of Payday candy bars, Hershey Kisses, and chocolate cupcakes made by Little Debbie— all the things Milan had once coveted (and sometimes been given for free) at Jeter's Market. Little by little, Elizabeth had also ac-quired the appetite that was born of her mother's impoverished childhood.

Now she peppered Milan with silly, over-wrought kisses. "I love you, Mims. Love you. Love you. Love you." Elizabeth and Milan had been this way with each other from al-most the moment Elizabeth was born. They were hopelessly smitten, eerily bonded— they even had their own language, like twins—lying around in each other's arms, cuddling, acting silly, calling one another by their pet names, most especially Mimi or Mims and Lils, the reason behind them nobody could remember anymore, or even if there had been one. Wood used to shake his head and say there was something wrong with them and that they were crazy. Even during Elizabeth's high school years, she and Milan rarely fought—which puzzled the other mothers, who regularly complained that there was nothing more deadly than a coiled teenage girl.

Though they reveled in their mutual affection and girliness—picking out bedroom fabrics, and clothes and jewelry, leaving each other notes and funny little cards—they were not confidantes. Milan didn't believe in that sort of thing between parents and children. She wouldn't dream of laying her problems at the feet of Elizabeth or Charlie, wouldn't hear of troubling one second of their childhood. She was a mother in every sense of the word, with rules and limits and close supervision, all the things lacking in the Lanier household (household?—what a funny name for that place). She was the Brownie leader, the room mother, the field-trip chaperone (the one who looked so different from the other mothers that Elizabeth once asked Milan if she was a movie star), and even though she sometimes got carried away with these things, making a fuss, showing up with ten dozen gingerbread men when a few boxes of cookies would have done—even though she could drive Elizabeth crazy—in the end, the daughter seemed to have been born knowing the intent of her mother's heart. And for an easygoing, forgiving girl like Elizabeth, that intent trumped any of Milan's annoying traits. Plus, a serious inventory of the Lanier siblings could only leave one with awe and respect for the kind of person Milan, by sheer will, had turned herself into.

Unlike some abused children, who ended up abusing their own kids, Milan tended to the physical and emotional needs of her offspring like an ever-vigilant lioness. In spite of the fact that she had Mrs. Denby, her sixty-year-old, white-haired housekeeper, Milan always insisted on working right alongside her, which included ironing all of Elizabeth and Charlie's sheets and bedclothes herself. Nothing pleased her more than making things look starched and fresh. And when her boy and girl were little, she had spent hours putting them to bed, reading them stories, bringing them ice cream and juice and even a single Ritz cracker in the middle of the night, making sure every stuffed animal was in its place. Then, after she had performed her self-imposed marital duties, she would often return to their rooms and sit quietly in the chair next to these flannel-clad cherubs, who had by now almost disappeared into the soft down of their beds—just sit there, absorbing the wonder of them, happy, safe, clean children. And in her mind, giving thanks that she had lived to see such a sight.

Brundidge was already in his office with his feet on the desk, holding the phone. He had just completed reading, as he did every day, via his computer, the *New York Times,* the *Washington Post,* and the *Wall Street Journal.* But it was this last paper that had provoked his ire. And now he was in the process of doing something about it.

A crisp female voice said, "Wall Street Journal."

"Yes, I'd like to speak to Mr. Charles Ahearn."

"One moment, please."

There was a wait as Brundidge fine-tuned some number two pencils on his state-of-the-art sharpener. Then the voice returned. "I'm sorry. Mr. Ahearn isn't in. Would you like to speak to his editor?"

"No, I would not. I've spoken with her before and she has an extremely poor attitude." There was silence, then, "All right. Put her on."

After a couple of rings, a thirties-sounding woman with a low, self-assured voice came on the line. "This is Charlotte Rampling."

"Yeah, I know. The girl from Smith, not the European actress."

"I beg your pardon."

"Charlotte, this is E. B. Brundidge. I'm callin' you from, as y'all like to say, down here in Arkansas."

The woman groaned under her breath, "Oh, shit. What is it now?"

"Oh, shit? Is that the way you talk? What kind of a professional deal is that?"

"I'm sorry. I'm having a bad day. What did he do this time?"

"Well, I'll tell you, it's the same ol' stuff, Charlotte. The guy seems to be incurable." Brundidge looked at his computer screen.

"Instead of using the name of our state, he's referring to it again as Dogpatch, with a little joke thrown in about inbreeding, implying that we're all a bunch of ignorant rednecks who sleep with our own kids. It's not good, Charlotte. You know, we're trying to raise formidable little girls down here."

"That's what I hear."

"I guess you're aware what the real number one incest capital of America is."

"Yes, you told me."

"Hey, that's okay. Don't feel bad. Hell, everybody's got problems."

"So, let me get this straight. You're calling to insult," slightly mimicking him, "New York City."

"Hell no. I love New York. The people of New York are some of the finest people I have ever met in my entire life. It's you and Mr. Charles Ahearn I have a problem with. You know who you all remind me of? France. And you know why? 'Cause you look down on America."

"I'll make Mr. Ahearn aware of your complaint."

"Oh, am I done? You're so abrupt and rude, I can never tell."

"It's two hours later here. I have a lunch."

"I'll bet you do. Gonna have a little sword-fish sashimi with a couple of rainbow rolls, are we?"

"I don't know yet."

"Sure you do. That's what you and all your friends live on. You ought to get your head out of your ass and come down here and eat some barbecue."

"Why in God's name would I want to do that?"

"Expand your horizons. Just remember, Charlotte, while you're sittin' up there on your little ten-inch café chair, ordering raw fish and seaweed salad, we're down here eatin' smoked pork and lyin' around in our big, soft Barcaloungers. I mean, how ignorant can we be when we're the ones who ended up with the killer food and the comfortable chairs?"

There was another pause, then, "Seriously, Mr. Brundidge, this is me talking now, not the *Journal,* okay?"

"Okay."

"I figure you're probably recording this, so you can imagine how much I must really want to say it. Fuck off."

Charlotte hung up. Brundidge looked at

the phone and smiled a little, unsure as to how he felt about her.

Elizabeth was gone now. The phone was ringing. Milan decided not to answer. Suddenly, she heard Mavis on the speaker, talking in a raspy, manlike whisper, "I know you're in that bed. And I know where you live. If you don't pick up, I'm gonna come over there and scrub off all your makeup, snap your picture, and put it in my store window."

Milan sat up in her bed, looking small and fragile. She lifted the receiver. "I'm up."

"And what are we doing with ourselves today?"

Milan yawned. "I don't know yet. I'm thinking about washing my house."

Mavis repeated it, like she was imagining it. "Washing your house. Listen, I know how you love to hose down the old homestead, but it's ten degrees outside."

"Oh, yeah. I forgot."

"I think we've lucked out with this Luke kid. He seems to be okay."

"Yep. That's the important thing. I'm just happy for my girl."

"And Duff was okay, too. You know, it could've been worse."

Milan lay down on her side. "He's falling in love with her. Again."

"That's ridiculous."

"Please don't deny what's happening. It just makes me feel lonely."

There was silence, then, "Want me to bring you an éclair?"

"No." Another pause. "What else have you got down there?"

Mavis looked around at her bountiful glass case and shelves. "Well, we've got a lot of sugar. But if you're coming, we can get more."

"I'm on my way."

Wood had been driving for over an hour before he realized he was already halfway to Excelsior Springs. The town where Duff lived. He hadn't intended to go there at all. But his 7 A.M. tubal ligation had been canceled because the patient's blood pressure had become erratic and he had called off the surgery. Now, he had no more appointments until after lunch. And he was thinking, those could be changed, too, if he said he wasn't feeling well. Wood never postponed appointments, so they would have to believe he was really sick. The only question that remained was, would Milan call his office? She usually didn't, because she respected his time at work. But she was not leaving anything to chance right now. She had watched him closely all weekend, refusing to go to bed, until he and Duff had done so, too—sitting up half the night, playing Scrabble, when she hated games, and then making way too much of the fact that she beat them both. What the hell was that all about? It was embarrassing. And then, never letting them out of her sight, except for the trail ride that she made certain Luke and Elizabeth went on, too—ensuring that the two old lovers were never effectively alone for the entire four days. It was pure Milan, so transparent, but thinking no one else could see how she was controlling it all. He was pretty sure that Duff could see. And he thought he had detected something else in her eyes, too. Pity. Pity that he would give his life to someone who had so little regard for him. Someone who would use a trick to marry him. And manipulate any circumstance just to keep him, with never a thought or inquiry as to his true feelings about anything. What a sad ending for a past lover and soul mate to witness. Maybe he was on his way to see Duff, because he needed to know if it was true that she felt sorry for him. If it was, then he would tell her that she needn't be, because he was happy. Or he would demand to know what the hell she was going to do about it. But of course, he could not do that. Because she might not give the answer he wanted to hear. And if she did, well, then he wouldn't want to hear that either.

The road was beginning to turn mountainous now and he had to pay close attention to negotiating the curves. It reminded him of the road from college in Durham that he had so often driven to meet Milan. They had rekindled their romance after Wood had broken off with Duff because she had sex with a fifty-year-old professor, something that she claimed fell under the category of youthful experimentation. It was Wood's first experience with betrayal and it wounded him deeply—even though he himself had never been able to completely wipe Milan from his romantic consciousness. During the time they were apart, he missed her and strangely worried about her and called often just to see if she was all right. And Duff

must've sensed his ambivalence, too, because she went out of her way to remind
Wood that Milan was not one of them. That
she was beautiful, but ordinary and not up to
Wood's intellectual gifts. And so it went.

Suddenly a car was honking and he realized he had drifted a little across the center
line. He quickly got back in his lane. Wood
was thinking about one weekend in particular now, the one when Tom Lanier killed himself. Luckily, it had happened when he and
Duff were estranged and Wood had driven
all night from North Carolina just to be with
Milan. For the next few months, they were together every chance they got, sometimes
meeting each other halfway. It was intense
and tender and just as Wood was making up
his mind to love her for good, she told him
the stunning news that she was pregnant. It
was stunning because she was taking birth
control pills. But had somehow screwed it
up. And even though she wasn't a person
who screwed things up and he wasn't even
in medical school yet, he embraced it. And
told himself that he was going to marry her
someday, anyway, and what difference did it
make if it happened a few years early?

He had been overjoyed when his daughter

was born and later, his son. And he and Milan had built a good life, but somewhere in
the place where such things are harbored,
there remained these nagging doubts—
even here today on this road, they were still
with him and probably with her, too. Each
one like an old library book they've already
read—a book that says something about not
being loved or being played for a fool—and
they keep checking it out anyway, perusing
it, rehashing it, and adding new evidence to
verify or impugn the truth of it, in order to believe whatever they need to believe to support their own behavior. He was sorry that
they did this and that they couldn't seem to
stop. It was exhausting and it had worn their
marriage out.

His chest was starting to hurt. A lot. It was
as though a tight band had been extended
around him and then there was a shooting
pain down his left arm. How many times had
he heard that one? Great! Now he was having a heart attack. And not a very original
one either. Now, when they found him, Milan
would know. There was no way he would be
this far out, on this highway, unless he had
been on his way to see Duff. The truth was,
he wasn't even going to see Duff. That was

the truth of it. He was just driving, letting off steam from the whole damn weekend, the pressures of his job, his dad dying. Wood was starting to sweat. Profusely. Maybe he could get off the main road and get to a creek or a park ground, so he could die there and it might just appear that he'd, on a lark, decided to commune with nature, because of his dad dying and everything. Because people had probably noticed he hadn't been himself lately. Now there was a knife in his chest, a sensation of actually being cut. Maybe if he could get to the woods and die outside the car, coyotes and wolves would eat him. Without many remains, they would have to consider foul play. Maybe his car had been driven there and his body dumped. But then again, what if the snow preserved him? Did coyotes and wolves eat frozen food? He didn't know. Wood wiped the perspiration above his lip with his shirtsleeve and then massaged his chest with the same hand.

Suddenly, the sun was so luminous against the windshield, he could hardly see. It was bouncing off the cars that whisked by him, like flashbulbs blinding him in glittering succession, like paparazzi recording his ill-planned, pathetic secret mission. Wood was now being peppered by a light that seemed almost as glorious as the one that had appeared through the stained-glass window on the day of his father's funeral—the day the air had turned a golden yellow and contained within itself a hint of glory or redemption or death or something—he wasn't sure. He steered the car as well as he could off the road and into a gas station. And there he sat for a while, hunched over, collecting his breath in his two cupped hands. Suddenly he was struck with a feeling of relief—and not just because he wasn't going to die here on this highway—but relief for his own father's death and the fact that he could no longer disappoint this good and loving man. Wood got out and walked, unsteady, toward the entrance and a sign that read FRIED CHICKEN, LIVE BAIT AND DVDS. But all he bought was a diet soda and some Tums. Then he walked back to his car, got in, steered the ancient Austin-Healy out into the traffic again, and turned toward home. Finally, the pain in his chest was going away. After a while, he shifted into an even smoother gear, grateful to be alive and back on the ride.

*   *   *

Mavis had no more hung up the phone with Milan than Mary Paige Kenyon, a short, stocky girl with yellow hair and a plump Scandinavian face, was standing at her counter. Mary Paige had grown up in Paris, but because Mavis was ten years her senior, the two women hardly knew each other. After going away to seminary school, and serving as a missionary in the Philippines and El Salvador, Mary Paige had now come home to care for her ailing mother. Mavis couldn't put her finger on it, but there was some kind of understanding in Mary Paige's eyes that always made Mavis not want to charge her for whatever it was she ordered.

"Well, Miss Mary Paige Kenyon, twelfth customer of the day. I guess you know that means your Danish is free."

Mary Paige looked at Mavis for a long time, her eyes filling with what Mavis assumed was gratitude. Then she began to sob, large, shoulder-heaving tears, till eventually she ended up gasping for air.

Mavis consoled her, "It's okay. It's just a Danish. Good Lord, I'm glad I didn't give you a free blueberry scone. I might've killed you."

Mary Paige laughed and apologized as Mavis guided her to one of the little café tables. Luckily, there were no other customers, allowing Mary Paige to tell Mavis her story. She was sorry to trouble her with it, but there was no one else she could talk to—at least not anyone who she felt would understand. Of course, she hadn't intended to tell Mavis either, but the unexpected kindness of making her the free Danish winner of the day had unleashed a river of emotion that was apparently just waiting for the right cue—the same way it happened when Sheriff Serious West, who could've been a preacher as easily as a lawman, used to get in the face of whoever he was interrogating and say, "Isn't there somethin' you want to get off your chest, son? Somethin' that's been lyin' heavy on your heart for a long time and could be lifted right here, right now; all you have to do is start at the beginning and tell Serious how you got to this terrible, sad place." You could almost hear the church organist playing in the background as the men broke and relieved themselves of their burdens. That's pretty much the way Mary Paige's story came out, too. Like it was something that just couldn't be kept inside any longer, once someone had offered even a hint of sympathy or understanding.

It seemed the First Baptist Church and its minister, Harlan B. Pillow Jr., had decided *not* to challenge the policy of the Southern Baptist Convention that prevents women from filling the pulpit—had, in fact, denied Mary Paige the chance to apply for associate minister of her hometown church on the basis of nothing more than the fact that she was not going to be able to come up with a penis. Mavis was incensed. She no longer attended church herself, but she and her mother had gone to the First Baptist regularly when she was growing up. And Brother Pillow's daddy, Harlan B. Pillow Sr., had screamed so loud and carried on so long about the fires of hell and damnation that he had scared Mavis and most of the other children half to death. Mavis had sat in the pew, next to her mother, wearing her little hat (always a hat) with her freshly washed white gloves and tried not to listen—tried instead to concentrate on things like what kind of salad dressing she would have once they made it to Cotter's Restaurant and Motel buffet. Brother Pillow would be screaming about little children who, even if they were good, would burn in hell if they were not washed in the blood of the lamb—and Mavis would be reciting, in her mind, Thousand Island or Ranch. Thousand Island or Ranch. Thousand Island or Ranch. Not listening. Not listening. Not listening.

Mavis knew several adults in Paris who had actually sought psychiatric help as a result of their time with Brother Pillow. Of course, they had gone to another town to do it. There was a retired psychiatrist in Paris who, it was said, was still willing to see special cases, but almost no one went to him because word had gotten out that the more you told him your troubles, the more he hardly said anything. Anyway, it had especially puzzled Mavis when Brother Pillow said he was doing the Lord's work. She couldn't help wondering how he could've gotten a job working for someone so important, when she wouldn't have hired him for anything. But the part she dreaded the most each week was when the good brother called all the young Sunday schoolers to come down front—and finally got around to saying something nice, like "Jesus loves all the little children." Only it didn't sound like a compliment, or a good thing at all, anymore. It sounded more like a threat, as in, Jesus loves you and you better love him back, *or else*!

As Mavis got older, it became more and more clear to her that Brother Pillow wasn't speaking for anyone but himself. And she finally stopped attending services altogether. All the talk about women keeping quiet in church and following the leadership of their husbands didn't sit quite right with her, either. She and her mother made all their own decisions and looked after themselves quite nicely. Why should they have to let a man lead them? Mavis's dad, the man they loved more than anyone, hadn't even had sense enough to come in out of the rain.

However, Mavis still felt that she was a religious person. Only she had decided to keep her religion inside her head. She didn't need a certain day or a place to go, to express it. Or any people to share it with. And she certainly didn't need some sweaty, red-faced preacher threatening her. Her religion was personal and private and tied to who she was. And nobody could attack it or question it, as long as they didn't know about it. It was when you put a sign out front and started attracting people and fighting over which one of you was right, that you got into trouble—the way her new friend was in trouble right now.

Mary Paige loved the Lord profoundly, had traveled the world on his behalf and was burning to tell others about it. It was the only thing she was burning to do. The rest of her, the regular person side, was shy, retiring, quiet. If she were denied this, then really, what was left? Taking care of her ailing mother. Growing old alone. And eventually, she would die, too, and all the beautifully unique religious thoughts, all the unspoken words and prayers that bore her personal imprint, would go with her.

Mavis didn't know how it happened, but when she looked down at her lap, she was holding Mary Paige's hand. And then she heard her own voice saying, "I don't know what we're going to do about this. But I promise you, we're not going to take it lying down."

Mary Paige nodded, grateful. Then, she bit into her Danish and smiled at Mavis, feeling renewed and wiping a little sugar from her pretty, turned-up mouth.

It was almost 11 A.M. and Slim McIlmore was still under the covers. She had gotten up earlier to feed her dead husband's dogs and then retreated back to her bed, barely bothering to shake off the snow.

The Brown Meanness that sometimes settled on her had come again, as she knew it would, and this time she would not have her husband's powerful, soothing presence to take refuge in. This time, because she was weakened from her loss, she would have no resources to fight it off. And she was sure it would take a little more of her each day, as it always did, until she would not even bother to eat the soup that Milan often left on her porch and eventually would have to get someone else to feed the dogs. And then would probably not even check to see if that person had done it—and finally would not even care if the dogs actually died and her along with them. That's how the Brown Meanness worked. That's how cruel it could get. It wasn't black or gray, colors that most people associated with depression. For Slim, black was night, which was exciting. And gray was up, forward, toward the sky. But brown was down, like the ground, muddy, hopeless. Dust. Nothing. Slim's mood was brown. It was something she had dealt with all her life. Something she despised—this evil, punishing shroud that kept her, not in darkness, which could have signaled a final resolution, but instead let in just enough light to keep her in the game. It stole precious days, weeks, months from an otherwise idyllic marriage and irreplaceable time with her son. No one had known the extent of her suffering, except her husband, her son, and her housekeeper, Mae Ethel.

Slim was a person who thought that every little thing about every living soul did not need to be seen or known. And the Brown Meanness, well, that was private. Her personal cross to bear. And if and when someday it all became too much, she would take matters into her own hands and leave this world, just as her mother had done, when Slim was only thirteen. Emily Longchamps, wearing her winter coat, gloves, and hat, had slipped into the family car on Christmas Eve and started the engine and sat there with the garage door down until she fell asleep and toppled across the steering wheel with her head and shoulders sagging and her hat now resting upside down on the dashboard—had done it with her three daughters and her husband sleeping only yards away, not even bothering to leave a note—so, as Slim thought later, you can imagine how much pain she was in, this loving mother and wife, to hurt her family in such a brutal way and forever ruin Christmas.

Slim reached out and picked up a small photograph from the nightstand. In it, she and her sisters, Lucy and Ava, were having tea on the porch of the Arlington Hotel in Hot Springs. They looked like young women who, after just having had their first bite of life, are now awaiting the main course and please don't be stingy with the pepper. Slim studied this early rendition of her face. In the picture, she looked slightly amused, head tilted down (just like her son to be), with eyes that stared seductively past the felt brim of her hat, past the person who is making the photograph and into her own eyes—*sixty years later.*

The Longchamps girls looked good. They could just as easily have been sitting with Ernest Hemingway or Henri Matisse in another Paris than the one they grew up in, and no one would have questioned it. She remembered the day vividly. The way she and her sisters had giggled at the men dressed like gangsters at the table behind them—the good-looking waiter spilling wine on Slim's new suit and the tears when she announced she was marrying Wood McIllmore. Of course, they all adored him, the town golden boy who played football and carried Rupert Brook in his coat pocket. Just the same, this was their baby sister, only nineteen, and he was going off to war. It was all too sudden.

But, oh, the fun they had, visiting her in Biloxi. Slim, a new war bride, still radiant from her first brush with real physical love, and later, much later, Lucy and Ava holding her hands while her husband helped deliver their beautiful, upside-down boy—blessed whole years of happiness together, raucous laughter, a capsized boat on the Champanelle River, black-and-white photographs— boxes of them with dressed-up people sitting at long tables, holding cigarettes and cocktails at the races in Hot Springs and nightclubs from Havana to New York, Wood in a cast at graduation (was it Sun Valley or a fall from Dapplegreys?). College dorms, Roman ruins, hot flashes, Charlene at the Beauty Hut suggesting ways to cover up her gray—what gray? Suddenly the little boy who delivered her newspaper turned into the middle-aged policeman who stopped her for speeding. And Mister Lindon, the butcher at the A&P who sliced her steaks and ordered her seafood, wasn't there anymore. And Mae Ethel, her housekeeper, Miss Purtle, her seamstress, all retired, all disappeared. People disappearing everywhere—sisters dying, son gone, holding onto her husband, holding onto love, dancing, always dancing, keep moving . . . gone.

The fact that it was over so soon had caught Slim completely off guard. Why hadn't she known about the brutal swiftness of life—the sheer velocity at which love, triumph, pain, and death all travel? It happened to the people around her every day. And yet, she hadn't even guessed that she herself would be subject to life's naturally evolving holocaust.

She traded the picture of Lucy and Ava for the one she liked best of her husband. She was glad the sun was in his eyes, because he would like that. He seemed like a man who had always just been outside. She remembered how deliciously cold his clothes felt and that he often smelled like the woods with a little Vitalis and pipe tobacco thrown in. She closed her own eyes. He was standing in their kitchen now, in the middle of the day. "I just needed to come by and see my pretty girl." Now they were out dancing somewhere and he, after all these years, was still aroused—his lips, touching her ear, "Let's go home." Later, as always, he would lie spent across the top of her, whispering, "My God, Slim, my God."

A strange pair of blue-veined hands put the picture back on the bedside table. She was still a girl in her head. Still madly, dramatically, in love with the boy they had just buried in an old man's body. She wasn't going to wallow in self-pity or bother anyone about it. But she knew this was nothing time could heal. Just as she knew that she would not be able to face the blank canvas of another day. Especially not now, with the Brown Meanness upon her.

Mavis and Milan were having coffee at the little table where Mary Paige had sat earlier. Mavis told only a little of her new friend's travails because Milan seemed upset. She was sure that Wood had dreamed last night about Duff because he had been laughing softly in his sleep. Mavis said, knowing Wood, that he was probably talking to his

horse. Rudy passed by carrying a tray of
freshly turned-out rolls and asked Mavis,
tongue in cheek, if he could get her anything
to make her two-hour break more enjoyable.
And Mavis answered that yes he could, he
could explain how he gets those popovers to
puff up so big when he can't get that little
thing of his to do hardly anything. And Rudy
had staggered off, mortified. That was the
problem with Mavis—overkill. Even without
the crazy hormones, you could just be kidding with her and the next thing you knew,
you were looking for an emergency room,
trying to hold your intestines in.

Milan had stood up to go when Harlan B.
Pillow Jr. arrived an hour early to pick up his
sandwich. Rudy started to wait on him, but
Mavis crossed and told Rudy that she would
handle it, and Rudy stepped aside, afraid,
and Milan sat back down, not wanting to
miss what was coming. Despite his name,
Harlan Jr. was no tall-haired evangelist in
some cheesy leisure suit. He was a good-
looking man, well turned out, with an up-to-
date haircut. Unlike his father, and many of
his fellow preachers, he did not call other
parishioners brother this and brother that.
He used their regular names and affected a

casual winning manner that was more akin to a good motivational speaker than a man of the cloth.

"How are you today, Mavis?"

"I'm okay. Your usual?"

"Yes, ma'am. And you might throw in one of those brownies, too." Then he added, "But don't tell Mrs. Pillow. She's a terror when I get off my diet." After that, he smiled as he did at the end of every sentence, hoping to deter any unpleasantness. Mavis frowned. "Is that a problem?"

"What's that?"

"Mrs. Pillow. Does she actually get to talk at home?"

"I'm not sure I understand."

"I'm not sure you do, either. In spite of the fact that I've been doing my best to make a nice sandwich for you for what—ten, fifteen years now?"

Harlan started to speak, but Mavis interrupted, "Excuse me." She turned and yelled to Rudy, "Turkey and Old Glory on white sourdough, easy mayo, one fudge espresso brownie, large 7-UP, no ice, walkin'."

Then Mavis turned back to Harlan with a smile of her own. "We're gonna work on that order for you, Reverend. And just as soon as

Mary Paige Kenyon is allowed to stand in
your pulpit, you can come back over and
pick it up."

Harlan Pillow Jr. wasn't smiling anymore.
He stiffened, momentarily unable to shake
off this attack on himself and his church. He
seemed to sense, almost immediately, that
this was no small gauntlet being thrown
down. Like other smart-minded, affable men
who made it their business to keep women
in their place, Harlan was proud that he was
a perfect gentleman about it, sure of his own
rightness. And being a man who can assess
things quickly, he was also already thinking
that Mavis was a woman to be reckoned
with.

Slim was on her knees in the gardening section of the Paris Fed-Mart Superstore. After
examining several cans of poison, she finally
decided on an econo-size and went in
search of a clerk. After a while, she finally
spotted one—a fat-cheeked girl whose
mouth hung slightly open, in a permanent
state of noncuriosity, and who said, trying to
feign excitement, the exact words on her
name tag: "Hi, I'm Kelly. Can I help you?"

"Yes, Kelly, I'm having a problem with my

yard. Actually, it's gophers. I think there's maybe ten or twelve of them. Can you tell me, would this be enough poison to kill, say, ten or twelve gophers?"

Kelly looked at the can, dumbly, like she had never seen anything like this before in her life.

"Gosh, I dunno." She examined the label. "All it says here is, if swallowed, what's this word?"

"Induce."

"Yeah. Vomiting immediately."

"Thank you, Kelly." Slim smiled and took the can back. Then as she was heading toward the massive row of checkout counters, she ran into Sidney Garfinkel, carrying a broom.

"Evangeline?"

"Please don't tell Wood you saw me here. I promised him I would never set foot in this store."

Sidney stared at the large can of poison. Slim defended it. "I have a gopher problem. A serious one."

Then she surprised herself by not wanting to go on with this story. It was as though, since she had nothing to gain anymore, she suddenly had nothing to lose, either. "If you must know, Sidney, I'm trying to kill myself."

Then she began laughing, gesturing toward the massive structure, "I should've known better than to come to the Astrodome to do it. Lloyd Case, down at the hardware store, would've known exactly how much poison you need to kill yourself. But then he would've also called my son. The only good thing about this whole dreadful place is the lack of personalized service!"

Slim laughed again, but Sidney just stared at her and said, "Could we get that cup of coffee now?"

Slim and Sidney Garfinkel were seated in a booth at the Motor Harbor. A waitress, who had leathery skin and looked like someone in her past had been cruel to her, sat two cups of coffee down in front of them. Besides some truck drivers and local farmers in coveralls, there was a boy and a skanky-looking girl with white-trash hair sitting at the counter. The girl wore a T-shirt that said, "Keep your hands off my squirrel." Some of the older farmers seemed puzzled by this and tried not to look at it. Several stopped at

Slim and Sidney's table as they were leaving and Sidney stood, enthusiastically shaking hands with them. Then he sat down and resumed his conversation.

"Don't do this, Evangeline. This will pass, as it always has."

Slim sat for a minute. Then she said, "I'm tired, Sidney. And I don't have Mac to help me fight it anymore. . . . My God, he was strong."

"Then use me. I'm strong, too."

"That's crazy. You don't even know me really."

"I know you're not ready to make this decision. Give me six months. And then if you still feel the same way, I'll leave you alone."

"Six months? Why? What can you do?"

"I'm a survivor. You must know I know things."

There was a pause as Slim pondered this. "Secrets?"

"Yes. And tricks, too." He raised his eyebrows in a way that told her not to doubt him. If Slim had not been suffering from the Brown Meanness, she surely would have laughed at this strange, tall man telling her he had tricks that could save her—this man who only days ago she could not have imagined telling her most personal thoughts to, much less that he would place himself as an obstacle to her leaving.

Mavis was in her Oldsmobile Cutlass, cruising by Mary Paige's house. She looked at the upstairs window each time she passed, hoping for a glimpse of her new friend. But the curtains were pulled and there wasn't even any smoke coming from the chimney. Mavis figured this was due to two women living there alone.

Then she went home and stood in her nightgown, staring out her own kitchen window. Unbelievably, it had started to snow again. This was more snow than she could remember ever coming before Christmas. She was thinking what it might be like to get out in this weather and build another person with your own child. And then come in and read that child a book by the fire. Mavis wondered if Mary Paige Kenyon might also be wondering whether she, like Mavis, was foolish to try and hold on to an old dream. She had not been able to get Mary Paige out of her mind. How simple and sweet she was— so good in her heart that she didn't even seem to hate the people who wanted to deny her most noble aspiration. This girl, who had risked being killed by guerrilla soldiers in order to spread the word of the very church that was now working against her. Mavis had known Mary Paige for such a short time and yet already she couldn't think of anyone who she admired more. And if Harlan B. Pillow Jr. wasn't going to do right by her, then Mavis was thinking that somehow she would. Exactly what that meant, she didn't know. But she had a feeling that it was going to involve more than denying a man his turkey sandwich.

Sidney Garfinkel's car was parked in front of Slim's house. Inside, she attempted to stir a pitiful fire with a bent wrought-iron poker, before Sidney gently took it from her. "Here. Let me do that."

Slim fell back in the easy chair in her den, while Sidney added several more logs to the flame. Wood had stacked these logs on the porch for her, not even a week ago. And she had gone out in the snow and brought several in before Sidney arrived. In spite of the warmth of the fire, she was still wearing her coat over a long silk nightgown with Dr. Mac's old fly-fishing boots. Slim made no effort to remove her gear. Maybe she was tired. Or maybe she still had on her winter coat because she was in a Mama-leaving-this-world kind of mood tonight. She wasn't sure.

Now Sidney was saying something about how perhaps he should not have parked where people could see his car from the road. Slim cut him off. "Sidney, I truly do not care what people think about you being in my house. Now, I want to know these secrets of yours."

She suddenly noticed what an incredibly appealing and impeccable human being he was, in his soft brown pullover sweater, starched blue shirt, and gabardine pants. And his smell was sublime, too. Of course, Slim couldn't have cared one whit about any of it. It was just a clinical observation, with no investment in it.

Sidney cleared his throat, then, "All right. You know my job, in the camp?"

"No."

"All right. Well, what I did . . . my job was transporting bodies from the gas chambers to the burial site." He cleared his throat again. "So, anyway, I started counting my steps. For example, it was 660 steps to the, uh, first mass grave. To go there once and back, was 1,320 steps. To go there and back four times was a mile. And so on. Then I found a foldout map of the world in the back of a passport. Ironically, it belonged to a gypsy. It even had a mileage scale. So I stole it. Each night I would mark on the map with a pencil that a friend and I shared a tiny, infinitesimal mark of how far I'd gone—until one day I was no longer in Germany, I had crossed into Austria and was staring into the face of the Alps. In eight months, I was completely out of Europe. By the time the Allies came, I was in India."

Slim searched for something to say. "How did you cross the ocean?"

"I walked. That is the power of the mind, Evangeline. It travels, just like the feet. That is what saved me."

She regarded him, unimpressed. He continued on. "Keep moving. Have a goal. One day you will arrive at a place that is better than the place where you were, even if it is only in your head."

After a while, Slim said without any respect for the idea, "So, you think I should walk?"

"Yes. With me. Every day. We can go anywhere in the world. But I would love to show you Morocco. Have you been?"

She lied. "Yes."

"Wonderful. We can compare notes." He stood up. "Well, I'll be back tomorrow."

Slim stood up, too. Sidney asked, "What time shall we start?"

She decided to name one just to get rid of him. "Seven."

"Perfect. Not early enough to gloat, but still entitles us to a certain smugness."

She sensed that he might be flirting with her. As she handed him his coat, she said, "Sidney, I have to say something. I'm an old woman. If I were going to have a romantic liaison with any man in this town, it would probably be you. But my husband's gone and I'm done with that part of my life. I just thought you should know that, before we start walking around the world together."

Sidney looked at her, bemused. "I'm sorry. I should've known better than to try and use the Holocaust as a tool of seduction."

Now, in addition to feeling hopeless, Slim was embarrassed. "No. I'm the one who's sorry. Please forgive me."

He smiled. "How can I not, when you're standing there in those boots?"

She saw the humor dancing in his eyes, but she wasn't up to meeting it. So instead, she merely shook his hand, said goodnight, and closed the door. Then she crossed to the sofa and lay down and fell asleep, just as she was.

Milan was sitting on the floor of the McIlmore great room, in the process of unpacking several dozen boxes of decorations and ornaments. This was her annual pre-Christmas inventory, the one she always did right after Thanksgiving, in order to determine what lights were working and what ornaments she wanted to use. Usually by now, she had a theme in mind like "A Nutcracker Christmas" or "An Old-Fashioned Christmas," but this year she wasn't feeling very theme-ish.

Right now she was putting aside all the large boxes of roses made of ribbon. Milan had taken a class in rose-making and for years these rose-shaped bows, which came in every color, size, and stage of bloom, were her trademark signature on all packages. Each petal had been gathered and folded and cut in a precise fashion. The work was painstaking, but Milan reveled in it, even covering the powder room lampshade and an entire twenty-foot Christmas tree until

Wood had finally said, "Don't we have enough of these damn roses around here?" But still, she didn't have the heart to throw them away.

Now she was removing a set of three hand-carved wise men, each the height of a small child. With their muted pastel-colored coats and realistic beards, they were probably the best-looking wise men in all of Paris—at least, that's what she had been thinking when she ordered them from a high-priced mail-order catalog. Milan loved catalogs. She stayed up half the night thumbing through all the exquisite merchandise that she could hardly believe could actually be delivered to your house. But now these wise men seemed dull and predictable. Not that she wanted to change the Christmas story or anything. She was just sort of wishing she could add to it, without offending people. For some reason, she was picturing ballerinas in blue netting. But that would be absurd. Who ever heard of ballerinas in a manger? Maybe she would just cover a Styrofoam star in pale blue netting embedded with rhinestones. Milan normally had excellent taste, if not style, but she felt Christmas was the one time of year when she could let herself go.

She looked at the clock now and saw that it was almost midnight. Wood had been in bed for hours, which was good, because he had looked so tired when he came home. She had drawn him a bath, but he took a shower instead. She really didn't know how he did it. Being in surgery all morning and seeing patients at the hospital till as late as nine o'clock at night. She needed to go check on Charlie, too. She and her son had fallen asleep together on the chaise lounge, watching an old movie. That's what woke Milan up, when she realized that her arms were empty, and that Charlie had slipped out of them. Why couldn't the people she loved just stay the way she wanted them to? Why does happiness never sit still?

She settled back into the chaise again and pulled several garlands of tinsel up in her lap, in hopes of untangling them. Lots of people had turned their backs on tinsel, but Milan still liked it, because it was happy and shiny and reminded her of some of the old store windows on Main Street. In a little while, she lifted her knees toward her chin, just as she had once done to make room for her brothers and sisters in bed, and finally fell asleep, with some of the silver strands draped across her.

Upstairs, Wood had fallen asleep, too, exhausted from his feeble attempt at infidelity. And unaware that the old woman across town, the one who gave him life, was now sleeping by a fire that had gone out. And that the one downstairs, who married him and who still loved him with all her might, was lying pitifully wrapped in her own Christmas tinsel. He slept like men who are good at it—not knowing that his mother would get up in the morning and start walking across Morocco in some crazy last-ditch effort to save her own life. And without understanding that his wife's effort would be equally valiant, when she arose and sought, like an old prospector, the ordinariness of another day.

CHAPTER 16

It was twenty degrees and the wind was whipping through the barren oak and sycamore trees all across Hillcrest Park. Just as Slim was thinking that she was cold and wanted to go home, Sidney informed her that they were now strolling along the beach between Cap Spartel and the Grottes d'Hercule, north of Tangier. It had taken them a week to get here, and although she didn't feel any less depressed, she had to admit that his descriptions of the Moroccan countryside were lovely—the whitewashed houses stacked like sugar cubes all the way to the Mediterranean—the only vibrant colors were on the clotheslines—and an impossibly blue Moroccan sky stretched across all of it.

Sidney told Slim he has not found this shade of blue anywhere else in the world, but that her hydrangea plants in spring have often put him in mind of it. Then, she confessed her secret—coffee grounds and orange peels. He was shocked.

Now they were passing the Paris County municipal swimming pool, which had been drained for the winter and was full of sticks and debris. Sidney was telling her about the Coves Malabata. And how, if you go out of tourist season, you can miss the European crowd and see nothing but lovely brown people for miles. He knows that it is wrong to single out an entire country for the physical characteristics of its people, but one cannot

avoid noting that the Moroccans are stag-
geringly beautiful.

But Slim was no longer listening. She was
thinking of the large square hole with the
sticks in it and remembering the day when it,
too, was filled with blue water and brown
children—a day when she had decided to
add three white ones to the mix—Carl Jeter,
Earl Brundidge, and her own son.

It all started because Slim disagreed with
something called "Colored Day." Tuesday
was the only time that blacks were allowed
to use the city pool. Afterward, the water
would be drained overnight before white
children could swim again on Wednesday.
Slim had a plan to do something about this
and got permission from the other boys' parents to implement it. The Brundidges gave a
reluctant yes out of respect for Slim and Dr.
Mac. But Hank Jeter had no such reticence.
He said, "I don't know why in the world they
won't let them kids swim together. It don't
change the water none."

The next Tuesday rolled around and Slim
drove the three boys to Hillcrest and tried to
buy passes. When the girl in the ticket booth
told her that the boys couldn't swim because
it was Colored Day, Slim was ready. Yes,

there was a rule that blacks could not swim with whites, but there was no rule that whites could not swim with blacks. It seemed no one had ever thought of this before. The girl finally let them in because she didn't know what else to do. Slim watched through the wire fence as Woodrow, Carl, and Earl emerged from the locker room wearing their Pierre Cardin swim trunks and state-of-the-art flippers and goggles. She was thinking that they looked more like midget astronauts than civil rights warriors. As they waded into the water, the crowd of astonished black faces parted, letting them through. The lifeguards stood up. No one knew what would happen next. Then someone reached out and stole Earl Brundidge's goggles. He hollered so loud that it made everyone laugh. Then the goggles were tossed from person to person. Earl dunked somebody and got dunked back. Pretty soon everybody was playing so hard, no one even noticed that something important had happened. Or even that the water in the Paris County municipal pool was the same clear bright blue it had been when the sun came up that morning, just like Hank Jeter said it would be.

It would be several more summers before

the municipal pool was officially integrated. But it was Slim and her boys who had started it all. Suddenly Slim realized that Sidney had stopped talking and was now staring at her, as though he could read her mind. He motioned in the direction of the pool they had just passed. "I don't know if I ever told you, but I liked what you did back there. I liked it a lot."

She smiled for the first time since the day she bought poison.

Brundidge was sitting in his office when one of his secretaries carried in a large bouquet of red peonies. Denny, from Dwight & Denny's Secret Garden, had said in a state of high agitation that these had to be special ordered because the caller insisted that only red peonies would do. Brundidge opened the card, which read, "I was wrong. But you're still an asshole. Charlotte Rampling."

Brundidge smiled. So few things in life surprised him anymore. You could've knocked him over with an eyelash. He picked up the phone and called her.

"I give. How did you get our local florist to print the word asshole?"

"I handwrote it. And mailed it."

Brundidge was still nervously fingering the card. "Oh, yeah, right. At first, I thought, by your large sweeping 'A' that you were a highly neurotic homosexual man. But I can see now that this is from a highly neurotic yuppie female, who is alternately attracted to and repelled by the populist themes in country music." This was going good. Sometimes Brundidge could think just that fast on his feet and it had thankfully happened when he needed it. He waited. Charlotte didn't say anything. Now he was worried. He had tried to sound hip and cavalier, but not smart-alecky. Then she said, "I'm coming to Little Rock on the fourteenth for a story we're doing about Central High. I thought it might be an opportunity to see if you're as offensive in person as you are on the phone."

His heart leapt and he didn't know why. He didn't even like her, really.

"Sure. What about dinner? I could drive over."

"Perfect. Pick me up at the Sam Peck Hotel. Seven-ish."

"Right." He hung up. Seven-ish. That's what she said. He'd heard people in Paris say it, mimicking people in old movies. But

Charlotte Rampling had said it sincerely. Seven-ish.

Word had spread faster than Cherry Smoke's legs that Mavis Pinkerton had refused to serve Harlan B. Pillow Jr. And Harlan, knowing that people would be watching, had given considerable deliberation to his response. In the end, he chose to ask his parishioners to boycott Doe's. He did this during a Sunday morning service, saying that Mavis's attack was not directed at just one member of their flock, but rather at the church itself and its beliefs. And that such overt meddling and defiance must be met with similar strength. Therefore, he was beseeching his followers to give up their cinnamon rolls and butterhorns and pain au chocolat. It was a lot to ask and he knew it. But he had been devoted to their congregation and because of his winning manner and good looks, they knew he could do better than the First Baptist Church of Paris. And now, many felt it was time to repay that loyalty.

Right away, Mavis felt the pinch. There were a lot of First Baptists in town, and their boycott cut her business almost in half. But what Harlan hadn't counted on was that many Baptists themselves did not agree with the ban on women ministers. They hadn't really said anything because no one had ever challenged it before. Most of these people had been on friendly terms with Mavis for years and, even more important, they had a sweet tooth. After only about a week, there was complaining in the ranks, fueled by what some said was plain ol' withdrawal from the best supply of sugar in town. Pretty soon, parishoners began arriving at the back door of Doe's, wearing sunglasses and darting furtively to and from their cars, clutching their profiteroles and baba au rhums and peaches-and-cream turnovers. Mavis and Mary Paige, who was now helping out, took to calling their back entrance "The Baptist Door." And some days, there was even a line that formed outside of it. Inside, Mavis had become emboldened by her ability to use food as a powerful tool. And she now decided to use it to deal with something that had annoyed her for a long time. A man from out of town was standing at her counter. Brundidge was next in line.

Mavis said, "Okay, it'll be a few minutes. What's your name?"

"Booger."

"No, what's your real name?"

"That's it."

"I'm sorry. We don't serve people named Booger. Mainly, because I would have to call it out and I'm not willing to do that."

Brundidge let out a long sigh. There were at least three other men in Paris with this same moniker and Mavis had wanted to say this for years. The man seemed confused. "I thought you didn't serve Baptists."

"No. That's not true. There's a door right back there that they can come through."

He asked sincerely, "Well, is there a Booger door?"

Mavis gave up. She waved her pencil. "Just gimme your last name."

Brundidge rolled his eyes. Late that afternoon, Mavis was adding up receipts when Brundidge returned with Wood, Jeter, and Sheriff Marcus West in tow. She had never seen them looking more somber. Sheriff West spoke first. "Mavis, I'm sorry to tell you this, but we've had a complaint that you're violating federal law here by refusing to serve certain customers."

Brundidge shook his head, disgusted. "I told you. That Booger thing. You can't discriminate against somebody just because they're a redneck."

Sheriff West removed a pair of handcuffs from his belt. "That's right. And now I'm afraid I'm gonna have to take you into custody. Would you put your hands out, please?"

Rudy and Mary Paige gasped. Mavis began sputtering and cussing. Sheriff West, undeterred, pretended to examine the handcuffs. "No, these are not the right size." He dug in his pocket and came up with a large teething ring, handing it to her. "Here, see if that fits you better."

Mavis stared at the strange new object, then slowly took it in her hand and looked quizzically at Wood.

He said, "By the end of summer, you should have yourself a little somethin' to go with that." Then he grabbed her, hugging her. "Merry Christmas!"

Brundidge clapped his hands, laughing. "We got you good! You little mother, you!"

Mavis covered her face with her hands. Suddenly Doe's erupted with shouts of relief and joy, so excessive they almost drowned out the dead quiet that lingered over the rest of the street. Jeter looked dazed and Mavis couldn't stop scolding them all and thanking them at the same time. And Mary Paige shook Wood's hand as though he were the father and Brundidge reminded everyone that he had been the driver until Rudy tried to clear it all up by telling a customer, "We are all the daddy!"

Later, as Mavis was hanging her closed sign in the window, Milan was already up in her attic, hunting for Elizabeth and Charlie's old crib. By the time Mavis and her Oldsmobile arrived at Fast Deer Farm, Milan was standing in the middle of the gravel road. Mavis screeched to a halt, got out, and walked straight into her old friend's arms. After a while, Milan said softly, "If it's a girl, I get to dress her."

Wood and Jeter and Brundidge were sitting on the side patio of the Pleasant Valley Retirement Villa. It was twenty-eight degrees and they were shivering in their winter coats and smoking cigars. Wood periodically gave Jeter, who was complaining about Mavis, a puff of his.

"Now she wants me to go to Lamaze class. I knew this would happen. I'm supposed to be her breathing coach. Hell, I can barely breathe on my own. I can't even keep that little plastic ball in the air anymore."

Wood said, "Oh, just go on and go. You can be moral support."

"She doesn't want moral support. She wants my family history, photo albums, the names of all my ancestors—"

Brundidge shook his head. "Man, she's got her hooks in you now. You know what's gonna happen next, don't you? She's gonna start buying your clothes and signing you up for stuff. Hell, you'll probably have to start wearing a damn cardigan."

Jeter glared at them. "This is all your fault, both of you."

Wood grinned as his phone went off. "Me? I'm just an innocent bystander." Then he lifted the receiver to his ear and heard Luke Childs's voice.

Wood was back on the road to Excelsior Springs. Only this time, he had good reason. Luke had called him from school to say that his mother had the flu and could Wood please phone in a prescription? Evidently, Luke had accepted his mother's assurance that her relationship with Wood had been nothing more than a little high school thing and certainly not something that he need trouble himself about. Certainly anyone could see that Duff was still fond of his future father-in-law, but as Luke knew all too well, being friendly and open was his mother's nature.

As a rule, Wood didn't like to phone in prescriptions without checking out the patient first. That was why he was now on his way to see Duff. Because it was the professional, not to mention decent, thing to do. An old friend who's sick, with no money or health insurance. And him a doctor. What choice did he have really? He was going to deliver medical attention and then maybe they would sit and talk. The idea was to experience her in some way that would satisfy him, even just a little, but not put either of them in jeopardy. Certainly, to attempt anything more would be insane. Having an affair with his old girlfriend, his wife's lifelong nemesis, his daughter's future mother-in-law—how destructive can a man be? Anyway, he had already proven that in spite of a now disappointing marriage, he could be faithful to Milan. This, in the face of overwhelming temptation and a growing awareness of his own mortality.

His most formidable test to date was a nurse at the hospital, a strikingly beautiful married woman, with plush breasts and hips, who didn't waste a moment of her time on foreplay—who just came right out and said, "I have a wonderfully thick bush. If you're ever in the mood, I'd love to show you." Had said some version of it on a number of occasions, and every time she did, Wood had smiled and answered something like, "I'm afraid my wife might think you were spoiling me." But in his head, his pants were already around his ankles and he was on his knees humping her like some big-dicked, red-assed monkey.

And she wasn't the only one, either. They were everywhere: the little pouty-mouthed girl at the pharmacy who held his hand too long when she gave him back his credit card; Brundidge's ex-wife, Darlene, who called Wood regularly and invited him to come hear her sing at the Tap Room, maybe they could have a drink afterward, and he could give an expert's opinion on her new boob reduction job; and a number of his patients, too, who in the middle of his examining them, had made all kinds of inappropriate remarks.

"I can't explain it, but for some reason, I'm real comfortable with you down there."

"Oh, how embarrassing. You can skip the lubricant, Wood. I'm ready."

"You know something? You feel me up better than my husband does."

Yeah, he'd had that happen more times than you'd think. Of course, it was always said as a joke, because a nurse was usually present, but they got their points across. Nobody ever talked about what doctors have to put up with. It was always doctors taking advantage of their female patients. Nobody ever said how women in labor could sometimes get sexually aroused. Or how certain ones let themselves go, with their poor hygiene, garlicky breath, and cheap cologne. Or how some of them acted, once they got undressed and slipped their heels into his footrests—opening their legs wider than they needed to, scooting down unnecessarily, trying to shove it all in his face, "Seriously, what do you think of my new Mohawk?" Once, in the middle of a breast exam, one of his older patients had even tried to unzip his pants. Wood had referred the woman to his dad, who said her hormones were out of whack and that she had waited for him, wearing only a slip, in his truck.

Anyway, that's how it was sometimes for a doctor who's around women all day—lonely, troubled women, whose husbands and boyfriends neglected them, but also bold, happy, healthy women who just wanted to get laid. And he had resisted them all. He wasn't about to change his plan now. Not even for one night of lovemaking with someone he'd had on his mind for twenty years.

The moon looked hard and cold when Wood pulled up in front of Duff's house. The exterior was ordinary, except that someone, probably Duff, had taken the trouble to paint it red. Inside, the rooms were cramped and unkempt, pretty much what he had expected. There were a lot of throw pillows and books everywhere, and the walls were covered with what appeared to be the works of local artists. Wood was now admiring one in particular, a watercolor of a giant pear.

He did this while running his hand down the long, naked curve of the woman who was lying next to him. When he got to her legs, he noticed that they hadn't been shaved recently and he was thinking how much he liked the imperfection of that—the unstudied sensuality of this small intimacy that they were both now in on. He pressed his mouth to the back of her knee and then lingered there.

The thing Wood had underestimated was the power of longing. People always talked about the power of love or hate or healing, but not enough had been said about longing. And if it had been, maybe he wouldn't have gotten into trouble. Because longing for someone you cannot see or have or hear is a powerful thing, indeed. Especially if you have been rolling it around in your head for half your natural life. That's how long he had been thinking of Duff.

And just being in her presence again had put him in mind of an old feeling that he was going to live forever. The same one he'd had while making love to her in the field behind his house, when they were still young, under a cluster of persimmon trees that always seemed to rustle softly as he came. That was the powerful longing that he could no longer turn his back on.

When he had first arrived, she was already feeling better. But he dug in his doctor bag anyway and attempted to take her blood pressure. As soon as the air had run out of the plastic arm cuff, he knew with certainty that he was going to make love to her. He knew that it would destroy him and his family and Duff and her boy and any chance for a wedding and peace and happiness on Earth and even grandchildren who could've belonged to all of them. But he went ahead anyway, because the longing had become larger than Wood himself. He had smiled and looked straight into her eyes, like Miss Lena Farnham Stokes had warned him not to, and given away all his power.

It had started with a simple kiss, but then he continued putting his lips on various parts of her, parts that were far away from one another and didn't make any sense logistically, but this was his way of telling her that he was going to take his time. And he could see by her look that she wasn't going to fight him, that she had already given every bit of herself to him and all that remained was for him to take it.

He helped her get out of her jeans and T-shirt, noticing that she had finally made the concession to underwear. He took his own shirt off and then turned back to kissing her, subtle, sweet kisses on her face and hands and arms, finally running his mouth over the cotton fabric of her bra and panties, wetting it with his tongue, especially around her nipples and between her legs. After a while, Duff began to cry a little and he held her like he would an infant, for a good while, just stroking her hair and soothing her. Then she crawled in his lap and put her arms around his neck and used her tongue to open his mouth, and they drew this out, too, savoring each other's lips like lovers who know that these things may not happen again. Wood then removed Duff's panties, but not her bra (because she asked him not to), and buried his face in her pubic hair, grateful to smell the same perfume that he remembered. After that, he put his tongue deep between her legs, and then stood up and took his pants off, and lay back down on top of her, still supporting his own weight with his arms, the way he did during his daily push-ups, and finally, almost reverently, entered her, asking at every increment if she was all right. She responded by clasping her legs more tightly around him. And since they were still approximately the same size as they once were, they ecstatically felt the glove-perfect fit at the same time, revisited. Wood increased his pace, then slowed it again just in time, and so on, until he stretched out their lovemaking longer than any other Duff could remember. As soon as they were done, he slipped off her as gracefully as he had gotten on, and then, lying on his back, placed her lengthwise on his chest, the way he often did Milan. He knew that was wrong, too. Repeating such an important, private gesture with another woman, the very thing Milan always asked him for after they had sex, "Don't go to sleep yet. Hold me over your heart." But he was already violating every dust fleck of intimacy he shared with his wife. What difference did this one now-diminished gesture make?

Maybe in some perverse way, he was finally punishing Milan for growing happier each year, as she acquired more of the things he was sure she had married him for. Punishing her for all the sex she insisted upon as a way of proving that they did indeed exist as a couple. We fuck, therefore we are. With Milan, it was never about love or romance or even longing. It was about making it look like love and romance. Leaving little flirtatious notes around with calculated messages that she probably got out of a woman's magazine, and getting herself all whored up in five-hundred-dollar negligees (Milan was incapable of understanding that seduction was vulgar), like it was a costume and he was the stupid animal who would have to respond to it, because the saleslady had said he would. Sometimes, he finished with her quickly, just because he hated that outfit so much. He was surprised she didn't give him a dog treat afterward. Anyway, these were the things she did while she participated in his life as though it was a role she had won, and now she would play to the crowd and do whatever she must to keep her costar and benefactor happy.

Duff, who was now folded along Wood's edge, had fallen asleep. And he was growing tired of staring at the giant pear. Suddenly, he was filled with desire again. He woke her up with his petting and eventually she guided him to the side of the bed, where she got on her knees and took him in her mouth. After a while, he told her that he wanted to see her breasts. She had tried to explain that she was a middle-aged woman now, and no longer sure of her gifts. Well actually, what she said was, that she didn't feel pretty anymore and something else about having nursed her son, but Wood had already turned her around while she was talking and pulled her backward into his lap and then unhooked her bra, and slipped each ample sagging tit out of its cup and into his own hands and held them there tenderly for a long time, like he was honored to do this, grateful for one more chance to rub the soft, fleshy talismans whose magical powers had so consumed and comforted his youth. And he stayed there like this, while resting his head against her back, until finally Duff could feel the wetness of his cheek. Then Duff turned and thanked him profusely with her mouth. Wood surprised her by switching on the little bedside lamp and then, holding her about a foot away from him, took a good long look, telling her how lovely she was, while kissing her nipples with the same intensity you would use to blow on a baby's stomach. Duff put her hands over her face and groaned and fell back on the pillow. This made him laugh. She laughed a little, too. Wood couldn't remember when he had felt this happy. Suddenly, he couldn't imagine ever leaving her. He was like a man who had broken into a house to steal some jewelry but was now going to get a truck and take the furniture, too. He wanted to be in her mouth again and to sleep in the sweetness between her legs and, right now, to turn her over on her stomach, which he did, a little too roughly (more like a teenage boy would've done it) and entered her vagina from behind, just a little at first until she got hold of the covers to balance herself, and then finally deeper, trying, as he would all night, to get to the middle of her. Outside, not long after Wood and Duff had come together again, most of the stars had faded away and the old, hippie wind chime on her front porch was as still as the trees.

Milan was on her way back from Hayti where she had delivered early Santa Claus gifts for her nieces and nephews. In spite of the fact that she and Wood hosted an annual holiday party for all the Laniers, which Wood had to annually get drunk for, Milan also liked to provide gifts for the children of her siblings to be put out on Christmas morning.

She shivered a little and turned up the car's heater. The road between Paris and Hayti was so dark at night, it made her feel lonesome and small. She slowed the Mercedes as a mother possum and her babies crossed in front of her. The larger possum looked straight at Milan with eyes like green marbles that seemed to be on fire. Now the blacktop and the ominous look from the two eyes in the dark were adding to the uneasy feeling that she had been fighting all day. Especially since Elizabeth had told her that Luke had asked Wood to write a prescription for his mother. And then Wood had failed to come home after work. It was nine o'clock now and she'd called his cell phone several times, getting no answer.

Later, when she pulled in the garage and saw that his car still wasn't there, she felt sure that he'd gone to Excelsior Springs. If Duff had the flu, as Elizabeth said, that would be the perfect cover for them to see each other. Milan went inside and turned the oven off and put away the leg of lamb that had been warming there. It was Wood's favorite and she'd asked Mrs. Denby to make it for him.

Charlie was spending the night with a friend, so she went straight to her bedroom and got undressed. Then she crossed to the window and looked out on the road to Fast Deer Farm. How many nights she had sat here, when she and Wood were first married, waiting for a glimpse of his car as it turned on to their gravel road. When it did, she would literally sail down the stairs to meet him and he would be happy to see her, too. Afterward, she would warm up his dinner, because that was the life of a doctor's wife and one that she reveled in. And then they would talk about their babies and the farm and whatever had happened at the hospital that day and maybe go upstairs and have a long hot bath together or make love and sit outside on the master bedroom porch afterward.

But these things didn't happen anymore and there were no car lights on the road to Fast Deer tonight. And Milan had to admit finally that the feeling she was getting was not one of mere ordinary unease, but rather of simply not being good enough. There was fear and shame and real dread in it and she crossed to the bed and curled up on her side of it, holding herself. It was the same feeling she used to get whenever she went anywhere with her family—riding in the back of Tom Lanier's old, rusted-out truck, with her and Frank getting to sit on the two broken pizza parlor chairs. To this day, Milan will not go to certain places, like the Dairy Queen, because of the way the owner would stare at

all of them as they poured into his establish-
ment like cockroaches and tried to cash in
their expired coupons. She had seen that
same look, in varying degrees, on the faces
of other merchants when the Laniers would
pull up outside their businesses. She could
almost feel their intake of breath and raised
shoulders, as though this were something
that would have to be suffered and then gotten rid of as quickly as possible—these children with their crusted noses and aluminum
foil sticking pitifully out of their shoes, who
smelled of pork fat and dirty hair—whose
clothes hung on them like the children themselves were the coat hangers and whose
eyes told you that there is nothing more you
will ever know about them other than what
you can see.

Certainly, there were well-intended church
people who held rummage and bake sales
in order to help the family. But the problem
was, they said it was for something called
"The Lanier Fund," which was then painted
across a twenty-foot banner. And the pro-
ceeds were always announced in church on
Sunday, which so horrified Milan that she
wasn't able to attend school the next day.
And perhaps worse, when all the youngsters

were called to come down front and form a prayer circle, Milan had been connected to a little boy whose mother, a woman with a kind smile, got out her handkerchief afterward and wiped his hand.

After years of that kind of reception, there is a sadness that one starts to feel about oneself. And finally, a curtain that goes down on that sadness, and there it stays. If you are smart, like the woman now curled like a fetus on her bed, it will be seldom visited. But also, never erased.

One of the places the Laniers did always feel welcome was Jeter's Market. All the children hung out there, but it was Milan who attached herself to the glass candy case like a small blonde barnacle. Most days, Pauline Jeter gave the Lanier kids free candy, as they knew she would, though she never said it was free. She said it was the result of something called "overstocking" or "taking in too much inventory," which Frank Lanier invariably fumbled and then finally giving up, would just ask, "Um, did that thing happen to you again?"

To which Pauline would unfailingly reply, "You know, I believe it did."

A block away, Milan also found refuge at

Lena Farnham Stokes's. She never went to Jeter's that she did not stop by the haberdasher's window first and stare at the picture of the buxom young monarch riding in her coronation coach and waving. One time, after Milan had told Hank Jeter that she would give anything to some day meet the queen, he had appeared to size Milan up, as she stood there conquering her free jawbreaker, and then he said, "She ain't so much. I think that ole gal would be lucky to know you."

This was electrifying information. For days, Milan couldn't even sleep. Someone thought the Queen of England would be lucky to know her! In her wildest imagination, she could not have come up with such an idea. And the person who thought it, was not just anyone either. He was a man who owned an entire store full of food and candy. And who would one day be put out of business by a two-hundred-thousand-square-foot superstore, which with all its power and might and money, would be unable to provide the familiarity or trust necessary for transmitting an idea of such exquisite discernment.

The one store on Main Street that Milan would never go inside was Sidney Garfinkel's.

The expensive clothes and seemingly formal atmosphere made her feel almost light-headed. Ironically, he was one of the few merchants who acted as though the Laniers would be welcome to come in if they had wanted to. It was somewhere in the way he smiled and said hello. Maybe the others didn't pick up on it, but Milan, with her fine ear for social interaction, did. And the fact that she never took him up on it did not stop her from pressing her face against the glass every day after school and staring in awe at the dazzling mannequins and their sleek, stylish outfits. She was respectful, too, never leaving a nose or handprint on the window, and especially if she had a cold, which was often, she always wiped the glass with her coat sleeve.

Milan would seriously study these resin women with their sunken cheeks, while writing in a small spiral notebook that she filled with childish sketches and minute details. Sometimes, at night, she would even practice their facial expressions, holding the little seashell mirror Tom Lanier had given her. She secretly named each one of the mannequins, faithfully describing the length of their hems, whether their sleeves were pushed up or left down, or how a certain coat looked better unbuttoned than buttoned. Her favorite was the brunette one with green cat eyes and short wavy hair. She especially liked that this girl seemed to be on her way somewhere, with her head thrown back, as though she would laugh if she could. Milan had given her the name that she herself wished was her own—Karen. Oddly, Karen was not a wife or a mother. At nine years old, children were the last thing Milan wanted more of. She already slept with sick, coughing toddlers who regularly wet the bed, and she had to spend a good portion of her day helping to shore up the rest of her siblings. No, Karen was not a mother. She was a stylish, independent career gal whose job caused her to travel, where she stayed in fancy hotels and sat in huge bathtubs smoking cigarettes and ordering pork chops and chocolate sodas from room service, and telling the hotel operator to please get her rich boyfriend on the telephone.

Milan especially loved imagining Karen at work. She loved how people depended on her and looked up to her and how her name sounded when they said things like, "Karen, can you bring me that file?" "Oh, Karen, are you free for lunch?" Or "Tell me, Karen, how do you do it?"

These were the sorts of dreams Milan had, standing outside Sidney Garfinkel's store window. But still, she never went in. She did, however, begin knocking on the door and inquiring as to the precise date and time he would next be changing out the clothes in his window displays. Unlike Wood and Jeter and Brundidge, who observed this ritual haphazardly while making their rounds on Main Street, Milan looked upon it as an event that should be scheduled and appreciated. And Sidney Garfinkel, who had never considered that he would have to come up with a date and time for such a thing, ended up doing just that—especially after he saw that Milan had gotten out her little notebook and written down everything he said in it.

Over the years, neither Sidney nor his faithful admirer ever missed a "changing of the mannequins" date. Once, when he had a terrible cold, he still came down to the store and changed out his after-Christmas window on the day and time he had told her he would. And she knew he must've gotten out of bed to do it, too, because it was the only

fashion faux pas she ever caught him in—
blue pajama tops under a wool overcoat.

As Milan got older, and even more striking
in appearance, she became Sidney Garfinkel's top model at local fashion shows, a
sort of Audrey Hepburn to his Givenchy. And
Sidney attempted to impart as much of his
own fashion sense and expertise to her as
he did to Brundidge. Although, to his regret,
Milan would never own the kind of inviolable
personal style that eclipses the mere wearing of designer labels.

Then, not long after a particularly notable
show in which their picture had appeared in
the *Paris Beacon* with their arms around
each other, something terrible happened—
an event that so mortified Milan, she avoided
Sidney Garfinkel for months afterward. The
newspaper had come out by two in the afternoon. By two thirty, someone had read it and
thrown it away, making it possible for Tom
Lanier to get one. Eventually, he had
propped the photograph up on the dashboard of his truck, which was parked to the
side of the Texaco station. There he spent
several hours drinking whiskey from a bottle
and talking to the man in the picture. Then,
he had found a dime wedged between the

seat cushions and after he tried for a long time to pick some hair and sticky stuff off of it, finally gave up, got out of his truck and called Sidney Garfinkel on the nearby pay phone.

"You filthy Jew bastard. Who do you think you are puttin' your hands on my girl? There ain't enough Jew money in the world for you to put your hands on my girl. Do you hear me? Not by a long shot. And when I get aholt of your slimy Jew ass, you'll wish you was back where you came from. Back at them ovens, where they said you was helpin' put away your own kind and stealin' their watches while you was doin' it. That's what they say about you! The only thing lower than a damn slimy Jew is a damn slimy Jew who will steal from another one."

Sidney Garfinkel had listened politely and then hung up. After that, Tom Lanier had started to cry. It was sudden and exaggerated, the way an actor in a comedy sketch might do it. Then he beat the phone on the side of the station and tried to throw the receiver down on the ground, but it stayed midway in the air, swinging from its cord. Finally, he got back in his truck and attempted to peel out, causing a brief screech, but he didn't have the power, so he just sort of coasted away. Like a stray dog who yelps at you, trying to be powerful, and then, getting no response, limps off.

Sidney never told this story to anyone, not even his wife or the female employee who had seen his face turn white. But Tom Lanier had told it all over town and changed the facts, too. He said that Sidney had tried to "get sweet" with Milan and that she had come home absolutely beside herself, which is why he had gotten in his truck and driven straight to the Garfinkels' house. After asking Esther Garfinkel to leave, he had threatened to kill Sidney, who got on his knees and cried like a little girl for forgiveness. And then Tom always ended the story with, "Idn't that just like a damn kike? Always got their hands in your pocket, but if it's in their interest, happy to get on their knees, too." But no one who knew Sidney Garfinkel could imagine him getting on his knees for anyone, except to pin a pair of pants. By the time Tom was done, everyone in Paris had heard the story, including most of the kids at school. Milan not only stopped going into Sidney Garfinkel's store, she stopped going to Main Street period, for fear of running into him.

And if she saw him pull up at the Stop-N-Go, where she worked in addition to Cotrell's, she would run to the restroom and not come out till he was gone.

A few months after the incident with Sidney, Tom Lanier had a complete nervous breakdown. This was around the time he told Milan that people were nothing more than blood and water and gravel with a hole punched in the top so they could speak and try to fool you. And then he started rearranging garbage, delivering it from one house to another, or just leaving most of it scattered in the street. This time, he was not taken to the county hospital (where poor crazy people went) but instead was transported to Milledgeville in Little Rock, which was about the most serious place they could put you for mental troubles. If someone said, "Well, you know, they've got him up at Milledgeville," that meant that person was in a bad way. The word was that Tom Lanier was even too sick to be seen by his own family. Not long after he arrived there, the official diagnosis came down: acute schizophrenia. Tom had suffered breakdowns before, but he had never been given a surefire diagnosis like this one. Pretty soon, it got all over Paris and the high school that the Lanier children's daddy was a complete schizophrenic. Far from being upset, Milan was happy. Finally a name upon which she could pin all the horrors of her childhood. The Laniers were not a litter of hopeless, ill-bred, hillbilly losers, after all. They were the offspring of a medically certified, card-carrying schizophrenic! The appalling food shortages, the notes from school nurses to please give so-and-so a bath, the shabby used winter coats and shoes, the drunken tirades and terrible violence (Milan was the only one Tom never hit, but she did always clean up the mess, whether it was spilt liquor or broken teeth), now it could all finally be placed under one forgiving, illuminating, exhilarating, all-encompassing banner! Schizophrenia! It was even better than cancer. She wanted to get in her drum majorette's uniform and strut down Main Street yelling it. Schizophrenia! It was the most beautiful sound she had ever heard. So wonderful it should be the name of whatever goes on the tops of sundaes—"Two scoops of vanilla, please, and a sprinkle of Schizophrenia!" Or a place with houses by the sea—"We're off to Schizophrenia!" Or a dance—"Come on everybody, let's do the Schizophrenia!"

About a week before Milan's graduation, Tom came home from Milledgeville. Strangely, he didn't seem to be crazy anymore. He didn't seem to be much of anything. He mostly sat around in a pair of camouflage hunting pants, and an undershirt, drinking orange soda and staring at a book he had stolen from the Milledgeville Hospital Library. It was a "How To" book for beginners on how to fix things. Milan, who normally didn't dwell on irony, thought how much Miss Delaney could do with that.

A few days later, when a magnificently wrapped package arrived at the Paris High School principal's office with Milan Lanier's name on it, the secretary became so excited that the giftee was called out of class to receive it. As soon as Milan saw the wrapping, she knew exactly where it had come from. And once she tore the paper away and lifted the lid, she had to cover her mouth to keep her excitement in check. Then, slowly, a few inches at a time, there emerged from the folded tissue a stunningly perfect dress of exquisite black linen with large covered buttons down the back and a wide chic belt and buckle made of the same fabric. And there was a blue velvet pouch, too, containing shoes with tiny, sling-back straps and impossibly high heels, which had been meticulously dyed to match the dress. And underneath the pouch, this, "A Paris original. The dress and the girl. With all good wishes, Sidney Garfinkel."

Milan must've drifted off to sleep because when she woke up, Wood was getting undressed and she hadn't even heard him come in. But then, she was sure he hadn't wanted her to hear him. She sat up in bed.

"How was your patient?"

The question did not seem to surprise him. "Fine. She has the flu. I, uh, tried to call you from the car, but it was out of range."

Milan lay back down. "Just don't say anything, all right?"

He started for the shower in order to wash off the evidence. Then he turned and added, "She doesn't have any money, you know."

If Milan had been a rapier wit sort, this was a golden moment, but she wasn't and it passed unused, as she put her head under her pillow and Wood went on into the bathroom.

CHAPTER 17

Mavis was making glorious beignets as Mary Paige read aloud names from a baby book. Mavis was thinking how happy she was and how much she liked the Christmas wreath Milan had fashioned from one of the holly bushes at Fast Deer Farm—the one that was now hanging on her door. But her reverie came to a screeching halt when she looked up and saw Lonnie Rhinehart and several of his redneck friends standing at the counter. She despised these men who loved her food and regularly came in to eat and swagger around, making lewd and inappropriate comments about Rudy, queers, and the physical endowments of many of her female patrons.

But what disturbed Mavis most deeply was the story that had gone around about how Lonnie had taken his pregnant beagle hunting and that when she prematurely gave birth in the snow, he and his friends had used their large heavy boots to stomp the puppies to death. It had sickened Mavis to have to wait on him and now that she was pregnant herself, and also fresh from her success with the Baptist door, she was determined to do something about it.

Lonnie attempted to give his order, but she stopped him. "You're not welcome here anymore. Actually, you were never welcome here. But until today, I didn't have the nerve to tell you."

He looked at her, amused, and then leaned his elbows on the counter. "Why ain't I welcome?"

"Because you stomped puppies to death in the snow. And it makes me sick to look at you. Now get out."

Lonnie drew back a little. Mary Paige felt sure that he had never been spoken to like this by anyone, much less a woman. She and Rudy held their breath.

Lonnie said, "Okay, if that's the way you wanna act." Then he lied, "Your food ain't that good. Anyway, looks to me like most of it's goin' down your own pie hole." The other two men followed him to the door. Then Lonnie turned back, smirking like the ominous costar of *The Donna Somebody Story.*

"I was thinkin', you should get yourself an alarm system here. A big ol' rough-talkin' girl like you—you just never know when some-thin' alarmin' might happen."

The men laughed, as though Lonnie had really outdone himself this time.

Mary Paige put an arm around Mavis's waist. Mavis swallowed hard, not yet know-ing what her courage would someday cost them all.

Brundidge was getting dressed for his date with Charlotte Rampling. He had decided to go with his black Tommy Bahama pullover, an oxford shirt, and jeans with Bally loafers because it all looked good with his tan dress coat. Cake handed him his burgundy hound-stooth scarf as she fanned the air. "Dad, that perfume."

"What's wrong with it?"

"Too much."

"Okay, well, get a washrag and get some of it off."

She went into the bathroom as Brundidge said to Lily, who was now on the bed, "Don't sit on Daddy's scarf, babe. I may still wear that one." He crossed and retrieved it. Cake came back out and patted his neck and chin with the wet cloth.

"Thank you, pancake."

He held up both scarves and asked them to choose. They picked the red one. He put it on, then clapped his hands. "Okay. Let's have it. Daddy's gotta go."

They ran to him, kissing his cheeks. "That's my girls. Whoa, that's good sugar!"

Brundidge's teenage niece, Deanne, came and watched at the door. "You mind your cousin, now. And I want you both in bed by nine." Then he said to Deanne, "Remember, you gotta check 'em for flashlights 'cause they'll stay up and read all night if you let 'em."

They were passing through the living room as Lily caught up with him and opened her hand. "Daddy, breath mints!"

Brundidge took the little roll from her. "Whoa! Can't forget that. Thank you, baby." Then he kissed them all again and went out the door, calling back, "Don't get Popsicles on the rug now. Eat 'em over the sink."

He was standing in the lobby of the Sam Peck hotel. And Charlotte Rampling was walking toward him. She was short, with a pretty, round face, plush lips, and glasses. Her brown hair was smooth and shiny and she was dressed completely in black. She wasn't what he was expecting, but overall, he was pleased, smiling. Then she said, "My God, you're bald! I can't believe it. Every man I go out with is bald!" She shook her head. "It's like I have some kind of hairless date destiny."

Brundidge stood frowning at her. Then he said, "That's it? That's your opening line? 'Cause if you're feeling like you blew it, I'm willing to let you go back and get off the elevator again."

She didn't laugh. An hour later they were sitting in a booth at Uncle Ned's Barbecue in Little Rock. Charlotte had hardly touched her food. Brundidge ordered two more margaritas and then turned to her. "See, here's the deal. I know you like those ribs. But you're so invested in, I don't know, your own superiority, that you won't eat them."

"How would my not eating ribs make me superior?"

"Oh, come on. It's that whole conversation we had about New York and Arkansas and how you should come down here and eat barbecue. I just can't believe you went to all this trouble just to show me that you don't like it."

"Here's a newsflash." She leaned toward him and said, sincerely, "I don't like it."

He regarded her for a moment, disbelieving. "Well, then, you're evil. You're the devil's spawn. Because there's no way in the world someone wouldn't like this if they were a normal person. Seriously, there's somethin' deep within you that's gone very, very wrong."

The waiter arrived with the margaritas. Charlotte took a sip. "I'm sorry. I'm not gonna eat some charcoal pig, slathered in unknown red sauce, just so you can feel better about yourself. If you can't deal with that, seek therapy."

"Hey, I don't have to pay somebody two hundred dollars an hour to listen to me talk. I've got real friends. And if it's something I'm too ashamed to tell anyone, then I just keep it to myself, feeling small and worthless for the rest of my life. Because that's the way it's supposed to be."

Charlotte was smiling now. "It's too bad this has gone poorly. Because I'll be honest, there's something about you that attracts

me. Of course, I know it could never go anywhere. But there's this sort of dense, impen-
etrable masculinity that you have—I don't
know, it's like I hate you, but I want to make
you yell out my name."

Brundidge's Tommy Bahama sweater and
all his other clothes were now neatly hung in
the closet of Charlotte Rampling's hotel
room. Her clothes, on the other hand, along
with her undergarments, were strewn everywhere. Right now, she had her legs wrapped
around his waist as he sat her bottom down
on the writing desk and humped her for a
good ten or fifteen minutes before she cried
out and fell spent across the hote con-
cierge's list of Things to Do in Little Rock.

A half hour later, they were in the shower
together and he was using the complimen-
tary mango shampoo to wash her hair while
pounding her from behind. Then, as she
cried out again, he covered her hands,
which were pressed against the tile wall,
with his own.

Just before dawn, he picked Charlotte up
and carried her out to their narrow third-floor
balcony. He placed a pillow under her rump
and did her face-to-face for at least another
half hour as the sun came up and several

cars came by and honked, which made it all the more exciting. By seven-ish, they had devoured everything under the silver domes that had been brought in by room service. Then they went at it once more with Brundidge on the bottom and Charlotte riding him, happy. Afterward, they lay exhausted in bed. Finally, she said, "I don't care what happens next. That was the best sex I've ever had."

He had his back to her. Charlotte put her hand on him. "What's wrong?"

Brundidge rolled over. "I have to tell you something. I've never done anything like this in my entire life. I mean, I always try to get to know somebody before we, you know . . ." He shook his head. "I'm sorry."

She was stunned. "What is this? Some kind of Bible belt thing? Are you crazy? It was wonderful. It was sublime. One a scale of one to ten it was a million."

"Even when I dated a topless dancer, we didn't do anything but have dinner for the first three weeks."

"Why?"

"Because. We're not animals, Charlotte. We need to have values and to care about

people's feelings. It's important. It's the backbone of civilization."

"Listen, I don't give a damn about civilization. I just know that we're here for a very
short time. And you and I fuck really well together. Therefore, we should do so whenever we can." She pulled the sheet up and
climbed back on top of him.

He said, "You talk terrible." Then, as they
got going again, "What I should really do is
wash your mouth out."

She was smiling. "Yes, you should. We'll
do that next."

Mavis was in her kitchen lighting a Christmas candle and rearranging the flowers on
the table. When it came to graceful living,
she was no Milan, but she had taken the
trouble to drive to Fast Deer Farm and cut
these flowers in the greenhouse. And even
though they didn't go with the Christmas
candle, she didn't care. Tulips in winter!
What could be more romantic?

A little later, when Mary Paige was seated
across from her, Mavis couldn't help thinking
how sweet her face looked in the candlelight.
Almost beatific. And that it reminded her a lit-

tle of the picture of Jesus that had adorned
the wall of her Sunday school classroom. She
had once marveled at how handsome he
looked, gazing upward, almost like a movie
star, as a similar light shone on his face.

Mary Paige couldn't get over the meal
Mavis had prepared. She had never tasted
anything like the pan-fried oysters with
caviar crème fraîche (which Mavis had special ordered from Gulf Shores, Mississippi),
the lobster mousse puff pastry bouchées,
and strawberry trifle. Afterward, Mavis put on
one of Dr. Mac's old tapes and asked Mary
Paige to dance. Mary Paige told her she
didn't know how and Mavis said not to worry,
that she would teach her. It was a slow number and Mavis wasn't very good either, but it
felt good just to be moving to the music together. For the first time, Mavis had someone in her arms who actually made her
heart soar, as they shifted from foot to foot,
heavy, plodding, with their heads on each
other's shoulders.

Suddenly, they heard someone knocking
lightly at the door, as though the person
wasn't sure she wanted to come in. When
Mavis answered it, Milan entered. She seemed
uncharacteristically forlorn, not even bother-

ing to ask Mavis how she looked. After speaking to Mary Paige, Milan crossed to the sofa and sat down, saying that the thing she had worried about for twenty years had finally happened. Her voice sounded numb and defeated as she told them how Wood had gone to see Duff and come home at 3 A.M. Because of the unbelievable fluke of Elizabeth's meeting Luke at college, Wood and Duff had now found the impetus they needed in order to live out their long-harbored desires. Milan almost felt she was fighting destiny. What she actually said was that Elizabeth should have gone to Vanderbilt, but that's what she meant.

Mavis tried to console her, when Milan suddenly got up. "It's so dark in here. Why don't you all turn on some lights?" Then she crossed to a lamp and did so, noticing the dinner.

"Wow." She looked at Mary Paige. "She fixes me spaghetti." Then she began studying Mavis. "My God, you've got on makeup. Who did that?"

"I did."

"Why didn't you call me? It looks liked you put that concealer on with a putty knife."

"What's concealer?"

Milan rolled her eyes to Mary Paige. "Hopeless."

Now both Mary Paige and Mavis were staring at her and Milan was getting a strange feeling that she should leave. Later, as she walked to her car, she was thinking that not since she was a little girl had she felt so utterly left out and alone.

Once Mary Paige and Mavis were in her old four-poster bed, they held each other, watching the moon come up and not even letting go when Chester jumped up and lay down beside them. From time to time, during the night, each one awakened and said things that she wanted the other to know. Mavis told Mary Paige that aside from a few clumsy experiences in college, she had never been with another woman before this, though she had known since she was a teenager that she wanted to. And Mary Paige told Mavis about her only other love, her roommate in the Philippines, who had tragically died of ovarian cancer.

Then they enumerated their dreams, one by one, as they held hands and rubbed Chester, who was lying on his back with all fours in the air. And after a while, each dream seemed not to belong to either woman anymore, but rather to both of them—what they should name the baby and all about Mary Paige's hero, Lottie Moon, the great woman missionary who gave her life for Christ in China and how they might start a little church of their own someday, combining the two things they were good at—Christianity and food. Mavis got up and crossed to her dresser, returning with a gold cross that had a small globe in the center with some sand in it that Jesus was supposed to have walked on. Lena Farnham Stokes had brought this to her from the Holy Land because Mavis was having such a hard time after her daddy died. She slipped it around Mary Paige's neck and kissed her, a sweet tender kiss that had in it the promise of all the words that had just been spoken, with Mavis thinking that wherever Mary Paige went from now on, she would go, too. And with Mary Paige saying a prayer of thanks that she was finally home.

Three long rows of first graders were lined up next to a fake green Christmas tree in the Pleasant Valley Villa cafeteria. The six-year-olds were there, as they were each year, to put on a show. Only this year, Judith Nutter

had insisted on a half-hour orientation be-
forehand in which she personally briefed the
children on how to act around the elderly as
well as why there was no reason to be
afraid. The last point must have struck home
because most of them were now looking
around while they sang, picking their noses,
scratching, and yawning as though they
were bored out of their skulls.

Afterward, there was cake and punch, enjoyed by all, because these little ones were
still too young to have caught on to the idea
that old people have no value. These children would actually laugh and kid around
and even sit attentively listening to a story or
two if some newly stagestruck geriatric soul
came alive long enough to tell it. It reminded
some of the more clear-thinking old folks of
how things used to be—children sitting and
listening to their grandparents' wisdom or,
even in the lack of it, picking up valuable tips,
remedies, and shortcuts that might not be
gotten anywhere else. It didn't make any
sense to seniors that just at the moment you
knew the most you would ever know, nobody
wanted to talk to you anymore. But what really rankled was when their own grandchildren graced them with a little ten-minute visit

and then acted as though they were going straight to heaven for it. Often, a grandma or grandpa would wait all day for a visit from one of these youngsters who, while being driven to a crushing array of appointments, rode in the backseats of cars like little heads of state. And when they did finally show up, it was their elders who had to keep things going, asking questions of young, disinterested faces that seemed dazed from too much attention, too many toys and time-outs. And their parents, the baby boomers and yuppies, seemed to think this was all just fine and that their own parents, the World War II people, were just fine with it—when in fact, though they didn't say so, the World War II people didn't think it was fine at all. And a few were even starting to wonder if maybe they hadn't sacrificed too much for their own children, if these adult offspring couldn't raise more considerate, less self-involved human beings than this.

After the music and refreshments, the tiny carolers had left, holding hands, two by two, and you could see how the sweetness of it all affected the old people. Certainly Serious West had smiled at Miss Delaney in a way that told her if they were six years old again, he would sure be holding her hand in that line. And the others were probably thinking that it wasn't so very long ago they themselves had walked in a line, two by two, and then, if they were lucky, gone home to their warm houses where their mothers gave them something good to eat and put them in their beds and felt their foreheads for fever and listened to their prayers. That was the shame of it—that old people needed their parents as much as babies and little kids do, but what they got was Judith Nutter and her five stages of grieving seminar, which almost no one attended, because frankly, most people felt one stage was enough.

It would be hard to know if it was the joyfulness of the children or the fact that Christmas was almost upon them, but Serious West had already made up his mind that tonight, he was going to hold Miss Delaney in his arms and kiss her and he hoped that she was going to kiss him back. Because they lived in the assisted-living section of Pleasant Valley, Miss Delaney and Serious came and went as they pleased. And the fact that her front door stood not more than five feet from his own had made his recent social forays into her world so much easier—five feet being the shortest distance that a black man has ever traveled to call on a white woman in Paris, Arkansas. Most who knew of these visits assumed the old English teacher was regaling the ex-lawman with her knowledge of literature, probably assigning him a book or two to read or something.

But Miss Lena Farnham Stokes, who lay about and languished as attractively as she could on the scaled-down movie set next door, had other ideas. She had seen the way Serious West looked at Margaret Delaney and she thought Tolstoy was the last thing he had on his mind. Which is why she kept her television off on the nights Serious visited, so she could monitor his arrival and departure—and also why, in spite of being half-deaf, she held a juice glass up to the wall, but was unable to hear anything except a noise that sounded a little like the wind.

Anyway, this night, Miss Delaney was in fact reading a book and listening to *La Traviata* on her CD player. She remained, even at seventy-nine, childishly astonished by the versatility of not only language, but also the musical scale. Astonished that after thousands of years, words and music could still be gathered into exquisite, artful arrangements that have never been thought of, expressed, or heard before. It was miraculous. Divine. And sometimes, when she came across a thought of such searing beauty and importance say, in a novel, then she would have to stop and put that book down, lay a hand on the middle of her chest, close her eyes, and just take it in. Then she would let out a sigh, almost of relief, that such things could still be absorbed in a world where TV reality shows allotted a full hour to finding out who peed in the camp.

A little later, Miss Delaney and Serious West were seated on her sofa watching the last scene of *The French Connection*. She had spotted in the paper that this movie would be shown tonight and, knowing how much Serious liked it, invited him to watch it again.

Now a perfume commercial had started and Miss Delaney, who was wearing her best long velour robe with the pretty sash in front, had gotten up to clear the coffee cups. But Serious had taken her hand and pulled her back down beside him. They sat for a minute, watching the couple in the ad, who looked emaciated and cold and mean—like they were incapable of loving anyone but themselves. They were kissing, but you could tell each would leave the other in a minute, if one of them got old or sick or ugly, and that the power of perfume would never be enough to keep them together.

Then Serious had picked up the remote with his good arm and clicked it off. He turned to Miss Delaney with as much deliberation as he might have used to deal with someone he had just taken into custody. And he said, "Margaret, I sure would like to kiss you. Now, I know how most people around here would feel about that, but I'm only interested in how you might feel."

She looked at him, a little dumbstruck. Then she said, "Well, I believe I would feel . . . honored."

That was when Serious took her in his arms and kissed her powerfully and hungrily—not like an old man, but rather like a man who has had a lot of experience doing such things but has not done them for a long time. They must've kissed for a good ten minutes before he untied her robe and rubbed his palm gently across the front of her. Pretty soon he put both his hands on her bare bottom and rubbed it good, too, and patted it. Miss Delaney couldn't help marveling how these Golden Glove hands, which had taken their toll on men and handled so expertly the ones who beat their wives, could be so kind to women. After that Serious used his long, graceful fingers, gently fondling her private parts like he would the soft folds of a favorite old cap. He did this for a long while, too, and the fact that his once powerful arm trembled only intensified her sensation. Then, he put his wide, generous mouth over hers at the exact moment she groaned with pleasure—allowing her, finally, gloriously, to add her own voice to the chorus of ecstatic lovers heard throughout her fifty years of teaching poetry. It would be the first time. But it would not be the last.

Wood and Jeter were in Fort Belvedere Christmas shopping. This was something they did together every year, since most of the good stores in Paris were gone and also because they refused to frequent the Paris County Fed-Mart Superstore. Brundidge had, at one time, been invited to go with them but had since been eliminated because of his incessant scorning of their selections and because he took too much time with his own. Wood and Jeter knew what they wanted from almost the moment they entered a store. They did not wander around aimlessly looking at merchandise.

Wood was already in a bad mood, in anticipation of the coming weekend's Christmas party for the Laniers. Sometimes he just sat in awe and wonderment that his wife could've sprung from such people. Milan seemed as out of place in their presence as Snow White standing in the middle of a bunch of chimps. He particularly dreaded how the Laniers spoke endlessly of celebrities, as though they were on intimate terms with them. And how they would interrupt dinner just to watch something like the *Celine Dion Christmas Special,* during which one of Milan's sisters might say to Wood, "You know, they say her dressing room is an exact replica of her house. And I think that's wonderful. I'm all for that, aren't you?" And then, horribly, he would have to answer.

Now Wood and Jeter were at a jewelry counter. Wood was holding a long mesh chain with a pendant that had an emerald in the middle.

"What do you think?"

Jeter said, pointedly, "For who?"

Wood was annoyed. "Who do you think?"

Jeter looked at the emerald. "I don't think it's enough."

Wood rolled his eyes and bought it anyway. His cell phone went off as he was paying. He answered it. On the other end was the one who wasn't getting an emerald. She was crying. Something about Dennis Childs, who, after being served with divorce papers, had come over and beaten her up. Excelsior Springs was closer to Fort Belvedere than to Paris and they made it in less than an hour. Jeter waited in the van while Wood went inside.

It wasn't long before a good-looking man pulled up in an old Corvette and got out. He stared at Jeter and then went inside. In a little while, the man came back out. The pocket on his jacket was torn and he was holding his side. He fished for some keys and then sort of staggered to his car and left. After that, Wood came out, too. When he opened the door, Jeter saw that his eye was swollen and there was blood on his shirt. Wood reached across the car seat and picked up the box with the emerald pendant in it. Jeter looked straight at him.

Wood let out a long sigh. "Nothing's changed. I'm the same person I've always been. Except that I'm insane." Then he closed the door and limped back inside.

On the way home, after they had gone about a hundred miles, Jeter said, almost to himself, "See, here's the thing. It's not just you having an affair. Now we're all having an affair . . . only you're the only one gettin' laid."

Wood looked at him in the rearview mirror but pretended not to hear.

A few days before Christmas, Ione Falkoff died, adding more sadness to the upcoming holiday. Milan was especially devastated by this news, because the ninety-year-old former owner of Falkoff's Drugstore had, like Pauline Jeter and Sidney Garfinkel, helped her survive adolescence. Many mornings before attending high school and always before special occasions, Milan would stop by Falkoff's makeup counter and use all the available free samples. Long before she was rendered obsolete by Fed-mart, Ione, who understood Milan's dire situation, acted as though she was a real customer, showing her new beauty products and pretending like she might actually buy something someday. Because Milan had loved a particular perfume named "Lilac," Ione made sure that a bottle was always left sitting out. And that's why on Christmas morning, Milan got up early, drove to the newest grave in Whispering Pines, and left, amid all the poinsettias and holly wreaths, a splendid array of that very flower.

The rest of the day came and went with less fanfare than usual. The McIlmore house was lit up like Milan's old fire baton, as though light might be an antidote to uncertainty. But inside, the two adults who lived there hardly spoke. Even the Laniers seemed more subdued than normal. Frank didn't even bother to entertain the children by pulling cigarettes out of his ears. Elizabeth and Luke went to Florida to visit the Duffers and Charlie stayed mostly in his room. Wood told everyone that his black eye was the result of having run into a door. But Milan never even asked about it. It was as though he could come home now with a spear stuck clean through him and she would only regard him a little curiously and then move on. Even when he had given her a lovely sapphire ring, which was much more expensive than the emerald pendant, she had pushed it back across the breakfast table and said, "Thank you. But I really can't accept this now. Maybe you can return it."

Not "Why don't you let your whore wear it while you're screwing her?" Or "What's wrong? Doesn't your little hoochie like sapphires?" But simply "Maybe you can return it."

It was so mature and decent. And he almost hated her for the way she was now killing him.

Chapter 18

Charlotte Rampling was returning to Arkansas. And not just for the purpose of fulfilling some forbidden Dogpatch sex fantasy either. Brundidge had already visited her in New York and it had gone better than she could've imagined. Her friends had been intrigued and amused by him, and he had taken her to several of his favorite spots, including a wonderful little restaurant named Erminia that she hadn't even known about.

Now they were on the interstate between

Little Rock and Paris and he was giving her instructions.

"Okay, when we get there, you're gonna stay in Cake's room. Cake's gonna stay with Lily."

"Why can't I stay with you?"

"Because I'm a father, Charlotte. I don't have women spend the night in front of my little girls."

"Okay. All right."

"Geez, it's like you were raised by wolves. I can't even believe you went to a good school."

"I'm sorry, they don't teach that at Smith."

He put an arm around her. "It's okay. You're in Arkansas now. We'll help you."

Later Brundidge sat her suitcase down in the middle of a bedroom that was mostly pink, except for the huge mural on the wall. "Girls, this is Miss Rampling."

She shook their hands. "I'm Charlotte."

He corrected her. "No, you're Miss Rampling. They don't call adults by their first name."

"Oh. Well, in that case, I'm Ms. Rampling."

Brundidge shook his head. "I'm sorry. They don't say Ms. either, because it sounds stupid. Cake, you need to straighten up all your animals on that bed."

Cake said, "What's wrong with them?"

"What's wrong is they ain't got no feng shui."

Lily studied Charlotte. "How old are you?"

"I'm thirty-three. How old are you?"

"Seven. You want some gum?"

"What kind is it?"

"Sugarless. It's the only kind he lets us have."

Charlotte looked at Brundidge. "That's mean."

"There has to be rules, Charlotte, or the whole fabric of society breaks down."

Cake and Lily were sitting on the bed, chewing their gum, watching Charlotte put on a little mascara.

Finally, Lily said, "Your eyes are pretty."

"So are yours."

Lily ran to her. "Do me." She turned her face up toward Charlotte, who dabbed her lashes with the wand, "Okay, hold still. I like your braid."

"Dad did it. He's got a whole book just on knots."

Now the girls were vying for her attention.

Cake said, "Are you interested in America, Miss Rampling?"

Charlotte thought for a minute. "Yes, I'd say I am."

Cake gestured toward the mural. "Tommy Epps painted our bedroom walls. He's a real artist."

Charlotte went over and studied it. There were no fairy tales or Winnie the Pooh characters here, but rather ten or fifteen significant historical events represented in some fashion. And Cake Brundidge was in the middle of all of them. And not just helping Betsy Ross sew a flag, either, but riding on the back of Paul Revere's horse and serving as the engineer for the Underground Railroad and doing a cartwheel next to the marines as they planted the flag at Iwo Jima.

Cake explained, "I wasn't really there. He just put me in it 'cause my daddy paid him to."

Charlotte said, still taking it in, "Very impressive."

Lily was lying on her back, with smudged mascara, playing with a gum wrapper. "I wish mine was all dogs."

Cake shrugged to Charlotte. "She's young.

She doesn't understand the meaning of history."

Brundidge was driving toward the McIll-mores' New Year's Eve party when Charlotte said, "So, you were a teacher?"

"Yeah. I had to quit when my parents got sick so I could take over the business." He said it nonchalantly, but the truth was it had almost killed him. Before his daughters, teaching had been Brundidge's greatest passion. He was the first one to arrive at school each morning and the last one to leave. And he had raised legendary amounts of money for historical field trips. His only flaw was that he cared too much, annoying some parents by sending home letters that said things like, "Are you aware that your child, in a recent pop quiz, has indicated that she thinks the Gold Rush is the name of a jewelry store, does not know why 407,000 Americans died for her in World War II, and hasn't a clue as to what continent she's living on? If we do not act soon, the children of Paris, Arkansas, may become as ignorant as children all over the country. Sincerely, E. B. Brundidge."

Charlotte was talking now. Something about his sweater. "I understand you only wear that one if you really like somebody. Is that right?"

"Is that what they told you?" She nodded. He laughed, shaking his head. "Well, that's not good."

For the first time ever, the McIlmores' New Year's Eve party was a bust. From the moment it began, you could sense the unease, as well as the disciplined hospitality. Duff had shown up unexpectedly with Luke and Elizabeth, looking more beautiful than Milan or Wood could ever remember. She said Luke had talked her into coming at the last minute, insisting that she needed to bring in the New Year with her son and future daughter-in-law and all her old friends. She told this story all night, each time throwing her arms around Luke and saying, "Isn't he the most divine thing you've ever seen? If I wasn't his mother, I'd date him myself."

Charlotte, who had taken an immediate dislike to Duff, could almost picture Freud slobbering on her.

For her part, Milan holed up in Wood's den for most of the night with Jeter. And Brundidge, for the first New Year's ever, did not do his Elvis impression because the idiot kid at the Little Rock costume shop had forgotten to hold Black Leather Elvis, which Brundidge had always rented, leaving only fat Vegas Elvis, which Brundidge hated. Anyway, too many people had done Elvis now and ruined it for him. Not to mention, no one was in the mood. Sadly, there was not even a rendition of Frank Sinatra's "Here's to the Winners," because Wood had said he did not feel up to it.

Charlotte, being a fresh arrival, asked if Wood and Duff were having an affair. And Brundidge lied that he wouldn't know, because romantic men do not talk about their affairs with women. That's just a rule. And then Charlotte wanted to know if Brundidge was a romantic man. And he told her that he was. At midnight, he kissed her in a way that proved it.

Then he broke another twenty-year tradition by leaving the party early. A few miles later, he and Charlotte were standing in the middle of his warehouse. Thousands of bottles of wine and liquor and beer lined the shelves and walls. She was impressed.

"Wow! What are you? Some kind of moonshiner?"

"Yeah. That's me. A moonshiner. Come here." He held her, burying his face in her hair. Then he led her into his office, which was literally covered with hundreds of trophies and photographs and all sorts of civic plaques.

"You know why we're here?"

"Yes. Because you're trying to have sex with me, away from your house."

"No. Because I'm trying to make love to you." He nibbled her neck. "'Cause I can't wait any longer. You're just so damn pretty and smart and when I watch how you handle yourself and the way you talk to people, it turns me on."

He was undressing her now and smiling. "I was gonna have a lot of candles here but I have twenty years of safety awards from the fire department."

He continued folding her clothes neatly and putting them on his desk, stopping only occasionally to kiss her. "Anyway, I like you. I like you a lot."

She stiffened a little. "I like you, too. But I don't think I'm ready—"

He said good-naturedly, "Hey, shut up, okay? I didn't say I love you. I said I like you. If and when I love you, I'll let you know."

When she was naked, he began removing his own pants and shorts and gingerly centered them across the arm of a chair.

"Then you can say, 'Well, hell, I was just using you for my exotic, hillbilly boy toy. I didn't know you were gonna go and get all serious on me.' And that'll be okay, too. And you know why? 'Cause I'll still be the one with the killer food and the comfortable chairs . . . who got to make love to the greatest woman in the world."

She was thinking that he looked terribly appealing in his freshly starched shirt and Missoni sweater mixed with all the pastels of an impressionist picnic and no bottoms. She gave him a beautiful white smile, which, along with her bobbed hair, put him in mind of the last thing she would ever be, a naked cheerleader. They made serious love till dawn and then went home and fell into their respective beds, where Charlotte stared at the wall and worried that the father of the little girl jumping up and down on the moon was slowly reeling her in.

Milan was back at Doe's, having lunch with Mavis.

"I can't believe those eyebrows are already growing out. I've got some wax in my purse. I'll heat it up in the microwave."

"I don't want you heating up wax here. Anyway, my eyebrows are not your business."

"Yes, they are. Any woman I love who has hair on her face is my business."

Mavis sighed. Milan shrugged. "Okay. Grow a unibrow. I don't care." She hesitated, then, "I wasn't gonna say anything, but maybe I should."

She waited. Mavis waited, too.

Then, "There's a rumor going around town that you're a lesbian."

Rudy, who was passing by, let out a half a guffaw before he caught himself.

Milan flipped open her compact and reapplied her lipstick. "Of course, you probably have Harlan Pillow to thank for that one. And here's the real kicker. I even heard,"— she pressed her lips together evening out the mocha color—"that I was your girlfriend."

Mavis, genuinely shocked, started to laugh. "Stop!"

Milan laughed, too. "Can you believe it?"

Mavis shook her head, laughing harder. "You . . . and me?"

"That's what they're saying—"

"Oh my God. That's just too—that's the funniest thing I ever heard!" Now Mavis was pounding the table, gasping for air.

Suddenly, Milan stopped laughing. "Okay. Now you're starting to hurt my feelings."

Mavis collected herself. Then there was a long silence while her eyes filled up with all the hope that she had tried to keep in check for most of her life. Finally, her voice came loud and clear as though she was in a play and these were words that she was trying out for the first time. "Milan. I am a lesbian. And I'm in love with Mary Paige." Mavis had thought she would feel like someone else once she said this, but strangely she still felt like herself.

Milan sat very still. Then she said, "That's not true."

"Yes, it is."

Milan shifted in her chair a little, then, "I want you to stop this. It's not funny. You're scaring me."

Mavis took her hand. "I don't mean to."

They stayed like that without speaking, the fragility of what was at stake caught in their breath. After a while, Milan's shoulders slumped and she began to weep a little.

"Why does everyone keep changing on me? I just wish everyone would stop changing."

Mavis got up and knelt down beside her. "I know it's hard. But I'm still who I was."

"Oh my God. How can you say that, when it was all a lie?" Her voice was suddenly cracked and tired. "How could I not have seen this? All these years of being best friends, you couldn't have said, 'Oh, by the way, I like girls?'"

Mavis said, "I wanted to tell you, so bad. At first, I was afraid that you would hate me. And then later, I was afraid because . . ."

"What?"

Mavis hesitated. "I don't know. I guess because you taught Sunday school."

Milan took this in. Then she stood up, shaking. "You know, I'm starting to think maybe I'm the one nobody knows around here."

Mavis stood up, too. "It's only a small part of who I am. It doesn't have to change things."

Milan looked into the plain, wide face that she had been telling her deepest secrets to since she was six years old. "No, it doesn't have to, but I'm pretty sure it already has."

Then she covered her eyes with her sunglasses. "And it's too bad, because you didn't even give me a chance. I might have surprised you. Now you'll never know."

CHAPTER 19

Charlie McIlmore made good on his promise. At Thanksgiving, he had told Miss Delaney and Brundidge that he would take them to a rap concert. Brundidge, who had tried without success to get his money back, had said it was the most appalling entertainment experience of his entire life. But Miss Delaney was now lying in her bed, listening to her new CD and thinking about the young black rappers who had sent her mind reeling. (She had even told Serious that she was too tired for their usual hot tea and whiskey nightcap.) Almost none of the singers and musicians who so captivated her students over five decades had intrigued her ear at all. But this was something completely different. She had never heard anything like this before in her life.

Yes, she'd caught bits and pieces of rap on her radio, but it had only made her angry—the vulgarity (as much as she could understand) and the lack of form. And even worse, she had seen one of these hip-hop characters on her television, standing in front of his multimillion-dollar, empty mansion. "This be my Escalade. This be my Bentley. This be my Jacuzzi where it all happens, dog." She had felt outraged that a society that had failed to educate these children was now throwing money at them and telling them that their little poem was really good. "Don't wanna suck on your sweet li'l thing. Just wanna do you doggie 'cause I'm the Bonin' King." But she knew if white educators like herself criticized it, then the money-grubbers would say, "Well, you just don't understand the black experience." Black experience? "I'm the Bonin' King." Where were Langston Hughes and Maya Angelou? What might these young street artists come up with if you laid a little Maya or Langston on them? That was her thought at one time and then she had forgotten about it until the concert, which was electrifying. And she had been right there in the middle of it—the charged-up people and the way they began moving and chanting to the exotic, erotic, hypnotic drumbeat that started on the stage and then drifted out across the audience, engulfing them in its easy, swampy vibe. And then there were the rappers themselves, who had at first seemed powerful and frightening, but somehow, before it was over, had shown her a sweetness inside of themselves and a depth of despair she had seldom seen in people so young. They railed about the things that poets have always railed about, the absence or presence of love—and also about the women who had given them life and then denied them the sustenance to maintain it and the grandmother who had pulled them back from the urban cliff, lifted them up, and breathed her own strength into their lungs, because strength was all she had.

This was heart outside the body truthtelling—"No matter how gangsta you are, you need that mama love." And then on top of the sweetness and the unmet need, there was rage. Miss Delaney was knocked out! It was the rage of Dylan Thomas, only born of the black experience. What might these ranting ghetto dreamers come up with if they actually read Dylan Thomas? Or Shelley or

Byron? Or even Henry Wadsworth Longfel-
low, the American rock star of his day. What
she would give to be teaching again, to have
a crack at these best of young people who
had been left behind, who were now telling
the truth of their lives but had not been given
the tools to do it with. So that all you had to
go on were these glimpses of raw genius
and promise. But sometimes a glimpse was
enough. And sometimes, as Margaret Delaney had once taught her students (and not
without controversy), even vulgarity is legiti-
mate—the rebel muscle of *Catcher in the
Rye* youth, flexing itself. And these rappers
were powerful, primal, and pissed, as they
skulked and strutted to a drumbeat that
seemed not to come from fifty-foot speakers,
but from Africa itself. "You brought us here.
It's been hundreds of years. You're out of
time." Miss Delaney had been thunderstruck
by the power and audaciousness of it. You
could hear in their awkward, righteous
tomes the voices of people who had been
chased like dogs, exploited, beaten, and
lynched. And these are the grandchildren,
who carry not shovels and dishrags, but
boom boxes—who have figured out that talking is even more powerful than singing and

playing basketball or winning the Golden Gloves. Have figured out that truth-telling to the drumbeat of their ancestors is exhilarating and profit-making and race-building. And what Miss Delaney was thinking, was, that if these children ever get books, *they can rule the world.*

After a while, she put on her robe and gathered up her CD player and carried it to a door across the hall. A door that had been closed for too long. This particular rap was something she wanted Serious West to hear. A few minutes later, she was sitting next to him on his bed. The CD was playing and she was telling him how she felt about it. Serious was lying on his side, taking her in and trying to picture her at the concert. As she spoke, she noticed his eyes were growing soft.

"What is it, Serious?"

"Nothing. You're just crazy, that's all. And I was wishing I was twenty years old so I had longer to love you."

She took his large, sweeping hand and held it to her cheek. Then she stretched herself along the full length of him. They had not spent a night together, ever. And for some reason, she was thinking that they should.

Or maybe it was just the need for this white
woman to lie in the arms of this black man
tonight, and have him hold her tenderly and
kiss her, as they experienced this mysterious and powerful new music together. So
that at least she might be reassured that
they and their kind were not yet lost from
one another.

Milan was in her garage, using a hair dryer
to defrost an old freezer that belonged to
Wood's grandparents. It was the kind of
thing she often did when she was upset. And
this morning, she had been up since 4 A.M.,
beating her rugs and cleaning out her cup-
boards. But so far, no amount of activity had
been able to quell the disturbing notion that
she was no longer in charge of her own life.

　　How could her dearest and truest friend
have failed to tell her one of the most funda-
mental pieces of information that one can
know about another human being? A little
thing? Was Mavis serious? They had been
sleeping together and putting suntan lotion
on each other's backs for thirty years. And
not once had Mavis ever had the presence
of mind to say that she was gay. Anyway,
what the hell was she doing, coming out

now? Just as Milan was losing her daughter
and trying valiantly to hold on to her marriage. Wood was already the talk of the town
and now, with Mavis's new revelation, it was
just a matter of time before someone came
up with the notion that Wood had left Milan
for Duff because Milan was sweet on
women, too. That's how information worked
in a small town. A few facts got seasoned
and rolled around and puffed up until they
became a big story that suited everybody's
liking. A story that wouldn't even faze Wood
or Mavis. The truth was he was too spoiled
and she, too insensitive, to give a damn
what people thought. But Milan did. She
didn't have the luxury of driving golf carts
into the pond at the country club or publicly
dating women. She knew and had always
known that with her, it was one false move
and she was out. Or at least that was the
feeling that always settled in, once she arrived somewhere good.

She had wanted to be brave. That's why
she had pretended to Mavis that she
would've been fine with the liking girls thing.
That simply not being told earlier was what
hurt. But Milan knew that wasn't true. She
wasn't fine with it. It was strange and new

and embarrassing, and she couldn't even fathom her lifelong friend dancing in the arms of another woman and meaning it. And that's why she was mad, why she was now chipping the last piece of ice with the tip of the dryer and blowing it to smithereens. Because Mavis had seen straight into her heart and called it right.

It was still early morning at Pleasant Valley and Judith Nutter was seated at her desk, weeping. An efficient woman, she usually cried only about things that pertained directly to her, but today, that was just half true. Rudy had arrived for work around six and found Tommy Epps frozen to death in the snow. The sometime artist was lying just outside the window to the maintenance room, the one the staff left open for him and the one he always climbed through when he was ready to go to sleep. Rudy checked the window and discovered that it was locked. Then he saw the empty whiskey bottle in the pocket of the Michael Kors shearling coat and decided that Tommy had been too drunk to figure out what to do. (He didn't like to stay at the bus station or the truck stop because he had been beaten up there by strangers.)

Now the entire nursing home and the town were in an uproar. Judith Nutter had decided to start locking the window because she did not want vagrants sleeping in the maintenance room, but she had failed to tell Tommy about it. Certainly, she felt badly about what happened, but this was obviously a young man who was deeply troubled. Some of the old folks agreed that he was indeed troubled, adding that was why they had left the window open for him.

Tommy was a true son of Paris. He had grown up here. People knew that he was a crazy misfit, but he was their crazy misfit. Like his counterpart in other small towns, they felt that he belonged to them. And now Judith Nutter had killed him with her arrogance and efficient ways. Even Serious West, who was the resident diplomat, could not help her on this one. Besides, he and Margaret Delaney had been offended when Judith had offered to convene a seminar on interracial relationships because she was getting a lot of questions about theirs.

Judith had spent a good deal of the morning wondering what she should do. She hadn't intended to kill anyone, but after all, she did have a responsibility to protect the residents and their possessions. Maybe she would call for a state regulatory commission to investigate this incident and then make new recommendations after determining what went wrong. Another option would be to have a panel discussion among the residents themselves. Or she could reach out to the community and put together a town meeting. Until Serious West had finally said, "Why don't you just say you're sorry?"

Brundidge paid for the funeral, just as he had always paid for Tommy's expenses. He told Cotrell's they could go ahead and bury Tommy in the Canali suit jacket that Brundidge had given him, adding that they might as well let him wear his old sweatpants too, which Tommy would be more comfortable in. At the service, Brundidge and Wood served as pallbearers and Miss Delaney read a passage from the Bible. Afterward, there was so much hostility directed at Judith Nutter that she ended up making the very first appointment with someone who had been twiddling his thumbs for months—the grief counselor.

For weeks, a pall hung over the residents of Pleasant Valley. They couldn't seem to shake off the idea that someone they had known, a person who was mentally ill, had been left out in the snow to die, and only a few yards from where they all slept. It didn't make any sense. What was so hard about leaving a window open that had been left open for years? They felt they didn't understand the world anymore or anything in it. This strange new place where rules took precedence over common sense and committees were formed to deduce things that children would know. Where people told all their secrets on national talk shows and appeared on the covers of magazines, not for their strengths, but their weaknesses. Where even criminals had no honor now, but killed people just for the fun of it and destroyed things simply because they were there. These old people were glad to be going deaf so they couldn't hear the songs that no one could hum. They were happy not to have cars, because there was no one left to put the gas in. And they seldom made phone calls anymore, because what they mostly got were recordings. Unbelievably, some had even switched off their television sets, giving up one of their last bridges to the outside world, because they could no longer comprehend the things that were on it, and especially not the girls who looked like Mary Tyler Moore but had semen on their faces.

Mavis and her dog, Chester, were in the kitchen, watching Brundidge savor the last bite of his apple-walnut pancakes. He was absentmindedly humming some juggling music from the old *Ed Sullivan Show,* a habit that drove Mavis crazy. Finally, when he was finished, he turned his fork over, the way Miss Phipps had taught him to. Then Mavis said, "I have something to tell you."

"Damn. I knew there was somethin' going on when you invited me over here for breakfast."

"I'm a lesbian."

He stared at her for a long time, then, "What in the hell do you want to go and do that for?"

"Because it's who I am. Until now I never had the courage to say so."

Brundidge let out a long sigh.

"Well, that's just great. Now we got one more thing that's gonna be fucked up. When did this happen?"

"It's always been true."

"Oh, man. Now you're gonna bring your girlfriend over to my house and I have to explain to my little girls how you're just like everybody else except nobody wants to be friends with Mr. Penis and then we're gonna have to go out and buy some stupid book called *Jeremy Has Two Mommies* and sit around and discuss it."

Ordinarily, she would've been fascinated by his colossal insensitivity, but not about this.

Her voice was trembling. "Okay, thanks. I just wanted you to know."

Now he could see that she was hurt. He opened an arm to her. "Well, come on. Come here. You don't have to get all *Glass Menagerie* on me—"

"You know, this was very hard."

"Okay, well, just shut up and let me give you a hug. Come 'ere." He did so, then, "You big ol' . . . lesbian."

Mavis broke away. "That's it. Get out."

"Hey, it's a joke."

"Well, it's offensive."

"Well, I'm sorry, but you just sprung this on me. I mean, give me time to shit or go blind here. What if I told you after forty years that I was queer?"

They regarded each other for a moment, then she asked sincerely, "You really had no idea?"

"Hell, no. I just thought you were . . . I don't know what I thought. I just know you always gotta take everything too far."

"You have absolutely no understanding of this, do you?"

"I get it, okay? I just don't do well with weird stuff."

"Why do you have to call it weird?"

"Because it is weird. It's not regular. Now I'll be imagining you lying around naked in bed with some girl."

She studied him for a moment. "I thought you men liked thinking about lesbians."

"Yeah. That's right. But not you and some big ol' missionary girl."

Mavis shook her head. "You know, it's funny, but I can't even remember now why we ever became friends."

He was starting to get mad. "Well, I'll tell you why. Because I've spent about half my life doin' stuff for you, including hauling around . . ." He sputtered, ". . . a bunch of baby juice and, and, all those discount bricks out there for your damn patio!"

"And I've fed you for twenty years! So let's don't go any further with the one-sided friendship crap!"

"No, let's do. If that's how you feel, then send me a damn bill!"

"Just stop it! Okay? Just go."

He started for the door. Then he turned back. "I think this went pretty well. I mean, you know, for somethin' dramatic like this. Just getting it all out on the table. That's the hard part."

She mulled this over. "Yeah. I guess it coulda been worse."

He laughed a little to himself. "Could've been a lot worse." He put his hands in his pockets. "At least we can still watch the Miss America Pageant together."

She smiled a little. "Right."

He opened the door and left. She sat back down and picked up a small notebook and turned to a page that contained a list of names. At the top, scrawled in large letters, were the words, "People to Tell." When she came to Brundidge's name, she drew a thick line through it.

In February, Rudy and Mary Paige threw a surprise shower for Mavis, to which about a half dozen of the most forward-thinking women in Paris and all the homosexual men

were invited. Right after Wood had determined that the baby would be a girl, Elizabeth went out and found a perfect old
clothbound version of *Huck Finn,* the same
gift her father had once given to her. And Milan, who claimed to be under the weather,
sent along a wonderfully huge English pram,
while Rudy spent a whole week's salary on a
baby bed, for which Dwight and Denny fashioned an over-the-top silk canopy made of
flowers and ribbon.

Duff, who had learned about the shower
from Elizabeth, mailed a card that said a
tree had been planted in the baby's honor in
some woods that had once been stripped.
Rudy and the two florists, who missed Milan,
simply could not get over this, asking party
attendees, whenever the opportunity arose,
"What in the world does a baby want with a
tree?"

It was spring and Sidney and Slim were
walking along the road to Fast Deer Farm,
having just entered Casablanca. In spite of
several months of dismal Arkansas weather,
they had made good time and today the sun
was out. Slim was actually beginning to enjoy the stories of pirates and the descriptions

of art deco influence on Moorish architecture, and she was even a little fascinated to learn that (Humphrey Bogart and Ingrid Bergman aside) Sidney had found Casablanca to be singularly unromantic. This led to a discussion of whether Slim was prettier than Ingrid Bergman, with Sidney insisting that, indeed, she was. Then Slim, who rarely said anything, told him she wasn't going to walk with him anymore if he was going to spout such ridiculous nonsense. And anyway, she had warned him about flirting. Sidney countered that she could call it flirting if she wanted, but that he was not going to stop speaking the truth. And that nothing could make him admit that Ingrid Bergman looked better than Slim. That he would rather die first than say it. And this made her laugh a little, an event he found so noteworthy, that he got out his small map and made a notation that she had done so outside the Mosque of Hassan II, whose minaret contains laser beam lights that shine toward Mecca (this in celebration of Slim laughing).

And then Sidney added that even though he was getting tired of doing all the talking, this fact would not discourage him from continuing their journey and that she had better

get ready, because when they got to Marrakech, he was going to make her laugh
again. Slim was looking at him now and
thinking that she had her doubts about that,
but certainly not his charm.

Chapter 20

Charlotte and Brundidge and the girls were
the first to arrive at the Champanelle River.
Once there, they set up a cabana, Brundidge's state-of-the-art grill, and every modern amenity known to campers. Charlotte
had never been camping or spent a day in
the wilderness and seemed alternately put
off and fascinated by all of it. On the way
there, they had passed a yard full of tomb-
stones with a sign advertising "Fresh Walnuts and Monuments." Charlotte simply
could not grasp a reason why these two
commodities would be sold together. Brundidge said it was common practice for country people to sell unrelated items. But
Charlotte couldn't let it go. "How does that

work? I mean, is it, like, a couple is out driving somewhere and the wife says, 'Oh, by the way, honey, on the way home, let's stop and get some nuts and some headstones for our graves.'"

Brundidge finally said, "I really couldn't tell you."

Later, she declined to spray mosquito repellent on him or his daughters, claiming that both the aerosol button and the liquid were harmful. When they went fishing, though she was excited to catch a bass, she refused to handle something called a crawdad. And Brundidge had to bait her hook for her, wondering out loud how she could eat raw fish if she couldn't even pick it up. Then, when he informed her that they would be staying after dark, she had something akin to a nervous breakdown. A picnic was one thing, but she was not about to stay in these woods at night. Now he was getting impatient.

"There's hardly anybody who lives around here and the ones who do are good people."

He got up and crossed to her, rocking the pontoon, and then bent down, nuzzling her neck. "Come on, can't you open up your heart to just one special hick? For only a few kisses a day, you'll receive a picture of him and his entire illegitimate family and the knowledge that you helped to change their lives forever."

Charlotte pushed him in the river. When he came to the surface, she and his daughters were laughing. That afternoon, after most of the others had arrived, they were treated to something called the Cypress Gardens Water Show. Charlie had come around the bend of the river in Dr. Mac's old speedboat, pulling three "skiers." Jeter, in his wheelchair, was fastened to a custom-made disc, designed by Brundidge, which was connected by a rope to the rear of the boat. He looked deliriously happy and drenched from the spray created by his two best friends, who flanked him, each wearing one ski. As they passed in front of the group, Wood and Brundidge performed a series of elaborate maneuvers, using sweeping feminine gestures like synchronized swimmers, making graceful arches over Jeter's head and then lifting their legs behind them in perfect unison. Most of the others seemed nonplussed by this, but Charlotte and Mary Paige were impressed. Milan explained that Wood's parents had taken him and Jeter

and Brundidge to a waterskiing show in Cypress Gardens, Florida, when they were ten,
and that they had perfected this routine and
been doing it ever since.

Mavis added that it was ridiculous, they'd
had thirty years to work on some new
moves, but instead they just kept doing the
same old things. It was that way with music,
too. They dragged out the same old songs
over and over, singing them unrelentingly
and unmercifully. Because it was tradition,
carrying on about stepping on pop-tops and
blowing out their flip-flops and searching for
their lost shaker of salt. Really, they just
drove everyone crazy. She hoped Charlotte
and Mary Paige would not encourage them.
Mavis was setting the table, wearing a humongous yellow maternity swimsuit with a
pleated skirt and sun hat when she said this
and Mary Paige was watching her, dazzled.

Milan and Mavis, who were still estranged,
had now settled into a kind of banal cordiality when they were all together. This had
happened without any prior discussion, and
though such an arrangement paled in comparison to their old friendship, each woman
was grateful for it.

No sooner had Milan begun spraying for

mosquitoes than Luke and Elizabeth pulled up in the Mustang convertible with Duff in the backseat. When Duff emerged, she immediately spotted Wood and the others and started yelling, "Oh my God! Cypress Gardens! I love it! I haven't seen Cypress Gardens in years!"

She was wearing sandals with little heels, camouflage short shorts and a crisp white linen blouse with the sleeves rolled up, cinched with a leather belt.

Charlotte said, staring, "Didn't those breasts used to be real?"

Mavis was also staring. "My God, she's had them done. How did you know?"

"It's a curse. I'm like a narcotics dog for fake boobs."

Milan, who was now busy putting out Mavis's lamb lollypops, cold couscous salad, and grilled pita bread, turned toward Duff. It was true. Her breasts were larger and riding higher than they had been on her last visit. There was no question she'd had something done. And the way she was striding, confident, with each expertly rounded plastic sphere causing tight folds in her blouse, you could tell she was proud of the effect they were having. Milan was thinking, well, so much for the girl who took her name off the homecoming ballot because she didn't believe in competition.

Oddly, the men didn't seem to notice anything different, except you could tell that they all thought Duff looked good. Milan figured that was typical—men getting the big picture and the women zeroing in immediately on what was really going on here.

Everyone exchanged greetings. Milan hugged Luke and Elizabeth, while Duff continued carrying on about the Cypress Gardens water show, explaining its origin to Luke and acting like she had gone to Florida with the boys herself, until Mavis mumbled that if Duff said just the words "Cypress Gardens Water Show" one more time, she would go into labor.

Charlotte got a beer and handed it to Milan. "Here. I think we may have to get drunk."

Milan smiled, appreciative of the unexpected camaraderie. After lunch, when almost everyone was floating on their inner tubes, Duff was lying straight across hers and not partially curled inside, the way a person who wasn't concerned with showing off her new breast augmentation might do. Mavis looked like a giant kernel of corn in

her tentsize yellow suit, which covered almost every inch of her inner tube as the little
pleats from the skirt hung off to the side and
her swollen abdomen stuck out about two
feet in the air. She and Jeter made a strange
pair of would-be parents, as he lay next to
her with his eyes closed, his skinny al-
abaster body stretched across his own tube
like a stringless marionette, while Mary
Paige swam around happily towing the two
of them. After a while, Jeter opened his
eyes. Mavis said, "It must've been a good
dream. You were smiling."

Jeter, feeling impish, said, "I was swimming the river with the baby on my shoulders. I was going faster and faster and then
all of a sudden . . . oh, forget it."

Mavis was suddenly touched. "What, tell
me. Your legs wouldn't move?"

"No, I won the Olympics. But I was dis-
qualified for having a kid on my back."

Mavis and Mary Paige splashed him. Not
far away, Brundidge and Charlotte were
floating together. Charlotte had never been
on an inner tube and could not get over the
fact that one could just drift along on one of
these old tires and end up in, say, Tennessee. Brundidge was now in the middle of

an old sports story, which Duff had encouraged him to tell, acting as though she had missed hearing it. ". . . So Alabama's beating Vanderbilt 14–2, and old Puddy Horton says [here Brundidge lowers his voice], 'Damnit, I'm gonna steal that son of a bitch's hat.' He stole the Bear's hat! Moonpie Wilson and his friends see him. These are not normal guys. These guys are superhormone enhanced. Puddy jumps on Moonpie's back. Moonpie peels him off and coldcocks him right there."

Duff laughed. Charlotte said with her eyes closed, "That's an incredible story. You really should get that down on paper before you forget it."

Mavis snickered, appreciating this new addition to their ensemble. "That's good, Charlotte. I like that."

Brundidge said to Wood, "That used to be a good story, didn't it?"

Wood mumbled, "I wasn't listening."

Jeter kept his eyes closed, thinking that nothing was what it used to be.

A long metal boat drifted by with loud music coming from a boom box. Charlie was in the rear, casting his fishing line. Luke was seated in the front watching as Elizabeth, looking glorious in her chartreuse bikini, was dancing on top of the center seat. Milan, who was ensconced on the sandbar, watched her daughter go by, wondering if she needed more sunscreen. Wood watched Elizabeth, too, and shook his head, laughing. Brundidge said, "Here comes Cleopatra on her barge with her pubescent male slaves. Now there's a girl with zest. You never see zesty people anymore." Then he trailed off to himself, "Everybody's gotta be cool now . . ." He noticed Milan looking prim and dry, sitting next to her giant stack of bridal magazines. "Looking good over there, Miss Milano." Then he said to the others, "Look at her with all that wedding stuff, would you? The ol' Milano's always got ever'thing under control." She lowered her sunglasses and acknowledged Brundidge, then returned to her magazine, pretending to read.

It was cruel and bizarre, having to socialize with the woman your husband was having an affair with. But in order to protect Elizabeth and Luke, she didn't have any choice. These days Wood was sleeping on the sofa, in the sitting area of the master bedroom in order to keep Charlie from suspecting that anything was wrong. Wood and Milan had never been willing to let their children know that their marriage was anything but good. And for years, they had improbably pulled together a rather fun, raucous family life, filled with friends and good times, in spite of their differences. But now, with an affair mixed in, their façade was growing thin. And Milan didn't yet know what she was going to do about it. Or if she was going to do anything. But she did have a vague idea that once the wedding was over, things were going to shake out one way or the other.

Milan noticed that Charlie had lost his hook on a snag. She watched, suddenly interested, as he began tying a new one to his fishing line. The movement of her son's hands or the way the afternoon light was now on him put her in mind of Tom Lanier and how he had looked just before he killed himself. Only he had been sitting on the front porch, tying the end of an old piece of string to a trigger. When Milan came out, he had turned and looked at her, like he was going to really show her something, like, "Watch this!" Then he grabbed the shotgun that was leaning against his chair. He did this the way a gunslinger might do it, snapping the barrel under his chin and the handle between his knees and then yanking the string, hard.

It happened in less than two seconds and it seemed to Milan that he was showing off for her. That he wanted her to someday tell people, "Boy, you should've been there. It was the fastest thing I ever saw!" Then, later, when she had been hosing off the front of the house, she couldn't get over how happy Tom had seemed just that morning. He had finally located a small snapshot of himself that he'd been trying to find for days. It had white scalloped edges and the picture itself had turned sort of brown. In it, he was wearing his old army uniform, which looked too big for him. His legs were apart and his hands were on his hips, as though he hoped this would make him look tough. Milan had never seen this photograph before and he told her, "Hold on to this, girlie! It could be worth a lot someday!"

She was jolted back to the present when she noticed that Duff's inner tube was now drifting toward Wood's. Eventually, when the tubes bumped together, Duff smiled at him and he returned it. Maybe it was because people who are lying on their backs, while floating around on something, often look smug, but Milan was thinking that Wood and Duff seemed especially pleased with themselves. Like they thought they knew everything. But she knew something they would never know. She knew, for example, that you cannot get brains off a house. Especially if the house is made of concrete. You can get the blood and the bone fragments off, but then weeks later, you'll be sitting on your front porch and you'll swear there's still a little piece of human tissue in there, somewhere. And no matter how many times you wash it, some of it is still going to be there. Maybe you can't see it. But it's there. It's just something you know.

That night, after the younger ones had gone back to town, the men put on Creedence Clearwater Revival and sang "Born on the Bayou." Sang it until Mavis had taken the extension cord connected to Brundidge's loudspeaker and thrown it in the river. The men had reacted with shock and dismay, eventually becoming depressed until Brundidge finally got the idea that they should all go skinny-dipping, the way they used to when they were kids. This was something he always suggested whenever they were on the

sandbar at night, as though it was a completely new concept. Charlotte had given
Brundidge an elbow, but he'd had too many
beers to grasp the delicacy of his suggestion. And then Duff took up his cause, saying
that she'd love to go and you could almost
hear the unsung chorus of female voices
saying, "Oh, what a surprise! We didn't see
that one coming! Any chance you'll be lin-
gering outside the water with your two new
friends?" Now Wood was saying he wasn't
going, which left only Brundidge and Duff,
forcing Charlotte to go, too. Then Brundidge
pressed Mavis, who exclaimed, "My God,
you're drunker than I thought."

"Come on, you and Jeet and Mary Paige
come."

"No."

"Why not?"

"Why not? Because I weigh six hundred
pounds. She's a missionary. And he's crip-
pled. Okay?"

Brundidge said he knew better than to ask
Milan. He explained to Charlotte and Mary
Paige that Milan was the only one who had
always refused to skinny-dip. Mavis added
that Milan never did anything daring or illegal. Mary Paige wanted to know what Mavis

had done that was daring and Mavis said that she had written "Mrs. Stevie Wonder" all over her notebook in sixth grade, which was way ahead of its time.

A conversation then ensued about how Milan was the one person who always volunteered to stay after school and help clean erasers—how she had actually been a hall monitor for three consecutive years—and earned every available Girl Scout badge (a group of teachers paid for her uniform) including even one for sanitation. Everyone laughed and Wood laughed a little, too, but told her with his eyes that he didn't like them picking on her, even though it was good-natured.

When they were done, Milan stood up and said, "Well, I think I'll go in now." After that she walked about a hundred feet away from them and climbed out on the large black rock that they had used to dive from since they were kids. Then, they all sat and watched as Milan, who even in PE had undressed in a bathroom stall, matter-of-factly shed her Capri pants and matching sweater with the little sailor collar and her under things, and then just stood for a brief moment in the moonlight.

Mavis said, in disbelief, "My God, she's going to get her hair wet."

Milan seemed like she was alone now and not even aware of them, which made it all the more compelling to watch. No one but her husband and daughter had ever seen her naked. And she was magnificent! Breathtaking—just the raw improbable beauty of her and no bad angle from which to view it. Wood was astonished and strangely proud and upset that she was doing this. And Duff was already thinking to herself that she was not going swimming after all. Jeter closed his eyes at first, because he was worried that there could be some new humiliation in this for Milan. Not that she wouldn't be lovely, but that the act itself might seem pathetic. But he needn't have worried. The fact that she had never done anything like it before lifted it from mere exhibitionism. And the fact that it was done in front of her husband and his lover was bold beyond words. Brundidge said, to lighten the moment, "Poor little old ugly thing. No wonder she was afraid to go in."

And Charlotte was thinking to herself, "She's standing on that rock, looking like that, for all the cuckolded wives everywhere, who've had to take a backseat to the other woman. This is the greatest fuck-you I've ever seen."

But that wasn't what was on Milan's mind. She was thinking that it felt good and free to be naked in the moonlight. And that maybe she had been missing out on something. Then she pointed her arms toward the stars and dove in, a perfectly executed swan dive, with her back slightly hollowed and her feet held together, forming a straight line from her curvaceous hips to her well-manicured toes, just the way Grand Scout Master Betty Barnes had taught her to, with Milan reminding herself as she landed, "the less splash the better." When she resurfaced, all eyes were still on her, except for Jeter's, which were now staring at Wood. He was wondering about an old football score that hadn't seemed to be enough for Wood either.

Milan pounded a gavel on the thick oak table that had been commissioned by her great-grandfather-in-law, Charles Longchamps, as a gift to the town. She loved doing this, because it seemed like something she had always seen important men doing. Then she declared that the second emergency session of the Twentieth-Century Millennium Time Capsule Committee of Paris, Arkansas, was now in order.

The first such meeting had been called months ago, in order to include the American flag from Dr. Mac's funeral. (Wood's dad had declined to give the committee his war medals, saying they were nothing more than the result of "unbelievable good luck.") After a unanimous vote, the capsule, which due to past vandalism now resided at a secret location, had been exhumed and the flag put in. Also included were Tommy Epps's dog tags from Vietnam, which he was still wearing when he died. Brundidge, a Millennium Committee member, had proposed that these be added to the capsule so that the lowest-ranking soldier would be represented right alongside Paris's most highly decorated veteran.

When Milan's brother Frank read about all this in the paper, he went crazy. He, too, owned an object of great historical significance. It was his one claim to fame and the committee had already turned it down. And now Frank, having been emboldened by the knowledge that the capsule's contents could indeed be revisited, had filed a lawsuit. He had done this after reading a book that a friend in prison had sent to him on how to become your own lawyer. And though he didn't like to read, he had been mesmerized by all the legal maneuverings that he might use to get his own way. This was a great book with real tips in it—not like that *Chicken Soup* shit that Milan sent him. Brundidge had tried to talk him out of taking any legal action. But Frank was insistent that the committee reconsider what he felt sure was one of the most important items to ever be associated with the city of Paris. And right now it was sitting on a Kleenex box that Frank had covered in velvet. (This was something he hadn't had last time.) It was a simple Coke can. Covered with all the signatures of the Rolling Stones. And Frank had something new to go with it, too. He passed out copies of the letter that he and his first-grade teacher, Miss Phipps, had recently worked on together. Actually, she had provided the big words and he the information. Here's what it said:

"On May 23, 1984, Auxiliary Sheriff's Deputy Frank Lanier observed someone throwing a Coke can out the back window of a limousine near Paris, Arkansas. Officer

Lanier proceeded to pull the limo over and issue a ticket. The people inside asked if he had any idea who he was talking to. When he admitted he didn't, they informed him that they were the Rolling Stones and that they were late for a concert in Little Rock. Officer Lanier responded that it is against the law to litter in Arkansas. The Rolling Stones then affected a high-falutin', New York City kind of attitude, telling him to call up their lawyer and using derogatory names like Goober and Chickens—. It was at this time that Officer Lanier took the Rolling Stones into custody, impounding their limousine and incarcerating them in the Paris County Jail. The next day, after paying a fine of $1,000, they returned to the site of their arrest, picked up the offending Coke can, and apologized for insulting the citizens of Paris. Sheriff Serious West accepted their apology on behalf of the town, saying, 'They seemed like nice boys who just needed a little supervision.' He also said they would be welcome to come back and visit anytime, but they never did. I swear all of this happened exactly as I have told it. Signed, Frank Lanier."

Then, Frank made a little speech. It wasn't very good. For one thing, he laughed inappropriately. This was something he had been doing since childhood. Over things like when somebody falls down or a squirrel gets electrocuted on a telephone pole. It's not that Frank was mean, it just felt good to see something else getting a piece of his diet. But this laughing also made him more nervous, because he knew he shouldn't be doing it. And also because he knew he could be next.

It took the committee less than five minutes to reject Frank's petition. After conferring with the others, Milan said as kindly as she could that while the letter told an interesting story, it did not provide any new evidence of historical significance. By comparison, she reiterated some of the more appropriate items that were already in the capsule—an old Civil War letter, Depression-era tin nickels that Jeter's Market had issued so that men couldn't spend them on liquor, Serious West's Golden Gloves, the homburg hat Sidney Garfinkel had been wearing when he first arrived at Ellis Island and in Arkansas, the championship football Jeter had tried so valiantly to catch, and so on. Then Milan added that, besides, the Rolling Stones were British and the commit-

tee had already included something from
England—Lena Farnham Stokes's picture of
the queen. After that, she pounded her gavel
and declared the meeting adjourned. Frank
was seething. Was she kidding? They already had something from England? A picture of a fat-assed housewife with a crown on
her head? What did that have to do with
Paris, Arkansas? Anyway, this was not
something from England. This was an American Coke can that belonged to the number
one rock group in the world, a group whose
members had insulted him and their whole
town and the entire state! And he had torn
them a new asshole for doing it. Name one
other place in America where something like
that had happened. It was historical, that's
what it was. And that was all there was to it.
Afterward, when Milan and Brundidge tried
to console Frank, he waved the Coke can in
their faces and told them that if he had to, he
would take it all the way to the Superior Court
of the entire United States. And even though
he got it wrong, they knew what he meant.

Midsummer. Hot. Marrakech. Slim and Sidney lost two weeks of walking because he
had eye surgery and then she sprained her

ankle while working in her garden. But today they were emerging from la Palmeraie, the gloriously abundant forest of date palms resting at the foot of the High Atlas Mountains. Sidney, who had been more quiet recently (reassured that Slim was now committed to walking, whether he spoke or not), had come back to life the minute their little map told him that Marrakech was in sight. And even though they were now really walking along the deserted Main Street of Paris, Arkansas, Slim had become a little excited, too, just listening to Sidney describe the exotic foods and vibrant colors and textures of all the fabrics that fill the souks of downtown Marrakech.

Something Slim had learned since leaving Casablanca was that Sidney, at the tender age of twenty, was a silk procurer for a major fabric house in Belgium. But the thing that completely dazzled her was his expertise and knowledge of silk. Right now he was explaining how Moroccan farmers carry the eggs of silkworms close to their chests in order to keep them warm, and also how they speak softly, so as not to startle them. Then, he said, after the eggs hatch, each worm spins a cocoon, which is then boiled until the end of the silk thread unravels. He described how each individual fiber is lustrous and strong on its own, but the more it bonds and is woven with other fibers, the more *fragile* and *delicate* the fabric itself becomes—so that eventually, if even one thread is pulled, the entire piece will be ruined. "But," Sidney added significantly, "without taking this risk, there would be nothing so beautiful as silk." Slim was wondering if they were still talking about fabric.

Then he casually mentioned that one client in particular, The House of Worth, used only silk from Marrakech because of the loving care the farmers gave to their worms. And that, in some cases, Sidney himself actually preselected these worms.

Slim stopped and stared at him for a moment. She told him that her wedding gown had come from the House of Worth. They excitedly compared dates and figured out that Sidney, being Worth's only supplier of silk at the time, had probably, indeed, selected the fabric and possibly even the worms that spun Slim's wedding gown. And that within a few months of her wearing it, he had been sent to Breendonk concentration camp while she had waited for her husband to return home from war.

They were walking again now. In spite of their initial excitement, they realized that this new information didn't really mean anything at all. It was simply interesting and unexpected—like finding out that someone on a train knows your cousin. But for some reason, they had both become quiet. And, for the first time, Slim held Sidney's arm all the way home.

Slim was sitting on her bed. Next to her was a large cardboard box. She hesitated for a moment and then opened it. She unzipped the plastic bag inside and then unfolded an exquisite white gown with long sleeves and a slender skirt and not an ounce of lace. Slim had relayed the story of this gown's origin to Elizabeth, who, now having second thoughts about her own dress, asked to see this one. Oddly, Slim had never imagined that her granddaughter might be interested in such a relic. And, on the heels of Dr. Mac's death, Elizabeth had thought the subject too delicate to broach. But Slim's conversation with Sidney had changed all that. And so, she had pulled the dress from her attic and now sat staring at it, feeling strangely unconnected to the day it had been worn.

Slim ran her hand tenderly across the fabric, as though she were trying to feel something more than mere silk, and noticed that not a single strand of thread had been pulled. Then she held the bodice of the gown to her cheek, caressing it and leaving it there, absorbing the texture. After a while, she rubbed her face with the skirt, too. Finally, she lay down on the bed, wrapping herself in the material, burying her face in the folds of it and drawing her knees up and moaning—at first, a low, soft, steady sound, followed by a louder, plaintive, broken noise that shook her shoulders. She wept for the delicate beauty that had remained intact all these years and for the man who had helped to create it and for what happened to him afterward and for the occasion of her wearing it and for the man she had worn it for and for all the things she had not wept over in a very long time.

Elizabeth, unheard by Slim, had come in and was now standing in the open doorway. She watched for a moment or two, and then crossed and put her hand on Slim's back.

"Grand-mère?"

Slim sat up and looked at her, startled.

Elizabeth sat down next to Slim. "This is what I want to feel someday. What you're feeling right now." Slim pulled her granddaughter close.

"Thank you, my darling. That's the best thing anyone's ever said."

It was after dusk on Main Street and the air felt just as hot and stale as it had during the day. Mavis was locking up Doe's as Rudy waited for her. She dropped the keys and he retrieved them since she was now too pregnant to bend over. Once they were under way, Rudy said, ". . . so Denny, he says to me, you know Dwight's not really feeling emotionally strong enough to go on a road trip with you right now."

Mavis sighed, "I'm sorry, Rudy, I can't get involved in your love life today. I'm too damn tired."

Since there were no cars or people around, they were now walking in the middle of the road. Rudy said, "Why do we stay here? Is it because we're afraid we can't make it anywhere else?"

Mavis groaned. "What are you talking about? Why does everyone always say that?"

"Say what?"

"That everywhere else is better, tougher. What a crock!" She waved her hand at all the deserted buildings. "Just look around. Hell, if you can make it here, you can make it anywhere . . ." Her words trailed off as she continued waddling up the empty street.

CHAPTER 21

Lottie Paris Pinkerton was born at 11:03 on the evening of August 3rd. Lottie was for Mary Paige's hero, Lottie Moon, and Jeter picked Paris for the town. It had been a most powerful moment when Wood caught the first glimpse of her coming down the birth canal. He couldn't help thinking of how his own father had put this little girl in motion years ago, when Dr. Mac had the foresight, long before it was common, to save a young man's lineage. After that, when Wood had taken the baby and put her on her mother's chest, Mavis drew in her breath, overwhelmed to see the trademark red hair that she and her father were famous for. Then

Wood laid his hand over Jeter's and they had cut the cord together.

Wood said, "What do you think, buddy? How about that?"

When Jeter couldn't speak, Wood covered for him, saying to Mary Paige, "Aw, he's just upset 'cause she didn't recognize him."

Ordinarily, Milan would've been in the delivery room, right there in the middle of it all, but she felt, under the circumstances, that this was an honor that now rightfully belonged to Mary Paige. And anyway, being present at a birth was such an intimate thing and Mavis had already proven that she and Milan were not on intimate terms. That's why Milan had stayed in the waiting room, along with Brundidge and Rudy and Mavis's mother, who regularly fainted at the sight of blood.

When Wood and Jeter had emerged, with Wood holding Paris in his arms, everyone cooed and carried on as Brundidge pounded Rudy on the back and a look seemed to pass between Wood and Milan that said this had put them in mind of their own babies.

Maybe it was the splendid moment itself, but Milan could not recall a time when Wood had looked more endearing, in his rumpled scrubs, with his hair partially matted by perspiration and one of his shoes untied. Several of the nurses had confirmed that it had not been an easy delivery and that Mavis's blood pressure had climbed to such a dangerous level, Wood had almost performed a C-section. Suddenly, Milan was seized with the urge to shake his hand and tell him how much she admired his unerring skill and good humor and that, even if he didn't want her anymore, she could still love him for guarding their old friend like the tenacious angel she knew he could be—at least, when he was at work. She was all too aware of the precautions he would've taken, the worry and second-guessing over someone who was probably too old and too overweight to be having a child. That was his way, attending to every small detail, anticipating and smoothing over every crisis and then acting like it was nothing more than a happy accident when it all turned out like a dream.

This was what she had wanted to say. But instead, she merely made a fuss over Jeter and his fatherhood and then stood paralyzed with rapture when Paris had wrapped her hand around Milan's finger. Later, she felt weary as the elevator carried her all the way to the basement when all she had wanted was to get off on one. Once outside in the parking lot, she stopped and looked up. There, on the third floor, the bright yellow light of the delivery room was still on. She knew that the man inside would be washing up about now, after which he would review the first words written about a little girl who was still less than an hour old. How much she weighed, how long she was, the color of her eyes—but nothing about the people who would annoy and challenge and love her and who she would probably find a way to love back. Suddenly, Milan hurried toward her car, trying to outrun the unbelievable thought that she might not be one of them.

After most everyone else had gone home, Wood, Brundidge, and Jeter sat up half the night in Wood's office, smoking cigars and drinking Glenfiddich scotch, with Brundidge mindlessly congratulating all of them on the fine progeny they had so far managed to spawn.

"I don't like to brag, but we got good-lookin' kids. Now that's just a fact. I'm sorry, but all kids are not lookers. You ever sit outside the entrance to the Magic Kingdom?

Whoa! I'm not sayin' the little SOBs don't have a right to be there. Hell no! Just because ours are better lookin' doesn't mean the others shouldn't get in. That's their God-given American right! And by God, I'll fight anybody who tries to stop 'em! I will now! I mean it!" Wood and Jeter stupidly agreed that they, too, would fight for homely children to be admitted to Disney World.

By 2 A.M., they were in Brundidge's van, sitting in front of Jeter's Market on Main Street. Now they were completely ablaze with the notion that living in a small town was the greatest birthright that could be bestowed upon a newborn baby. Determined that little Paris should have a childhood at least as wonderful as their own, they vowed to personally rebuild the entire street in her honor. Then they were quiet, steeped in the relaxed and loving familiarity that now enveloped the van. After a while, Brundidge said to the others, "You ever see a big-city bus pull up late at night? With all those sad-faced people sittin' inside all lit up? That's the lonesomest sight in the world." Wood and Jeter agreed that it was. Then Brundidge expressed his undying gratitude that the three of them would never have to be on that bus and neither would their children, which made him start to cry a little and finally kiss Jeter, who told him to get away.

Around four, they went back to the hospital and demanded that the maternity nurse go in Mavis's room and retrieve Paris, which she did. Then the three men, having marinated themselves in cigar smoke and liquor, huddled over this tiny female person, who in spite of having just arrived out of nowhere, had already managed to consume their interest. After a while, she opened her eyes and, getting a good look at them, or a good whiff, or both, began shrieking at the top of her lungs. Jeter was so shaken by this, they quickly returned her to the nurse and hurried down the hall. With Wood saying she probably had a little gas. And Brundidge worrying that she might have too much Mavis in her. But her father was already thinking that he would try very hard never to make her mad.

It was early morning. Slim and Sidney Garfinkel were walking when they spotted an enormous tomato garden not far from the gravel road. In the distance was a little farmhouse.

Slim exclaimed, "Sidney! Would you look

at those tomatoes? Really, we have to stop and buy some."

"There's no sign. I don't think they're for sale."

"Well, then we have to steal them. Because I refuse to leave here without having one."

They crossed to the garden and crouched down in front of the tall staked vines. Sidney whispered, "We're in Algeria now. They have death by hanging."

Slim said, while picking several of the largest ripe ones, "It'll be worth it. These are nothing like store bought."

Sidney gathered some, too. Suddenly, shots rang out. They seemed to be coming from the front porch of the little house. Sidney and Slim took off running. Now a man on the porch was hollering and cussing as he fired a gun into the air. The tomato thieves never looked back. They ran until they were exhausted and finally collapsed in a little ravine under a tree. They were lying on their backs now and laughing so hard they could scarcely catch their breath. Finally, Slim sat up and took a bite of her tomato.

"When did we get to Algeria?"

"Last week. I didn't tell you because I was

afraid you would stop walking with me." He waited, then, "Have you been there?"

"No." Then she lied, "But I've always wanted to go."

He smiled. She took another bite of her tomato. "My God, these are sublime. We may have to steal some more."

Sidney ate his, too, with a little of the juice running down his chin. "I never knew you were immoral."

"Really? I thought that was why you liked me."

He smiled again. After that, they stretched their legs out side by side, savoring the meat of the tomatoes and the day.

In spite of having stayed out all night, Jeter was up by eight and watching worriedly as Rudy counted out bills on an old metal nightstand. When he was done, he grandly announced that Jeter had $57.29. Then he placed the paper money in Jeter's nylon jogger's wallet (a gift from Miss Phipps on a day of confusion) and put the change back in a shoebox. Jeter was pleased because he had even more money than he thought—especially after selling a couple of poems to something called the *Three Penny Review*.

Shortly after that, Jeter's wheelchair was sailing up the concrete ramp of the public library with Rudy running behind it. Once inside, Jeter told head librarian Susie Minetree that he was here to obtain a library card for the town's newest citizen. And he had a reading list to go with it, too. At first she was stunned. Nobody had ever applied for a card for an infant before, much less tried to put a reading list on file. Then, having no one to tell her it was against the rules, Susie decided it was the greatest idea she'd ever heard. A few minutes later, Rudy promptly filled out all the appropriate documents, writing the word *bébé* next to "age."

Jeter and Rudy were at Dwight & Denny's Secret Garden now and Jeter was staring at a soft-bodied young girl with nickel-sized hands and a porcelain face. He asked, "Do you have any . . . modern dolls?"

Denny sniffed. "If you mean dolls with breasts, you should try Fed-Mart. We don't approve of dolls with breasts."

Jeter didn't know what to say so Dwight added. "These are priceless heirlooms from the Madame Alexander Collection. This is something that is passed down from one generation to the next."

Rudy careened a little, thinking that Dwight looked good in his tight black jeans and white T-shirt. Jeter gestured with his head toward the one he'd been considering. "How much for her? I mean, if there could be a price."

Dwight stood on his tiptoes and retrieved her. "Oh, that's Jo from *Little Women*. She's not for sale. She's part of my personal collection."

Rudy said, "It's for his little girl who was born last night."

"Oh, right." Dwight stared at the doll now. Then he seemed to remember something. "You know, Amy was really the pretty one but they were out of stock." Then to Jeter, "Did you ever see the movie with Katharine Hepburn? Jo should never have cut her hair."

Jeter was confused now. "So . . ."

"How much do you have?"

"Fifty?"

"Sold."

Wood was making rounds when something at the end of the maternity-ward hallway caught his attention. He stopped and looked at the man who had pulled his wheelchair up as close as it would go next to the nursery glass window. Jeter wasn't laughing or smiling or doing any of the things that people usually do when viewing a baby. Wood could see that he had a strange look on his face—not unlike the look that Wood had once worn when he'd stood staring at the end of Jeter's hospital bed—as though he had to come by one more time to make sure that the thing he thought had happened had really happened. After a while Jeter shook his head a little, then started up the wheelchair, and rode away.

It was Lodusky Phipps's birthday. Because they had done so for years, Jeter, Brundidge, and Wood attended the party. Milan, who had a cold, sent along a beautiful bracelet, which was much more expensive than the cherub pin with the blue rhinestone eyes that she had given to Miss Phipps as a child. But the former first-grade teacher, who was having one of her final days of clarity, insisted that she would now wear them together. After cake had been served, most of the residents who had been well enough to attend went back to their rooms. Serious also left early in order to visit his son. Because Miss Phipps was having such a good day, Miss Delaney asked Rudy to put on some of Dr. Mac's music. Then Wood, who had decided to leave, for some reason stayed—maybe just to hear some of his father's old songs. In a little while, Etta James drifted out of the nursing home speakers, singing "I Only Have Eyes for You." Shockingly, Miss Lena Farnham Stokes asked Wood to dance. Not knowing what to say, he accepted. Brundidge, feeling awkward, invited Miss Delaney to dance, too. It was immediately apparent that they were all four good at it. Then Lena Farnham Stokes began resting her head on Wood's shoulder. Wood saw that her eyes were closed and that she looked content, as though she were thinking of some long-ago love. He smiled, feeling happy about this. Then, he began to worry that perhaps she was thinking of him.

Outside, Jeter and Miss Phipps were now sitting on the porch. A conversation unfolded, without either knowing that it would be their last. Miss Phipps said, "A lot of lightning bugs out tonight."

"Yep."

"My son used to tie thread to them and fly them like little kites." For a moment she seemed sad. "You never sunk yourself in what might've been, did you?"

Jeter struggled to come up with an answer. "Well, I guess I just tried to dream up somethin' better in my head."

"Is that what you were doing all these years? You were so quiet, I never knew." After a while, she added, "Maybe that's what heaven is . . . you know, getting to live the life we dreamed of." Then she said, almost to herself, "If so, I'll finally get to raise my boy." Miss Phipps got up and crossed to the door. She usually called him Mr. Jeter, but tonight she didn't. "I hope I'll see you there, Carl . . . And that you'll be running."

Mavis was going out of business. She was sitting at her desk now, in the back of Doe's, Paris sleeping in the crib next to her. After going over a pile of receipts, Mavis sighed and got up and just stood, taking in the place that had been at the center of her life for the past fifteen years. Yesterday, she had told Mary Paige and Rudy what they both already knew.

Doe's was the last business remaining on Main Street, except for Brundidge Beer and Beverage. That would always be there because, as Brundidge said, people needed to get drunk after they got a good look at what was left of the town. Dwight and Denny had finally given up and moved out to the inter- state in order to make their small enterprise more convenient for one-stop shoppers. The simple truth was there was no foot traffic left now. Even Tommy Epps was gone, leaving behind his two miles of graffiti.

The Baptist feud had taken its toll, too. The line that had formed outside the Baptist door each day got smaller as word got around who was standing in it and pressure was brought to bear. Also it didn't help that Mavis had refused to conceal her relation- ship with Mary Paige and was now per- ceived as a full-fledged lesbian. Apparently, for some people, there was a limit as to how much sin sugar could trump. And there was also the fact that more folks had moved out- side the city limits and it was a lot of trouble to come all the way downtown just for a bear claw.

Mavis felt a kind of bittersweet pride that she had held on as long as she did. She was honored to be the last hurrah of this fading boulevard. It was here that Clarence and Dauphine Doe had helped to heal a father- less girl's broken heart and allowed her to attend one of the world's great cooking schools for free. And now, just being here at the end seemed in some small way to repay that debt.

Suddenly, there was a commotion up front and she went toward it. She saw that Lonnie Rhinehart and two of the puppy stompers had come in. They were wearing boots and hunting clothes and reeked of beer. She was suddenly nervous, but strangely thinking at the same time that they could be a heavy metal rock group, "Lonnie Rhinehart and the Puppy Stompers."

She headed them off. "I told you I'm not serving you. Now you all need to go on."

She saw Brundidge's van as it pulled up outside and Wood and Brundidge got out. Then they opened the back door and Jeter started down the ramp. Paris began to cry. Mary Paige went to get her.

Lonnie said, "Is that your little bastard baby you got back there?"

Mavis didn't answer, but instead stood there marveling at the spectacle of Lonnie Rhinehart, history's bad gene. It didn't matter what era he lived in, or whether he was in the KKK or the SS or just a group of agitators like himself. He was the same guy, the one who just keeps coming, who never becomes extinct like some species or goes out of style or mutates into something better— but instead, just keeps on swaggering around the world, fearing women, blacks, Jews, and queers like Kryptonite and spouting the same old tired lines, "You're not from around here, are you?" "What you need, little lady," "Let me tell you somethin', boy." Blah, blah, blah! Mavis was sick of it.

She knew he was here to gloat, as though she were going out of business for standing up to him. And she had already made up her mind that he would leave empty-handed. What she had learned recently was that having a child makes you either more brave or more afraid. And she wanted to be brave, if not for herself, then so that the next incarnation of Lonnie Rhinehart would have to think twice before he messed with Lottie Paris Pinkerton. Mavis pulled herself up and accentuated each word. "Get out of my store. Now."

Lonnie came closer. "You know, you ought to appreciate my business. Most people don't care to come in a place where two big ol' dykes have had their hands in all the food."

He leaned against the counter. "Now what

is it exactly that y'all do together? I can't quite figure it out."

One of the men laughed. "I bet they sniff each other's panties."

Rudy said, nervously, "Let me just wait on them."

Mavis stopped him. "No. They're leaving."

Lonnie turned to the others, "Man, it's just full up with queers in here, ain't it?" Then, to Rudy, "What do you say, tiny dancer? I got something you can suck on. I just have to run outside and git it off my gun rack."

Mavis was now toe-to-toe with Lonnie. She pictured him in the surrender position, naked, on his back, legs apart in a final homage to women, blacks, Jews, and queers. Then, wishing she had her stun gun, she said, "I'm warning you, I'll kill you."

Now the whirring of Jeter's wheelchair could be heard coming through the door. Wood and Brundidge entered behind him, but Lonnie didn't turn around. He was now too involved with Mavis. "You know, I hate to hit a woman, but since you ain't one, I guess it won't count none."

Brundidge was on him first. He literally leapt a good three feet and took Lonnie down to the floor. Then, when Lonnie's friends tried to intervene, Wood knocked one of them down, causing the other to throw him against a table. Mary Paige crouched, covering Paris with her body, and Rudy grabbed a bottle of Doe's best extra virgin olive oil and threw it, missing everyone, but jumping up and down, excited, anyway. The brawlers periodically changed partners whenever one or the other was thrown across the room, shattering dishes, tables, and chairs. Then, what happened next was seen only by Mavis. Unbelievably, when Jeter got a clear shot at Lonnie, he used his good finger to start his wheelchair. At first, Mavis couldn't comprehend it. Then, after it was too late, she screamed, "Noooo!"— drawing it out and accelerating the loudness of it in proportion to the speed of Jeter's chair as it went careening into Lonnie, knocking him into the brick wall.

Then, Lonnie, who seemed to have been stunned by this, impulsively picked Jeter up and tossed him through the air. And Mavis, who was still hollering at the top of her lungs, caught a fleeting glimpse of her child's father as he passed in front of her with his body waving like a flag or some kind of rag doll that was being shaken. After that, there was

a thunderous splintering of glass as Jeter
landed against the bakery case, filled with all
the fresh pastries that Mavis had made only
that morning. Some flour, from a sack that
had busted open, lingered in the air. Then, attempting humor, a meek voice came from inside the case, "My neck . . . I think it's
broken."

Before Mavis and Rudy had even swept up
the glass, everyone had heard about the terrible fight at Doe's. And how Carl Jeter was
now in the hospital and that Lonnie Rhinehart had gone to jail for putting him there. In
spite of his substantial injuries, Jeter was
positively euphoric over his unexpected par-
ticipation in such a no-holds-barred brawl.
And he felt strongly that if the town bully was
prosecuted for beating up an invalid, it would
negate the idea that Jeter had seriously defended the mother of his child. Anyway,
since Jeter said he was the one who attacked Lonnie, it looked like Sheriff Marcus
West was going to have to hold his nose and
let Lonnie go.

But Wood was worried about something
more serious than Lonnie Rhinehart's incarceration. The X-rays were already showing

him that Jeter's kidneys had been severely damaged when his back had struck the bakery case. Wood knew this was something that was potentially life threatening for someone in Jeter's condition. He hadn't even treated his own cuts yet. Right now, with help from his nurse, he was tending to Brundidge's sprained arm. And Brundidge was still emitting fumes.

"I never liked that son of a bitch. Even in a parade, he was an asshole. Always had his trombone slide in the back of my neck. Steppin' on my heels so my feet would come outta my shoes."

Wood said, "Yeah. Somebody ought to kill him."

Wood's nurse looked at him, surprised. He didn't care anymore. He was caring less and less about civilized behavior. Wood hadn't been in a real fight since junior high and lately he'd managed to have two. One with Dennis Childs and now the one at Doe's. He was starting to feel reckless, like maybe he could kill somebody with his bare, bloody hands if they pushed him far enough or killed his best friend, which right now, though he didn't say so to Brundidge, loomed as a real possibility.

Brundidge was on his way out, shaking his head. "I thought it was just a friendly fight. I didn't know we were gonna be picking people up out of wheelchairs and flinging them through the air. Shit."

Wood went home around midnight and stayed holed up in his den. He put on one of the Edith Piaf tapes that his mother had given to Elizabeth. Then he lay down listening to his favorite song on it, "Les Trois Cloches." Even though the lyrics were in French, the melody put him in mind of the more mournful American version "All the Chapel Bells are Ringing." He turned it off. By the time the nurse called to say that Jeter's fever was 103, he was already up and putting his pants on.

Wood made it to the hospital in less than seven minutes. Over the years, he and Jeter had been through at least a dozen medical crises together. Jeter could be as fragile as a piece of paper that has to be kept afloat by someone blowing. And that someone was always Wood. Or sometimes Jeter would grow strong and he and Wood and Brundidge would take a trip together. It was an ever-unfolding situation that required daily vigilance. He'd had pneumonia three times, hepatitis, a bleeding ulcer, septemia. Once he had even flatlined and Wood had revived him. But now it seemed that Wood had pulled all the rabbits out of his hat and that the hat was finally empty. No one had to tell Carl Jeter this. Anyway, his doctor was a lousy actor, which is why Jeter had once replaced him as Meriwether Lewis in a sixth-grade play.

Jeter asked to be moved back to his room at the nursing home. He wanted to be in familiar surroundings, among his own things. Using his stick, he typed a final letter to his daughter, to go with all the one's he'd already written. Miss Phipps was having an off day, but most of the old folks, like Miss Delaney and Serious, came by to see him, although no one told them Jeter was dying. In fact, because he had come home, they all thought he was doing better. But Milan and Mavis and Brundidge understood why they were there. Mavis brought a bottle of champagne and Milan poured it into Jeter's plastic bottle. The five of them drank and told funny stories, mostly about all the good times they'd had together. Jeter especially wanted to relive some of the trips he and Wood and Brundidge had taken. In spite of his injury, they had managed to go fishing in the Bahamas, Key West, and even Egypt.

It was there on a deep sea fishing venture that Brundidge had mooned the Egyptian Port Authority (mistaking it for the yacht of some Euro-trash assholes) and then tried to convince them that his misdeed was nothing more than a friendly American gesture meaning "Hello. Good to know you." Wood, Jeter, and Brundidge were all detained, while Wood lamented that Milan would be out buying a new outfit every day so she could beg for his release on CNN.

Pretty soon they were all laughing enough that some had to wipe their eyes and sigh afterward. For a moment, they almost forgot the real reason they were together. Wood had been laughing, too. And when his eyes met Milan's, it seemed for a second that they were young and in love again, acting silly with their friends and that everything was going to be okay. After a while, it was obvious that Jeter was getting tired and so they each took a turn saying good-bye while the others waited outside.

Brundidge got upset because Jeter had decided to be cremated, an idea that disturbed Brundidge greatly. They actually had words about this. And then Brundidge had said, "Man, I hate all this. I hate this so bad."

Jeter spoke softly, "It'll be okay."

"No, it won't." Then he dug in his pocket and retrieved a scrap of paper. "I wrote a few words here, so I can, you know, say it just right."

"Ever'thing's already been said."

Brundidge stared at him, holding the paper, unhappy. "No, it hasn't. And you haven't even heard it yet."

"Why do you need to load people up just as they're leaving? You're just gonna upset me—"

Now Brundidge was mad. "I don't see how you can be upset when I haven't even said anything! I mean, goddamn, I just wanted to tell you . . . well, I can't even read it now because you've gone and ruined it. Now it's gonna sound stupid, like we're at a goddamn banquet or somethin', so just forget the whole goddamn thing, okay?" He pushed the small piece of paper back in his pocket.

And that's how it stayed for a while, until Jeter finally said, "I know you love me, Earl . . ." Brundidge didn't answer, so Jeter pushed on. "And I, uh—"

Brundidge interrupted. "All right. That's

enough. You don't need to get all theater-in-the-round on me." Jeter smiled. Brundidge stepped closer to him. "So what's the deal? Are we done here?"

"Yeah, we're done."

"Well, all right then . . ." Brundidge hesitated, not wanting to leave it like this. He seemed not to know what to do. Then, in a little while, he got a mischievous look on his face, as though he was already appreciating what was coming. And little by little, he began to back slowly toward the door, singing low and soft. "See you later, alligator, after a while, crocodile, see you later alligator . . ."

Jeter was grinning now, and each could tell by the other's relieved look that they had finally settled on a satisfactory ending.

Brundidge pointed a finger directly at Jeter, singing louder, "She said I'm sorry, pretty baby, you know my love for you is true. She said I'm sorry, pretty baby—" He looked fearless and a little pouty, as though he were defying death to try and interfere with something as classic as this. Then he continued facing his old friend as the words trailed him out the door and down the hall. "She said I'm sorry, pretty baby, you know my love is just for you. . . ."

After that, Mavis came in, carrying her humongous purse and Paris. Jeter asked her to hold the baby up to his face so he could kiss her. And then he wanted to kiss her hands. So Mavis pressed each tiny palm to his lips, which made Paris and Jeter both laugh a little. Mavis laughed, too, and in the middle of it all, noticed that Jeter's face was now contorted and that he was no longer laughing, but was actually weeping, which caused his words for Mavis to sound choked and harsh. "Damn you. I've been ready to go for years. Then you had to go and do somethin' like this."

Now Mavis was crying. She lay Paris on the bed and began digging in her purse. When she came up with several photographs, she held them up toward Jeter. "You have to pick. It's for her dresser."

Jeter studied them for a moment. "The one in my football uniform." He laughed a little. "That way you can tell her her old man was a big stud."

Mavis stared at him as tears continued rolling off her fat cheeks and onto her blouse. "Don't ever laugh at that." She gestured toward Paris. "Look what you did there. Her old man *is* a stud. And Mary Paige and I get on our knees every night and thank God for that."

"Come on."

"Are you kidding? You're the biggest fucking stud in this entire town."

He gazed lovingly at the daughter lying next to him and said to Mavis, "You're crazy."

"You know anyone else around here who's knocked up a two-hundred and fifty pound lesbian?"

Jeter had to admit that he didn't. And even though he knew it was silly, he rolled the idea around in his head now, taking it in like an unexpected, last minute windfall.

Then it was Milan's turn. She came in just as a sliver of moon appeared in his tiny window. She crossed and opened the curtains wide, the same ones she had made for him because there was a snow scene of a small town on the fabric that she had known he would like. When she turned to face him, they smiled, the way people who have loved each other for a long time can smile, knowing that this will be enough. Then she crawled into bed with him and held him in her arms, like he belonged to her. And they stayed that way until Jeter fell asleep.

When he woke up, she was gone. He

wanted to know the score of the local foot-ball game. Wood turned on the radio and they listened to the last quarter together. After a while, Jeter saw an old look settle on Wood's face. Finally, he spoke. "It doesn't matter whether you should've thrown that ball or not."

"We don't need to talk about that."

"Listen to me. All that matters is, I tried to catch it. Because that's the way we played. You and me. And if I could get out of this bed and be eighteen, I'd do it again. Do you understand?"

Wood shook his head that he did, as each one realized this would never be resolved. After that, Jeter laughed a little to himself.

"Man, that was some serious whup-ass yesterday. Did you see the surprised look on that son of a bitch's face when he saw me coming?"

"Yeah. It's not every day you get attacked by a quadriplegic."

"That was almost worth dyin' for."

They laughed together. Then Wood said, "God, I'm gonna miss you."

Jeter met his gaze. "I wouldn't mind if it wasn't for my little girl . . . I wanted to see what color her eyes are gonna be. You know, they keep changin'."

Wood smiled.

"Don't let her go with the boys who drive fast, okay?"

"I won't."

Around 4 A.M., Jeter woke up and stared at Wood, who was sleeping in a chair, illuminated by the light from the nurses' station. Then he said, "Woodrow?"

Wood opened his eyes. He got up and crossed to the bed and put his hand next to his old friend's cheek. The same one that Cherry Smoke had once placed herself so lovingly against and that Hank and Pauline, in search of a sensory route to their son, had kissed hundreds of times. After enjoying the warmth of it for a moment or two, Jeter died. Wood stayed alone with him for a while, thinking that his eyes looked peaceful and innocent, not unlike those of a deer they had shot when they were thirteen. He remembered how they both cried afterward, admitting that neither had wanted to do it and vowing never to do it again.

Then he rang Milan and said, "It's over."

She thanked him for calling and went and sat in her favorite window, dry-eyed, imagining Jeter without his chair. After a while, she called Mavis, who picked Paris up and started a fire in the kitchen, even though it was warm out. And then Mavis and the baby had sat rocking, next to Chester, where they would stay for most of the morning.

Brundidge had heard the phone, but didn't answer. He already knew what it meant— this cruel middle-of-the-night ringing that nothing good ever came from. He lay there quiet till the sun was up. Then, when his little girls came and got in bed with him, he held them tight and wept.

Slim was already in her kitchen, drinking coffee, when she got Wood's call. Afterward, she went outside and worked in her garden till Sidney arrived. When she told him, he reached for his perfectly pressed handker-chief and walked away from her for a while. After he collected himself, he helped her move a climbing oleander to near the old tree house where her son and his friends had spent so much of their time.

Back at the nursing home, Wood had re-moved all the tubular appendages that had for so long encumbered his greatest friend. And Rudy came and gave Jeter a bath. He did this while humming "Hernando's Hideaway," the song his parents had been dancing to when they became the national tango champions of Cuba. This was to keep his spirits up and also because Jeter had always liked it. Miss Delaney, who once taught that restraint is the most powerful emotion in all of literature, kept to herself for most of the day. She felt especially sorrowful when she realized, too late, that she had let several of Jeter's plants die since falling in love with Serious. But it was Miss Phipps who was inconsolable, parking herself in a folding chair outside of Jeter's room. When Cotrell's came to collect the body, she wailed so loudly that one of the attendants asked if she was a relative to which she replied, "Yes, he was my husband."

That afternoon, Brundidge and Wood were going through Jeter's meager possessions. They saw the letter on his computer that he had typed for Paris. But there were no final thoughts or a last will and testament as one might expect. Just a simple log of who had come to see him and what time they had done so. At the bottom of the page, he had put the day's date and then this man, who had been so prolific and masterful with words, had written simply, "I died."

Brundidge and Wood sat looking at each other, absorbing the clarity of it. Then, Brundidge, who had been sifting through the cardboard box under Jeter's bed, showed Wood that it was filled with old newspaper clippings and photographs, mostly to do with Wood. His years as the quarterback at Duke, articles about each game, the announcement of his marriage, his acceptance to and graduation from medical school and all the Dean's list stories in between, his affiliation with his dad and the local hospital, stories about his practice, the birth of his children, and on and on. Wood couldn't get over it. He had to go out in the hall and walk around for a while. It was as though, since nothing had happened to Jeter after his injury, he had begun to collect the things that happened to Wood. Things that Wood himself hadn't even kept a record of. When he came back in, Brundidge said, without any unkindness, "Well, I guess somebody liked your life."

Wood, feeling his strength waning, said nothing.

Then something even more shocking hap-

pened—something that could not have surprised him more if he had learned that Jeter
was an alien. Rudy had produced the key to
Jeter's small filing cabinet, the one that contained all of his poems and short stories. Inside, there was an especially thick folder,
which was labeled simply, "Her." Wood
hadn't intended to read any of the contents
now, but after he saw some of the titles, he
became, for some reason, uneasy. And later,
when he read a few of the passages, even
though a name was never mentioned, he began to feel that he knew who these lines had
been written about—knew her very well. And
it had started to actually make him feel sick.

There was "The Woman in the Window"—
a poem about a young wife who mines solitude and comfort out of a loveless marriage.
And "The Rose Maker"—a mythological tale
about a poor girl who cannot stop making
roses out of ribbon. And "A Painting of a
House"—a touching vignette about a
teenager who attempts to repaint her family's house after her father's suicide.

Of course Jeter, like all writers, had uti-
lized only what he needed, mixing up some
facts and embellishing others. For example,
Milan had painted the Laniers' house long

before Tom died. But it was clear that she had been the sole inspiration for all of these poems and stories. The same woman whose conversations and inquiries Wood regularly dismissed had apparently been nothing short of mesmerizing to someone else. Someone with far greater artistic gifts and sensibilities than Wood would ever be privy to.

No wonder these works had never appeared anywhere. And had certainly never been shown to him. There was no attempt at subtlety. And no need to name the source of Jeter's rapture. "The perpetual blush on her luminous cheek, fueled by simple candy." Even Wood's children would know who that was. Then there were references to the mystery of (Milan) and her unsettling contradictions.

"The breathlessness of her soul, as though everything she did was being done for the first time." And "The achingly beautiful eyes that did not let strangers in." Wood felt sure Jeter wanted him to read these words, otherwise, he would've asked Rudy to destroy them. And he was certain he saw himself in "The horse lover who wipes his boots on his wife's clean floor and brushes past her without speaking." And there was also this: "The unremitting sadness of a man in a coma, lying next to treasure."

Brundidge had been reading them, too. Finally, Wood said, "My God, he was in love with her."

"I know."

"You knew?"

"Yeah. I've always known. Didn't you?"

"No. Why didn't you tell me?"

"Because. It's not something you talk about. It's just something you know."

Wood shook his head.

That night, he and Milan had dinner alone. Neither of them spoke until toward the end when Wood said, "I brought a box of his things home. You know he saved every little scrap about us."

She corrected him. "About you."

"I, uh, read some of his stuff. Some poems and . . . stories. A lot of them seem to have you in them. Did you know that?"

"I knew there were some."

"He let you read them?"

"No. He never asked me to."

"But you knew that he was in love with you?"

"I wouldn't go that far."

"Well, he was. And I'm apparently the only one who didn't know."

He looked at her, exhausted, not caring how it sounded. "What else don't I know?"

She got up and crossed to him. "He was your best friend. He had maybe six square inches of his face where he could actually feel. Are you really worried that while you're off screwing someone else, he and I might have done something *there*." She got closer to Wood. "Because if you are, I'm not sure I want to know you anymore." Then she left, leaving Wood to feel the way she, until now, would never have wanted him to—small, mean, miserable.

Since Jeter had not belonged to a church, there was a memorial at the high school gym. It happened a few days later and was brief, as he had requested. The Paris High School Choir sang the Lord's Prayer because it had been Pauline Jeter's favorite song. And Miss Delaney, on behalf of the Paris Literary Society, read some passages from his poetry. Brundidge and Wood both spoke, with Wood making a mess of it, periodically losing his place and his composure.

Duff had ridden down for the service,

along with Elizabeth and Luke. She wore an impossibly short red skirt and a body-hugging matching jacket that were too young for her years. She insisted she had worn this for Jeter, as opposed to something somber, because it was more in keeping with who he was. But Milan was pretty sure that the white silk camisole, which allowed glimpses of the lacy half-bra underneath, was for Wood. Duff topped it off with an un-expected embroidered clutch purse and little black T-strap heels. You could tell, just as she had once successfully contrived a see-through peasant blouse and riding pants, that considerable thought had been put into this ensemble. Milan imagined how Duff must have stood in front of her mirror and practiced different moves in order to see which ones showed her lace-framed cleav-age to the best advantage. Men were so naive. They had no idea women like Duff did these things—women who liked to pretend that every ounce of their appeal had been born with them.

She also saw that Duff, especially during the music portion of the service, had tried to visually engage Wood so that they might share a moment. But Wood seemed oblivious to it. Not that it mattered to Milan. She already felt so sad about almost everything. Today, Duff and Wood could make love in the center circle at half-court for all she cared.

Afterward, everyone went to Milan and Wood's house. As usual, there were abundant flowers and food everywhere. And Brundidge played all of Jeter's favorite songs over the sound system. But it wasn't like Dr. Mac's funeral, where people told funny stories and felt good about a life well lived. Jeter's life had been cut short and at least half of that had been a continuous struggle for survival and whatever dignity can be gleaned from pretending that one doesn't mind having one's ass wiped by strangers. And baby Paris was passed around constantly, almost as reassurance that Jeter had indeed experienced some sense of normalcy and happiness. Milan had watched as Duff held the baby in her arms, in Milan's opinion for too long. It was clear that Duff was becoming emboldened by her liaison with Wood—more sure of herself and her rightful place among them. Each visit now rendered new evidence of her growing sense of entitlement. And it almost seemed that today, if Wood wasn't going to notice her, then she was going to make sure that everyone else did—and that her uncharacteristic loudness increased in direct proportion to his seeming indifference. And now it appeared that Duff was using Paris a prop in her one-woman show, prattling on about how she had known her daddy forever and how, when she got older, she had some stories to tell her. Then Duff had laughed and added, "Well, maybe a few that will have to be censored."

If Milan hadn't felt so numb, it would've been galling. A woman who had barely seen the deceased for twenty years, proclaiming herself as the one with stories to tell. And then hinting that there might be something off-color in them, too. Milan knew for a fact that Jeter had been immune to Duff's artifice. The acquired rebelliousness and affected soulful empathy that seemed to dazzle Wood had left Jeter cold. It was a response that he and Milan shared. They were people who had real things to go up against. Naturally, they resented the ones who had the luxury of inventing the drama of their own lives.

But perhaps even more annoying, Duff

was continuing to speak to Paris as though the infant were an adult. Unlike many of her peers, Milan believed that babies should be spoken to in baby talk. Unable to take anymore, she turned her back now and began talking with Miss Delaney.

Then Duff, in a sort of final dramatic effort to distinguish her presence, had a little crying jag. She apologized profusely for being so emotional, saying it was what she hated most about herself, "this terrible inability to simply shake things off." Blah. Blah. Blah. Finally, Mavis had had enough of this woman, who seemed so puffed up by her recent conquest that she could no longer judge the inappropriateness of going to a funeral and trying to steal attention from the corpse. She walked directly over to her and took Paris back. Then, in a quiet measured voice that only Duff could hear, she said, "You know, this is a real sad day. And you've got on a short red outfit and you're making a whole lot of noise. And I'm just wondering, why is that?"

Duff sat for a moment, surprised by this abruptness from one who had always been cordial. Then, she said, "You're right. I'm trying too hard, aren't I?" She felt strangely relieved and grateful for Mavis's candor. "That's what I love about you. How you always tell it like it is. You know I'm like that, too." She looked straight into her eyes now, seeking validation. "I'm sure you can imagine how stressed and alone I'm feeling."

Mavis was taken aback. "Wait a minute. I'm not your friend." She turned and made sure Milan wasn't paying attention. Then she leaned closer into Duff's face and said evenly, "That's my friend. Over there. Don't ever be confused about that. I'm not."

Mavis turned and walked away. Duff decided to let it go. To tell the truth, she was almost glad it happened. The more people came forward with how they felt, the sooner she and Wood might just be compelled to do something about it.

That same day, as the sun was going down, Wood, Milan, Brundidge, and Mavis, holding Paris, released Jeter's ashes from the roof of his parents' grocery. Wood said softly, without a hint of self-consciousness, "There you go, buddy, you're free now. Go long. Go wide."

A breeze came up and for a moment Jeter was moving again. Wood had hoped the wind might carry these ashes to all the other rooftops, like Tillman's Electric and Falkoff's and even Doe's at the end of the street. But they mostly just drifted near or around the old store. The quartet stood watching, as though they were waiting for something else to happen. But nothing did, except some crows appeared and circled above their heads, adding an even more somber note. Afterward, in Brundidge's van, there didn't seem to be any song that was right for this occasion—returning a man to a town that wasn't there anymore. So his four best friends sat together, riding in silence, while his daughter fell asleep in her mother's arms.

Chapter 22

Duff was lying on her back with her buttocks raised off the carpet, counting. When she got to twenty, she collapsed. Then, she stood up, removed an exercise tape from her VCR and lit a Marlboro. She hated working out. She always had. That's why she was so often listed as "observing" in PE, which was a euphemism for menstruating. Unlike Milan, who clumsily ran around panting after every ball, always talking up something called "team spirit," Duff had natural grace and agility. And nothing to prove to a bunch of jocky girls who insisted on calling each other by their last names. Unlike Milan, who openly sought the approval and camaraderie of other females, Duff was a man's woman, which is why she had, at this late date, decided to start exercising. Now that Wood was back in her life, she realized that she could no longer take for granted the considerable physical blessings of her youth. Her butt was getting back into shape. It had always been one of her best features. But she hoped to lift it just a little, now that there was someone worth lifting it for. And also, now that she had seen his wife naked. Thank God Duff's breasts now looked even better than they had in high school. And most important, Wood seemed happy with them, though, as a doctor, he was opposed to implants, period.

She was reading again, too. Mark Twain, Kurt Vonnegut, Saul Bellow, and some of the other authors whom she remembered Wood liked. She looked at the phone now and wished he would call, but at the same time felt embarrassed by this longing, which, for her, seemed singularly uncool. She wasn't happy with her behavior or his at Jeter's funeral. She was now painfully aware that she had overplayed her hand, which was completely alien to her natural, easygoing temperament. It wasn't like her to go anywhere and make a spectacle of herself. She was the girl who always picked out the most intriguing person in the room and then holed up quietly in a corner with him, laughing over some charming and mutually appreciated observation. And now she was not only embarrassed by her own behavior, but also by the knowledge that Mavis had probably been right to call her on it. She couldn't help but blame Wood a little. After all, she understood his grief better than anyone. They were soul mates. But he had scarcely spoken to her. Of course, when she thought about it, she really didn't see him speaking to anyone. But then again, there was also the idea that when a man has spilled himself inside of you, he needs to come up with a little something on public occasions, too. She picked up the phone now and dialed. She knew it was brazen, but if Milan answered, she would ask some little something about the wedding. And if it was Wood, well then, she had something to say. He answered on the second ring. She said, sounding a little breathy, "God, it was hard to be near you today and not touch."

He was obviously startled. He hesitated, then, "This is probably not a good time."

"Is she in the room?"

He sounded uncomfortable. "No."

Now she made her little speech. "I got pulled over by a state trooper on the way home."

"I told you not to drive fast."

"He offered to tear up the ticket if I would have dinner with him. You know, he was one of those big ol' country boys who's always got a hard-on."

"I don't like this story."

"Don't worry. I'm not going. But I should, because you were so mean."

He hadn't meant that he was jealous, although maybe he was a little. But mostly he was surprised by the immaturity of her wanting to tell this story to him. Especially on the day of his best friend's funeral. He said, "I'm sorry. I'm feeling pretty low right now."

"I know. I loved him, too."

Wood heard someone pick up on the line. Duff sighed. "I wish I could take you in my mouth and make all your pain go away."

Wood cleared his throat. "Okay. So, I guess I should go—"

Someone hung up. He said, "Listen, I care for you. A lot. But this is not good."

"Would you rather not see me anymore?" Nice recovery. Now she was showing him some backbone.

"Don't be crazy. We'll talk."

"Okay, but my phone may get turned off. If that happens, I'll get a phone card at the 7-Eleven and call you."

They hung up. Wood felt sick. It was either Milan or Charlie who had picked up. And right now he couldn't decide which would be worse.

Duff went into the bedroom and put on her nightgown. She was getting a disturbing vibe that Wood was becoming less sure of his feelings for her. She stared at her breasts through the thin fabric. Suddenly, she felt stupid for having paid over four thousand dollars for something so artificial that, in her youth, she would have ridiculed. How had she let things get this far? It had cost her an old car, a ton of tip money, and her entire income tax refund. She had always been the girl in the catbird seat. The girl who things came to. Not the girl who chased things. Now here she was calling him at home, acting desperate. After years of choosing wrong men, had she become completely blinded by what appeared to be a second chance at happiness? She was spending her life savings, losing her dignity, risking her son. It was insane. And strangely, it was also why she now had to prevail.

At Fast Deer Farm, Milan was in the shower trying to wash off the phone conversation between her husband and his lover. But she was feeling extremely calm. And strong. The first twenty years of her life had been filled with nothing but drama and she was thinking how much better she had liked the last twenty. How in spite of Wood's indifference, there wasn't a single day that came to mind that she would take back, except of course for Dr. Mac and Jeter dying.

When she had arrived home from scattering Jeter's ashes, she had gotten out the poems and stories he had written about her and read them all for the first time. And she had been stunned, not only by the meticulous portraits of her own psyche (as though he had seen inside of her) but also the obvious love that had gone into creating them. She had already memorized her favorite line: "For whatever was heroic in human beings lay not in the smart observer, but rather in the one who feels deeply and then endures. And that person was, and always would be, the rose maker." There it was. She was an *endurer,* which was its own kind of heroism. A most powerful idea from someone who thought she was worth all his beautiful words that now coursed through her veins like a much needed transfusion. There was Main Street coming through for her again. How she loved the son of the man with candy. It was almost as electrifying as when Hank Jeter had said the queen would be lucky to know her.

Wood came into the bathroom. She saw a hazy version of him through the steamed glass. She was thinking it was fitting that his image was murky because she wasn't sure who he was anymore. He might as well have panty hose on his head and have come in here to rape or rob her. He seemed to be looking for something. He was all hunched over, slamming drawers. Suddenly, she felt sorry for him and knew with certainty now that she no longer wanted to participate in all of this. She wanted it to be over. Then, for the second time in her life, she did something completely impulsive, something she had neither imagined nor planned. Without even turning the water off, she opened the door and stepped out. She reached for her thick white terrycloth robe and wrapped it around her. She was dripping wet and her hair was plastered to her face. Wood was startled, but no longer wondered who had picked up the phone. Then she stepped in front of him and said matter-of-factly, "All my life, I trusted you. Until now, you never lied to me. You never let me down . . . So I think, I finally see how important this must be to you. And that there's really no reason for me to get up early anymore and put on makeup or read all those books that you suggest I read . . . because I get it now . . . I get that all the vacations I can plan and having our friends over and fixing up this house and raising our children is not going to be enough for you." Here, she struggled to keep her voice steady. "But I want you to know, Wood, that it's been more than enough for me. And I have only you to thank. For Elizabeth and Charlie. And a real home . . . and love . . . and, and Christmas. I could never repay you. So, if this is what you want, then go on and do it. Because I owe you that . . . and also because I do so love you." Wood stared at her, disbelieving.

"But right now, I just need for you to leave."

He marveled at how different she looked without all her products. He used to stand at her vanity and peruse them all and say facetiously, "My God, nobody's that ugly." And now she was standing here, barefaced, exposed, telling him he could go and she had never been more gracious or looked more lovely, with drops of water caught in her lashes as she tried not to cry.

Wood's life had been a smooth, straight ride for so long. It seemed like all the things one never sees coming had been saved up for the moment he arrived on the threshold of middle age. He had gotten off his horse to look around and everywhere he turned, there was a sucker punch waiting. He had done what his father had taught him never to do, put his oar in the water in the middle of a good, long glide. And now, in spite of everything, here was his own wife giving him her blessing to leave, telling him she loved him, *thanking* him. This was even more unexpected than finding out that his best friend had been in love with her. And it wasn't some woman's magazine ploy either. He could see that. Could see her pain and the genuineness of what she was saying. If Milan was conniving something, you could tell it a mile away. And she would never know that you knew either, which made it all kind of endearing. She could be so childlike—laughably transparent in her plans to get her own way, excited about her birthday weeks in advance, incapable of hiding how much she wanted to please you—and yet, so utterly adult in her responsibilities to her children and family and friends. It was confusing, the contradictions. Maybe Jeter had been right to be fascinated by the terrain of her. Maybe she was worthy of poetry, even though she didn't like it much herself.

But could any wife sincerely thank her philandering husband and then give him her blessing to leave? Could such a thing be true? What was she? Some kind of Neiman-Marcus-shopping,   Mercedes-Benz-driving saint? Had he really so misunderstood her all these years? He honestly wasn't sure anymore. He just knew that she was hurting and he had never felt sorrier about anything in his life. He wanted to pick her up and hold her and dry her hair and tell her that this had all been a terrible mistake. But he knew that would be too easy a solution for his crime. And he also knew that he had someone else's feelings to consider, now. And that wherever he turned would be a betrayal in some fashion. Wood kept his hand on top of her head for a moment. Finally, he said, "If you need me, I'll be sleeping at the office."

Then he left, realizing for the first time that the woman who lay crumpled on the bathroom floor was stronger than he was.

None of the people in the painting that Wood was standing in front of looked happy. It was not an important, artistic observation. It was just something he noticed and it depressed him—these strange humans with their sour, jumbled faces. He wasn't in the mood. And he didn't give a damn what was Cubed. He had already mastered rejecting the play of light on form in Miss Phipps's first-grade class.

Duff had gotten tickets for the Picasso exhibit months ago. Wood hadn't felt like picking her up and then driving all the way to Fort Belvedere, but they hadn't seen each other since Jeter's funeral and he could sense that this was important to her. Then, Milan had asked him to come by and help pick out wedding music. But rather than admit that he had plans, he said he had to tend to Trudy Davis, who was dying of bone cancer, when only the dying and the cancer part were true.

On the way home, Wood and Duff were discussing Picasso's notorious misogyny and Duff had told Wood how the artist got all his women to cut his toenails for him. And Wood had said the guy needed his ass kicked. And Duff laughed, telling Wood that he was the only man in the world whose toenails she would cut. And he had said he wouldn't want her to do that, or that he wouldn't like it, or something. Whatever it was, it hurt her feelings.

Then, just as they got to the outskirts of Excelsior Springs, Duff announced that she wanted to go see the springs themselves.

She could tell he hadn't really enjoyed the day and now she was determined to make up for that. And not wanting to hurt her feelings again, he made the turn. They found a secluded spot and, in spite of the fact that they had on their good clothes, Duff immediately got out of the car and jumped in the water, not caring that it was the end of summer and that these springs were always cold. She was standing in the middle of them now with her hands on her hips. Her clothes were wet, her blouse was transparent, her skirt was hiked up around her thighs. And what he was thinking was how lovely and natural his wife had looked when she dove from a rock in the moonlight and when she stepped out of the shower that night. The night she had asked him to leave. And that *this* seemed staged and forced and even exhibitionistic and he wished he was somewhere else.

Duff was calling him a slacker now and daring him to come on in. He couldn't leave her out there alone, if for no other reason than it would be rude. So he took off his belt and shoes and socks and waded in, shocked by the coldness and impressed with her ability to withstand it. She splashed him until he was as wet as she was. And then she unzipped his pants and tried to make love, which surprised him because the water was around fifty-five degrees. And he had to explain to her that it was physiologically impossible to have an erection under these conditions. And then he was annoyed, remembering that she had made A's in science but still didn't seem to believe him. After a while, it became apparent that they were just two people standing around in cold water, so they went back to the car.

Once they were under way again, with the heater turned up, Wood was thinking of a thick white terrycloth robe that matched Milan's. Duff began to pout. It was in the way she sighed and held her cigarette and leaned against the window looking out. Finally, he pulled over and asked her what was wrong. She said she felt he didn't want her anymore, that he had just come back after twenty years to get some old romantic notion off his mind. And he claimed that absolutely was not true, all the while wondering if it was. He couldn't help noticing the two large, wet outlines of her dark nipples pressed against her blouse. He put his hands there and caressed the hardness of these recent purchases, trying to reassure her, kissing her lips. She removed her panties and he slid across the seat. But she said, "No, not here."

He was puzzled. She pointed to the highway. "There."

He knew exactly what she meant. When they were seventeen, they had put on the Beatles' "Why Don't We Do It in the Road" and done just that. In commemoration of the song, they had done this on the road from Paris to Hayti. It had been exhilarating. And they had gotten away with it, too. But for Wood, the idea had lost its freshness. And though they were still not back to the main highway, a car could certainly come along this road and he would scarcely have time to get his pants up. She was out of the vehicle now and on her way to the center line, determined to mine something memorable from this day—danger, forbidden sex, some kind of crazy intimacy? Wood felt that much of it had already been a disaster, plus his manhood had been impugned at the springs. Then again, he had to admit it wasn't every day that your old girlfriend lies down in the middle of a road with her huge, custom-made-for-you tits pointing toward heaven and her legs apart, waiting.

Wood got out of the car, feeling more duty bound than excited. A few minutes later, as Duff's pleasurable cries took on their own rhythm, he found himself wondering what had happened to the boy who used to ring doorbells and confess that he was the one who had knocked a ball through the window. But he didn't really need to ask that question. He knew where he was. He was in the middle of Arkansas County Road 121, humping a woman who was not his wife and using the last painful gasps of a dying cancer patient to cover it all up.

It was Monday morning and the wedding of Elizabeth Marie McIlmore and Lukas Duffer Childs was scheduled to occur on Saturday at two o'clock. Workers had already begun to arrive at Fast Deer Farm and large metal stakes, intended to secure a four-thousand-square-foot tent, were being driven into the lawn. Dwight and Denny came every day, fussing over the construction and floral embellishment of a giant trellis. Though they mostly bickered between themselves, they were unfailingly solicitous of Milan, the one person in Paris they worshipped. And they rode herd on all the other workers, too, even those not under their jurisdiction, saying things like, "We would never show that to Mrs. McIlmore. It simply won't do."

For her part, Milan was glad not to have a moment of quiet. In order to give the caterers extra space, she had gotten up at 4 A.M. and moved hundreds of Wood's grandmother's old canning jars out of the garage. Because if she was awake and idle, she would start to feel a sort of paralyzing sadness that would make her not want to get up ever again. And so she never stopped moving. She was either doing something or she was asleep. No in between. No downtime to think. And she held on to all of her notebooks, going through seemingly hundreds of pages of lists, as though the coils that held these papers together were magical charms that somehow gave her strength.

Mavis was in the McIlmore den, talking to a seafood supplier on her cell phone. Obviously, the person on the other end was not saying what Mavis wanted to hear, which caused her to pace and groan and increase her volume. Milan, who could hear her all the way in the kitchen, rolled her eyes and sighed. Even though she and Mavis spoke only sparingly and out of necessity now, there had never been any question as to who would cater the most important event ever to be held at Fast Deer Farm. Especially with Mavis being Elizabeth McIlmore's godmother.

Milan hurried to the oven and removed a tray of chocolate chip cookies. Because Elizabeth was getting all of the attention lately, Milan had made these for Charlie and his friends. Actually, she had sliced them from a refrigerated roll and then baked them, after eating a good part of the dough herself. She finished putting the cookies on a plate. Mavis, still on her cell phone, entered and turned up her nose at them. Milan picked up the plate and breezed by Mavis without acknowledging her.

Rudy entered, struggling with a box of four hundred linen napkins. Mavis barked into the phone, "Look, I just need to know that it will still be packed in dry ice when it gets here." Rudy stopped and stared at her.

"My God! Are we ordering more sperm?"

Mavis scowled, waving him off.

Upstairs, Milan paused outside the door, listening to a conversation between Charlie and several other boys as they played a video game.

"What are you, man, some kind of pussy?"

"Oh, look at that! He's running away! Just like a little pussy!"

"Pussy. Pussy. Pussy."

Suddenly Milan's face felt hot and she was filled with anger. She didn't know if this had something to do with the disrespect that was currently being inflicted on her by her own husband, but hearing her son speak so disparagingly of women both surprised and infuriated her. And also caused her to use a word that she had never used before in her life. When she entered the room, the boys had immediately stopped playing and looked up at her.

Milan said evenly, "Charlie McIlmore, if you want to use that word, then you better learn to use it correctly. How dare you say that pussy is weak! Pussy brought you into this world. Pussy . . ." she was searching now, "holds your head when you're sick and, and . . . irons your pajamas." Milan set the cookies down, looking around.

"Who do you think painted this room? Who do you think spent four hours driving to

Little Rock and back to get you that video game that nobody else could find?" Charlie looked unsure. Milan said, "Well?"

He guessed, softly, "Pussy?"

"That's right! As a matter of fact, I don't think there's anything in this entire house that you can eat, drink, or wear that wasn't brought here or made possible by pussy. And there's nothing bad or scared or weak about it! I think I can speak for all your mothers when I say the next time I hear you boys using that word"—Milan couln't think of anything, then—"you better give it some serious thought."

Charlie and the others were frozen, speechless. They had never seen this side of Milan and she had never seen it herself. Then she smiled and said sweetly, "Now I brought you all some cookies. Would anybody like one?"

They nodded, hoping that was the right answer. "Well, I'll just be downstairs if you need anything else." Then, she left, feeling better. The way people who have little control over their lives feel when they have finally drawn a line somewhere.

*   *   *

Across town, the man who hadn't helped with the wedding music was installing an intrauterine device when his nurse came in and said that Kathleen Duffer was on the line and that it was important. He took the call in another room and was shocked to hear her sounding hysterical. He thought something had happened to Luke or Elizabeth. And when she assured him that this was not the case, he relaxed a little. Then she said, "We need to talk. I can't tell you over the phone. It's too important. You have to come here tonight."

Wood left Paris immediately after scraping a cervix for cancer cells and drove the two and a half hours to Excelsior Springs without stopping. All that time, he was wondering what the hell this was. Was she wanting to end it or maybe give him some kind of ultimatum? Suddenly, he felt irritated that she had refused to tell him anything on the phone. Maybe driving three hundred miles round trip in one night across mountainous terrain was fun if you were twenty. But Wood was thinking he was tired and that he was too old for this kind of nonsense. He wasn't sleeping well on his office sofa and now he could hardly keep his eyes open. If he were having an affair with Milan, she would never ask him to do something like this. She would be concerned for his safety. Or, at the very least, meet him halfway, as she had in college. Or better yet, tell him not to come at all, because that's what phones were for.

He wondered if he got killed on this treacherous road, whether Duff might wear red to his funeral and then tell everyone that he would've wanted her to be gay. He suddenly realized that they had never even discussed what she should do if something happened to him. Now he had a sick feeling that if he died, then sometime down the road, she might tell their story to her son and he, in turn, to Elizabeth. No! No! No! Wood was horrified just at the thought of it. Their children would never be old enough to hear something like that. Not if they lived to be a thousand! Now he was bothered by the feeling that Duff might not have the good judgment to know such things. And for the first time, he realized, just as he pulled up in front of her darkened house, that he really wasn't sure how much he trusted her.

She answered the door wearing his old

high school football jersey and no panties. He was shocked because he hadn't seen his jersey in years. Hadn't even known that she had it. And then, before he could even remove his jacket, she had jumped in his arms and wrapped her bare legs around him, probing his mouth with her tongue. He was thinking that she tasted like cigarettes and beer and he didn't know why he hadn't noticed this before. She took his hand and led him to the sofa. "God, I'm glad you're here."

There were lavender-scented candles burning everywhere. She said she had gotten off work too late to pay her electric bill. She sat opposite him with her legs half-folded, taking in a deep meditative breath. "Something terrible has happened. I know you're going to be angry, but just listen before you say anything. Okay?"

"Okay." Right now he was wondering if she knew that her legs were apart enough that he could see everything or that maybe because she was so upset, she wasn't aware. He was thinking, "I look at this all day and then I drive all night to get here and the same damn thing is staring at me."

She began, "Luke read my journal."

"What journal?"

"The one I write in. Every day."

"About what?"

"Personal growth. Observations. You and me."

"Shit. You've got to be kidding. Why would you do that?"

"I've always done that."

"Why? That's stupid." He got up. He was angrier than she had ever seen him.

She said, "It's an outlet."

"Maybe for teenage girls! That's why there's a teenage girl on the pink plastic cover! What the hell's wrong with you?"

She was genuinely hurt. "I can't believe you're talking to me this way. I've always collected my thoughts in journals. I thought you knew that."

As bad as this was, she'd had a strange confidence that it would bring them closer together.

He tried to calm himself. "Okay. Just tell me what was in it?"

"Everything."

"What do you mean, everything?"

Now she was yelling. "Everything we've done together! Everything I think about it! Everything!"

Wood began pacing. "This is unbelievable. This is a damn nightmare." Then he crossed to her. "You can't just write down general information, like appointments and dates and things to do? You have to actually get a piece of paper and put our names on it and the fact that we fucked? I don't get that! How could you be so careless?"

She looked at him for a long time and then said, evenly, "You're the one who had to get married."

He sat for a while and hung his head. The lavender from the candles was starting to burn his eyes. "You do understand, don't you, that this will destroy our children? I mean, forget what they think about us. They'll never be able to have anything together now."

She was smiling but there was no happiness in it. "And when did you realize this? When you were lying on top of me or between my legs?"

He nodded, acknowledging her point. After a while, he asked, "All right, tell me what Luke said."

"He said he was too upset to talk and that he wanted to discuss it with Elizabeth first."

"Well, that's great. That's great." Wood was laughing now to himself. "I don't know what

to say. Alienation. Death. Destruction. We got
it all now."

She crossed and put her arms around his
waist, laying her head against him. "I'm
sorry. I thought it was locked."

Wood nodded as though he understood.
He held her and patted her, trying to feel
something. After that, he left.

For the next few days, Wood wandered
around in a stupor. He didn't attempt to con-
tact Duff or Milan, but he tried constantly to
reach his daughter at her dorm, where she
refused to take his calls. He stopped eating
and dark circles appeared under his eyes.
His patients began asking if he was ill. One
day, when he was sitting in his office telling a
woman about her options for menopause,
he noticed that a pair of his underwear was
actually lying on the sofa and he was sure
she had seen it, too.

Duff rolled into town on Thursday in her little Toyota and set up camp at the Holiday
Inn. She hadn't been able to speak to Luke
either, but she took that as a good sign, fig-
uring that if he and Elizabeth were going to
call off the wedding, they would've done so

by now. She was here to oversee the preparations for the rehearsal dinner, which her parents, who would be coming in from Florida tomorrow, had agreed to host.

The dinner would be held at a place Duff had long ago rejected—the country club of Paris. But now she was grateful to be staging this important event there. Because she could only imagine the tricks Milan had up her sleeve for the wedding. She wouldn't be surprised if the Tournament of Roses Parade came down the aisle. Certainly Duff didn't feel competitive about money, but she didn't want her son to be humiliated by a rehearsal dinner at IHOP either.

What she was concerned about at the moment was that she hadn't heard from Wood. Duff felt ill herself just thinking what he must be going through. As painful as it was for her and Luke right now, they at least had shared their many past troubles together. She had sheltered him from nothing. That's why they were so close. She knew it had to be so much worse for Wood and Elizabeth, who had been supremely buffered from most of life's hardships.

To tell the truth, Duff was starting to feel

that maybe it was best for everyone that Luke had read her journal. She certainly hadn't wanted their children to find out about her and Wood in this fashion, but maybe there was no good way to tell them. And at least now, it was out in the open, which was exactly where Duff liked to operate. She had always been a person of integrity and deeply resented being forced into shadowy terrain. At least now she could be honest and forthright with her son, having regained the side of herself that she respected most.

Duff spent a good portion of the afternoon conferring with the chef at the country club, along with Mr. Leonard Stiles, who had been the manager for over thirty years. Today, he seemed overly solicitous toward her, having remembered that she was the first and only woman to go topless there.

That night, Wood called to say that he had to tend to a longtime patient, Trudy Davis, who was dying. He didn't care that she had actually died the day after the Picasso exhibit. He no longer had the energy for new lies.

Duff ordered some Bailey's Irish Cream from room service and signed her daddy's name to the tab. By nine, she was smoking in bed and watching some insects eat their young on the Discovery Channel. She was wondering if this was some kind of cosmic message, cheap symbolism, or merely a coincidence. She noticed a rogue hair of mysterious origin on the thin bedspread and, repulsed, kicked the cover onto the floor. Then, she lay back down on the sheet with her hand over her eyes, unhappy, emitting smoke.

At Fast Deer Farm, the list maker was propped up in her clean, fluffy bed surrounded by all of her notebooks. She had on her favorite peach nightgown and her skin looked luminous in the romantic restaurant lighting that she had long ago had installed in her and Wood's master bedroom. Right now, she was conducting a sort of mental wedding rehearsal by outlining the ceremony on paper. She spoke softly to herself, enumerating each step. When she got to the part where the mother of the groom and the mother of the bride would be seated, she wept a little, but never even stopped to wipe her eyes. Then, she went right on with the rest of the make-believe ceremony, as though it had been only slightly interrupted by a small summer shower.

Even though it was past ten o'clock, Wood was still seated at his desk in his office, re-folding a fast-food wrapper and talking to Charlie on the phone.

"I don't get it, Dad. Why can't you just come home?"

"I can't right now, Charlie. Your mother and I've got some things to work out."

"Well, you better not wait too long. She's acting crazy."

"Why? What happened?"

"Nothing. She just came running in my room and gave me and all my friends this big lecture about how pussy is strong. And we better not ever forget it. I'm not kidding, Dad. She must've said it fifteen times."

Wood was puzzled, then he said, a little weary, "Well, I don't know what to tell you, son. Those sound like words of wisdom to me."

Mavis's big Oldsmobile Cutlass was speed-ing away from Whispering Pines Cemetery. Mavis was driving and Milan was in the back-seat with baby Paris, after having delivered a lush bouquet of Elizabeth's wedding flowers to Dr. Mac's grave. This was Milan's way of including her father-in-law in the festivities and a small opportunity for Mavis to show thanks for the little girl in the backseat. Right now, Milan, who always got dressed up to go to the cemetery, was singing "Jimmy Crack Corn" to Paris. She did this mainly so she would not have to speak to Mavis.

Mavis said, "You should sing 'In This World of Ordinary People, I'm Glad There's You.' She loves that."

Milan frowned. "That's no baby song." Then sweetly to Paris, "Is it? You should tell her that's no baby song."

Mavis made an abrupt turn onto a black-top road, tipping Milan over. After about a mile, she pulled into a driveway and parked the car in front of a trailer. Before the three had even reached the porch, a minuscule country woman named Yankee Epps, who was Tommy Epps's cousin, came out to greet them. Even though Mavis made all of Doe's wedding cakes, it was Yankee who spent painstaking hours adding the sumptuous details. And now Mavis wanted Milan's approval before this one made its final journey to Fast Deer. The cake was exquisite and Milan graciously found words of praise for both women, but directed it all to Yankee.

Once they were back in the car, the glow

from the cake had faded. Now Milan was wetting an antique handkerchief with her mouth and rubbing Paris's face with it.

Mavis watched in the mirror. "Please do not spit on my child."

"We're freshening our faces. Mind your own business."

Then, suddenly, out the window on her right, Milan noticed Wood's Austin-Healy sitting in a car wash stall and saw that Duff, holding a long metal wand, was the one washing it. Duff had on tight cutoff jeans with a long-sleeved turtleneck tucked into the waist and was standing with one hip cocked as she sort of cavalierly slung the wand around.

Milan yelled to Mavis, "Stop the car!"

"What? Why?"

"Stop the car! Now!" Mavis pulled over and Milan jumped out. Then Mavis picked up Paris and placed her in her baby sling and began running after Milan. Now Mavis could see where Milan was headed.

She called to her, "Do you really want to do this?"

Milan didn't answer but picked up speed in her high heels. Mavis said, reassuring Paris, "It's okay, sweetie. Don't be afraid. Auntie

Milan's finally having that nervous break-down."

Duff looked up and seemed happy to see Milan coming toward her. As Milan spoke, Duff continued working.

"If you want to have an affair with my husband, there's plenty of other towns to do it in."

Duff said, "Who are you, the sheriff?"

"I'm asking you to not stand here, on this street, in that outfit, washing his car, when you know everyone's aware of the two of you and it's the day before our children's wedding."

"My car broke down. He loaned me his. I'm washing it as a thank-you."

Milan was calm. "No, you're not. That's not what you're doing at all."

Suddenly Duff didn't look friendly any-more. She coolly pointed the spray, which was now on soap cycle, toward Milan. "You ruined my life."

Milan didn't even flinch as the suds hit her. "No. You did that yourself. And now I guess you're working on messing it up for the next generation."

Then Milan tried to take the handle away from Duff. As they struggled, Duff said, "Stop it! You're hurting me! You're always so damned enthusiastic."

Milan got the wand. Now Duff was yelling, "You never forgot to take a birth control pill! You never forgot to do anything in your life!"

Milan sprayed her with suds. "That's right. I'm a responsible adult, not a carefree, fornicating goat!"

(Carefree, fornicating goat! Not from the *Reader's Digest* vocabulary quiz, but from simply having had enough!) Duff lunged at her, causing them both to go down. Milan said, as they struggled, "I don't have to explain myself to you. All that matters is that I got a wonderful daughter out of all of it who's made your son very happy. If I were you, I'd be glad for that."

They were rolling around on the concrete, completely covered in soap when the water went off. A crowd was beginning to form.

Milan yelled, "Put another quarter in, Mavis."

"What?"

"Put another quarter in!"

Mavis said, "I don't have another quarter! Anyway, it takes four." She turned to several people, explaining, "She doesn't know. She washes her own house and car."

An elderly man handed Mavis some coins. "Here, I've got a couple."

A redneck type came up with the rest. "Hell, I'll give 'em a dollar if they keep it up."

Mavis took the coins and, carrying Paris, ran to the control box and deposited them.

Milan yelled, "Put it on water, not soap!"

And Duff added, "And kill the wax!"

Milan seconded this. "Oh my God. That's right! Kill the wax!"

Mavis shook her head, yelling, "All right! I heard you!" Then, as she fidgeted with the box, "I'm trying to read the damn directions, here. You'll take what you get!"

When Milan got her breath back, she said to Duff, "Just so you know, I've told Wood he's free to do whatever he wants."

Duff was floored. She took this in, and then said, "Do you mean that?"

"Yes." They looked like two overwhelmed laundresses, their clothes heavy with water and suds. Milan said, "All I ask is that the two of you not do another thing to ruin this wedding."

Duff affected warmth, "That's the last thing I want."

"Good. Now, I'm the mother of the bride and you're the mother of the groom. We are going to get up and shake hands and show everybody that we can still make this work."

Milan stood up and extended her hand. Duff stood up and shook it. Some in the crowd applauded just as the water came back on. Realizing that the sprayer was too long for Milan to use on herself, she asked Mavis to do this for her. Then she stood ramrod straight, mustering as much dignity as she could while Mavis begrudgingly hosed down her front and backside. After that, Duff turned around and Mavis stepped closer to her, causing Duff to jump as the spray stung her legs. Mavis smiled. "Sorry. There's just somethin' about having your own wand." Then emboldened, she made Milan jump, too. Milan glared at her, as some of the spray landed on baby Paris, who laughed.

CHAPTER 23

On Friday, the bride and groom arrived in Paris. Wood was so inconsolable by now that he told a patient she didn't need a hysterectomy, when in fact, she did. But he simply wasn't up to discussing it. He made a mental note that he would call her later and tell her he had made a mistake or that he was getting out of medicine completely and would give her a referral. Wood may have become an adulterer, but he had never been unprofessional. Now he couldn't even seem to summon the stamina required for an ordinary workday, much less the kind of show-must-go-on energy that his wife was fairly famous for.

He could only imagine the shameful scene that was now taking place across town in his own house. Even though Milan knew of his affair, he had never specifically admitted it. Until she had so poignantly stepped from the shower and told him that it was time for him to leave, they had coexisted with some sort of mutual "don't ask, don't tell" détente. But today, he felt sure, as close as Milan and Elizabeth were, there was no way his daughter could keep her terrible secrets to herself. Nor did he want her to be burdened alone with it. Well, maybe he did want that just a little.

Wood hated thinking of all the things Duff might've written on the pages of her now infamous journal but a good number of the sexual positions and words that had been uttered in ecstasy while he was comprising one-half of those positions now ran through his mind. There was the "Excelsior Springs Can't Get It Up Chilled Dick Dip" and the "Arkansas County Road Fuck Fest," just to name a few. It was hideous. Unfathomable. As many times as he and Jeter and Brundidge had seen the movie *Fatal Attraction* and been terrified by it, that cautionary tale was nothing compared to this. Please! Let some snaky-haired, psychotic bitch come at him with a butcher knife! What a blessing that would be! He would give all his wealth just for the chance to wrestle such a creature around his own master bathroom, if that event could stand in place of this. Because this was hell on earth for adulterers. Who needs locust and plagues? This was hubris punished unparalleled, unlike any other he had come across on his own library shelves. Even William Shakespeare had not come up with this particular brand of male suffering. And it had all been brought about by a silly predictable mistake that could've been committed in any one of Milan's bourgeois romance novels.

As it turned out, Wood knew his daughter very well. She hadn't intended to tell her mother about the journal at all. But whether it was from the stress of the wedding or the affair or both, as soon as Milan's arms were around her firstborn, the tears came, flowing as effortlessly as the news of her father's betrayal. The last thing she wanted to do was hurt her mother. But the sun had always shone on Elizabeth McIlmore and, unlike Milan, she was unable to keep such things inside. However, she did have the maturity and foresight not to wound her mother with details. And for some reason, Milan didn't press her for these things. It almost seemed to Elizabeth that her mother already knew.

A few miles away, a DO NOT DISTURB sign had been placed on the door of an ordinary motel room. Inside, Kathleen Duffer was dealing with a drama of her own making, unlike any of the ones she had created in the past. Her son, who had set his suitcase down and was now standing a few feet from her, seemed to be waiting for an answer.

Duff lit a cigarette and stretched her legs out. "I don't know. He's just someone I never got over. I suppose I was looking for something."

"Well, you shouldn't have been looking for it here. This was my deal."

She seemed unprepared for his harsh attitude. "Luke, I grew up here. This is where I'm from."

"Oh, I'm sorry. So what are you claiming? Fucking rights?"

She smacked him hard and lost her cigarette. He blinked, trying to comprehend her, while brushing the ashes from his face. She reached for him, apologizing, but he pushed her away with his hands and a profanity. She was on the floor now, saying how sorry she was and trying to find the lit cigarette.

He said, as though he were finally resolving an old curiosity, "You know, Grandma and Grandpa are right. You do only think about yourself. They gave you everything and you just pissed it all away."

Finally, she retrieved the cigarette and snuffed it out in the cheap plastic ashtray. Then she got another one and lit it before she spoke.

"I know you're very angry at me right now. You have every right to be. But don't let them use this to turn you into some Republican country club asshole. That's not who you are."

"Yes, it is, Mother. If the fact that I like not getting my credit cards cut up and knowing where I'm gonna be living next month and that my mother is not gonna be screwing my future father-in-law makes me a Republican country club asshole, then that's exactly who I am."

She got up and crossed to the sliding glass door and stared out at the empty swimming pool.

"I know it doesn't look that way, but until now, everything I've done has been for you."

"That is such a lie. What did you do that was for me? Get knocked up by a loser who beat the hell out of both of us? All you do is make bad decisions."

Duff exhaled, put out her cigarette again, and gave up. "Okay, you want your pound of flesh? You can have it. You're right. I'm a fuck-up and a loser." She sat down on the bed and stared at the floor for a long time. Then, she said, "I've been trying for so long to get things together before you were old enough to figure out what a mess they were in." She laughed a little. "I guess I lost that race, huh?"

Luke sat down next to her. She turned toward him. "I know you can't forgive me now, son. Or maybe ever. But I've worn that waitress uniform for a long time and you know a lot of worthwhile things because of me. And I don't care what I've done, you can't take that away. Because it's a fact. And also because it's all I have."

Then she looked away from the eyes that seemed to have finally decided about her.

Elizabeth removed some bits of apple from her coat pocket and held her hand out to Sook, who licked it clean through the wooden bars of her stall. Then she walked over and leaned against the tack wall, next to Luke, who had been watching her. Neither spoke, but Elizabeth audibly took in the air, which was ripe with the smell of horses and wet straw. She was thinking that there was something comforting about a barn, which changes even less than a house. No one ever rearranged or recovered things here. She could come home and, here, it would always be the same.

When she turned, she saw the outline of her father in the massive doorway. He looked around and then started walking toward them. Sook, sensing Wood's presence, began to dance a little. Luke unfolded himself, as though he was getting ready for something and Elizabeth crossed her arms, calling out.

"Daddy, I know why you're here. But this is not something that can be fixed."

Wood took this in for a minute and then kept walking. "I just want to tell Luke, this wasn't your mother's idea. None of it. It was all my doing."

Luke crossed to Wood, took his fist, and knocked him down. Wood made no attempt to defend himself. He was momentarily stunned. Sook shook her head and blew gushes of air through her nostrils, as though she were disapproving of this unpleasantness. Wood got up and wiped the dirt from his face.

"Okay. I'll give you that one."

Luke started for the door.

Wood called after him. "You know, it'd be hard to find a worse mess than this one. But it shouldn't keep the two of you from doing whatever the hell you want."

Luke turned to Elizabeth, "I'll call you later."

Wood went after Luke. "Listen, I took your punch. Now I'm asking you to sit down."

Luke thought about it, then walked to

where there were several bales of hay and did so. Elizabeth joined him.

"Thank you." Wood sighed like a man who already knows the futility of his own words. "Now I know this is hard to understand. We're dealing with an old situation here that's got a lot of strong feelings in it. And Kathleen and Milan and I are not going to explain those feelings to the two of you. But, Luke, what I can do is promise you that it will never happen again. And Elizabeth, I promise you, that I will love and honor your mother for the rest of my life."

"Well, that's great, Dad. Now maybe you can also tell us how we can have a wedding, or a baby, or, or . . . even a cup of coffee together, when we can't even all be in the same room."

"I understand it's gonna take some time."

Elizabeth stood up, losing her composure. "You just don't get it, do you? You can't make this okay. These are our mothers you're messing with!"

"All right, calm down."

"You ruined everything and for what? Some stupid piece of nostalgic ass."

Luke admonished her. "Shut up, Elizabeth."

"No, I won't shut up. If it was more than that, then please tell us, Daddy. Because it must have been so wonderful that it was worth hurting my mother in such a cruel and humiliating way. It must've been the greatest piece of ass in the whole wide world."

Luke whipped her around. "Okay. That's enough! Now stop it!" He threw his arms up and headed for the door. "I'm out of here."

Elizabeth and Wood watched him go. Then she turned away from her father, not in anger now, but simply wanting him to disappear.

Wood tried again. "Baby—"

She didn't answer. He gently turned her toward him.

"Listen to me. If you love that boy, then go on and marry him. And pray that if one of you screws up so bad and does the worst thing you've ever done, the other one will say, it's okay. You're gonna be okay. Just come on home." He put his eyes level with hers. "That's what I want for you."

"No. That's what you want for yourself. My God, you're incredible. You think something like this can be forgiven?"

He thought for a moment and then said, sadly, "No. But I have to believe it a little, if I'm gonna get up tomorrow."

She was crying now. Her nose was running and she brushed the sleeve of her sweatshirt across it.

"I was just thinking how when I was a little girl . . . and you would have Uncle Brundy and Uncle Jeter over and you all would get drunk and carry on about these men that you loved so much, like Emerson and Tolstoy and Shakespeare." She wiped the tears off her cheeks with both hands.

"You said their names so often, and the way you said them, I actually thought that you were a friend of theirs."

His voice was a hoarse whisper. "I didn't know that."

"Well, I did. But I just wanted to tell you, I've got it straight now. I don't think that anymore."

He winced a little.

The rehearsal dinner was still hours away. Elizabeth was lying in bed now, with her face half-buried in a thousand-thread-count pillowcase. Her antique French nightstand was littered with the paper wrappers of miniature Mr. Goodbars. Milan was stroking her daughter's hair. After a while, Elizabeth said, "I don't think I've ever hated anyone before."

Milan's hand went still for a moment, then, "Just remember, this is only one of the things your father's done. He's also come home every night for twenty years and given us a wonderful life together."

"You always give him a free pass."

Now Milan continued her stroking. "Honey, do you have any idea how hard he works down at that hospital? He's got more patients than anyone in this town. And he never turns anybody away."

"That gives him the right to have an affair?"

"No. But if we're gonna count up the bad stuff, we're gonna count up the good stuff, too."

Elizabeth raised up and looked at her mother, astonished. "You're gonna take him back, aren't you?"

"I wish it were that easy."

Elizabeth lay back down. "Well, you go ahead. But I never will. Not only for this, but also for . . ." She was unable to finish.

"What?"

"I don't know . . . not loving you the way you . . . deserve."

Milan tried to underplay this, the way parents do when confronted with the unsparing, dead-on observations of children.

"That's what you think?"

Elizabeth wouldn't look at her. "Yes. I'm sorry, but I've always thought it."

Milan lay down next to her. "Oh, Lils, I wish you could've seen us when we were first together. If I just walked in the room, your daddy couldn't keep his mind on anything else. And when I was pregnant with you and Charlie, he was over the moon—"

Elizabeth stopped her. "That was a long time ago."

"I know that. But things always come in cycles. It's like your Grandpa Lanier. He was crazy. Then he was not crazy. You're loved. You're not loved. Everything comes around again. That's just life."

Elizabeth took Milan's hand and held it in both of hers. She had chocolate on her mouth. "Mother, that makes me so sad."

"What?

"You're happy just to remember love?"

Milan thought for a moment, as she rubbed the chocolate off with her thumb. "It's not sad. It's . . . hopeful. I'm just a hopeful person. I always have been." She shrugged, smiling at her daughter. "I guess it's just a gift."

*   *   *

It seemed that everyone in Paris had an opinion as to whether the rehearsal dinner would go on, but it did, simply because no one stopped it from happening. It was as though the wedding cruise had sprung a leak, but until there was a complete damage assessment, no one was willing to tell the passengers that it was over. And so, a good seventy-five people, the ones who were the closest and dearest to the McIlmore and the Duffers, got dressed in their second-finest outfits—the finest having already been reserved for the social event of the year—and drove to the country club of Paris, where they dined on prime rib and roasted squab and praline soufflés and even though everyone, except strangely the Duffers, who arrived from Florida, had heard by now what was going on, they sat politely through dinner and all the required toasts.

Duff and Wood astutely avoided each other as even she, by now, understood the gravity of their situation. When Wood rose to say his toast, he simply welcomed Luke to the family. Then he turned to Elizabeth. "When you were a little girl, I swam the Champanelle River with you on my shoulders." He shook his head a little. "Sometimes its hard for a father to believe that his daughter doesn't need those shoulders anymore. Or that there's nothing much left for him to do but . . . stand in awe." He picked up his glass, rubbing it. "Your mother and I, we had some dreams for a girl who hadn't even put her hand in ours yet. Mostly, I guess . . . about the kind of person she might be. We never told you what they were. Because they seemed too much, overreaching, unfair." Wood stopped, overcome. Finally, he raised his glass toward Elizabeth. "And then you went and surpassed them all."

A number of people were moved. But Wood's daughter was not one of them. Brundidge buried his face in a napkin as Charlotte, who had come down for the wedding, attempted to comfort him. When Luke stood up, he avoided mentioning Wood altogether, but said something nice about the McIlmore family in general. Then he thanked his grandparents for being "the rock that I have always counted on." And he, too, raised his glass toward his intended, saying that he had planned not to get married till he was thirty, but that falling in love with Elizabeth was like getting run over by a long, beautiful train.

Everyone laughed so warmly and appreciatively that Milan, the one who was good at feeling hopeful, started to feel that way again. Started to feel that maybe this wedding could actually come off, after all. And then Luke finished his litany of superlatives regarding Elizabeth with one last thought. "But I guess what I like best about her is her complete openness toward life . . . this spirit of adventure. I don't know exactly what you call it. I don't have it myself. But I've seen it before, in another woman I love. My mother."

If he had been looking at Duff after he said this, he would've known that she had stood up and tried to acknowledge him by touching her heart. But he never looked her way and she, now embarrassed, had left. Milan, who knew the anger Luke was feeling toward his mother, was impressed. She had supported this puppy love in the hope that it could grow into something more. But here was her daughter's fiancé indicating that he was already capable of more—that there was a part of him that was not just a boy, but was, in fact, a man. And even though her lifelong enemy was the recipient of this unexpected generosity, it made it no less meaningful. If a boy so young could express this kind of love and empathy and forgiveness, what would he be like in future years? Wood raised his eyebrows at Milan and both understood that they were sharing the same thought. For a brief moment, it united and bolstered them, just this lovely glimmer of what their daughter might be getting herself affiliated with.

And then, it all turned awful when the Duffers got up to speak. They were supposed to tell everyone to eat, drink, and be happy. That the bar was unlimited and on them. But being the affable Duffers, they wanted to do more. And it became apparent, almost immediately, that they were the only two people in the room who had been kept in the dark about all the events leading up to this evening. And you could see by the worried looks on the faces of people who had failed to tell them these things—you could see that these people now knew that was a mistake.

Tom Duffer, who had clearly had too much to drink, started out by announcing that a lifelong dream was finally coming true tomorrow—a Duffer McIlmore union. And that such a union had almost happened twenty years ago, but didn't, which just goes to show, when it's right, you can't keep a good idea down. And then Susan Duffer helped her husband regale everyone with how much Luke and Elizabeth reminded them of Wood and Kathleen at the same age. How darling they, too, had looked together and so in love. And they had funny stories to go with all the accolades. It went on and on. And was so mortifying that no one seemed able to move or to stop it. Wood set his jaw and stared at the centerpiece. And Milan looked straight at the Duffers and never stopped smiling. And Duff, who had now come back from the ladies' room, watched for a minute, horrified, and then left again. Mavis, sitting with Mary Paige, began to say that someone should put an end to it. She looked right at Brundidge. Charlotte began nudging him with her elbow. And he had whispered, too loudly, what the hell did they want him to do? Now everyone was looking at them and suddenly Brundidge jumped up and waved his arms in the air and said, "Sorry, Tom, but I'm on the meter here. Paying the babysitter eight dollars an hour. I say everybody loves everybody. Let's boogie."

It was incredibly rude and even after the music started, and Brundidge and a reluctant Charlotte had begun to dance, Tom still looked confused. Later, somebody said Eliz-

abeth and Luke could be heard arguing out
by the driving range. And that the Duffers
and their daughter had spoken to one another, but never touched.

After it was over, Wood walked Milan out
to the parking lot and asked if there was anything he could do to help her. And without an
ounce of sarcasm, she said she didn't think
so. And then she got in her car and drove
away, feeling both powerful and sad that her
husband was getting smaller in her rearview
mirror.

C H A P T E R   2 4

It was after midnight and Wood was lying
around in his shorts. The leather from his office sofa periodically stuck to the back of his
legs. His clothes were piled in the chair beside him. He rubbed his jaw where Luke had
hit him and winced a little from the pain. But
he was thinking that it also felt good, even
earned, like a tender muscle after a hard jog.

He got up and crossed to his grandfather's

old glass medical cabinet. He retrieved a bottle of cough syrup and took a long swig. He didn't care that he had already had several drinks at the rehearsal dinner or that he always warned his patients not to mix their medicine with liquor. He just wanted to be unconscious and, so far, that hadn't happened.

Wood returned to the sofa and lay down. He was thinking how miserable he felt and how it was fitting that he should feel this way on this particular sofa where he had inflicted so much misery on others. It was here that he had told Carrie Shoemaker, a mother of six, that she had pancreatic cancer. That was a hard one since she already had Crone's disease and multiple sclerosis, too. Seriously, how much bad news can you deliver before you simply burst out laughing and say, "Hey, you know what? Let's just all go home." This was also the place where he told Joe and Shelby Dunne that their only son's leukemia had returned. And where he held Laura Cahill in his arms because her twins were already dead inside of her—a boy and a girl, facing each other and sucking their thumbs. Whenever his own filmography drifted through his mind, that picture was now forever a part of it. Whenever he kissed his own children goodnight, the Cahill babies were always there with them.

And there were hundreds of other sad stories in which the participants had sat meekly, holding hands, attempting to swallow the sickening lumps in their throats as they tried to steel themselves against the conveyor of all bad news, Wood McIlmore. Yes, this sofa was exactly where a man with his past deserved to be.

Now he was looking at all his academic and medical degrees on the wall. He couldn't have cared less if somebody came along and pissed on them, but he had never really noticed before how much he liked their frames. Milan had chosen a sort of ebony-toned wood with mattes made of cream-colored grass cloth and a thin line of silver. It must have taken her a long time to pick out all the components. He wondered whether, if she had completed her own teaching degree, she would have bothered to frame it with these same ribbons. He decided that she would not have.

Suddenly, he was hungry. He had barely touched his food at dinner. He reached for a sucker in the glass jar on the coffee table and unwrapped it. These were usually given out to children and he wondered how long it had been since he'd had one himself. Years. He lay there in his underwear with his eyes closed, savoring the sugary lemon taste and thinking that he should eat suckers more often. Now he was trying to imagine a time and a place when they would all laugh about these silly goings-on. Maybe a Thanksgiving or a Christmas with family and friends—the grandchildren off playing in another room and he and Milan and Charlie and Elizabeth and Luke and Duff and everybody sitting around the fire: "Oh, man, your mother was sooo mad, she wanted to kill me."

"And your mother! Hell, she had me sleeping at the damn office!"

Laughter.

Now a grandchild wanders in. "Hey, what's going on?"

"Nothing. Just tellin' about the time your grandpa was doin' both your grandmothers."

More laughter.

See? No matter how he arranged it, it just didn't work. As a southerner and a McIlmore, Wood could pan a little nugget of humor out of almost anything. He could laugh about death, defeat, humiliation—southerners were especially good at that. But infidelity, the arsenic of all human intimacy, he now realized could not be laughed over, even with time added. This was something he hadn't considered before and, frankly, it surprised and depressed him.

Suddenly, there was a knock at the door. Someone was calling his name. Someone else was groaning. Wood got up and opened the door. It was Brundidge with Frank Lanier, who was all bent over, holding himself. They entered and Brundidge asked, as though it were important, "What the hell are you eating?"

"A sucker. What's the matter with him?"

Brundidge said, "He OD'd on Viagra."

Frank groaned and fell on the sofa. Wood looked at him. He was sick and tired of everyone in Paris bringing their genitals to his doorstep.

"What the hell's wrong with you, Frank? Where'd you even get Viagra?"

Brundidge answered, "Your wife uses it on her flowers and apparently gives it to him by the truckload."

That was typical of Frank Lanier—embracing anything that renders the most basic acts of human existence unnecessary: Crock-

Pots that do the cookin' while you're out carousing, electrodes that exercise your muscles while you lie in front of the TV, and Viagra so you don't have to get your own hard-on.

Frank mumbled, his mouth pressed into the leather sofa, "I was trying to kill myself."

Wood said, "It's not poison, Frank. Just because you take a lot of something doesn't mean it's going to kill you."

Frank curled up, hugging himself, unable to comprehend that this, like so many of his other problems, was the result of impulsive excess. He had decided, after being laid off by the sheriff's department, that he had bipolar disorder. This was something he accidentally came across (while channel surfing) on a program called *Nightline.* This caused him to spend his life savings on a very expensive mail-order light, billed as a "Mood Rejuvenator." He had also earnestly filed a lawsuit after finding a wad of gum in a McDonald's hamburger, but the case was thrown out after the gum was proven to be Frank's. He had even attempted a brief flirtation with fame, shipping a thousand headshots of himself, five hundred laughing, five hundred crying, to a so-called Hollywood agent. Frank's entire life had been nothing but one treacly drama after another. There was only one thing he seemed to have done right, and that was to stand down the Rolling Stones. And now no one wanted to give him credit for it.

Wood sat next to him. "Why do you want to kill yourself, Frank?"

Frank said, into the sofa, "Nothin' to live for."

Brundidge spat out the words, "It's because the Millennium Committee turned down that Coke can of his! I am sick to death of hearin' about that damn Coke can!"

Frank looked at Wood, his eyes, pleading. "Can't you give me somethin'?"

"I'm sorry, Frank. There's no medical antidote for Viagra. Did you try whacking off?"

"Yes."

"And?"

Frank's voice came from far away. "Nothin'. When I was done, it was still hard."

Brundidge walked away. "Aw, man, I don't even want to know this. Forget the Coke can, Frank! What we should do is amputate your damn dick and put it in the time capsule, 'cause that's the thing that'll be here a thousand years from now."

* * *

A few minutes later, they were in the van. Brundidge was driving. Wood was drinking. Frank was lying in the back, moaning. They had already been to Frank's house and picked up the Coke can and several shovels.

Brundidge said, "We're gonna put it in for you, Frank. It's not worth killin' yourself over. Now, I'm one of the few people who knows where this capsule is buried. So, if you ever tell, you won't have to off yourself, 'cause I'll do it for you."

Frank mumbled, "I'm not gonna tell."

"All right then. See that you don't."

Within an hour, Wood and Brundidge had dug a considerable hole, while Frank sat on a rock, hanging his head in agony. They were not far from the Champanelle River now and about a sixth of a mile from Sheriff Marcus West's house.

Wood offered Brundidge a sip of the whiskey he had pilfered from a crate in the van. Ordinarily, he might have told Frank to go on home and sleep it off, but since Frank was Milan's brother, Wood felt in some small way that he was doing something for her. But that was just the liquor thinking, because it was Milan who had denied Frank's request in the first place. Wood put the bottle back in his jacket pocket and leaned on the shovel.

"Are you sure we're in the right spot?"

"Hell yes. I was here when they put it in. But they used a backhoe."

Wood said, "Well, I've got a backhoe. Let's go get it. I can't stand here diggin' a damn hole all night. I've got a wedding to go to."

Suddenly, Frank started to cry, not just quiet tears, but real girlie crying. "I cain't believe you boys are doin' this for me! Nobody ever did nothin' for me in my whole entire life!" He was sobbing now, overwhelmed. "Man, I just love y'all so much."

Brundidge said, "All right, Frank, calm down. Don't get all *Long Day's Journey into Night* on us."

When they got to Fast Deer Farm, Wood climbed up into the large driver's compartment of the backhoe and started the engine. Then he backed it out of the barn and went toward the gravel road where Brundidge and Frank were waiting in the van. It must've awakened Milan because when Wood looked up at their bedroom window, he saw that she was watching him. He waved and smiled stupidly, and she waved back, as though nothing that he could ever do again would surprise her.

Wood used only back roads to wind his way to the spot where they had all just been. Once there, he worked the backhoe, which farmhands had taught him how to operate as a teenager, and in a while, he had made the hole twice as deep. And still, there was no capsule. After a while, it was 3 A.M. and Wood and Brundidge, who were now drunk, announced that they were going home. Frank, who was also drunk and still hurting, became hysterical. He had known it wouldn't work out. Nothing in his whole life ever had. And this entire Coke can thing, keeping it out of the Millennium capsule was just a payback from Milan for losing their daddy's ashes! That's all this was, payback! No matter what he did, she was never gonna get over it. In spite of Wood's inebriated condition, he suddenly became alert. This was a story he hadn't heard before. He went over and sat down next to Frank.

"What do you mean?"

"Nothin'. I don't mean nothin'."

"No. Go on, Frank. You started it. I wanna hear."

Frank shook his head, "It's nothin'! She's just always been pissed at me, that's all."

"For what?"

"Ever'thing. It all started 'cause she couldn't fix Daddy's face on account of the gun shot was so bad. So Cotrell's had to put him in the furnace. So now she's even more upset 'cause, you know, she's the one who seen it happen."

Wood said, "Wait a minute. Slow down, Frank. Saw what happen?"

"He did it right in front of her."

"Did what?"

"Blow'd his head off."

Wood took this in. Then he said, softly, "Shit. She never told me that."

"That's 'cause she don't want nobody to know. You know Milan, always puttin' on the dog." Frank pointed to under his chin. "Stuck it right here." Frank made a clicking noise. "And he was smilin' at her, too. Anyway, so Mr. Cotrell calls me to come pick up the ashes. After I did, I went to get my truck washed and to the Dandy Dog. I don't know. Somehow, they got throwed away. Hell, they was just in a box. They looked like any ol' thing. So I went back to the car wash and the Dandy Dog, but the trash had already been took away. And Milan, she just freaked out— about how Daddy cannot go back to the Paris dump! That's all there was to it! And so we're out there all night, siftin' through garbage and shit and she's cryin' and car- ryin' on, 'We gotta find Daddy, Frank! We gotta find Daddy!' See, she was always his favorite. At the end, he wadn't even botherin' to use the toilet no more. He was just lettin' her take care of it."

Brundidge came over and said, "Hey Frank, shut up. You shouldn't be tellin' this."

Wood said, "No, let him finish." Then, to Frank, "Go on."

"Well, then all of a sudden, she ain't cryin' no more. She gets all crazy and starts laughin'. And I'm thinkin' maybe she's caught the schizophrenia. I'll never forget, she found this old box of Tide and she's pourin' it ever'where and sayin' 'Lookee here, Frank! Could that be Daddy?' And then she'd just fall on the ground laughin'. I mean, she was gone! Pickin' up shit where people had emp- tied their ashtrays and askin' me, 'Hey, Frank, look at this! Do you think this is Daddy?' And then she'd laugh and say, 'Nope, that's just old cigarette butts! That's not Daddy!'"

Now Wood had tears in his eyes. Brundidge said, "That's the worst story I ever heard."

Frank said, "Well, she ain't never forgive me for that." Then he looked at Wood and added as an afterthought, like it was nothing, "That's the weekend she went back to school and you knocked her up."

Wood looked pained. Brundidge said, "I mean it, Frank. Shut the fuck up."

Frank, seeing the effect of his words, was feeling important now. He said, "Well, it's the truth. That's what caused the real trouble. 'Cause she got so mixed up about ever'-thing, she forgot to take them pills and then she got pregnant. And that's when she come to me, wantin' to know if I know somebody who would marry her. And I say, any man would marry you, Milan, 'cept they all know whose kid it is." He smiled at Wood. "She said she wasn't gonna make you marry her and ruin your life. And so, I asked a couple people for her. And just like I thought, they said they'd sure like to have a go at her, but they weren't gonna marry nobody that was havin' your baby. And she acted like I hadn't really tried at all, but I did."

Wood was staring at Frank now, dumbfounded. Every false assumption he had ever made about his wife, had, in five drunken minutes, been cleared up by the town idiot. Why had he never asked her these questions himself? He didn't know. Could people really lie next to each other for twenty years and never once discuss the thing that seems to be lying there between them? Never once asking, "Say, by the way, did you mean to . . ." or "Oh, no, surely you didn't think . . ." Resentment and suspicion piling up like weathered old tax notices, pinned to the door of a rotting house, not unlike the Lanier house, until one day the foundation gives way and everyone inside is buried alive by the sheer pathetic weight of it all.

Wood had not known that he could feel such sadness. This was worse than being unfaithful. Discovering that not only had his wife not trapped him, but she had apparently been wandering around in the middle of some Wagnerian hillbilly nightmare, trying to find someone else to marry her. It was staggering.

He had been so sure that this great sweeping joke had been played on him, with Milan seeming to get everything she had ever wanted out of it. But nothing, he knew in his heart, that was given in complete love. And so, she had set out to earn that and each day fallen a little farther behind because the person she hoped would someday love her had already made up his mind. It seemed he had misunderstood the terms of their relationship as badly as Jeter had misjudged his and Cherry Smoke's. Wood was sitting on the ground, holding his head in his hands, mumbling.

Suddenly Brundidge, who had continued digging, let out a yelp. Then he tapped the hard surface of something with the tip of his shovel. "Okay. There she blows, boys."

Frank jumped up and began dancing around. "Hot dawg! I knew it! I told ya'll it was there!"

"Yeah, you told us, Frank. You're a regular divinin' rod."

Brundidge struggled to lift the time capsule. Frank jumped in the hole and attempted to help him, jumping around like a game-show contestant who already knows the answer. Brundidge, noticing Wood's distress, called out, "Hey, what's goin' on over there? We're gettin' ready to have a ceremony." Then harshly, "Step back, Frank! Give me some room here."

Now Frank was clutching his Coke can and weeping tears of real happiness.

Wood fell back on the gravel, looking up at the stars and thinking of the role fate or the randomness of life or something had played in his story. There was no question that he was the major villain, but he and Milan were also the victims of poor timing. Just as he was about to propose, she had told him she was pregnant. If he had only spoken first, their entire marriage would have been changed. For him, it was the difference between volunteering and being drafted, and, for her, knowing that she was loved. A missed opportunity, occurring in the span of a moment, as painfully hard to accept as the way, say, Mavis's daddy had drowned. Wood took another swig of whiskey, thinking about that now—about the randomness of life that can sometimes be softened by alcohol and sometimes not. And how beautiful it can be when the DNA from a dead man lying face-down in one inch of water can get together with a little thawed tadpole swimming around in a petrie dish thirty years later and make a little girl named after an entire town. Or how awful, like Wood and Milan's poor timing. Or like when, as Rudy had once told him, if the White Sox had given Castro five hundred more dollars for a signing bonus, Rudy's entire family and all of Cuba would now be free. It was enough to make you want to hold on to something that was true and steady—something like what Wood had already let go of. Now Miss Delaney's voice was in his head. "The overriding message that one may take from all of literature is simply the idea that getting up in the morning is a remarkable act of human courage." And there were also voices from the Literary Society of Paris, reviewing the story of Wood and Milan:

"Well, ever'body kept a tellin' him how wonderful he was, and finally he just got to believin' it."

"Then it turns out, he's just another man, and not a very good one at that."

"It's an old story, but I thought his wife was the best person in it."

Wood was interrupted by Frank and Brundidge carrying on about something. Frank said excitedly, "That ol' boy was tryin' to warn me!" Brundidge brought the soda can over to Wood.

"Do you believe this? Look at what's on this can!"

Wood took it, reading it to himself. "To Frank, Keep a cool tool. Mick Jagger." Wood looked at Brundidge stupidly. Brundidge took the can back and stomped off. "Son of a bitch was a damn psychic!" Wood was thinking this was enough to do him in. A drugged-out rock star giving prophetic, spot-on advice to a hillbilly loser he's known for five minutes. And Wood couldn't even discern the obvious good intentions of the woman who sleeps next to him. Or at least used to.

He was headed for the van now. Going to trade in the whiskey for some scotch. He caught a glimpse of himself in the van's side mirror. He was thinking what a flaming ass-hole he was, and that he should have flames all around his head, like the hood of Frank's car. What made him the grand prize in his and Milan's marriage, anyway? A mere accident of birth. She could just as easily have been the only child of Slim and Dr. Mac and he the teenage caretaker of an incontinent, schizophrenic garbage man. But he was born lucky. He got to be the carefree gilded boy lying around in cheap motel rooms with his lips pressed to her cheek, whispering, "Don't worry, baby, it'll be okay." That was his contribution back then. And never a moment of slipping himself into her marrow. With all the roar of his cheering family and his blue-chip education, that had been the best that Woodrow Phineas McIlmore could come up with.

Brundidge was yelling, "Come on! Let's get the hell outta here! Marcus West just turned his lights on."

Wood got up and lumbered over and looked at what was now a shallow hole and a capsule that didn't seem to be buried very deep at all. He said, almost disinterested, "Damn. You all didn't stick it back in very far."

"We got it back in there good enough. Let's go!"

Brundidge handed Frank his car key. "Frank, you take my van home. I'll get it later."

Frank said, "Where are you goin'?"

Brundidge said, gesturing toward Wood. "I'm riding with him. He's too drunk to drive this thing alone. Go on. Get going."

Frank hugged them both, fighting more tears. "I'll never forgit you all for this."

Brundidge said, "No, Frank, you have to forget. Don't ever mention it again."

"If I ever have a boy, I'm gonna name him Woodrow Earl."

Knowing Frank's other kid was named Doral, after the cigarette, Brundidge said, "Well, then, Lord help him. Now get the hell out of here!"

Brundidge and Wood climbed up on the backhoe. Wood started the engine. Brundidge said, crouching next to him, "Can you still drive this thing?"

"Yeah, I can drive it. But see, here's the problem . . . I don't have anywhere to go." He said this like he was completely out of ideas, like he might not even bother to take his next breath if Brundidge didn't tell him to.

"What the hell's wrong with you?"

Wood didn't look at him. "You know what's wrong with me."

"I don't know nothin'."

"Sure you do. I threw away my life." He hesitated, then, "And I'm not gonna get it back . . . am I?"

After a while, Brundidge said, "I really

don't know." This simple truth coming from someone who put the best shine on everything pierced Wood like nothing else. He reached for the gears and shifted, attempting to steady himself. Then, once they were under way, he shook his head, laughing softly. "You ever see mold?"

"Yeah, I've seen mold."

"I'm talkin' about slime mold. That's the lowest thing on the food chain, Brun." He leaned close like he was passing along a secret. "Other bacteria will not grow on it. Will not touch it."

"So?"

"My God, don't you get it? Even bacteria has a line it will not cross."

"What do you wanna talk about shit like that for? I don't wanna hear it."

"'Cause that's what I studied in med school. See? That's what's so funny." Wood was laughing more now. "I was taught that. I actually knew it."

Brundidge frowned. "Just keep your eyes on the road, okay?"

They drove a while longer. Wood turned morose. "I remember when I used to go down to the hospital and watch my dad in surgery. You remember that?"

"Yeah."

"I'll never forget how, when he would cut people open, he had this way of holding human tissue in his hand. I've never seen anything like it. He did it . . . like it was an honor. Just a big fuckin' honor." Wood stared straight ahead into the darkness. "That's the kind of man he was."

Wood had been adamant that they not drive by Marcus West's house because he was up now and would hear them. And the only other way out was the interstate. But Brundidge, who was not as drunk as Wood, had a sinking feeling there was a darker reason that they were now riding in a glass cab, one story up, on an eight-lane highway. Wood was looking for more trouble—some kind of punishment for all the things he'd done. Because sometimes, engaging something dramatic or dangerous was better than simple anguish, at least for a man. They had gone only a couple of miles when something dramatic and dangerous presented itself.

Just as they were passing the Paris County Fed-Mart Superstore, they saw it. Lonnie Rhinehart, with his two henchmen, sitting in the middle of the empty parking lot. Because Fed-Mart closed at midnight, Lon-

nie often used their vast facility for after-
hours socializing. Like a redneck "Big
Daddy" overseeing his concrete plantation,
he would sit around in his pickup truck till all
hours of the morning, drinking beer and listening to country music on his tellingly large
speakers. Lonnie also hung out at the con-
venience stores and truck stops, but Fed-
Mart was his flagship venue. There was just
something irresistibly seductive about a
place where you could buy ammo in bulk,
along with condoms and a lawn mower, all at
eleven thirty at night.

Brundidge said, "Well, well. Looks like
Christmas is gonna come early this year."

Wood stared for a minute. Then, shifting
gears, he turned into the parking lot. Suddenly, he increased their speed and began
heading straight toward Lonnie's truck.

Brundidge said, "What are you doing? I
just meant, let's finish the fight."

"No. We've already had the fight. Now
we're gonna take the son of a bitch out!"

Brundidge was alarmed. "No. No. Wrong.
Come on, stop it now. Let's get a plan here."

Inside the truck, Lonnie and his two
friends had become riveted by the backhoe
that was now barreling toward them. Lonnie

said, "What the—?" He had no sooner begun to speak than he could see that it was
Brundidge and Wood who were inside the
thing. "Holy shit! What the hell are they
doin'?"

The three rednecks could also see that
Earl Brundidge's mouth was wide open and
that he seemed to be yelling about something. And that Wood, who never took his
eyes off of them, didn't seem to be listening.
Just before the backhoe slammed into them,
Wood stomped on the brake, which caused
a long drawn-out screeching noise, with the
shovel ending up only inches from Lonnie's
front bumper. After that, the five men sat
there, staring drunkenly at one another—the
air heavy with alcohol and testosterone.

Now Wood noticed that Lonnie's lip was
curled in a little sneer. And this made Wood
mad. In fact, it enraged him. The idea that
this man could kill their greatest friend and
still wear a sneer like that. He quickly read-
justed the shovel and once he had engaged
the bottom of Lonnie's bumper, he lifted the
pickup as high as he could, until the front
end was pointed skyward. More howling
could be heard from inside the truck's cab.
Then Wood released the shovel, dropping

them. Wood smiled at Brundidge, pleased. Lonnie frantically fumbled for his keys, but Wood maneuvered the backhoe behind the truck and repeated the procedure. This time, he catapulted the trio into the dashboard, causing their faces to press hard against the windshield. The men's screams could be heard all over the parking lot, with Lonnie's trumping the others. "Shit! This mother's gonna kill us!"

Wood released the shovel again, slamming them to the ground. Brundidge said, "I like that. That was good. Now let's go home."

Wood looked at him and said a little drunkenly, "I told you, I don't have a home."

Then he repositioned the backhoe and began pushing the men and their truck toward the Paris County Fed-Mart Superstore. "Anyway we can't quit now. This is for Jeet. We have to finish it."

Brundidge was dumbfounded. No one hated these two hundred thousand square feet of cinder blocks more than he did. But he was also half-sober. "What do you mean? Kill 'em?"

Wood replied, "I don't give a damn what happens to 'em. They killed Jeet and he hated this store. Looks to me like a twofer."

Brundidge was yelling now, almost drowning out the noise that came from the bulldozer pushing the truck. "You crazy SOB! We can't take this out! It's a superstore!"

"Bullshit. There's nothing super in there. Anyway, it's ruined everything. It has to go."

As the truck neared the building, Lonnie and his cohorts increased their hollering and pleading. Wood was pushing the accelerator full-tilt now. Brundidge looked up, awed by the vastness of what they were approaching. "Jesus. We're really gonna do this."

The truck and the backhoe then careened through the plate-glass window, setting off the alarm and scattering an enormous display of clothes that had been designed by a movie star. The air was suddenly littered with cheap shirts, thin sweaters, and poorly hemmed pants, a few of which landed haphazardly on the windshields of both vehicles. Wood continued pushing the truck toward what turned into a sort of escalated scenic tour of redneck Paradise, mowing down aisles of products, barreling through the automotive section and sending stacks of tires bouncing into the air, past sporting goods and beer coolers and on into patio furniture, destroying several sets of tables and lawn chairs before Lonnie's crumpled pickup finally came to rest inside a large portable swimming pool. After that, the backhoe climbed unceremoniously up on top of it. Then it was eerily quiet except for the sound of a distant alarm. After about a minute, Lonnie and the two men crawled out of the truck and limped off, groaning. Brundidge and Wood got down off the backhoe. Other than a bad gash over Wood's eye, on the same side of his face where Luke had struck him, they were remarkably unscathed. They stood there for a while, like a couple of dazed shoppers, taking in the seemingly endless rows of still untouched merchandise.

Finally, Wood said, squinting from the blood that had leaked into his eye, "Good God, we didn't even make a dent. How big is this piss hole?"

Brundidge leaned against a self-cleaning outdoor grill, trying to collect himself. "I dunno. Three or four football fields." He ignored the approaching sirens. "And they're everywhere. There's thousands of 'em."

Wood absorbed this, then kicked the crumpled remains of a buglight made in Korea. "Okay. Well, that's a start."

*   *   *

Wood was lying on the bunk in his jail cell. Brundidge had gone to make his one phone call to Charlotte. Wood didn't have anyone to call. He was out of excuses for his own behavior and couldn't think of a single living soul who might care to speak with him. He was counting on Charlotte, the out-of-towner, to bring Brundidge's checkbook and post bail for both of them.

In spite of the life-changing events that he had just participated in (he had to admit that he had enjoyed destroying Lonnie's truck even more than a small section of the Paris County Fed-Mart Superstore), all he could think of now was getting home to Milan. There was so much he had to tell her, but mostly he just wanted to be in her lovely, safe, warm presence again. His mind was still reeling from the story Frank had told him. He could finally see how he had used all the wrong clues to build a stereotype of his own wife. "Blonde, Simple, Needs Money, Loves to Shop"—a stereotype that was just as false as any that Lonnie Rhinehart could conjure up. He had actually looked down on her for her devotion to the very things that made his life easy. And in her own fashion, she had whipped him good for it, too. She had stood naked on a rock in the moonlight and reminded everyone what a fool he was and then set him free and told his girlfriend that she could have him. And to top it off, she had done everything humanly possible to protect their children from his recklessness.

Brundidge returned from making his call. As one of the deputies opened the cell door, Wood asked, "What did she say?"

Brundidge said, "What did she say? Well, she's pleased, of course. It's five-thirty in the morning and she's now on her way to see Fishbait Oliver, the Bailbondsman Who's Also a Friend. Oh, yeah, I'm impressin' the hell out of her. I just told her, 'Hey, while you're there, go ahead and pick up a bucket of minnows for yourself, too. It's on me.'" The deputy closed the cell door and Brundidge sat on the bunk below Wood's. "Damn. What am I doin'? I really like this girl."

The both lay quietly, then Wood said, "You know what an intrauterine device looks like?"

Brundidge sighed. "My God, are we gonna start this again? Don't you know any normal shit to talk about?"

Wood leaned over the top bunk. "I'm serious. It's that thin, like a little coil." He showed Brundidge, with his fingers almost touching. "*That thin.* I can put one in with my toes."

"Yeah. So?"

"Nothin'. I was just thinkin', what I have to do to get my wife back is . . . even more delicate."

"Yeah, that's the ticket. Now you're thinkin'."

In a little while, Brundidge fell asleep.

When Wood looked up, Marcus West was staring at him. Marcus took his key and unlocked the door as he spoke. "Woodrow, I don't know where you boys are goin' when you get outta here. But I have a suggestion. Home." Wood smiled.

CHAPTER 25

The sun was just stirring the Champanelle River when a red Mustang convertible pulled up to the sandbar and two young people got out. Without speaking, they undressed and then started running toward the water, two beautiful, high-rumped backsides fulfilling a long-suppressed desire. The girl's shiny straight hair bounced from side to side as she raced the boy—raced him on well-shaped legs that people said looked just like her mother's, only longer. As they reached the water's edge, she grabbed the boy's hand and they dove, he, a little awkward, she, with her back slightly hollowed and feet together, just as she'd been taught, with both landing at the exact same moment like a couple of show-off porpoises. When they came up again, they found each other, and the girl's laugh, which people said was too loud, could be heard up and down the river.

Wood was running along Main Street now. He hadn't slept in days and was still a little drunk. But when he had stepped away from the jail and taken in the long view of the boulevard—the cobblestones that had once sounded so right under the hooves of his horse, and the old boarded-up stores that had so carefully sheltered his boyhood—he had the feeling that for the first time in a long time, he was going in the right direction. And that he had come from a very long distance to be here.

He had just passed Gift Chest Jewelers and Tillman's when he saw someone standing in front of Jeter's Market. She was a large woman and was carrying a bag of groceries with one hand on her hip as she smiled at him and shook her head a little. He knew that look very well, knew that she was saying, "Mmm, hmm, went and got ourselves into some trouble, did we? Well, that's all right, Peaches. You're on the right road now."

Wood smiled back at Mae Ethel, wanting to cross toward her, but then Hank and Pauline Jeter emerged from their store, startling him. Wood could see that age hadn't weighed them down yet. Hank wiped his hands on his meat apron and, with a stick match, lit his pipe. He nodded to Wood, as though he were telling him that it was just another day. Wood nodded back, grateful, and then noticed that Pauline was calling to someone up the street. He moved on, trying to see who it was. As he neared Case Hardware, he saw the back of a little boy, maybe six or seven, who was bent over, laughing.

When Wood got close, he could tell that it was Jeter. God, it was good to see him like that. Then, two other little boys came running up. Brundidge had Wood in some sort of a headlock and they were all laughing. The older Wood tried to approach them, but the trio quickly untied their horses from a parking meter and rode off. As Wood stood watching, Jeter turned around and waved at him in a way that said he would see him again.

Wood was in the street now, running past the Grecian House of Beauty, Blackburn's Shoes, and Arkansas Tire and Supply. Someone behind him was honking. When he turned around, he saw his grandparents in their old Buick. There was a JUST MARRIED sign on the bumper and his Grandfather McIlmore seemed to be in a hurry. He wagged his finger at Wood, and Wood didn't know if it was because he was standing in the street or that he had an affair, but you could tell there was some love in it. Belle reached both her arms out toward Wood, but his grandpa sped up, leaving her to only blow him a kiss. Wood returned it and moved on toward Garfinkel's, where a crowd had gathered around a window as one of the well-dressed mannequins seemed to have come to life. She was shy and luminous and looked to be about sixteen, as she twirled in her shimmering blue skirt. When he got close, he could see that it was who he thought it was. She cocked her head as she turned and looked straight at Wood and told him with eyes that matched her skirt that she loved him. Then the crowd looked at him, too, as though they were expecting him to do something about it. But all he did was take off running, past Lena Farnham Stokes's and Falkoff's, toward some music that was playing up the street.

As he got near, he could see another crowd of spectators who were riveted by something going on at the center of them. Wood recognized many of his friends' parents and people from Main Street he hadn't seen in years. They were young again, the way he remembered them, including the Brundidges, who didn't have cancer yet and looked wonderful. Then Mr. Brundidge and some of the dads gave him the thumbs-up, the way they probably had to Dr. Mac on the day Wood was born and the way they had throughout Wood's entire life, even for something as small as a touchdown or as easy as fathering a baby or delivering one of theirs. And the mothers were smiling at him in the same way they always had, as though he were their son, too.

Wood began walking toward them, wanting to embrace the mothers of his friends and shake their fathers' hands and they seemed to want to speak to him, but one by one they disappeared, leaving only the couple who was dancing in the middle. Dr. Mac was in his military uniform and Slim had on big earrings with her hair swept up in a roll—just the way Wood had seen them in pictures. They looked good together, as his father spun his mother around, holding one finger perfectly still in the air, while he continued his deft moves. Wood always thought most people looked silly doing the jitterbug, but his dad looked like a man who knows exactly what he is doing. Like Gene Kelly. Dr. Mac saw Wood and motioned to Slim to look who was here! Now they were both smiling and waving to their son. And it seemed to Wood that his dad had something he wanted to say, too. But as the music got faster and faster his parents and their dancing were slowing down and starting to go away. Someone was honking again. He was getting angry at his grandfather when he turned around and saw that it was Brundidge and Charlotte—saw them so clearly that it startled him. Brundidge rolled down his van window and said, "What the hell are you doing in the middle of the street?"

Wood wanted to grab him and say, "I just saw your parents and they look great!" But instead, he shook his head, collecting himself. "Nothing. I was going to meet my mother at the cemetery."

"Get the hell in the van."

Wood was too tired to argue. He got in, smiling at Charlotte, who didn't even bother anymore to regard him curiously. Brundidge then sped off before Wood could get the sliding door closed.

Brundidge grumbled, "It's not enough we just got out of jail! You gotta go wandering up the middle of the goddamn street!"

There was still a chill in the air as morning dew lingered on the grass and the headstones at Whispering Pines. Wood had promised last week to meet Slim here, knowing that the two of them had agreed to visit Dr. Mac on special days and Elizabeth's wedding was such an occasion. Some of the flat grave markers were over a hundred and fifty years old, and Wood noticed that the Lanier family patriarch, Lucius, no longer had a birth date that was legible. A large standing angel with "Rhinehart" scripted under it seemed to stare at him disapprovingly. Wood moved away. He was glad Jeter had been cremated. He was thinking how it wouldn't be right for him to end up in the same cemetery with the man who killed him. And that there should be a cemetery for SOBs. Then he was wondering if he himself might be buried there.

It startled him a little when Slim pulled up in her station wagon looking considerably older than when she had been dancing on Main Street. Wood crossed and opened her car door and took out the robust blue hydrangea that she had brought for his father. He sensed immediately by her manner that she was completely aware of his drunken lawless activities. For one thing, his mother was a good friend of Serious West and Serious knew everything that went on at the police station. He would not have called Slim to gossip, but rather to give her a heads-up and to say that he would be there if she needed him. Slim coolly surveyed Wood and then said with sincerity, "Well, how was your brief incarceration? Did it provide you with some quiet time to think?"

He smiled a little. "You know, it did." They were walking toward Dr. Mac's grave now. She took his arm.

"Good. You needed that, Woodrow. It seems you haven't been thinking as well lately as I know you are capable of."

Wood sighed. "It's true." She had always been this way, somehow able to communicate disappointment and confidence in her son, all at the same time. Understating, but never underestimating. Even when he got injured playing football and people sitting in the bleachers would encourage Dr. Mac to go to him, Slim would always stop her husband, saying, "Don't worry. He'll get up." And Wood always did.

Suddenly, they stopped, noticing that some graffiti had been spray-painted on Dr. Mac's grave marker, as well as those of Wood's grandparents and several others in the area. Slim caught her breath and Wood cussed under his. They stared at it for a long time. It didn't appear to be personal, just some nicknames and numerals, spray-painted by reckless kids. Wood fell to his knees and, using the sleeve of his jacket, tried to rub the paint off.

Then he said, surprisingly anguished, "Who would do this to him? There's no town here anymore. If there was, this wouldn't happen." He scrubbed the granite harder until his mother finally said, "Son, stop it!"

Wood looked up at her, surprised by the harsh tone. Slim said, "Don't you get it? That's not the monument." She stepped closer to him. "You're the monument." Her words cut him like a sharp, clear knife. He stood up and looked into her eyes. She nodded and smiled in a way that put him in mind of all the people he had just seen on Main Street. Could that have been what they, too, wanted to say? He pulled his mother close. They stayed that way for a long time, both knowing that something important had changed.

Wood was standing in the doorway of Duff's motel room. He was breathless, having run all the way from the cemetery. She was looking out on the little concrete balcony.

"Kathleen—"

"Please don't say that you would take it all back."

He closed the door and told her with his eyes that he would.

"My God, you can't even let me have that?"

He crossed and stood next to her. He stared at his shoes, moving them around a little. Then, finally, he spoke.

"I could never leave my wife. And I'm pretty sure I already knew that." There was a long silence before he added, "I don't expect you to forgive me."

She sat for a while, then, "I lost my son. I'm gonna need a little more than an embarrassing cliché here." He was quiet. She went on, "What I was thinking was, we now have nothing to lose. We could go on seeing each other and it would be so awful and so terrible of us that no one would ever suspect or know."

Now he was completely off-balance. "Well, see, here's where they get you on that deal. We would know."

"I see. Now we have morals. And a conscience. I don't know why, but I keep expecting something more original."

Wood stared at her for a long time. "Kathleen, I'm in love with her."

She recoiled a little, as though he had

struck her. In her list of potential reasons Wood might give for not seeing her any-more, this was the only one she hadn't con-sidered. They sat for a while, like two old friends who can immediately calculate the distance now between them.

Seeing that Wood looked tired and hun-gover, she said, "Don't look so sad. At least you made an old, beat-up woman feel pretty again. That's not a little thing, you know"—she cleared her throat—"to remind someone of who they used to be. But," she added softly, "not worth a son."

His eyes were red and swollen and full of regret. "I guess I could tell you some things, but nothing that would mean much now."

"No."

"All right, then. I won't."

"You know them, anyway."

"I do."

"Okay, then."

"Okay."

Wood was at the gate to Fast Deer Farm. He had run all the way from the Holiday Inn, stopping only to dash in the nursing home and tell Miss Phipps that today was the cut-off date for wearing white shoes. He knew she would be coming to the wedding and he had promised to do that for Jeter. Strangely, he would not have thought of it yesterday, even though, as it turned out, it didn't matter. Since Jeter's death Miss Phipps had gone completely downhill. She had ignored Wood's announcement, brushing the sweat off his forehead and telling him, "You've been playing too hard again, haven't you?" Then she added that if he didn't get his alphabet work in by tomorrow, she would have to grade him down.

Now Wood could see his house in the distance. He felt sure that Milan had heard about his arrest. For one thing, her mother and siblings used police scanners for entertainment. There was so much he wanted to say to his wife and yet he knew he didn't have a right to say any of it. What he figured was that he would walk through his favorite pasture and try to collect his thoughts. But by the time he arrived at his barn, he hadn't come up with a single sentence that seemed credible, much less not laughable. All the usual generic excuses, "We were drifting apart," "I was having a midlife crisis," "The grass is always greener," sounded like lame, catchall impersonations of the truth.

For the first time in his life, he hadn't a clue as to what Milan might be thinking. He had always been sure of her and now he wasn't. She had been so calm the night she told him to go. And at the rehearsal dinner. Now his palms were sweating. What if she had finally made up her mind about him, the way he had once made up his about her? Milan had already mastered her half of the most noble symbiosis that can occur between two people—loving someone else more than yourself. Could he really now expect her to also perform the most extraordinary human act on record—forgiveness? He didn't know. But right now he had to stay focused. Yes, they had a wedding to get through, but first he wanted to at least plant the seed of reconciliation and then, who knows? Maybe by Christmas, her favorite time of year, they could start over again. He stopped inside the barn long enough to pat Sook, reminding himself that Milan did not care for long speeches. He would apologize and then lay out all the reasons for staying together. Maybe suggesting that they discuss it again in a few weeks.

Wood thought he had pretty well organized what he wanted to say. But when he got to the top of the stairs, he didn't even knock. He just opened the door and, seeing her standing over by the window, said none of the things he had planned, but instead crossed to the middle of the room and stood there, panting, like a dog. Milan turned and looked at him. . . . "You're having kind of a hard year, aren't you?"

He didn't answer, but just continued standing there, thinking she was like a little round mirror that you put under someone's nose to see if they're still alive, and that maybe she had just shown him that *his* now had a small spot of mist on it. Finally, he said, "I was running down Main Street this morning and I saw you in Garfinkel's window. You were about sixteen and you had on one of those full skirt deals and you were twirling around. Do you think I'm crazy?"

"Yes."

Wood went on. "You were smiling at me and I ran away because I knew I was gonna disappoint you . . . and then I ran all the way here to tell you how sorry I am for that. And

that I know I'm not the man you thought I
was . . . but I think I know the man that I
could be." Then he said with his voice sounding hoarse and emotional, like he hoped it
wouldn't, "I don't expect you to answer right
away, but if I just keep coming here . . .
could you picture yourself ever letting me
hold you again?"

She looked at him for a long while and
then, thinking how much he looked like
their children, said evenly, "I'm picturing it
now."

Wood decided not to breathe. His eyes
were so full of his feelings, he could hardly
see her. "That can't be true."

She seemed to have thought about this
before. "I've watched people throw things
away all my life. That isn't for me. I love you. I
won't waste one day of that."

This caused him to weep. In the space of
twelve months, he had lost his father, his
best friend, and his wife. And now it seemed,
miraculously, that he might get one of them
back. He grabbed her, holding on, the way
he had once held on to logs in the Champanelle River when the current got too
strong.

CHAPTER 26

It was almost 10 A.M. and Fast Deer Farm resembled an Aztec village with scores of people moving about and performing their assigned tasks. Four hundred white wooden folding chairs were lined up with the same precision as crosses at Normandy. In front of them, an enormous rounded trellis was dripping with diaphanous ribbon and Cecil Bruner roses. A huge white tent loomed majestically near the pond, which was strewn with an armada of gardenias floating on lily pads.

Upstairs, Wood was now in the shower. He lathered his hair with Milan's expensive shampoo for people with highlights, not caring that he didn't have any. He let the steaming hot water wash over him. He rubbed a circle in the mist that had accumulated on the door, creating an oval through which he now saw Milan remove his tux from a cleaner's plastic bag and brush it, almost respectfully, with her hand. Then she hung it on the hook of the bathroom door, so that the steam might take care of any unseen wrinkles.

He suddenly realized the he hadn't even thought about his tuxedo, much less made an effort to see where it was or if it needed to be cleaned. He rubbed soap under his arms. She had to have gotten his tux cleaned when she was still mad at him. That was so Milan. Not letting the sorry behavior of others interfere with the things that needed to be done. Wood turned the water off and stepped out of the shower. He could see a stack of thick fresh towels sitting on the bed. He entered the bedroom, on his way to retrieve one, and noticed that Milan was seated at her dressing table. He was thinking how much she still looked like that girl on Main Street. He crossed to her. Then he leaned down, wrapping himself around his wife, his naked body outlining her and the little velvet stool with the crown-shaped back that she was sitting on. He stayed that way, his face buried in the softness of her neck, getting her slip and her hair wet, which felt good and right to both of them. After a while, he went back to the bed and picked up a towel.

Milan brushed her hair, but continued watching him in the mirror. There was something so comfortably masculine about him. A trait that was deeply imbedded and that he himself was completely unaware of, which made it all the more appealing. For some reason, she was thinking how much she liked his ability to shake his head and laugh while lying in the ditch. And that she also liked the way he was leaning over right now, unself-consciously drying himself off, his genitals resting against his thigh. For a moment, she forgot to breathe. She felt like a newlywed. He caught her watching his reflection. She looked away. He smiled to himself, grateful, thinking of the days that lay ahead, and then reluctantly put his shorts on.

The window was open and the sound of an argument was drifting up. Dwight and Denny were in bitter disagreement over the number of lily pads in the pond.

"You've got too many. It's contrived. It's looks all . . . Jungle Cruisey."

"No, it doesn't. And you don't have to be so darned snippy."

"How many times do I have to tell you, you never want an even number? Nature is odd."

Milan and Wood laughed a little together. It wasn't much, but it felt good, too. There was a knock at the door. Then, without waiting, Luke and Elizabeth entered.

"We have to talk."

Milan stood up, "Sure, honey, come on in."

Wood struggled to finish dressing.

"Excuse me, I'd like to get my pants on here."

Elizabeth brushed past him and said without humor, "Yes, we'd all like that." Then, she struggled to begin. "This is hard. So, I'm just gonna say it. Luke and I have decided to call off the wedding."

No one made a sound. Finally, Milan found her voice. "Are you sure?"

"We've gone back and forth all morning. But yes."

Luke spoke up. "We appreciate all the trouble you've gone to. But considering everything that's happened and the stress at the rehearsal dinner . . . it's just not how we want to start off."

"Now wait a minute. Let's not lose our heads here. People get married under all sorts of adverse conditions, even when one of them is shipping off to war."

Elizabeth and Luke gave him a look that said that his opinion counted less with them than a child's. Then Elizabeth pressed on, "We did, however, decide to go ahead and consummate our relationship."

Milan said, "Oh, my God."

Luke was embarrassed. "Lizabeth, you don't have to tell everything. That's not their business."

Wood was dumbstruck, "You're a virgin?"

"I was. Until a couple of hours ago."

Milan said, "Oh, my God."

"You and mother taught me that morals and respecting yourself are very important. Remember? And since I didn't fall in love with anyone before Luke, I didn't have sex. And since I knew right away that I was going to marry him, I decided to wait. You know, to make it kind of an old-fashioned thing."

Wood stepped away a little. "Okay, this is more information than I want."

"Well, I'm sorry, Daddy, but I didn't have sex based on your moral code. I see now that that was stupid, but I would like to get credit for my sacrifice."

Milan gestured toward her bathroom. "Lils, can I see you in here please?"

Elizabeth obliged her mother while Wood awkwardly finished dressing with Luke watching him.

Once they were in the bathroom, Milan spoke first, "What are you doing?"

Elizabeth hugged her, excited. "Mother, it was wonderful. I love sex! And I didn't even know! It wasn't awkward at all. Everything fit together perfectly!"

"Oh, my God."

"It's okay. You told me to save myself for someone I love and I did. Be happy for me!"

"All right." Milan seemed overwhelmed. "I am. I will."

She hugged Elizabeth back, wondering if this was appropriate.

Elizabeth said, "Good. But right now we have to go tell Kathleen and the Duffers that the wedding's off." She held Milan by the shoulders, excited. "Then, we're gonna go somewhere and do it again!"

Milan followed her daughter out. "Oh, my God. You need to calm down, young lady." When they returned to the bedroom, Wood was waiting.

"Look, honey, I appreciate your fine

morals. If you want me to admit that you're a better person than your old man, I've known that for years. But you've got a whole lifetime to punish me. This is your day. If you're not gonna use it, then make it for a reason that's about you, not me."

Elizabeth didn't even seem angry when she said, "Well, I wish I could, Daddy, but the truth is, that's just not possible now."

Wood started to pace and swear a little under his breath.

Luke said, "Look, we're not calling off the wedding to spite you. But we can't get married just to make you feel less guilty either."

"I get it. I understand." He paced some more, then, "All right. You all just do whatever you need to do." He looked at Milan. "Are you okay with this?"

She met his gaze, steeling herself. "Yes. I think so."

Wood shrugged. "Okay. I don't give a damn what it costs. The important thing now is that you decided this together and that we'll all live to see a better day."

Milan was getting into gear now. "Oh, my God. I've got to tell Dwight and Denny." Then, to Wood, "You better get your doctor bag out. Somebody's gonna have a heart attack. There's four hundred pounds of lobster, the flowers, the cake. What are we gonna do with the cake?"

Elizabeth threw her arms around her mother. "Oh, Mims, I'm so sorry for you."

"It's all right. I know. We'll freeze it. That way it can stay beautiful forever!"

A little later, valet parkers had assembled a mile's worth of cars on the road to Fast Deer Farm. The folding chairs were half-full of carefully turned-out people and a small orchestra was playing Corelli's "Pastorale."

Inside, Mavis was supervising last-minute touches on the wedding buffet, which was designed to resemble a sumptuous country picnic. All of these things were continuing to happen for the same reason the rehearsal dinner had gone on. Because no one had yet stopped it. Everyone sensed that the previously tenuous situation had now escalated. But Milan, still unwilling to risk the hysteria of the two florists, among others, had stopped short of publicly saying that the wedding was off.

Elizabeth and Luke had gone to the hotel to tell Kathleen and the Duffers about their decision. The rest of the wedding party, the bridesmaids and ushers, were upstairs, lounging around on the beds and watching television, still unsure as to their fate. But several of the more perceptive girls were starting to cry.

Wood and Milan were now huddled in the den with their Episcopal minister, Dr. Regas, trying to figure out the best way to proceed while incurring the least amount of damage. Charlie, Slim, and Sidney Garfinkel were also present. A few feet away, Charlotte watched Brundidge practice the flower-girl walk with Cake and Lily looking on. On the small chance that this wedding might still be given a reprieve, he carried one of the little baskets on his arm, advancing slowly. "See? They're like baby steps. And don't worry if you mess up. Your daddy's gonna love you anyway. Remember, you just throw your little petals like this and smile."

Charlotte said, "I don't know why you just don't do it yourself. You're good. You're really good."

Miss Delaney and Serious had come inside because Serious had gotten a splinter in his hand from one of the chairs. Milan found a pair of tweezers and began working on the offending sliver. Mavis came over and listened to the discussion that was unfolding. Dr. Regas was speaking. "I don't think we need to offer any detailed explanation. I think we just say these young people have simply decided that they need more time."

Slim said, "Right. Anyway, who cares what people think? If only this could be the worst thing that ever happens to us."

Now Miss Delaney and Serious had to be let in on everything, and Miss Delaney, with a newly awakened interest in romance, tried to hide her disappointment. Then Wood told the minister that he would go outside himself and let people know that the wedding had been called off. And that was when Milan started saying something about how maybe they should go ahead and have a party any- way. People were already here and dressed up and the orchestra had come all the way from Little Rock. And the truth was, frozen cake is never really very good. She had just said that to make her daughter feel better. And then she said something that would al- ter not only the outcome of this day, but would forever change the town of Paris and many of the people in it. Would divide fami- lies and friends in a way that nothing else had since the Civil War. And it had all begun quite innocently, when all Milan said was that it was a shame there wasn't someone else who wanted to get married today. And Brundidge, who had been crossing with several Bloody Marys and sipping one, literally almost choked on it, like a comedian with perfect timing. And Charlotte had told him not to flatter himself—that he had nothing to worry about. Everyone had laughed a little, except for Mavis, who didn't laugh at all and was now staring at Mary Paige as though she was already picturing the two of them standing in front of the Cecil Bruner rose trellis. And she was not the only dreamer in the room, either. Miss Delaney took Serious out into the hallway and the others could see that an intense discussion was taking place.

Now Milan was beginning to question what she had just put in motion. She watched as Mavis crossed to Mary Paige, then flirtatiously leaned down over her and began whispering. Milan marveled that she had never seen Mavis look so happy, noticing that even the childishly overdone eye shadow could not detract from her newly acquired radiance. When the two women's faces touched softly, they laughed, and in spite of the old uneasy feeling that was starting to build inside of her, Milan was struck by how much this put her mind of the scene upstairs that had just unfolded between herself and Wood.

A few minutes later, Mavis and Mary Paige were seated on the sofa in front of the minister. Mavis's initial excitement had now been tempered by fear and her hands were trembling so badly that Mary Paige had to hold them. Mavis had assumed that lesbians could at least get married spiritually, but now Dr. Regas was explaining that, while he had no personal objection to their union, Episcopalians could not officiate at same-gender marriages as long as they were illegal.

Out in the hallway, Serious West had other concerns. "Margaret Delaney, do you want to get us both shot?"

"Why not? We've already lived past our normal life expectancy."

He could see that she was completely earnest. "Serious, I don't care one whit about that piece of paper, but I would like to let people know how I feel about you. I think that's an important part of loving someone. And it might settle down all the talk at the nursing home."

"You think you and me getting married is gonna settle down the talk?"

"I don't know. I just know that when you kiss me, it would be legal. And I'm getting too old to be a nonconformist."

"Girl, you've got a strange way of looking at things."

"You still haven't answered. Will you marry me?"

"What do you think?"

Then Serious picked her up and swung her around so forcefully that Miss Delaney lost one of her shoes. They didn't have to explain their decision because people could see by now what had happened. Wood had gone over and reassured them that he and Milan would be pleased to host their wedding. And everyone had begun to congratulate them, but all Miss Delaney could see were the deeply wounded faces of Mavis and Mary Paige. And she stopped the well-wishing immediately and planted herself next to the two women on the sofa, declaring, "We'll get married today. But only if Mavis and Mary Paige are standing up there with us." Then she added, "I say if we're gonna break one rule, why not break them all?"

Milan and Wood exchanged a look of uncertainty and, strangely, each seemed not to
mind it. In the spirit of good manners, everyone else smiled. Some smiles stayed on
longer than others as people took in the full
measure of what was happening and also
what the consequences might be. A little
daring is sometimes called for when a plan
has gone awry. But now this was beyond
daring. This was do or die social suicide.

Fifteen minutes later, the wooden seats
were completely full. The harpist had started
"Cavalleria Rusticana Intermezzo," which
was the last song before the wedding music
was to begin. Dwight and Denny were frantically attempting to reassemble some of the
bridesmaids' flowers into another wedding
bouquet. Denny added drama to the situation by claiming that he had actually been
forced to slap one of the girls who hadn't
wanted to let go. A newly returned Luke and
Elizabeth struggled to soothe the hurt feelings of the wedding party, as well as to comprehend who they themselves were being
replaced by. Elizabeth was ecstatic over
these new events. She had always been
fond of Miss Delaney and had long ago begun to think of her Aunt Mavis as something

of an icon. Luke was just relieved that his grandparents and mother were now on their way home. The Duffers had finally learned from several of their friends about Wood and Kathleen's affair. They had thought that nothing their daughter did could shock them anymore, but they had been wrong. And Luke was thinking that if they could see who was replacing their grandson and his fiancée in the society wedding of the year, it would probably finish them off.

Rudy, who was now in charge of the entire kitchen crew, began barking orders as though this were the precise moment, since coming to America, that he had been waiting for. Margaret Delaney and Serious were busy talking to his son Marcus and Marcus's wife, Janine, who had been summoned inside to hear their big news. And you could tell just by looking that Marcus did not think this was a very good idea. But you could also tell, by Serious's demeanor and the way that he placed his hand on Marcus's shoulder, that he was letting his son know this was a done deal. That Serious was not in asking mode. He was in notification mode. After a while, Serious and Marcus broke away from the women, with Serious pulling him closer, whispering in his ear, and you could see with every nod of Marcus's head that the father was winning the son over with his signature arsenal of intimidation, charisma, and charm.

Slim and Sidney had ventured outside with instructions to present as normal a front as possible. They shook hands and greeted people warmly. Sidney seemed invigorated by his status as a conspirator in the daring plot that was now unfolding. Slim told him that he was smiling too much. And that he seemed more demented than merely happy. Then Sidney said that she didn't seem joyful enough for the grandmother of a presumed bride to be, which led to a few more disagreeable words before they realized that this was their second fight (the first one having occurred over Ingrid Bergman) and another silly one at that, which got them both to laughing, causing even more speculation as to what was going on.

Inside, Cake and Lily Brundidge were seated on the sofa, on either side of Charlotte, with their feet dangling and their little baskets of rose petals in their laps. The heels of their matching patent leather shoes annoyingly hit the front of the Chinese coffee

table, until their dad, huddled in deep conversation with Wood, told them to stop. Then
he went back to his discussion, lowering his
voice.

"Now, I want to get this straight. You're
gonna go tell all those people who got
dressed up and came here today that your
daughter is not gonna marry her boyfriend
after all. But what we do have are two fat lesbians and an old black man who wants to
marry an old white woman. And then you
want me to let my little girls go out there and
sprinkle rose petals for them. I don't know,
Call me a worrywart, but I don't have a good
feeling about that. I don't have a good feeling
at all."

"You know those people out there might
just surprise you."

Brundidge got as close to Wood as he
could. "What did you do? Fuck all your
brains out? They're not gonna surprise me.
They'll tear those girls to shreds. There won't
be anything left. Hell, I'll be lucky to find a little piece of ribbon."

Wood sat, leaning forward, mulling this
over. Then he said, "Let's just cross one
bridge at a time, okay? Right now I'm more
worried about finding a minister."

Frank Lanier, who was in the kitchen stuffing his coat and pants pockets with little pastries, suddenly perked up, like a bird dog going on point. Then he crossed to where Wood and Brundidge were. "Hey! Is somebody lookin' for a minister?"

Upstairs in the master bedroom Milan was putting the final touches on Mary Paige's makeup. A newly gathered bridal bouquet was on the dressing table. Elizabeth was lying on the bed playing with baby Paris. *"Bonjour, mon petit chou."*

Mavis was complaining that Milan was making Mary Paige look like a streetwalker, or even worse, a damn corpse at Cotrell's Funeral Home. And the husher had answered, "Oh, hush. I'm just giving her a little color. You can't get married unless at least one of you is blushing. Which reminds me, I need to take yours down a notch."

Mavis was offended. "Why can't I blush?"

"Number one, you've already got on way too much. And number two . . ." Milan hesitated.

"What?"

"Well, it just seems like, you know . . ." Her voice trailed off. "You should be the man."

Mavis narrowed her eyes. "What do you mean?"

"I mean, you're both wearing pantsuits. People are gonna get confused. I just think Mary Paige should carry the bouquet."

"Why don't I get a bouquet?"

"Because, you know . . . you're the man."

"Stop saying that! I am not the man! Why do you need labels?"

"I don't need labels. But if I have a wedding in my backyard it has to make sense. There has to be a bride and a groom."

"Why?"

"Because there just does. Otherwise, nobody will understand it. Why do you have to argue? Just decide who's the bride, who's groom, and then, after the ceremony, you can be whatever you want."

Mavis shrugged to Mary Paige. "Do you believe this?"

Elizabeth said, without even looking their way. "You might as well give in. She made me learn calligraphy."

Finally, Mary Paige said softly, "We've never even discussed which one's the bride."

Milan was astonished. "Okay, but I just think this is a mistake—"

Mavis cut her off. "All right! Give her the

damn bouquet!" Mavis picked up the flowers and tossed them to Mary Paige. Then to Milan, "There. I'm the one who changes the tires and kills the spiders! Happy?"

Wood and Brundidge and Dr. Regas were now huddled over a certificate that Frank Lanier had produced from his wallet. It carried a large stain that Frank said had been caused when his girlfriend spilled the juice from a can of Vienna sausage on it, adding that even though the juice was clear, it was still hard to get out. Brundidge shook his head, repulsed by this explanation. The paper, which had Doctor of Divinity scrawled across it in enormous gold letters, certified that Frank Lanier had successfully completed a seven-week course by mail from the University of Esoterica. Dr. Regas examined it, mystified, but finally declared that while highly irregular, he certainly couldn't say it wasn't valid. Then there was a discussion about calling in one of the several judges present, or a lawyer, for an expert opinion, when Charlotte spoke up and said, "I'm a lawyer."

Brundidge was shocked. "You're a lawyer? How come I didn't know that?"

"It never came up." Charlotte looked at the certificate.

Brundidge smiled at Wood, proud. "She's a lawyer."

"Yes. I got that."

Then, Charlotte shrugged. "Looks okay to me." Brundidge was dubious. "The University of Esoterica? Are you kidding?"

"It's bullshit. But you could probably make a case for it. The right to declare yourself a religious entity is very broad and varies from state to state."

Frank said, "That's right. It also means you don't have to pay no sales tax on hooch and smokes."

Wood said to Charlotte, "Are you sure about this?"

"Not the hooch and smokes part. But what are you worried about? People who are completely intoxicated are married every day by idiots wearing Elvis suits."

Brundidge looked at Wood. "Well, there's your answer." Then he regarded Charlotte, not quite sure what to make of the Elvis comment. And he also noticed that she seemed to enjoy him the most when he was not quite sure.

Frank smiled. He was on a roll. Not only was his most prized possession now safely ensconced inside the Twentieth-Century Millennium Time Capsule, but he was also about to officiate at the most important wedding of the year. Okay, it had turned into a three-ring circus and had some elements he didn't approve of at all, but that was just the price you paid for being around Wood McIllmore and Earl Brundidge, who had a habit of letting situations deteriorate into something like this. He looked straight at Wood and Brundidge and began to sing, suggestive, cocky, "You can't always get what you wa-aant. But if you try you might get what you ne-eed." Then Frank paused and just stood there, shaking his head up and down, as though he were now absorbing the glory of having made such a fine point.

That was the problem with Frank Lanier. You couldn't give him a hand-up, because the minute he got on his feet again, he was insufferable and full of himself. Wood and Brundidge knew exactly what he was referring to, and they each gave silent thanks that the other crime they had committed last night was still unknown.

Brundidge said, "Shut up, Frank. You look

like hell. You better go comb your hair if you wanna be in this rodeo."

Frank sauntered off, still singing. And Brundidge took Charlotte off to the side, wanting to know what else she hadn't told him.

Across town, Marcus West's dog, Tracee, who was of about the same pedigree as Frank, was on his stomach, sniffing and pawing the strange new object that he had just managed to unearth. This had been easy to do, since it was near the surface of the ground and apparently wasn't even sealed. And now Tracee had his head buried deep inside of it, trying to make a choice. Eventually, what he came up with was an old soda can. If he had been able to read the words on the can, he might've understood its significance and put it back. But because Tracee wasn't capable of this, he did the next best thing, which was to bend it with his teeth, squarely on the part that said, "To Frank, Keep a cool tool. Mick Jagger." Then Tracee started running wildly up and down a hill, proudly displaying as much of the can as he could in his mouth. After a while, he got bored and started chasing the large white envelope that had blown right by him when he was running. Once he caught up with it, he shook it mightily in his mouth and then began shredding it with the help of his paws—shredding all the words that had been so carefully crafted by a partially senile first-grade teacher as proof that her former pupil had stood up to the most famous rock band in the world on behalf of the dignity of all hicks everywhere.

Wood was calling for Milan and someone said she was upstairs with Mavis, who was now sick. He was starting to feel a little sick himself, as he stood at the bar and poured another one of Brundidge's Bloody Marys. Wood didn't need Frank Lanier to tell him you can't always get what you want. All he had to do was look around. Compromise and half-victories were everywhere—an old couple who were coming to love a half-century late and to some still the wrong color, two lesbians who would get married today but not legally, and a man and a woman who had been together for twenty years, just now getting to know each other. Even Brundidge, who had his arms around Charlotte's waist, was a living testament to compromise, albeit, one that was in his favor. Maybe you get a major New York City newspaper to admit that you come from a good and decent place, but apparently you could, if you played your cards right, make love to one of their representatives.

Brundidge and Charlotte came over and stood next to Wood. As Brundidge freshened their drinks he said, half-kidding, "I don't know, buddy, I just don't know. You wake up in the morning thinkin' you're gonna get a son-in-law. By nightfall, you got a cross burnin' on you lawn."

Wood frowned. "Thanks."

For the first time Charlotte was afraid.

Upstairs in the master bathroom, Milan and Mavis were kneeling in front of the toilet. When Mavis was done retching, Milan wiped her old friend's face with a washcloth and then held her. In a little while, Mavis's expansive chest was racked with sobs.

"I'm so scared."

"Of what?"

"My mother. Everyone."

"Come on, you took on an entire church . . . and men, with guns."

"Yeah, but these are people I love." Mavis blew her nose. "Can you believe Mary Paige thinks I'm the strong one and she was captured by rebels?"

Milan seemed thoughtful. Then, "Maybe you're not the man."

"My God, will you please stop worrying about that?"

Now the tears were Milan's. "I'm sorry. I just don't want you to get hurt. Look, I don't give a damn which one you are or what you are. All I know is I love you."

"Then why do I feel like you're ashamed?"

Milan shook her head, disbelieving. "You think I'm ashamed? Of you?" She sat for a moment, reflecting on this. "Do you remember in high school when you looked in my purse and found those homemade Kotex made out of old rags and rubber bands?" Mavis stared at her, unsure what this was about. Milan went on, "I thought I would die when you saw that. But you never said a word. To anyone." Milan could hardly speak. "And I knew right then that you would always be my friend."

Mavis took Milan's hand in her own. "And I will. But I need you to . . . not look down on me."

Milan put her hand over Mavis's, thinking of all the times the two of them had taken turns placing their hands on baseball bats and batons, until the last hand at the top won.

"My God, I'm in awe of you. You were the only one who would spend the night at my house. Do you have any idea what it meant to have you lying there next to me while my dad was tearing everything up? . . . . Thirteen years old. You did that."

Mavis's eyes were amused now, the way Milan remembered them.

"What was that cheer? We used to do it over and over to drown him out."

They sat there for a while, trying to conjure it up, reveling in the memory of their old bravery. Finally, they thought of it. Then, as though it were planned, they began to chant, soft as a whisper, huddled on the floor with one or the other carrying it.

CHAPTER 27

The brand-new wedding party was now standing just inside the door of the McIlmore den. As Wood made his way past them, toward the considerable gathering outside, Rudy actually crossed himself and others gave thanks that they were not in Wood's shoes. After shaking hands and greeting people, Wood made his way to the rose trellis. There were some cheers on his behalf, as he used his hand to make a small awning over his eyes, surveying the crowd. Finally, he began.

"First of all, welcome to all of you. It, uh, looks like we've got ourselves kind of an awkward situation here. And believe it or not, the awkward part is not that I just got out of jail this morning."

There were a few gasps and some laughter.

"I had to get out because my wife says it's rude to be in jail when you're giving a wedding." More laughter. Milan, who was watching from the upstairs bedroom window, exhaled. She had decided to observe Wood's speech from the place where she felt safest. Then, afterward, she would come downstairs and attend the ceremony, if there was one.

Wood continued, "Our daughter, who so many of you have helped us to raise, and let me say here thank you—"

Applause and cheers.

"Anyway, our, some might say irrepress-

ible, daughter and her considerably wise beyond his years fiancé, Mr. Luke Childs, have
decided to delay their marriage."

Groans of disbelief. Wood forged on.

"I think anyone can see that these two are
pretty gone on each other. In my opinion, this
wedding will happen. It just won't happen today." Wood looked toward Elizabeth and Luke
who, hidden from the rest of the crowd, gave
him nothing. He rubbed his hands, uncharacteristically nervous. "So, what do we do?
You're here. You're all dressed up. Milan has
bought somethin' like $950,000 worth of
food—apparently this is very special food that
comes in all kinds of little shapes and stuff."

Laughter.

"And Mavis has made you all a hell of a
cake. Which is why we've been kicking
around the idea of going ahead and having a
wedding anyway. I mean, all we need are
two willing people. And that got me to thinking about how easy it is to get married the
first time . . . when everybody looks all shiny
and new." Milan folded her hands under her
chin, wondering where he was going.

"You take that person home and, I don't
care what anybody says, you know in your
heart you can return 'em."

More laughter. Brundidge muttered to Charlotte, "Lord help us. Now he's a comedian."

"But the real test comes after you've had 'em for a while, had a chance to open 'em up and look inside and find out that they don't look so hot, after all."

Wood turned toward Elizabeth and Luke again.

"That's the real test. And then, if you're lucky, one of you says, in spite of it, Hey, let's try this for another twenty years."

People were beginning to squirm.

"And that is what has happened to me this morning. So, I was thinking, maybe this could be a second chance, something few of us ever get in this life, for me to stand up here and say . . . how much I love her. I'm not sure I said it loud enough the first time . . . I'm gonna say it loud today."

There was scattered applause because people were unsure what to do. Milan stayed perfectly still, trying to keep her emotions in. Elizabeth, watching from below, studied her mother's face for a response and was disappointed to see that she was moved. Wood searched the crowd for Milan, and not finding her, became more nervous. It was one thing for his wife to *privately* take him back and quite another to do it in front of everyone they'd ever known.

"So, that's what we're gonna do . . . If she'll have me." Now he clapped his hands, like a man who is trying to give himself momentum. "And, as it turns out, we'll be joined by two other couples." Wood said this like it was an afterthought. Like, Oh, by the way, there'll be punch and cookies, too. He tried to smile winningly. "People who also love each other and want you to know it." He looked in their direction. "Miss Mavis Pinkerton, who wants to marry, at least in spirit, Miss Mary Paige Kenyon. And Miss Margaret Delaney, who has decided to marry Mr. Serious West."

A current of shock and disbelief traveled through the assembled guests, as though Wood had plugged in a cord somewhere that they were all attached to, bringing them to life as one howling, wounded chorus. It was a noise and a response that he wanted to unplug immediately. Mary Paige's mother had been too ill to attend, but her Aunt Frieda and Uncle Neal, who were patients of Wood's, were now up and moving. They had come to see his cute blonde daughter marry the Duffers' grandson, not to be humiliated by having to witness their own niece flaunt her relationship with the big, lesbian loud-mouth who had taken on their church. In fact, on the day they heard about this "ro-mance," they gave all their bread that came from Doe's to the birds. And they liked to tell people about how the birds had refused to eat it—liked to say that it was a sign or something. Mavis's mother had also stood up, but for some reason had thought better of it and sat back down. Mavis and Mary Paige had seen all of it, standing in the door-way. Mavis squeezed Mary Paige's hand and Mary Paige took a deep breath, as though air were a fortifying substance against meanness. A few feet away, Serious West, with his good arm around Miss De-laney's waist, said to no one in particular, "Well, there's no point in havin' a party, is there, if it ain't gonna be excitin'?"

But Margaret Delaney didn't hear any of it. She was thinking what a privilege it was to look into the face of this good man and see her own future, or what was left of it, and she had never felt so sure about anything in her life. Wood had his hands in the air, motioning for everyone to settle down. A few other people gathered themselves to leave as he continued.

"Now, I know that may not sit right with some of you. Two women who love each other. Black mixing with white."

Maybe it was Brundidge's Bloody Marys, or what Slim had said to him at the cemetery, or even the exuberance left over from his run down Main Street, but he was wound up now, determined to see this through.

"I know it's hard to let go of your old feelings and resentments." He noticed that Elizabeth was no longer standing next to Luke. "It's something I've had to do myself. But what I want to tell you is that it feels good. Feels real good." Finally, he looked up and saw Milan in the window, saw that she was with him.

More guests got up to leave. "This is the same old bullshit that killed Carl Jeter." He paused and met some eyes in the crowd evenly. "And I don't want any part of it. If you want to hate people for who they love, then you do need to get off my property." There were audible gasps and some applause. Several of Mae Ethel's grandsons cheered.

"And don't come around asking me to fix you up anymore, either. 'Cause I don't want your business." Then muttering halfway to himself, "And I sure as hell don't want to look up your ass."

Slim closed her eyes at her son's vulgarity. Wood looked up again and smiled at Milan like she was the sweetest thing he had ever seen.

"I'd rather stay home and make love to my pretty wife. . . . She is pretty, isn't she?"

He pointed now. "You see her up there in that window? That's her spot." Milan smiled. Wood walked directly toward the crowd. "I know you all think I'm drunk. But I'm just happy. Happy to be here with all of you, because now I know, you're the ones worth knowin'."

There was some laughter mixed with tentative relief.

"We got that taken care of, didn't we, Sheriff?"

Serious smiled and said, strongly, "Yes, sir."

Wood clapped his hands again, glad to be unburdened. "And now we're gonna have ourselves a wedding. Not a damn lesbian wedding or some kind of interracial deal, but a wedding for these fine people. And it's gonna surprise ever'body, too. 'Cause you

know what they say about us . . . about a little *southern* town—they say *we're not up to
the task*. Isn't that right, Charlotte? You know
they say that, don't you?"

Charlotte nodded a little, half smiling.
Wood smiled back.

"That's a cute hat. I like that." Then to the
others, "Isn't that cute?"

Charlotte seemed flummoxed. Wood
pressed on, now even more emboldened by
his spur-of-the-moment dream for his
town—no doubt caused by liquor and life-
altering circumstances, but a dream never-
theless.

"Well, I'm gonna tell you somethin'. I think
we are exactly the ones who are up to the
task—all of us who grew up here in this
place where . . . familiarity turns so easily
into . . . understanding. . . . And where, if
you'll just think about it, all our triumphs and
our failures are met with the same embrace."

Miss Delaney was nodding now with her
eyes closed, the way she always did when
words from one of her students began to
sound promising.

"This is the place where, more than anywhere else on earth, we have the chance of
being truly loved in spite of who and what we

are." Wood expanded his arms to include everyone who was left. "We are exactly the ones who can get out there ahead of everybody else and say right here today, in my grandfather's backyard, that we are gonna put a stop to this hate that gets passed down from generation to generation." He was gesturing toward Serious, Miss Delaney, Mavis, and Mary Paige now. "We are exactly the ones to stand up and say, once and for all, where there is love, by God, I want to be there!"

Slim McIlmore was looking at her son, as fascinated as she had been on the day he was born. Sidney turned to Slim and started to speak, but instead, cradled her arm in both of his. Charlie had a puzzled smile, still waiting for the punch line. And Luke had looked at Wood, in spite of himself, and shared with him a glimmer of something. Brundidge was on his feet now, clapping, trying to infuse the moment. "That's a good speech! A damn good speech!"

A fair number of people chimed in, but more were now starting to get up and leave. Some, because they had been too polite to interrupt Wood. And others, because they had to. People like Windola Thacker and her

son, Kirby, who have an unspoken agreement that he will spend the rest of his life
driving his mother to the beauty shop and
taking up the slack at heterosexual dinner
parties. And then there was coach and
church deacon Wally Faber, who believes
that homosexuality is a choice, like deciding
to try for a field goal on third down instead of
kicking it. He left with Mrs. Faber, who believes whatever Wally believes. And also, the
Metcalfs, from the Duffers' guest list, who
fought and lost the right to raise the Confed-
erate flag over the country club every morning. But in spite of that fact, Trudy will be the
first to tell you that they once met Muham-
mad Ali on a train and he was just the nicest
person you could ever want to know—soft-
spoken and not an ounce of big shot in him.
Anyway, those were some of the people who
left, including a few more who made a mental note that they would never speak to
Wood McIlmore again—this drunken, bleeding heart asshole who they allowed to feel
their most private parts, but who still didn't
know them any better than this. But improbably, amazingly, most stayed, if not in out-
right support, then just to see what would
happen next. And the Laniers, who re-

mained oblivious to all social issues, held on, hoping for dinner.

Milan watched from the window as Wood continued to work the crowd. Periodically, he looked up to make sure she was still there. But what he could not know yet was that he had finally become some kind of real hero to her. For the first time, had actually earned it—this half-drunk evangelist sinner, reborn lover, whose veins now coursed with the newly fired blood of the just forgiven. She didn't have to wonder anymore if he loved her. He was standing here, proclaiming it. Proclaiming his love for love, proving that the ecstatic lover's journey is a short one toward the rest of humanity—black, white, old, poor, queer—Wood was saying they could all get together at his house. Even for a boy raised by progressive parents in a town of ordinary social barriers, this was an adventurous leap. As a little girl, Milan had stood with her family outside those barriers. She had been a nigger, a queer, a misfit herself. This was solvent for an old wound she hadn't even known she needed. And she had never loved her husband more for providing it. Here were scores of people fleeing her house, running from a gamut of social faux pas and insults that violated not just their sense of propriety, but their most deeply held values and beliefs. Far from wanting to stop them, she couldn't have cared less if Wood had turned the garden hose on them. She wasn't going to use it to wash her house anymore. She had nothing to hide. Like Wood, she was out of jail. The whole town knew he had been unfaithful. The whole town had seen or heard about her at the car wash, acting like white trash, beating the hell out of Wood's old lover. And now her best friend was marrying a woman and she was giving her a party for it.

Unlike Mavis and Miss Delaney, who had willingly allowed themselves to be known, Milan had been dragged here. But she was standing up now, applauding and cheering. Now that her façade was gone, she could see so clearly what was at stake. And she knew there would never be another afternoon like this one, where people have stepped so bravely and so far from the main road and yet were still demanding a place on the map. She could see by the tentative faces below her that everyone was now feeling at risk, the way people do when a lesson is about to be learned, one way or the other.

And she wanted to seize this opportunity, to stand up with her husband, in front of all of them, and say, yes, I support this. This is who I am. She wanted, finally and gloriously, to be *known*.

When Milan turned around, she was startled to see Elizabeth standing there, holding Slim's gown. Then her daughter said matter-of-factly, "I don't know if I'll ever get married. Or even wear a wedding dress. But if I do, I'd like it to be one that was worn by my grandmother . . . and my mother."

Downstairs, someone must have cued the little orchestra, because it began to play "Jesu, Joy of Man's Desiring." Cake and Lily Brundidge started down the aisle, carrying their little baskets, matching their steps and giggling, unaware that they, too, were now civil rights warriors, just as their dad and uncle Wood and uncle Jeter had once been on a day only a little warmer than this one, when they had tested the waters of the Paris County municipal pool. As the girls scattered their petals with too much abandon, they could not have known that they were helping to challenge the social and legal fabric of the United States of America—the very country that their daddy had shown them on their bedroom walls was the greatest one in the world. And right now, this same man was tracking their every step with his raised eyebrows, nodding, smiling, and then monitoring faces in the crowd for their response. Charlotte watched it all with amusement and wonder. Who were these outrageous people who had drawn her into their strange world through a thousand-miles-away telephone call? A world that seemed oddly familiar— aggravating, unpredictable, audacious. The fact that she was starting to feel a little at home in it made her, at the same time, uneasy. She made a mental note to tell Brundidge that she could not come back for a while.

Suddenly a murmur raced through the crowd. It seemed that something was happening at the end of the long white runner. As heads began turning, it became clear that what that something was, was Milan. They would've stood anyway, because in spite of the fact that she was already married, it was the mannerly thing to do. But it was mostly the mere sight of her that brought them to their feet. Although Milan's beauty was widely acknowledged, no one was prepared for the lovely way she filled out

Slim's gown or how the sun shone through her hair onto the slightly faded fabric and made the full measure of her seem almost golden.

When she started down the aisle, Othelia Lanier wept. And Slim nudged Sidney excitedly, confiding that this was the dress he had helped to make. Because Milan was shorter than Slim, the gown's hem cascaded onto the lawn, and made a silky whispering as she passed each row of guests. When she swept by Slim and Sidney's aisle, even Slim gasped a little and Sidney literally held on to his chair, overcome to see the garment that so singularly and lovingly connected the life he had once known to this one.

And Wood, standing in front of the trellis, watched in wonder while Milan made her way toward him. As she got close, he shook his head and stamped his foot softly, trying to keep his composure, and then failing, had to turn away.

Finally, the new wedding party was lined up in front of the Reverend Frank Lanier, who identified himself, though Wood had specifically told him not to, as a Doctor of Divinity with the Church of the Meaningful Word. There were some snickers, which

caused Wood to stop and explain to the remaining guests that Frank was indeed an or-
dained minister with the full authority to
marry people, which only seemed to invite
more doubt.

Afternoon shadows were climbing up
Frank's polyester suit by the time each couple had said some version of wedding vows.
Wood had said his the loudest. As luck
would have it, Frank had pretty much memorized the traditional marriage ceremony,
which had apparently come with his ordina-
tion certificate. Only a few parts seemed
incoherent, like when he threw in "abomina-
tion" for no reason and stumbled over the
phrase "man and wife" in regard to Mavis
and Mary Paige, finally settling on "wife
and . . . wifey." But people got the general
gist of what was happening and the legality
of such a preceding, or the lack of it, could
be dealt with later.

While "Ave Maria" was being sung by Sam
Blackburn III, Wood glanced up and saw
Elizabeth, wrapped in a sheet, watching
from her upstairs bedroom window. Luke,
without a shirt, was standing next to her,
looking happy. Wood wondered how many
others had seen it, too. Jesus. People had to

be thinking by now that they were all insane. Everybody getting married but the bride, who was already upstairs on her honeymoon.

After the ceremony all three couples made their way down the aisle, amid a blizzard of rose petals—a blizzard because, as always, Milan had ordered too many. And it seemed that these petals were being thrown even more enthusiastically than usual, as though the revelers who released them were trying to make up for all the guests who had gone home.

Now in the middle of the flower storm, Wood pulled Milan close to him. Though he shielded his eyes, he could still see a patch of magnificent blue sky, not unlike the one that had served, almost a year ago, as an umbrella over his father's funeral. That day, like this one, had all the warmth of summer in it as well as the achingly tender light that comes with fall—a light as complex as the color of the Champanelle River—and seems to carry within itself a feeling that something is being left behind and also the idea that something new is coming.

The wind came up and blew some hats off, as the guests rushed toward the three couples. Mavis's mother nervously shook hands with her own daughter before spewing in a loud rush of breath, "Just be happy." Then she hurried away, fanning her eyes with the wedding program. Mavis ran after her mother and when she caught up, spun her around, holding her without either of them saying anything. Then Mrs. Pinkerton, who seemed to feel better after this, straightened her daughter's collar and, starting to cry again, ran toward her car.

Across the yard, Mary Paige was being embraced by all of Elmer Tillman's grandchildren, whom she had babysat throughout most of high school. There was some laughter over how Mary Paige was the only sitter who would allow them to go outside and holler and beat on pots and pans on New Year's Eve. And Lloyd Case, with his daughter Melanie and her husband, Dennis, were pumping Serious West's hand, thanking him for asking about their little boy, who had some kind of spinal problem, and not saying anything about all the years Serious, on his own time, had cruised Main Street just to make sure everything was okay before heading home. Instead, Lloyd said that if he had known Miss Delaney was the marrying kind, he would've beaten Serious to the punch. And there were a lot more after that, who, if they didn't say congratulations, said something that let Serious know that they were not going to oppose his happiness. Like prosecuting attorney Doug Riffel, who said he was against this marriage, not on the basis of race, but because Serious was pig-headed and obnoxious. And Serious had let out a delighted hoot that rolled across the crowd like good music and reassured every-one that they were right to stay.

Margaret Delaney had been embraced by so many people that her little hat was now crooked—people who wanted to tell her about some book they couldn't put down or to remind her how their grown children had been ahead of the pack at college because of her devotion. Or how the McCurdy's son, Jesse, was one of the stars of the Gulf War, because when they had been waiting out in the desert, he was able to regale his fellow soldiers with a chapter by chapter account of a different novel every night. Miss Delaney had heard such comments before, but she knew these people needed to retell them to-day, to reassure her and themselves that nothing had really changed between them.

Now the sun was in Slim's eyes as she pressed her palm against her son's cheek and whispered something. And then Wood got behind his mother and enclosed her in his arms. When he saw his own son watching all this, he said, "Hey, Charlie, you know what I say when people call me a mama's boy? I say thank you."

Charlie smiled. Slim shook her head at Wood's silliness. Wood motioned for Charlie to join them, but he declined. His dad grabbed him anyway and, as they started to roughhouse, Slim stepped back and watched, feeling farther away than usual from the Brown Meanness.

A few feet away, Sidney Garfinkel shook Milan's hand. Then she took her hand back and threw her arms around him, not knowing of his role in creating the dress she was now wearing, but instead thinking of the one that had arrived over twenty years ago and blurting out what she had been too shy to say then, "I love you, Mr. Garfinkel!"

Sidney was so taken aback that he impulsively kissed her on the mouth and then, embarrassed, removed an expertly folded handkerchief from his pocket and rubbed the lipstick from his own lips. Milan saw that he missed a spot and knowing this was her forte, she took the handkerchief, with Sidney submitting his face to her, just as he once might have to his own mother when he was still a schoolboy back in Belgium.

Elizabeth and Luke had now rejoined the party. Elizabeth pulled Slim aside and whispered, "Grand-mère, I've been upstairs having sex and I love it!"

Slim stared at her.

"Don't worry. I'm not gonna tell anyone. I just wanted to tell you. But seriously, it's wonderful, isn't it?"

"I'm not discussing this with you now."

"Okay. But don't get too prissy on me." Elizabeth grinned, raising her eyebrows. "I know you stole tomatoes with Mr. Garfinkel."

Slim laughed a little, marveling at the wondrous communication network of Paris and thinking that if she did have a secret worth keeping, her granddaughter would be one of the few who she would trust with it.

Brundidge sidled up to Wood, holding one of the little carryall bags that belonged to his daughters. "Don't worry. I've got the top of the cake covered."

He unzipped the bag, allowing Wood a clandestine peek at the two dolls inside.

Brundidge smiled, "Lesbian Barbies." Wood was nonplussed. Brundidge added, "In fact, that may be the new name for our movie." Brundidge moved on, pleased with himself and how the day was turning out.

Wood was now gazing across his lawn at the several hundred people waiting in line to say something encouraging to the ones who they knew needed to hear it. He was wishing his dad were here to see such a sight, this man who loved to rub up against wrong ideas until they looked all worn out. Right now, he would have his arm around Wood and he would be saying, "Well, son, you sure got yourself into something today, didn't you? But that's okay. I've already told people that your mother and I have just given up on you. That it's all in the Lord's hands now." Then, he would proudly pat Wood on the back and walk away.

Wood was looking at his grandfather's house and imagining how puzzled the older McIlmore would be by the strange event now occurring on his property. How he would probably not understand any of it, except maybe the love behind it. Because love was one thing the McIlmore men were good at— whether it involved their wives, children, patients, or their little town. They were good at love, or they had been, and Wood resolved to be as good as the rest of them. Especially now that he had been given a second chance with his own wife. His daughter was another story. Beyond the wedding guests, he could see Elizabeth sitting in the tire swing that hung from one of Fast Deer Farm's massive oaks. And he could hear her complaining, in the distance, that Luke was not pushing her high enough. Just as she had once complained to him. Suddenly he felt a sadness that he knew could not be lifted by anything that would occur here today. How to win back a daughter who once thought her father was a friend of Shakespeare's and has now found out he's more like a fool in one of the old bard's plays. Wood felt sad because he knew there were some things that cannot be earned back. And that like the Purple Crackle, a new incarnation of whatever has once been is sometimes more pitiful than nothing at all.

Milan had taken baby Paris from Mavis and was holding her in the air and showing her off to everyone. And Paris had tilted the large head that babies have, as she closed her eyes and smiled serenely. Wood was thinking how much she looked like someone he used to know. And how he would find a way to do right by her, would someday read her all the poems that her daddy had left behind, and take her down to Main Street and tell her about the people and their stores and their stories and how it had been there—where three boys on their horses had once ruled.

Sidney, who must have been feeling a little reckless after kissing Milan, had now accepted Paris in his arms and was sort of cooing to her in his soft Belgian accent. It was a strange sight—Sidney Garfinkel holding a baby and cooing. But it seemed fitting to Wood, on this day when love had gotten out ahead of hate, that such a thing should happen. For Sidney Garfinkel had lived in a time when love had fallen behind. And the people of Paris, Arkansas, had, without even knowing it, made up for that in some small way—people who lived so very far from the distant hole that held almost everyone he had ever loved in it. And yet, somehow seemed to be so very much like them—these ferocious teachers who cared passionately about learning and parents who were so decent, their little boys wanted to fight Hitler for him, and all the merchants on Main Street who had rebuilt half his store before he even knew his windows had been broken.

Wood could see now that not only Sidney, but virtually everyone in the world who mattered to him, was at this moment engaged in some sort of loving act. Even Brundidge and Charlotte, who thought no one could see them, were making out a little over by the bar. New York and Arkansas, French-kissing. Wood made a mental picture of all of it, knowing that such large-scale goodness is always fleeting. The same way he knew that some of these well-intended souls would get in their cars in a couple of hours and express doubt about what they had just been a part of. Being a student of literature and history, Wood figured that good stays, on the average, about one sprinter's step ahead of evil. Love, ahead of the kind of people who want you to believe that birds can hate enough not to eat bread. He was lucky. His entire life, along with the hope of all humanity, could be contained within the distance of that one step, or beyond. He had never known poverty or bigotry or fear. Even his other worst mistake, throwing a football when he

didn't need to, had been paid for by someone else. Love had never fallen behind in his
life, like it had in Sidney Garfinkel's and Milan's and, in some measure, Jeter's. And, as
it so often does, in places all over the world.
When it happens, a person or a town or a
country has to come in afterward and say
okay, let's clean this mess up. Let's start
over. And then miraculously, love steps off
again, ever hopeful, everlasting.

Wood was now thinking that he no longer
wanted to live within that small, rarified
space that had once contained him. He
wanted to stay on the hunt for this feeling
that had come alive, if only for a few hours,
in his own backyard. He wanted to be worthy
of his own life. To go where love had fallen
behind. And to his sorrow, he now understood that he wouldn't even have to leave
home to do so.

The air was turning cold as a breeze rolled
off the Champanelle River and the little orchestra struggled to hold onto their sheet
music. Inside the billowing white tent, wait-
ers relit candles and began lifting the lids
from enormous silver bowls as everyone
made their way there. Ordinarily, Milan
would be directing all this, but today she felt

more like watching. She came over and leaned her head on Wood's shoulder. Without thinking, he kissed the top of it. He was starting to feel tired. He had almost destroyed a superstore, his marriage, and his family, and had taken on the moral convictions of an entire community. Frankly, he would be glad now when all these people went home. For the first time in many years, he wanted his wife to himself. He was already planning how he would get up early and chop wood and stack it close to the fireplace so that in a month or two, he wouldn't have to go out in the snow so often. He was going to make a fire every night this winter and let the girl who had loved only one boy for her whole life know that that boy was now ready to listen to whatever she needed to tell him. Ready to hear about what had worried her or scared her or made her feel small. And she could tell him these things a little at a time or not at all, but he would be there. And if she needed to wake him in the middle of the night and have him soothe her, or to use him as a light against the darkest parts of her childhood, then he would be there for that, too. As true and steady and unmovable as he would be when the need for building fires has long passed and some distant winter has come to cover the prince of Paris and his first love with a fresh new blanket of snow. He was as sure of that as he was that he would be back on his horse tomorrow morning, riding toward the sun.

Epilogue

Some children were running alongside the Champanelle River. There were five or six of them and they were racing a dog with a can in his mouth. Seven-year-old Marcus West Junior, who lived nearby, was one of them. And Cake and Lily Brundidge were there, still in their flower girl dresses because their daddy had said they could wear them to Marcus's house if they wouldn't get them dirty, which they did anyway. And then there was Milan's little niece and nephew, India and Travis Lanier, and Mae Ethel's granddaughter, Elizabeth Brown, too. Right now, Cake and Elizabeth had stopped to catch their breath. Cake was bent over, panting, looking like a small jock wearing a formal. Elizabeth finally asked, "Who got married today?"

"Ever'body."

"Uh-uh."

"Mavis Pinkerton married some ol' gal."

"Did not."

"Did so. And Marcus's grandpa married an old white woman."

"Who?"

"I know her, but I forgot."

"You're tellin' a story."

"Am not."

"Wood and Milan McIlmore got married again, too."

"Why?"

"I dunno. Guess it didn't take the first time." Elizabeth seemed worried.

"Well, you better not ask me to marry you."

"Who said I wanted to? I'm never gettin' married. I'm gonna live with my daddy."

By the time they were off and running again, the others had already come across the strange, mysterious box, along with its former contents, which had now been scattered across a wide area. Marcus spotted the American flag that had once draped Dr. Mac's coffin and said, "Man, this is cool. I'm keepin' this."

As he gathered it up, India Lanier already had on the homburg that Sidney Garfinkel had worn when he first arrived in America. It covered her eyes and with typical Lanier bad taste, she also put on the World War I gas mask and then, after Tracee barked at her, discarded it. And Elizabeth Brown picked up the long drum majorette's baton that Milan had carried during the last parade on Main Street. Cake put the chain with the dog tags around her own neck and Lily and Travis got into a fight over Serious West's boxing gloves, which Lily won. But her hands were so small, she had to struggle to keep them on. Travis then scooped up the football, along with a little sack of tin nickels from Jeter's Market, declaring that he was going to spend them somewhere. Cake told him they weren't worth anything, but he put them in his pocket anyway.

What had been only a breeze all day now turned into the kind of wind that whips laundry around on a clothesline. Marcus's mother came outside to collect her linens and called to her son, but he was already too far away. She struggled to remove some sheets as the metal circle that held the clothesline started to clang against the pole. Marcus and the others were running along the top of the river bank, heady from the excitement of their find. Lily was out in front, taking powerful steps that rustled her skirts as she punctuated the air with the boxing gloves. Marcus and Cake each held a corner of the unfurled flag and, even though it was horizontal, like a tablecloth, the wind lifted it and caused it to ripple as they ran. Tommy Epps's dog tags from Vietnam beat against Cake Brundidge's chest and India Lanier tossed the championship football back and forth with her brother, whose pockets jangled with make-believe money from the Depression. And Elizabeth Brown strutted, holding the baton across her chest, while the dog periodically circled her.

They were all laughing as they picked up speed, running against the current of the river—unaware that they carried with them just a few of the most noble items from the twentieth century, along with some others that didn't amount to much at all. But none that would be left behind now for posterity. It was enough to make you think that maybe you can't put a town in a box, after all. Or inside a two-hundred-thousand-square-foot superstore. There are some people in Paris,

Arkansas, who will tell you that theirs was once set down on a place called Main Street. But that place is gone now. Leaving some to wonder that there is nowhere left to put the town but inside children like these.